The KEY CLUB MURDERS

CHARLENE PREWITT

To my best friend, Nora who passed away in 2002 along with her hubby Rick. Writing her in as a character and she was a character, helped me keep her alive in my heart.

The Key Club Murders

Copyright © 2017 by Charlene Prewitt - All rights reserved.

Interior Print Design and eBook Interior Design:

Dayna Linton, Day Agency

ISBN 978-1548562595 Paperback

First Edition: 2017

10 9 8 7 6 5 4 3 2 1

Printed in the USA

The
KEY CLUB
MURDERS

PROLOGUE

ONE OF THE THINGS I most like about my best friend Nora, is she always has my six. One such time we were walking out of the mall loaded down with packages, looking across the parking lot for the car, when out of Nora's peripheral vision she could see a couple of degenerates closing in on us. She dropped her packages and clotheslined one guy with her left arm, bringing him down to his knees, then with her foot shoved him on the ground holding him down. Meantime, the other perp grabbed my bag and started running. Nora, who does multitasking better than anyone I know, saw this and took her whopping big Vera Wang purse, tossed it around the feet of the runner, bringing him down face first. I ran over to him, stuck my foot in the middle of his back, holding him down while dialing 911.

When the police arrived, they started laughing at the two thieves who were hog-tied with newly purchased scarves and tights.

After taking pictures with their cell phones, they handcuffed the perpetrators and returned the scarves and tights to us. We immediately tossed them in the trash can near the mall doors.

They took our report and said they would be in touch. They led the culprits to the patrol car, still laughing.

One of the officers yelled back they would call us to come in for a review of the report once it was written up.

We loaded the car and decided to stop for lunch on the way home. As we ordered our lunch, an older man was choking and about to pass out. This time

I kicked into action, as I'm an RN. I ran over to him, put my arms around him from behind, and pumped a couple of times until the food lodged in his throat came shooting out and he was able to breathe again.

He was so grateful he paid for our lunch and insisted on a hundred-dollar reward for saving his life. We tried to refuse his offer, but he wouldn't hear of it. We headed back to the mall.

A few days later we were called to go to the police station to review the police report and sign it. That was the day I met my honey, Detective Jackson Boxley.

CHAPTER 1

I'M CHARLA O'HARA. I am an RN and a sleuther. I have had defense training and am good with a gun, though I haven't had to shoot anyone. YET!

I moved in with my longtime boyfriend, Jackson Boxley, about five years ago. He's a homicide lead Detective for GPD. I'm proud to say that my sleuthing has more than once helped Jackson out on a few of his cases. He referred to my help as "accidental flukes."

I keep a poster of Ryan Reynolds stapled on our bedroom ceiling. Not because I'm being a teenager again or because of sexual reasons, but because Jackson looks so much like Ryan Reynolds, brown eyes and all. Besides, I love waking up and seeing the poster when I first open my eyes, especially if I roll over and don't see Jackson in the flesh. He doesn't mind the poster.

Andy Carpenter has Tara, a Golden Retriever. Stephanie Plum has Rex, her long-time Hamster. I have Morris the Cat, except my cat is a grey tabby and his name is Bozo. I have had him just a smidgeon longer than I've had Jackson. Bozo's the constant in my life. He runs the neighborhood by day and stays in by night. He has always greeted me, no matter what, and it's comforting to know that.

My side kick and sleuthing partner is Nora Weston. We have been best friends most of our life. People always think we are sisters.

I'm 5'6" and I may be a few pounds overweight. I have green eyes that Jackson says appear very light in color sometimes and are mesmerizing. *He is prejudiced.* I have mousey blonde hair, with high lights, that I wear for the most part in the same fluffy ponytail. It's simple. I wear my clothes slightly tight. My nails are a mess. I use the bare essential of makeup almost every day. I do know how to doll up when needed. I get by.

Nora is also 5'6", but other than that, the similarities end. She has big blue eyes and lots of fake. Her eye lashes are fake. *Never goes without them.* Her finger nails are fake and longer than they should be. She gets them done every Wednesday, without fail, along with her toenails. Though she's redheaded, she colors her hair even redder. She teases the heck out of it to make it puffed to its full extent *Fake.* But her boobs are real. Recently she got a breast reduction to help with her back pain. Though it helped, she's still huge. She could go down a couple of more cup sizes. She always wears a lot of makeup, especially her eyes, and doesn't leave home without any of it. She sprays a whole bottle of perfume on herself before leaving her house, and you can smell her coming before you see her. As far as perfume for me, I spray it in the air and walk through it. *If I remember to wear any.*

I don't wear much jewelry; just a simple promise ring Jackson gave me a couple of years ago, a thumb ring, hoop earrings, a watch and a plain gold chain. But Nora is loaded down with jewelry, even a couple of toe rings. *Diamonds.* I don't see how she can hold her hands up or keep from tilting over from her gigantic boobs. How people thought we could be sisters was beyond me.

We both have permits to carry concealed weapons. While taking shooting lessons at the gun range, I had no trouble hitting the target and passed with flying colors. Nora's fake nails messed her up, making her have to try and try time after time. She couldn't get her fingers through to the trigger because of her nails. Her nails came off and she finally passed on her *fifth try.* The nails went back on, but not as long as they were before. She feared she might not get a shot off in time, if needed. *Like she would ever shoot anyone.* Nora's gigantic boobs got in the way when shooting her .38 lever action rifle. She couldn't remove her boobs, but she did learn to adjust where and how she shot the rifle. It was an adjustment. I had no trouble.

We plan on getting our Private Investigation license sooner rather than later. We've gotten pretty good at investigating and solving crimes, though not always in the conventional way. Practice makes perfect. We have been helpful to the police on numerous occasions, sort of.

CHAPTER 2

NORA AND I WERE planning on going shopping. It's another favorite hobby of ours. Hers more than mine.

Jackson was kissing me good bye and Nora said, "Get a room," which she said every time she saw us kiss. Bozo my watch cat rubbed against my leg, wanting me to take the time to feed him. I am sure he thought I forgot.

Jackson's smart-phone rang in the middle of our kiss. He slightly pushed me away and answered. He repeated the name and address while writing it down. "Louise Stafford, 8992 W. 95th. Homicide, uh-huh. She was shot and found dead by her neighbor . . . Jeanne Hughes.

"Right, right, on my way," Jackson said. He turned and continued writing in his nifty notepad as he hung up. Jackson ran back to the bedroom and grabbed his shield, gun and jacket.

He came back out to where he left me at the door, but this time he was the one leaving.

"Gotta go, ladies," he said as he looked at both of us. "I know you heard my side of the conversation. Mrs. Stafford's neighbor has gone every Wednesday for coffee, for months. I guess she won't be going anymore."

"Wow, Jackson, that's cold," I grimaced. "Keep me posted."

"No," he said, knowing full well he would end up telling me. *Jackson always tells me.* He leaned in for another quick kiss then said, "Apparently, Jeanie, the neighbor, knocked and when no one answered, she walked in, found Louise sprawled out on the kitchen floor, blood streaming from the head. She screamed and called 911. The dispatcher told her to stay put." He went out the door.

Nora and I looked at each other. "Louise was one of our Writer's Club members," she said.

We didn't know her outside the club. She was certainly interesting and was a great contributor to our club. We liked her, though she was very private.

Then Nora said, "We better cancel our shopping trip and head to Louise's address."

"Yep, she's a writer club buddy. We need to help," I said, concerned.

"I'll drive," she said, pulling out her keys from her big ass bag. *I have never understood why she prefers that large of a bag, but she thinks she does.*

"Whoops, I have to feed Bozo," as Bozo meowed, reminding me. I did a 180 and stepped back inside. Bozo looked up at me with a little meow. I said, "You're welcome."

✦》》《《✦

WE PULLED UP TO Louise Stafford's home just as Jackson and a new, young Detective Scott Edwards was just going into what appeared to be a very well kept house.

We tried to go under the crime scene tape and were stopped just short of getting through. The uniforms were holding strong on not letting unauthorized personnel in. We knew one of the uniforms, a Ryan Glenn. We grew up together and went to the same school. Nice guy.

We called Ryan over, and asked, "How about letting us through?"

"Jackson's orders said we can't let anyone through."

"Well, then if it's Jackson's orders, he'll be happy to see us." I bent over slightly showing a little cleavage.

Ryan looked over at Nora, whose cleavage always showed, as she flashed her fake eyelashes at him.

"For Pete's sake, you two. You're married," he said looking at Nora. Then, he looked at me. "Charla, what will Jackson say if he saw you trying to sexually seduce me to get past the Crime Scene tape? Good grief," Ryan muttered.

"Jackson would welcome the help," I pouted.

Ryan rolled his eyes, and shook his head, "N . . . O . . . no!"

No matter what we tried to do, Ryan didn't let us through.

He motioned for us to come in closer to him, then he whispered, "Louise Stafford was shot in the head twice by what looks to be a .22 caliber. She's lying in the middle of the kitchen floor. She dropped the coffee pot, and there's water and coffee grounds all over the floor. Poor lady had blood pouring out of her head . . . She was getting ready for her weekly coffee clutch with her neighbor. I wished I hadn't gone in there now," He said, hanging his head in what looked like a little prayer.

Ryan has a hard time keeping things from us as well. He's worked with us before.
"Come on Ryan, let us through."

"NO . . . !"

"What about Jeannie Hughes?" I asked. "Can we talk to her?"

Ryan shook his head no and nodded toward the house. "She's still in there."

We shrugged our shoulders and moved around to the other side of the yard with hopes of convincing another cop to let us through. We saw an opening in the corner by the porch that no one was manning. Just as we approached it, Ryan came running over.

"Uh, I don't think so, ladies. No still means . . . NO!"

Nora and I felt helpless. Our hands were tied by not being allowed into the crime scene. We decided to work the perimeter where neighbors and passers-by stood gossiping and gawking.

The police were already questioning the neighbors. We hopped in.

We nonchalantly strolled over to a neighbor lady who was crying. We introduced ourselves as Louise's writing club friends. We also told her that we were helping the police with interviewing. A twofer.

Her ears perked up. She said, "I didn't know Louise was in any club. Though I did know she was always writing stories or in a diary or something."

Carol Hershey, who clearly was the neighborhood gossip, started spilling the beans, *without any prompting from us,* on what she observed and what little bit Louise mentioned to her over the fence.

"Louise's husband LEFT her just a week or so ago," Carol Hershey said, with disgust.

"Husband?" I repeated.

"Yeah, she wanted his help with the boys."

"Boys?" Again, I repeated.

Nora and I looked at each other, confused. We really didn't know Louise.

"So what was wrong? I mean, why did her husband leave and what was wrong with the boys that Louise needed help?" I was fishing for clues. Anything would help.

"Louise wanted Joe to put the hammer down on their son Joe Jr. He's fifteen, getting into a little trouble lately. He broke his curfew *numerous* times, and when confronted he smart mouthed his mother."

"Well, why wouldn't her husband help her?"

"Ah . . . , Joe wouldn't discipline Joe Jr. because he had a bad childhood with his father. Joe's father was strict with him so he didn't want Joe Jr. to turn against him like he did his father. He would rather leave Louise."

"Nice. . . " Nora mumbled.

"How old is the other boy?" I asked, as I glanced at Nora, who clearly was displeased with Joe as I was.

"Let's see, hmm. I believe Ricky's thirteen. Just yesterday Louise was telling me Ricky's the good son. She said that Joe Jr. has such a smart mouth and teased Ricky all the time. Ricky learned to stand up for himself though, and was getting tougher. Apparently, Louise was a buffer between the two teens. What's going to happen to those boys now? I was probably her closest neighbor, uh, friend with the exception of Jeannie."

We thanked Carol, handing her our rather unique business card. Yeah, we have business cards.

Charla O'Hara 555.555.5515

Nora Weston 555.555.5516

P I

PERSONAL INVESTIGATION

Because we really didn't want to mislead people with the PI thing, we put across the very bottom of the card "PERSONAL INVESTIGATION" in really tiny letters. I guess we should apply for our Private Investigators license.

"Carol, call if you think of anything else."

"I will."

"Wow," I said to Nora as we walked towards another neighbor. "We didn't know anything about Louise. Did you know she had two sons, or a husband?"

"No, I had no idea," Nora said, looking surprised.

"You know, we should review Louise's stories she shared with us at the Writer's Club. There might be a lead or two in those stories," I suggested, as we moseyed over to the next person to interview.

When we approached another assumed neighbor, he looked deep in thought.

"Hi, I'm Charla O'Hara and this is Nora Weston. We're Louise's um . . . friends." We reached for his hand to shake.

As he shook our hands, his head bobbed back and forth, "I'm Harold Stonewall. I live across the street here," he pointed to his house.

He looked at us and said, "I was wondering who would take care of this beautiful lawn that Louise took so much pride in."

We turned and looked over the yard and it was landscaped and groomed perfectly. Flowers bordered the porch area and down each side of the sidewalk to the street. Baskets of flowers hung all around the wraparound porch. It was beautiful.

I thought, *"Martha Stewart in the flesh."* Oops! Not so much now. I gave myself a mental head slap for being so insensitive.

I turned back to Harold who was saying, "Look how the cops and suits stumped all over Louise's flowers. That's a crime in itself, don't you think?" as he turned, and looked at me then Nora.

We again turned and looked over the yard. I had to agree, and Nora nodded yes.

Harold went on to say, "Louise was grooming her yard just yesterday. Those boys of hers never helped or that husband. Worthless bunch," he muttered. "Who's going to take care of it, now? What a shame, what a waste," as Harold was now referring to Louise. "Who could have killed that poor woman?"

"We hope to find out," I answered.

"Hey, Harold, where's the boys?" Nora asked.

"I'm pretty sure Mutt and Jeff are in school," he said. "I'm sure they don't know about their mother, yet."

"Hang in there Harold." Nora handed our handy dandy business card to him. "Call if you think of anything."

We excused ourselves, patting Harold on his arm as we moved by him. He was physically upset but we didn't know if it was over Louise's death or her yard. He looked at our card and then squinted to read the bottom. He moved the card out and then back close again. I'm not sure he ever picked out what it said. No one does.

We gathered up all the information we could from all the neighbors and passers-by that would comment. We would talk to them all again, later.

Some people were visibly upset and some not so much. We scanned the perimeter of people to see if anyone stood out. Nora the Text Queen, with the most current electrical and digital devices, shot the perimeter of all the people standing around. We would review it later.

Nora was scanning the people standing across the street in front of Harold's house. She picked up on one guy who was watching us. When Nora pointed her camera towards him, he quickly turned his face and hurried away. We definitely would check that out.

Once again, we found an opening at the crime scene tape. Again, we fell short of getting through. *Damn that Ryan.*

About that time, Jackson came out into the yard and saw the two of us. He walked over.

It just turned me on, watching him walk towards us.

Nora did a double take at me, shaking her head in disgust. I guess she doesn't see Ryan Reynolds like I do.

"Oh brother, what are you two amateurs doing here?" He smiled down at me.

"We know Louise. She is . . . was . . . in our Writer's Club. When you got the call this morning, we knew we had to come." I turned on the charm.

"Stay out of it. Let us do our job." He was still smiling, as he knew there was no way we would be staying out of it, especially since we knew her.

"Has anyone notified her husband, Joe, or her boys?" I asked, like I knew more than I really did.

Jackson said, "The husband's on his way. He wanted to be the one to tell the boys," he said, a little too smugly.

"Here he comes now," a reporter yelled.

We watched the police car pull up with Joe Stafford sitting in the front seat. Or so we thought. He got out and hurried toward the house.

News stations and reporters were now flooding the scene, shuffling for position. Joe didn't want to talk to them.

The officer accompanying Joe stopped, turned and looked at the reporter, and said, "Give him a break people, he just got here."

Joe walked straight into the house with the officer following close behind.

Jackson gave a loving squeeze to my hand, trying hard not to let anyone see. He started back towards the house, but not before he said, "Stay out of it." *He has to go through the motions.*

He started walking again, then turned, and did that finger thing where he put two fingers to his eyes then pointed them to us. "*I'm watching you,*" he mouthed.

Fat chance we would stay out of it. I did the, *I'm watching you,* back to Jackson. He kept walking. We tried to fall in behind him. We would have made it, too, if Jackson hadn't caught us. He motioned an officer over, and the officer led us back behind the crime scene tape. *Darn!* We really wanted in that house.

CHAPTER 3

STAFFORD LOOKED DOWN AT his wife lying in a pool of blood. He had to look away. He turned to leave the kitchen, and ran into Jeannie Hughes who was standing by to answer more questions. They looked at each other and did a slight hug. Jackson and his partner, Det. Donnie Harper, who just got there, led Stafford to the living room. Stafford and Jackson sat down. Harper stood. Jeannie Hughes stood back just out of earshot with another junior detective, watching Joe Stafford's every move.

Donnie Harper has been Jackson's current partner for the last year. Jackson's last partner of five years, died of a heart attack from too many late night burgers. Det. Donnie Harper was 5'10, 145 pounds, dark brown shoulder length hair. She had deep brown eyes and she was drop dead gorgeous. And I hated her.

Stafford stood while Steve Houston, one of the Crime scene techs, tested him for gunfire residue on his hands and clothing. Stafford looked disgusted about the routine, but cooperated.

Jackson said to him, "I am sorry for your loss," then asked, "Where were you about eight this morning?"

"I picked up the boys at seven and took them to school. Then I went to work. Louise was cleaning up the kitchen. She seemed to be okay," he replied looking Det. Harper up and down.

"Where were you before coming to pick up your kids?"

"I've been staying at Hotel Hybrite for the last week and a half."

"Why is that?"

"I left Louise."

"Why is that?" *Jackson has a way with words.*

"We couldn't agree on how to discipline the boys."

"How so?"

"She wanted me to step up to the plate especially about our oldest son, Joe Jr. I just couldn't."

"Why's that?"

"I had trouble with my dad growing up. I didn't like him much. I didn't want that same kind of relationship with my sons. Hey man, I really need to go get my kids," he begged, standing up to leave.

Jackson rose from his seat on the sofa, stood back as if to say go ahead, and then said, "We still need information. We need to do a follow up."

"I understand, but first I need to get to my sons," Joe said, upset. "I really want to be the one to tell the boys. I don't want them to hear it from anyone else, or read it over the internet." He looked Det. Harper up and down again saying, "I realize the spouse is the first suspect," then turned to go out the front door.

Joe Stafford left the house just thirty minutes after arriving. He wasn't prepared to see his wife like that. *Or was he?* He avoided the yelling questions from the reporters. The same police officer that brought Stafford held up his hand as if to say "not now," led him back out to the police car to go get his sons.

"Hey Mr. Stafford, what happened? Who killed your wife? Did you kill your wife?" yelled the same reporter.

"The insensitive a-holes," I muttered.

Nora returned the mutter, "You got that right."

Joe Stafford kept walking and doing his level best to ignore them, but they kept yelling questions and comments as he closed the door of the patrol car.

Jackson would drill Joe more, later.

Nora and I walked back toward her car, but not before we tried to cross the crime scene tape one more time. And we were turned away.

CHAPTER 4

"Daniel"

AFTER DANIEL NIELSEN LEFT the house of Louise Stafford, he returned to his home, to his wife, Vivian and their two kids, Stone and Pebbles. He gave his wife a hug and kissed her on her cheek.

Daniel's two kids came running to him. Daniel hugged his ten-year-old son, Stone, a strawberry blond with freckles and then reached for his eight-year old daughter, Pebbles, with her blond curly hair bouncing in a ponytail. Both the kids were adorable, with blue eyes that matched Vivian's.

Daniel nicknamed his children Stone and Pebbles as soon as Pebbles was born. He thought it fit. They reminded him of the old Flintstones series from when he was kid. He loved those two kids and their mom, but something was missing. Always missing, until he figured it out one day several years ago. He needed extracurricular activity. He needed exciting sex with a stranger.

He would go scratch that itch again on Friday night. He went on Friday nights frequently. He belonged to the "Key Club" at "The Cheer Up." Friday, he would be back at the club.

His rule was IF the same woman pulled his hotel key out of the hat for her fifth time with him, he would give her the time of her life, but then he would have to end it once and for all. He wouldn't want them to feel like there was something special coming out of such a chance meeting. Five times, whether it was accidental or not that the same person would pull his key out, he would have to stop her from letting the cat out of the bag, as it were. He could not EVER let his sweet Vivian know.

After last seeing Louise Stafford a few weeks ago, on her unfortunate fifth time pulling his key out of the hat, it was time to pay her a visit and stop her from ever mentioning it to anyone. He couldn't take the chance; he had to make that visit soon.

Daniel thought to himself as he visited Louise, he hated this part. He really felt bad, but it is what it is. It was after all the fifth visit. Daniel took solace in that he showed Louise the night of her life. He curled her toes. She screamed in sheer lust, delight and satisfaction.

Instead of Daniel being the dominate and she the submissive, he wanted her last time to be all straight sex without black leather restraints, whips or any of the dominate sex acts or toys he liked. It had to be pure real passionate sex with all the bells and whistles. Yes, he gave her the time of her life. Then he had to end her life.

She didn't even know he had slipped through the garage door right after her sons left with their father. He waited until he felt the coast was clear, then quietly crept in behind her just as she was pouring herself coffee. He had the silencer on the gun already so as not to make any noise. He stood three feet behind her and POW, POW. Just so happened, Louise was his fifth POW. Four had fallen before her.

She fell to the floor. "Good night, sweet Louise. Sleep tight." He turned and left without anyone ever knowing he was there.

Daniel watched Louise's neighbor bend over and pick up her newspaper. She turned and walked back into her house without noticing him.

Whew, Daniel exhaled. That was close. He hurried down the street to his car.

He couldn't help but remember just a few short days ago; he attempted to visit Louise and was stopped short of saying goodbye to her then. Apparently, there was no school that day for whatever reason. There were kids out up and down the block. One of Louise's sons was shooting hoops in the driveway and didn't look like he was going anywhere soon. Daniel aborted his mission. Louise would live a few more days.

But now the deed was done.

CHAPTER 5

JUST SO HAPPENED WE had Writer's Club that afternoon. There wasn't much more we could do with the police hell bent on keeping us out.

We sat down and told the group what had happened, even though it had been on the news and the group had seen Nora and me on TV.

"Who was that hunk that came over to talk to you guys?" Loraine asked.

"Oh him," I smiled. "That's my honey, Jackson."

"Yeah, and he doesn't look like Ryan Reynolds either," Nora rolled her eyes just before she heehawed.

"Uh-huh, does too," I yelled at her. "He does."

"Well he could play Ryan Reynold's double," Loraine giggled. *And can eat crackers in my bed any . . . time,* she thought hoping Charla couldn't read her mind.

Childishly, I said, "See, Nora."

Once again, she rolled her eyes.

"At least he doesn't look like Col. Sanders, like Rick does."

Nora laughed and said, "Rick does remind me of fried chicken."

All of us had a good laugh. The truth was, Rick does have a goatee with light hair and has packed on a few pounds in the last couple of years, BUT no real resemblance to Col. Sanders. *Yet.*

"Let's review the stories Louise brought in for the club. See if we can find out who, what, when or why," Nora announced.

We gathered up all we could find of Louise's stories, but only found a couple among us. Spreading the stories out on the table, we divvied the pages out to each of us to start reading.

We tried to compare notes but came up empty.

I had a hard time concentrating on the club that day. Everyone did.

After sharing stories about Louise, we figured out we really didn't know Louise, nothing about her personal life, nothing at all.

"I know you girls will try your hardest to find out what happened to Louise and why," Katy said.

"Yeah, if you need our help in anyway, just call," one of the girls offered and everyone agreed.

"Thanks everyone, we may take you up on it," Nora said.

I nodded my head in agreement, and then we all said our goodbyes.

CHAPTER 6

I TALKED TO JACKSON and he said that Joe Stafford and sons would not be going back to the house for the time being. They were going to stay with family.

It was late afternoon. The CSI and police should have been done with their investigation. The coroner would be gone by now too. Nora and I decided we should go back to Louise's house.

Nora called Rick and told him that she would be home in an hour or so. He is used to her and my shenanigans.

We pulled up and saw Harold, the guy we talked to earlier, looking over Louise's yard still shaking his head. *Or is he back looking over the yard?*

"Well, if it isn't the sleuther twins," he smirked.

"Oh, you figured the card out," Nora smiled at him.

"Yeah, I had to get the magnifying glass to read it though. P. I's. Clever." He shook his head more with amusement.

I've never seen anyone shake their head so much. *Maybe he's really a bobble head . . . ? I just amaze myself.*

"Harold, have you been here this whole time?" Nora asked.

"Nah, just came back over to check to see how much more damage to the yard there was. I'm thinking about trying to put as many flowers back upright for Louise as I can. I think I'm going to water them too," he said, still shaking his head.

A Ford Edge pulled up. A woman who looked a lot like Louise got out. She looked so much like Louise we had to do a double take. Twins? She wore jeans with a Tee and a navy blazer. Her hair was bobbed and highlighted. She talked to Harold for several minutes. Nora and I leaned in closer.

Harold looked at her and said, "It is a rotten shame that the police just trampled Louise's yard. They just ruined it."

We looked the yard over and it was clearly worse than this morning.

"Where's my manners? This is Louise's twin sister, Rita Brownstone. Rita, these here ladies are friends of Louise, Nora and uh, uh."

I interrupted Harold.

"Hi, I'm Charla," I held out my hand.

I handed her our business card with Nora and my phone numbers.

Rita took the card and looked at it and then looked at it again.

Harold just smiled.

"We are so sorry to hear about Louise," Nora spoke softly.

Rita asked, "How do, did you know Louise?"

I took her hand and patted it, "We were in the same writer's club."

"Then you have a lot in common with Louise," She commented.

I thought, *not so much, as we now know.*

But instead I smiled and said, "Yes."

Rita said to Harold, "I really appreciate you keeping watch over Louise's house," She said, then paused. "Excuse me." She started walking towards Louise's front door.

"Rita," I yelled after her, "we need to investigate what happened and why. We were wondering if we could get our hands-on Louise's stories. We have a few, but we would like to look through her stories to see if, by chance Louise would have mentioned anyone we could possibly follow up on."

Rita looked at us and cocked her head. "What?" she looked at us confused.

"Nora and I have helped the police on numerous occasions, and had some luck on solving a few crimes. I thought if you didn't mind, we could look over Louise's stories just to see if anything at all would pop out. We would keep them safe and sound." I was trying not to sound pushy, but man I wanted those stories.

Rita thought for a few seconds and then said, "I guess it would be okay. Come in with me and I'll get them. If you think they will help. I just want to know what happened."

"Rita, do you think the originals are on Louise's laptop? If so, we won't have to physically take her stories."

"Come on in," she said.

We followed Rita inside Louise's house. Outside of what the investigation had done to the house and, of course the crime scene, Louise did keep a tidy house. Very nice, indeed.

On our way back to a small office, we had to walk through where Louise had been lying on the floor with only a chalk outline of her body remaining. We glanced at the bloody kitchen floor, trying not to stare. Rita clearly got upset. She stopped and stared at the floor. Nora about ran into her and me into Nora.

Rita started crying, "It's so unfair. Louise wouldn't hurt a fly. Just not fair. My God, she was my twin."

Nora gathered her into her arms. "There, there, Rita," Nora said, patting Rita on her back.

We stood silent for what seemed like minutes as she pulled herself together, and then we followed her into Louise's tidy, but small, office. She had stacks of stories.

Apparently, Louise was working on something just this morning and left her lap top open and unsaved.

First thing Rita did was hit "save." It came up as "Another Lie." *Hmph.*

"I wonder why the police left the computer on or even left it here." Nora stated out loud.

"Well," I said sarcastically, "that was an oversight. I'll have to ask Jackson. Strange! But I am glad they didn't mess with it or take it. Someone's butt is going to be chewed."

We got in the program where Louise had her stories, one after the other, in her word document.

We matched the hard copies to the laptop and Rita said, "This is going to be a lot. I'll put them on a flash drive for you. Louise always has extra flash drives."

There were a few stories that were sitting on the desk that we couldn't find in the laptop, so Rita said, "Just take them and here's a journal I found buried here."

"Rita, I will copy them and get the originals back to you."

"Take what you want," Rita said, as her voice trailed off. "I hope they help. I wish I could help, but Louise was the creative writer. I just wouldn't know where to start."

CHAPTER 7

As WE LEFT, WE told Rita we would be in touch.

When we got back to the house, I walked into the dining room which doubled for an office. I started printing off hard copies as Nora handed me a bundle of copy paper. "Crap, I ran out of copier ink and I don't have much paper left."

"I'll pick both up on my way over tomorrow," Nora said, picking at a broken nail. "Damn, I've got to get a nail appointment."

She pulled out her cell and stepped into the living room to make her call.

Bozo came in and started talking and brushing against my leg.

"Hi boy, you're home early," I said, as I bent down to give him some lovin'.

Bozo has a collar on that allows him to come in and out of an electric doggie door all he wants. No other animal can get in, we hope, unless they sneak in with him. We are able to lock his door when we want him to stay in at night.

After Bozo got enough love from Nora and me, he hopped up on the sofa, turned three times, then flopped down to take a catnap.

We spread Louise's stories over the table and started reading through them.

"Some things make more sense now. She wrote about Joe and the boys. *A lot*. Or so I think they're about them," I said, looking them over and setting the last story I read back down on the table.

Most of the stories were short stories, which made it easy to compare notes.

"Some of these seem more like an elaborate diary of a day to day accounting of daily occurrences. Hmmm. Now this could be interesting," Nora said, thinking out loud.

"I think so, too. I keep a daily accounting of my efforts each day, but nothing this elaborate. Mine are more like scattered notes every which way on the current calendar page each day. Main thing is, it helps and I understand them," I laughed.

"Yeah, but no one else can," Nora laughed harder. *It is always a competition between us.*

We decided to set the daily occurrences aside until later.

"Nora, do you have any stories about a Jesse Baines over there? He's described as a thirty-year-old that lived down the block from the character, Joan Hannity. Apparently, he has a crush on Joan. I have the same characters in a couple of the stories."

It wasn't unusual for the same characters to be used in story after story. Heck, my idol, Janet Evanovich has repeat characters. One such series is on Stephanie Plum who is one of my favorite characters. James Patterson has Alex Cross and Michael Bennett, among others. So it was the norm to have repeated characters or heroes in different stories.

Nora went through the stories she had spread out. "No, I don't see anything. She shuffled through the papers and something jumped out at her. "Looky here," She pulled out a page with Jesse Baines' name on it.

"Jesse Baines, but it doesn't mention Joan. There's a different crush, a Marilyn Crain. Wow, this guy was fickle," Nora kept shuffling through more stories, "Or a playboy of the major kind."

Then I found another story with Jesse Baines.

"Okay, this could be a lead. Let's just go through all the stories and pick out any and all with Jesse Baines." I suggested. "Or any multiple names or occasions."

Louise had several stories that are short stories, about seventy pages or so. Some looked to be nine thousand words.

Bozo came in and jumped up into the middle of the table. He laid down among the stories and started licking his paw, and washing his face.

I picked him up and sat him back on the floor. He looked up, disappointed. I patted his head. He flopped down right there.

Nora stood up. "Gotta go to my nail appointment. I'm taking a handful of stories with me to work on tonight."

She bent over me and gave me a hug. "That's okay, don't get up," she snarled.

"Tomorrow when you come back, bring the video you shot of Louise's neighbors and passersby' with you."

"Will do. I looked it over earlier but nothing stood out, except that one guy who clearly didn't want me taking his picture." She threw up her hand good bye and left.

Bozo jumped into my lap, settling in a comfy position. I gently petted him as I continued to read.

I recognized some of the stories. "These are the ones Louise brought to the writers' club meeting for the club to read and *critique as* we do for each other. But this one, she hadn't brought in," I said, now talking to Bozo.

"I wonder if it would be a good idea to ask the writer's club if they would want to help? They did offer. I'll check later," I said still talking to Bozo.

Jackson came in and looked beat. He threw down a pizza box and took out a cold beer he just brought in.

He leaned over and kissed me with a little tongue. Oh my . . .

He gave Bozo a quick pat on his head that just popped up.

He looked over at me and said, "I don't even want to know."

I opened the pizza box and we each picked up a piece.

I took a bite, "This is good, Jackson. Better than the last pizza we had." I took a draw off my beer.

"Do NOT try to butter me up, Charla. It's the exact same Italian sausage, mushroom, and pork sausage with green pepper that we always have."

"Well, for some reason, it tastes better. You know some people make it better than others, is all I'm saying."

He glared at me a nanosecond and said, "Whatever."

Curiosity finally got to him.

"Whatcha got there?" He picked up a story.

"These are Louise's stories that her twin sister Rita loaned us. We thought maybe we could find a connection."

Jackson took another bite of pizza, he looked at me and once again said, "Stay out of it."

"So, Jackson, your people never even touched Louise's computer. It was exactly the way she left it. Thank goodness or I wouldn't have all these stories."

"That's interesting. I WILL find out." He was not happy. "Someone didn't do their job."

I shrugged and took another bite of my pizza followed by a long draw of my cold beer.

I thought, when I find substantial evidence, he won't be saying, "Stay out of it." I shrugged again and took another swallow of beer.

I pushed Bozo off my lap, got another piece of pizza and headed to the living room. With my hands full, I dropped down on the sofa in front of the TV.

Jackson grabbed another beer and brought his plate full of pizza and joined me, as did Bozo.

I ate until I had to unzip my jeans. Jackson took that as an invitation. He took my hand and led me to the bedroom.

"Make up sex," he said.

"I love make up sex," I giggled.

CHAPTER 8

WE TURNED ON THE baseball game. The Royal Socks were headed for the playoffs and it was the first time in years they stood a chance. They were so much fun and exciting to watch this season. With the Royal Socks the game wasn't over until it was over. They always found a way.

Since the baseball season was about over and the football season had already started, my mind started drifting while watching the game. I thought the baseball uniforms looked like pajamas. In fact, most of the baseball team's uniforms looked like P.J.'s

My thoughts turned to football. I didn't like the backside of football pants either and how you can see their jock strap across their butt cheeks. I gotta say though, I like the frontal view. Yep, I do. If anyone besides me looked at the packages in the front of football players uniforms, then they would know what I am talking about. I smiled and snapped to.

The Royal Socks just won a squeaker over the Philly Steamers, 4-3

AFTER A GOOD NIGHT'S sleep, my eyes popped open and OMG! I had been dreaming of the frontal packages of football pants. Whoa! I sat up and looked over for Jackson who was gone, so I looked up at Ryan and smiled.

Darn, I needed Jackson after all those football packages. I opted for a cold shower instead.

I just had to unlocked Bozo's electric door, and put out his food and water, when Nora pulled in with coffee. She brought a couple of that new five dollar, croissant, chocolate donut thingamajiggy, called a Cronut.

And let me tell you THAT'S SOME GOOD STUFF.

We oohed and aahed, with chocolate goo running down the corners of our mouths. That was one of the best things I have ever had in my mouth.

After we finished our Cronut, she bent down, picked up a bag, and said, "Here's your ink and paper." She tossed the bag on the table. "I also put the video on a CD so we could watch it on your computer."

We started viewing the CD. We were looking it over carefully, when lo and behold, we both picked up on something at the same time.

"See that?" Nora asked me.

"Yes. As soon as you pointed your camera at that guy, he clearly pulled down his hat and turned and walked away as fast as he could."

We backed the CD up and watched it again and again, trying to see if this guy was in any other shots. What showed up was a small part of him behind another neighbor. Not enough to even say it was the same guy, but it was. He had a yellow baseball hat on, pulled low over his face. Sunglasses covered most of his face. He was wearing what looked like a pale-yellow hoodie that he had pulled up over his baseball hat. We neither one were sure of the hoodie color. It wasn't the same guy that we saw earlier walking away quickly when Nora pointed her camera at him.

"Well, could you pick him out of a line up?"

Nora looked again, then answered, "No, not even if my life depended on it."

I picked up a page of the story that I was reading last night. "I noticed in this story that there's a guy who lived across the street with a thirty something son, that just moved back in with his dad. Apparently, he's just newly divorced. But it looked like he has issues with women."

"Hmph, maybe we should go back to Louise's neighborhood and ask more questions."

We grabbed more PI's cards and left.

No one was around when we pulled up to Louise's house.

"Harold's been busy. It looks almost perfect," Nora said, as we looked over the front yard.

We headed across the street toward Harold Stonewall's home, and rang his front doorbell.

"Well, well, to what do I owe the pleasure of the sleuthing twins visit? Uh, Nora and uh, uh."

"Charla." I said smiling. *How could anyone keep forgetting my name?*

"Yeah, yeah. Charla."

"Well Harold, we were wondering if you know of anyone around here who has a family member that moved back in with them."

He thought for a second and looked up toward the sky and said, "Not as I can recall."

About that time, a thirty something man stepped out of Harold's house and walked toward him. "Oh, meet my son Oliver." Oliver reached out his hand.

Nora and I looked at each other. *This is curious.*

Nora took his hand and did a quick shake. Then I took his hand, looking him up and down with curiosity.

"Nice to meet you," Oliver said, looking at one of us and then the other.

"Harold, you made good on your word." I pointed to Louise's yard.

"Oliver helped me. We worked on it last night and this morning. Just got through an hour ago. Some of the neighbors came to help. Going to water it this evening," Harold said, proudly.

"Louise would be very pleased."

Just then Rita pulled up. She motioned for Nora and me to come over to her. *I really wanted to ask Oliver some questions. I guess they could wait.*

We could tell she had been crying all night. Her eyes were red and she had bags and dark circles under her sad eyes, but looked sharp in her tan corduroy jeans and brown plaid shirt with the sleeves rolled up. It made her green eyes pop in spite of the red in them.

"I just left the boys. Joe Jr. is taking it harder than I thought," she said, as we walked towards the door.

"He can barely look at me since I look so much like his mom. It really bothers him. He kept saying he was so sorry he gave her such a hard time lately."

Rita noticed the front door ajar. She stepped back. I moved in front of her cautiously and pushed the door open, and then Nora gave me a shove.

I turned and gave her *the look.* "Stop it," I whispered, as I pulled my gun out of my gun size purse.

She snorted like it was funny as she was searching for her gun in that big hulking purse she *has* to carry.

We stepped into Louise's house. Someone had been there. Things were topsy-turvy. Drawers were pulled out, cushions on the floor. It was torn up. We heard the back-door slam.

I ran after them, jumped off the back steps, and started to chase the perp. I tripped over a rake left there by someone. *Harold.* I was flying in midair, landing on my left knee. A big wide-open gash was filling with blood. I had to sit there for a moment while the guy got away. I finally was able to limp back into the house.

Nora was standing next to Rita with her gun hanging down by her side.

"I checked the interior of the house. All clear," Nora said, putting her little .22 derringer away.

I mentioned to Nora several times she should get a larger gun. She couldn't kill a fly with hers.

"Oh, my God, what is going on?" Rita said, clearly crying again.

While Nora tried to comfort her, I called Jackson.

Nora looked down at my knee which was oozing blood down my leg. "Charla, you need to get that knee cleaned up and you probably need a couple of stitches."

I brushed her hand away as I was concentrating on my phone call to Jackson.

"Yeah," but it wasn't Jackson's voice. It was Donnie.

"Good grief," I muttered.

"I am so sorry, Charla. I shouldn't have answered Jackson's phone that way."

"No, you shouldn't," I said, clearly ticked. "Where is he? I need to talk to him . . . quick."

I tried to be nice, but it's hard to do sometimes with Donnie being so close to Jackson. I wanted to pull her hair out even though she has been nothing but nice to me. *Okay, I am a bit jealous. My green eyes were greener. After all, he looks like Ryan Reynolds.*

"Here he comes now," she said, as nice as she could to me. Hmmm?

"Yeah?" he said.

"What's with the damn attitude about answering the damn phone with the yeah crap?" I asked, disgusted. I probably sounded worse than I meant to, as my knee was really hurting.

"Sorry, babe. The commissioner wants answers. And he wants answers now. Apparently, Louise isn't the only housewife to be shot in the head while making coffee."

"That's what I'm calling about, Louise. Wait. Not the only one who got shot in the head? I don't know about anybody else getting killed." *Well, I guess Jackson doesn't tell me everything. Hmph.*

"So why did you call?

"We're at Louise's. Someone broke into her house and trashed it."

"I'm sending a couple of cars and we'll be right there," Jackson said, with concern, hanging up.

"So, did you get a look at the guy who ran out of here?" Nora asked.

"His back side, mostly. He had a bright blue hoodie, washed out blue jeans, and red tennis shoes. I think. When he made a left turn out and over the back fence, he kinda did a semi- circle with his body, and I could see he was young and blond, maybe twenty or so. I saw all that as I was tripping over the rake. *Harold.* I am not sure I could pick him out of a line up."

"Why didn't you just shoot him?" Nora snorted. "That would slow him down," another snort. *She thinks she's so damn cute.*

"And if you had shot him, it wouldn't even sting with that itty-bitty gun of yours," I retorted.

Within ten minutes a couple of patrol cars pulled up and five minutes later, Jackson and Donnie arrived at the same time as the CSI team.

In the meantime, Rita brought out peroxide, Neosporin and butterfly bandages to clean my leg up and doctor my knee.

"Thanks Rita. Damn, I tore my favorite jeans."

I picked my gun up off the chair where I was sitting and slid it back into my gun purse.

I gave the intruder's description to Officer Ryan who said, "Always in the right place at the right time." He shook his head in approval, but smirked. At least, I think he shook it with approval.

I pulled the curtain back and looked out front.

Harold was back out there in front of Louise's house yelling, "Show some respect! Stay on the sidewalk. Stay off the grass. Watch the flowers."

For the most part, everyone cooperated. And Harold stayed out there making sure.

I watched the CSI guys dust and gather bag after bag of evidence. It surprised me that they could come up with so much after bagging up so much the day before.

"By the way, what were you doing here?" Jackson asked me.

Rita interjected. "The girls are my sister's friends and I asked for their help. After all they are PI's."

Jackson grimaced. *Again.* "I guess staying out of it is out of the question. Did you read their card closely?" Now he's looking at Rita.

"Oh, come on, Jackson, we won't be in the way and you know we help more than not," I fluttered my eyes.

He threw his hands up as if he was surrendering. "Stay out of their way." He pointed to the CSI team and officers.

"Rita, why were you here?" Donnie asked.

"I dropped by to pick up some clothes for my nephews."

Donnie nodded she understood. "Oh."

Always the intellect, I thought.

And then Jackson saw my knee.

"What happened here?" He pointed to my knee.

"We heard whoever was here flying out the back door, and I went after them. I tripped on a rake." *Harold.*

"C h a r l a . . . don't chase any . . . one." Then snickered and said, "Let Nora."

"I have my gun." I said, as Nora stared down Jackson, searching hard for a rebuttal.

"Oh my god . . . oh my god, oh my god, you are so . . . so frustrating." He threw his arms around me and said, "Please be careful."

"Always," as I hugged him back.

Rita has now figured out that Jackson and I are an item. She smiled sweetly, watching Jackson fuss over me before he walked away.

Nora and I snooped around trying not to interfere with the police investigation. We went back to Louise's little office just as a young CSI intern was walking out.

We were alone in there, when I spotted something wrong with Louise's computer . . . It was gone . . .

We called out to Rita. "Do you see anything unusual?" I asked her when she walked through the door.

"No, but the picture frame Louise had the boys' picture in is broken on the floor and, oh, wait," as she looked around. "Her computer's gone."

"You mean you don't have it? You didn't take it with you yesterday?" Nora said, hoping.

"Nope," Rita said.

"We were hoping you took it for the boys."

"Nope," she was in shock, looking around and shaking her head. "No, I left everything here just as you saw it yesterday. What is going on?"

"We will find out," I said.

Nora left to catch up with the young CSI intern.

"Hey," Nora looked down at the young intern's name tag. "Hey, Carlos, did you take a laptop just now?"

"No ma'am, no computer."

"Did you see anyone with a computer?" she asked the same intern.

"No, I didn't see anyone with a computer."

"Thanks. Let us know if you see anyone with one," Nora handed Carlos our card and walked back to Rita, leaving Carlos squinting at our card.

I limped over to Jackson. "So, big boy, someone took the computer, and it wasn't your guys, or us. Did you find out who dropped the ball in Louise's office yesterday?"

"No, but I will," he frowned. "I am researching as we speak." He glanced in Donnie's direction.

Donnie heard Jackson and hung her head as she wandered over. I smiled. But it killed me.

"Donnie, I need you to follow up on who dropped the ball yesterday," as he looked back at me. "I want that computer found, asap," he said. *But he felt it was her that dropped the ball.*

"Yes, sir!" she smirked. Saying "*Yes, Sir,*" was clearly a joke between them. I would find out later.

We said good bye to Jackson and walked out with Rita, helping her carry the boy's clothes. I should say I limped out.

I hoped the lab boys would find out what happened to Louise's computer. They were still there when we left.

I had a feeling ole Harold would keep a close eye out on them.

"Rita, would it be alright if we talk to the boys? Could we follow you there and you can introduce us to them?"

"I don't see any harm, but if either of them gets upset, you will have to go."

"Agreed," we both said.

We followed Rita to her parents' home where the boys were staying, and their father was just leaving from his visit. Joe Sr. nodded to us, but kept walking to his car. Hmph, I wonder why he's in such hurry? *We found later he was on his way to see Jackson.*

We entered the house. Rita said she would round up the boys.

The three of them came in and Rita introduced us to Ricky and Joe Jr.

Nice looking boys. I just wondered why Louise didn't talk about her family.

We talked to the boys for a few minutes about general things. We didn't want to spook them to where they wouldn't talk to us in the future. I only asked one question and as gently as I could.

"Do either of you boys know a twenty something blond guy from around here that wears red tennis shoes and a bright blue hoodie?"

Joe Jr. hung his head, then looked up, stared into space for several seconds and then answered, "No."

I knew he knew someone that fit that description, but was clearly too scared to acknowledge who.

"If you think of anyone, let me know," I said, trying to get Joe Jr. to look me in the eye. No luck.

Ricky said he didn't know anyone and I believed him.

"One more question boys, and then we'll go," Nora said. "Do you know who your mom's best friends were besides her neighbors?"

"Our mom's best friends are Carol Sue Faxton and Bev Martin. At least, that's who called her all the time," Joe Jr. said, still not looking Nora or me in the eye.

Rita got into Louise's cell phone and pulled up the two friends' numbers.

Nora wrote down the numbers and said she would follow up today and tomorrow. Rita forwarded the pictures and phone numbers to Nora's cell. God, I love technology.

We didn't want to be pushy under the circumstances, so we said thank you to the boys.

About that time, Joe Jr. came over to me and gave me a hug, then Nora. Ricky followed.

We got out to Nora's car and I said, "That took me by surprise."

"What did?" she asked.

"Oh, the boys, being so sweet. I wasn't expecting it after all we've heard."

"I think Joe Jr. has been re-thinking how he treated his mother now that she's gone. I think he's truly sorry," my old buddy said to me.

CHAPTER 9

FOR A COUPLE OF years, I have worked at Westside Memorial Hospital two days a week, and on call every 4ᵗʰ weekend. I grabbed my scrubs and said good bye to Nora as she dropped me off.

I started my twelve-hour shift and so far, so good. Not much happening. I checked in with my patients and introduced myself to each one. Because it was slow, I was able to spend some one on one with each of them longer than usual.

I answered the call light of Mrs. Joan Cosby. I helped her to the restroom, then fluffed her pillows and helped her back into bed. She thanked me, and all of a sudden she said, "Didn't I see you on TV just yesterday with a redhead with rather large bosoms?"

"Yes, that would be my best friend, Nora. We were there trying to find out about a . . . err-a . . . friend Louise Stafford."

"Well, you know, I know Louise Stafford. Or I should say I'm friends with one of her aunts. Louise's father's sister, Marge Barnover, spoke of Louise on occasion. I have seen the twins off and on over the years."

That piqued my interest. I pulled up a chair and got off my poor injured knee.

"Mrs. Cosby, Nora and I knew Louise from Writer's Club. Since we are not busy, how about sharing information?"

"Call me Joan. Yes, Louise was a writer. She has always loved to write. Some of her stuff was pretty good, or so her Aunt Margie told me. She apparently had a bit of a wild side."

I looked surprised at Joan's comment.

"What's the matter, dear?" she asked.

"The two girls couldn't be further apart in personalities."

I glanced down at my hands and noticed my jagged fingernails, so I tried to tuck them under the long sleeves of the sweater I wore over my scrubs. "I'm just surprised."

Just as I was about to ask Joan what she meant, a code blue was announced. Because I had a bit more experience in cardio, I had to go.

I helped with the emergency, zapped the guy back to life, and helped move him to ICU. We were lucky, or I should say, Mr. Holbert Jones was lucky. He was going to make it.

It was an hour and a half later when I got back to Joan and she was sound asleep.

I asked the nurse's aide, Susan Maxlina, when was the last time she checked on Mrs. Cosby. She said she checked on her about thirty minutes ago. In fact, Susan said she had made all the rounds for me.

"Mrs. Cosby said she was tired and wanted to take a nap. I helped her with her pillows and she closed her eyes. She dozed off pretty quick," Susan said. "A few minutes before you came back to this wing, Caroline, *(who is also an RN but since I'm nurse in charge of that floor today, I'm her supervisor)* checked on Mrs. Cosby's chart against Mrs. Cosby's I D bracelet. She took her blood pressure and temp. Mrs. Cosby grumbled, as she wanted to sleep."

"Thanks, Susan, I'll check with Caroline."

I found Joan's chart and then I found Caroline.

"Caroline, I noticed Mrs. Cosby's temp had peaked a bit, and you didn't give her anything."

"My judgment was since she wanted to sleep it wouldn't hurt to wait a while before giving her anything. So I let it slide," Caroline said, annoyed.

"I wished you would have given her something for the fever, was all," I said, just as annoyed.

"It was my judgment call." She sounded peeved. *Not the way to talk to her boss.*

I stood and looked at her and said, "We're not done talking about this."

Caroline frowned and said, "I'm sure."

"Drop the attitude by the time I come back," I told her, as I walked away to make my rounds and checked back on Joan who hadn't moved. As I walked over to her, I noticed her shallow breathing and that her temperature was even higher. Her blood pressure had taken a dangerous drop. I buzzed for help. We worked on reviving her by putting cold packs on her forehead, then elevated her head. I gave her a shot of vasoconstrictor. She started to come around, but was very weak. After I hooked her up to an I-V drip, I called the doctor on call and he checked her vitals which were slowly getting better by the second. Her blood pressure was coming up and her temperature was coming down. Her eyes slowly opened and a faint smile came across her lips. The doctor said that my quick action more than likely saved her life. We agreed we should put Joan in ICU, just in case.

"Better safe than sorry," the doctor said, "until she's out of the woods."

I looked at Caroline and said, "So Caroline . . . what happened?" *I was livid.* "Looks like you might have put Mrs. Cosby in danger. Your judgment call about killed her."

Caroline wasn't so cocky now. She said, "I didn't mean to . . . to mistreat her. I thought . . ."

"What did you think Caroline?" I said, still livid. "At least I got there in time and she's going to make it." *But I wanted to say no thanks to you.*

I checked on Joan again before I left for home. She had tubes coming out all over her. She opened her eyes as I touched and patted her hand.

"Sorry, Charla, we didn't get to finish our conversation about Louise. I have a lot to tell you," she said in a weak voice.

"Tomorrow, Joan, tomorrow, when you're more up to it," I squeezed her hand and watched her doze off. I hobbled out of her room and left for the day.

CHAPTER 10

SINCE MY TEN-YEAR-OLD EXPLORER was in the shop, I hitched a ride with Paul Overland, a nurse who worked the ER and just happened to live down my block.

I got home just after midnight. Jackson was in bed, but Bozo stretched and came over to me.

"Meow."

"Well, hello, big boy."

He kept looking up at me with his tail straight up, rubbing against me.

"Did Jackson forget to feed you again, Bud?"

"No, Jackson most certainly did not forget to feed him. You know he wouldn't let me have any peace until he was fed," Jackson said, reaching for me.

"Well now, this is a nice surprise," I rose up on my toes and kissed him.

"If you think this is a surprise, come on to bed and I will show you a real big surprise."

"Oh, Jackson, you devil you."

He led me to the bedroom where he had put rose petals all over the floor and bed.

Bozo sneezed.

Jackson picked up the cat, tossed him out of the room, and shut the door.

Jackson was absolutely wonderful, romantic, and delicious.

Afterwards, I was too tired to eat. I rolled off of Jackson and took a deep breath, smiling.

"Good night," I mumbled. But just as I was going out like a light, I whispered, "Yahoo, baby, thanks."

"No problem, the pleasure was all mine," he said with a little giggle.

"Hmmmmm," I moaned.

CHAPTER 11

THE NEXT MORNING, I woke up to Bozo meowing and walking across my chest, rubbing his head against my face. I noticed Jackson was already out of bed, so I glanced up at Ryan with a smile.

I dragged my tired body out of bed and jumped in the shower.

The water made my sore knee burn, but I dried it gently, put my robe on and hobbled down the hall to the kitchen where Jackson was pouring coffee. He came over, put his arms around me and said, "Baby, you were on fire last night." He kissed me, then handed me a large cup of black coffee.

"Meow."

I looked down at Bozo and said, "Okay, boy," as I gave a little slap to Jackson's derrière.

I put his kibbles out, fresh water, and unlocked his electric door.

I took a sip of my coffee and said, "I like spontaneous. The roses were a nice touch. It was indeed a surprise."

"You were the Sur . . . prise. I can't thank you enough, even if you were looking up at Ryan Reynolds half the time."

"I did not look up. I would never . . . Why should I when I have you in the flesh?" I teased, flipping the dish towel at his butt, missing contact.

Jackson loved to tease me. It would bother most men having Ryan Reynolds looking down on them, but Jackson's very secure in his manhood. He was okay with the poster overlooking all that we do.

He pulled me close to him, kissed me and said, "Thank you again," as he patted my fanny. "See you tonight." Then he was gone.

I got a couple of donuts and poured myself more coffee. I pulled up the news on the Internet, but it was the same old political B. S. "I wished you guys weren't so self-serving. What about this country?" I said out loud. "Good grief, it said that China was now the world economy leader," I slammed the lid down on my computer in disgust. "Come on America . . . step it up, and grow a set," I mumbled.

"Meow," Bozo looked up at me. "Meow."

"Oh, big boy, I'm not mad at you. I thought you went out already."

"Meow," he said as he headed toward his doggie door.

I limped to the bedroom, put my scrubs on, brushed my hair, and did a couple of passes with my mascara. "*Good enough,*" I thought as I hobbled out the door to my ride. Paul was kind enough to pick me up.

"So, when are you going to get your car back?" he asked.

"For some reason, it is taking longer than they thought."

"What happened to it?" he asked, turning his head to look for traffic before pulling out into the street.

"I was driving home, sitting at a stoplight when I heard a lady scream, 'He stole my car!' I went into my Good Samaritan mode, and chased after the car. The guy slammed on his brakes, jumped out of his car and headed for me. I slammed on my brakes and the engine blew. Thing was, the guy was her husband."

"I swear, Charla, you're an accident waiting to happen. What did he do when he came after you?"

"He stopped short of the car when he heard the engine blow and just stood there laughing. Apparently, they were fighting, and the little wife yelled out what she thought would get her help. It worked. She ran up to my car, looked at me, shrugged, then went over to her hubby, kissed him, and they made up. Yet, I'm out the cost of a new engine. Go figure."

When I got to work, I immediately did my rounds leaving Joan for last, and then I hobbled in to see her.

She wasn't there. Her room and bed were empty and she wasn't anywhere to be found.

I rushed to the nurse in charge. Norma, where's Joan Crosby?" I said, in a panic.

"Charla, Mrs. Crosby's down getting tests done. Her doctor wanted to know why she crashed yesterday." She put her hand on my arm and said, "You look so pale."

"No, no, I am okay. After yesterday I was fearful something else happened to her," I said, relieved.

Finally, I was able to see Joan. She had her test and was back in ICU getting ready to move back to my floor.

I was so happy she was okay, as I felt sure something was suspiciously wrong. Just a feeling and it wasn't a good one.

A couple of hours later, Joan arrived in the exact room she had before. She was tired when I checked on her, so I let her get some rest. I would be back later and we could finish our talk.

After checking on Joan several times, it was getting close to the end of my shift. I limped back in to see Joan one more time for a short conversation.

I dragged my butt home via Paul. Once again, Bozo and the other bozo were there, ready to greet me when I came in. I petted both. One rubbed against me and the other handed me a freshly cooked bacon and egg on toast sandwich. That was actually what I needed. I left a little egg and tiny bite of bacon for Bozo *the cat.*

Jackson and I walked down the hall to the bedroom, and Jackson feeling somewhat frisky, asked, "You wanna have a repeat of last night?"

"Are there rose petals?"

"Maybe, a few not so fresh, but the rest are going to be real fresh," he giggled.

"Okay, but this time you have to do all the wooing. I'm beat so don't move me too much."

"Oh, babe, it's as much for you as it is for me," he said. And he proved it.

CHAPTER 12

NORA WAS OVER BRIGHT and early. We sat down at the dining room table with our coffee and cronuts. I think I already said this, but boy, those things are good.

We talked about the weather, the writer's club, and what she and Rick had done over the last two days and nights while I was at the hospital. Nora doesn't even text me when I work at the hospital. That was the number one rule for us, unless it was a complete emergency. So far, it's been emergency free.

"So, I went over to Louise's friend Carol Sue Faxton's home, and she said for years that she, along with Louise and Bev Martin, went out many Friday nights. They hung out at a favorite bar called, are you ready for this? It's called 'The Cheer Up.' Though Carol Sue said Louise only went once a month most of the time."

"That's crazy," I said, taking a sip of coffee.

"Yeah, it is, but it's their favorite place to hang out and hook up."

"What? Hook up?" I said shocked.

"Yep, hooking up. Carol Sue made it sound like it was a key club. Once a month, the guys get a room at the Hotel Endormier , then head to The Cheer Up, throw their keys in a hat, then at the end of the evening, the interested ladies draw out a key, and leave with the key owner to the Hotel Endormier out by the airport. I drove by it and decided to go in. It is actually a beautiful upscale hotel," she said, finally taking a breather. "The name means to fall asleep but I bet there isn't much sleep going on," she noted with a giggle.

"Maybe Louise was doing research for a story. Maybe her friends were helping," I said. So how did these keys in the hat develop? How did it start? When did it start?" I asked full of curiosity. "And who names an upscale hotel . . . Hotel Endormier?"

"Oh, for Pete's sake, Charla . . . keep up . . . Anyone who is interested meets up at The Cheer Up, drinks a little, gets acquainted a little; and then the guys who have the rooms at the Hotel Endormier throw their keys into an actual hat kept at the bar. The ladies that are interested pull out a key, say the number out loud and the prospective man who belongs to that room number takes his key and the lady back to the Hotel Endormier for a little HO HO," Nora giggled. "There are always takers and no keys left at the end of the night. I feel like I am repeating myself."

"Ohhhhh. A night at the Hotel Endormier for a night of extracurricular activity," then I giggled. "I get it. Yuck."

"Yesterday I went and talked to Bev Martin. She pretty much said the same thing, only not so descriptively. She was somewhat embarrassed. She hung her head a lot. She said she felt so bad for Louise. Both Carol Sue and Bev said they would help in any way they could. Neither one knows why this happened to Louise," Nora said, taking a breath and another bite of cronut.

"We need to get the three ladies' pictures and take them to 'The Cheer Up,' I said, pausing to take another bite. Still chewing, I continued, "We need to talk to the bar owner, or anyone working there, and the customers hanging out there. I'll call Rita and see if she can get us some pictures. Maybe Louise had a few pictures on her cell. Could we get lucky or are you the only one who wears their cell out snapping pictures?" I teased her.

"Good idea. Now, what did you find out from your patient?" she asked since I told her a little about Joan Cosby earlier that morning.

"You know, Nora, I was so suspicious. I was afraid someone tried to kill her. No reason for it, I just had a bad feeling. Thank goodness, she's okay."

"It does sound like someone slipped her something or stuck her with a needle . . . ," Nora reiterated.

"Joan told me that Louise was a wild child. Her twin was an angel. They were identical in appearance, but complete opposites in personality. Louise was like a back window in a car. She was always looking back to see where she had been and watching the past get smaller. Rita was like a front window of a car, always going forward and things getting bigger and bigger."

"That's deep!" Nora interrupted.

"Yeah, well, Louise had some demons, I guess. Joan said she was always writing stories, and some of them were true stories. Some were pretty good. I would like to drop by to see Joan today. Just keep an eye on her. Maybe she can shed some more light on our victim."

We read through a couple more short stories.

I called Rita and asked if we could meet with her and asked her to bring Louise's cell.

She agreed to meet us for lunch at Rosa's Café.

We arrived at the hospital to see Joan who was sitting up in bed still covered with tubes. She was surprised to see me.

"Well, young lady, what are doing here on your day off?" she asked.

"Nora and I wanted to visit a minute with you. This is my friend Nora."

Joan raised her hand, "Hello."

"Charla said you gave her quite a scare the last couple of days," Nora said, sitting down and making herself comfortable.

"I reckon I did," Joan acknowledged.

Meantime, I left Nora with Joan and limped back to the Nurses station to take a look at Joan's chart.

When I returned, I asked her how she was feeling.

"Better today. The doctor came in a while ago, and said someone gave me a shot of insulin by mistake. Of course, they don't know who did it. It wasn't on my chart. But the test found insulin. Funny treatment for a possible gall bladder attack."

"I just read it on your chart. I am surprised how such a mistake could happen," I said, but I knew I would have to investigate this so-called accident. I was ticked. *Maybe I should advise her to seek council on her hospital charges for the near-death experience and the charges that would accrue because of it.*

"So, tell us a story about the twins," Nora said.

"Well, for the most part the stories about them came from their aunt," she said. "Marge just couldn't get over how different the twins were from each other from the start. Funny thing, Rita was the ornery one and Louise was reserved.

Then somewhere in their early teens they switched personalities," Joan said, just about to nod off.

"You're getting tired now. Maybe we should go. And Joan, don't let anyone give you a shot, or anything, without the nurse on duty being here too."

"Will do. You coming back tomorrow?" she asked.

"We'll try, but we have errands, and the next day we're going to Louise's funeral."

"Well, if you get a chance, pop in, I'll be here a couple of more days."

Nora walked with me as I limped straight to the nurse's station. I wrote on Joan's chart that the nurse in charge had to supervise all activity concerning her. Then I wrote in big letters on a sticky note "FYI, READ INSTRUCTIONS" and attached it to her charge. I felt better leaving Joan now.

CHAPTER 13

WE GREETED RITA, SAT down, and ordered lunch, filling her in on what we had found out to this point.

"I am not surprised. Louise had a bit of a dark side. Yet she was a great mom and tried to be a good wife, but Joe was a hard case himself. He came with baggage, too," Rita said.

"That's what we heard," we both said in unison. Nora punched me and said, "Jinx, you owe me a coke."

"Really," I said, punching her back.

"Do you remember Joan Cosby?" I asked.

Rita thought for a minute then said, "I believe she's a friend of my Aunt Marge. I don't know her that well. Only saw her a few times with Aunt Marge. Nice lady from what I've heard."

Rita pulled out Louise's cell phone and we looked at all her pics. There were several of the boys, a frowning Joe, a few scenery pictures and one of a yacht. There were several pictures of Louise with her two buddies, Carol and Bev. Rita kept flipping through and, voila', a picture of Louise with a couple of rather good-looking guys that appeared to be a bit younger than Louise. She was nestled between them. One of the hunks had his arm around her, and the other was leaning in touching his cheek to hers.

"That's interesting . . ." Nora thought out loud.

"Okay, we need to go to The Cheer Up and the sooner the better," I said. "Forget going in as investigators.

"We?" Rita asked.

"That would be ideal if you could go as well. Maybe pretend to be Louise. Wear a wig that would look more like Louise's style." I stared at Rita, "I think you could pull it off."

Rita said, "Oh, my gosh, did you see how Louise was dressed in that picture and her make up?"

"She looked like she was having fun," I said, looking at Louise with the two hunks again. "Clearly, they were not looking into the camera. No selfie. Maybe these two guys didn't know the picture had been taken. You don't have to work this with us. I just thought it might make our contact with these guys easier, you know since you look like Louise. They might think you're her."

"I have to think about it. I am not my twin. I don't think I can pull it off."

"I understand," Nora said. "We do have to be careful in so many ways."

"We need to think about a plan of action. And you are right. If someone from The Cheer Up was going to the Hotel Endormier for a little HO HO then killing them, we do have to be careful," I said.

"I am single now. I divorced two years ago. I could leave my kids with a sitter. I just don't know."

"You don't have to act like Louise, just look like her."

We enjoyed our meal, chatting about things other than Louise. As we were leaving, I reminded Rita to wait for our call. She had time to think about helping us and could decide on her own without pressure from us.

We went back to the house to read more stories. We had to go through them one line at a time.

I thought it was times to call the Writer's Club girls in to help. But the first call I had to make was to Jackson.

"Hey Babe," I said, as he picked up. Only it was Donnie again.

"Hi, Babe, back at ya," Donnie laughed. "I'll get him."

I waited without a reaction to Donnie when Jackson came on the phone, finally.

"You got diarrhea or what?" I said, disgusted. "What would it take for you to answer your own damn phone?"

"Whoa, hold on, hon. What's got your panties in a wad?" He laughed. *He knows me.*

"I have a murder to solve. And just once I would like for you to answer your own phone."

"Again, hold on, hon. YOU have a murder to solve?"

"Okay Jackson. I don't need this . . . I need your help. I need information and in return, I have some information to help you out."

"Wactcha need?" He reluctantly asked.

"You mentioned another woman got shot in the head while in the kitchen, just like Louise."

"Yeah, but that murder was several weeks ago. Louise was actually the second one," he said.

"Jackson, I need to know about her. Please tell me about it. Please," I pleaded.

"I can't tell you now. I'll be home after a while, and I can share with you then," he said.

We hung up and I called the Writer's Club gals while waiting for Jackson to get home. Everyone could come over the next day. Nora left feeling good about our plan of action.

CHAPTER 14

JACKSON CAME DRAGGING IN about six, after finishing his fourteen-hour day week for the last couple of weeks.

I had dinner made and was ready to sit down when he came in.

"Make up dinner," he smirked.

"Noooa." *Yes.*

We sat down to spaghetti and meat sauce with a salad and garlic toast. It smelled fabulous.

We sipped Pinot Grigio red wine, and not the cheap stuff. I even lit candles on either end of the table.

We were enjoying our meal when Bozo popped in. He smelled his favorite meal.

"Meow, meow," as he brushed against my legs.

"Okay boy." I dished him up some spaghetti.

"That's amazing," Jackson said.

"What?"

"How Bozo eats the pasta first leaving the meat sauce."

"It's his favorite," I said, listening to Bozo purr while he chowed down.

We cleaned up the kitchen, grabbed another glass of wine and sat down at the table where I had spread Louise's stories out again.

"Jackson, tell me about the first murder. I need to compare notes."

"You know I shouldn't, but living with you and sharing EVERYTHING, then, okay, I know what I tell you will be kept between us. Oh yeah, and Nora, your faithful companion." *Little did he know we weren't sharing everything with him, yet!*

"It's the same modus operandi. Victim Lora Janeson was found by her neighbor, except Lora wasn't expecting her neighbor. The neighbor, a Mrs. Yardley, noticed Lora's car still home, and she knew she always worked. She went over to see if Lora was sick or something. When Lora didn't answer the door, Mrs. Yardley, always the nosy neighbor peeked into each window until she saw Mrs. Janeson lying in the middle of the kitchen floor. She dialed 911. We haven't connected the dots yet," he said.

"Okay, I have a theory," I replied.

"Really . . . a theory," he smirked. "Let's hear your *theory*."

"Smirk all you want, but my theory is good," I said to him, half pissed.

I told him as much as I wanted him to know at this time. I didn't want him to spoil my investigation. I mentioned The Key Club etc. but didn't want him to know just yet of our plans of going to The Cheer Up to check out the "Hotel Endormier" key in the hat thing.

He gave me Lora Janeson's address and background with his up to date notes. I am so glad he shares better than I do. He glanced over Louise's stories. "This is interesting stuff." He started reading again.

CHAPTER 15

I DOCTORED MY KNEE which was better than yesterday. Nora picked me up bright and early as my ten-year-old car still wasn't ready. The "I Fix Cars" mechanic said it would be another few days before I could pick it up. Meantime, Nora hauled me around, or I would drive Jackson's old Ford Fusion he had for a backup tucked away in his garage.

When Nora and I got back from the grocery store, Nora pulled the rotisserie chicken off the bone while I cut up the rest of the things needed to make chicken salad sandwiches. I opened up the chips and poured them in a large bowl. We got out assorted drinks; put a bucket of ice out with glasses, arranging the buffet style lunch to make it easier for serving. I slid my mini office back into the closet. It is a small compact table with a couple of shelves and rollers that has most of my things I need for an office. I can roll it away to have more space for entertaining when needed in the dining room.

The Writer's Club girls arrived, and we said our hello's, then we lined up to fill our paper plates. *Yes, paper plates. Nothing is too good for company.* We sat around the table and started eating. We were chitchatting about everything from the weather to Louise's family. We wondered how the boys were coping. The funeral was tomorrow and we all planned to attend.

"Meow, meow." Bozo headed for me.

"Hi, big boy. Oh, if anyone's offended by cats, speak up or forever hold your peace," I announced, as I reached down to pat Bozo's head. No one objected. Bozo was welcomed.

I heard the doorbell. "What a pleasant surprise, Rita. Come on in."

"Thanks, I just want to discuss what we talked about yesterday," she smiled.

"Come on in and meet The Writer's Club. They are all here to help. Everyone, this is Louise's sister, Rita." They all looked up and did a double take.

"Identical, except for the hair," Loraine mentioned. "Louise's hair was longer and darker."

"Yes, we were identical twins," Rita smiled. "Louise colored her hair." She paused, then looked around and said, "I want to help find out what happened to her."

I offered her a sandwich while everyone took a story. She declined.

Reading page after page, we again came up blank. They appeared to be just stories.

"This is the deal . . . tomorrow's Louise's funeral. On Friday night we, *I looked at Nora*, are going to The Cheer Up club.

I filled the club in on most of The Key Club information.

"Oh, wait a minute," Loraine said. "I think it would be fun for us all to go. Kind of a girls' night out and we just happened to go to The Cheer Up."

"You know, that would be a great way to go undercover," Nora sounded excited. "We can doll up and act like we are celebrating a birthday, someone's 30th maybe. Great cover."

Now everyone was getting excited, even Rita.

Bozo was excited too, as he meowed and rubbed against everyone's legs while getting petted by everyone he brushed.

"We all will go to Louise's funeral, then Friday night we meet up and go to The Cheer Up," I said.

The plans were made.

CHAPTER 16

NORA AND I MET the rest of the Writer's club at Louise's funeral. We all tried to sit together.

I could see Louise's sons were having a hard time being strong, especially Joe Jr. Rita was sitting between them with her arms around each of them, with her own kids sitting next to Ricky.

Joe was nowhere to be found, but at last he came in, and sat down on the other side of Joe Jr. within seconds of the service.

The Rev. Harry Shapton introduced himself.

"May we pray?"

All you could hear was the rustle of heads moving to the down position with a sniffle here and there, while the boxes of tissues were being passed around.

The silent prayer was over, and the good Rev. Shapton continued.

"We are here today, not to say good bye to Louise Rita Stafford, but to remember her in all good light. She served in this church for many years as the church editor and writer of the newsletter each week. As you all know, she loved to write. She has a twin sister, Rita Louise Brownstone." Everyone turned to look at Rita.

Rita Louise, Louise Rita. Hmph, strange, I thought. *Well, they are twins.*

The good Reverend continued, "Louise spoke highly of her and often told me she wished she could have been more like

her twin, Rita, who seemed to have it all together. Louise said she was the half empty cup and Rita was the half full cup."

Rita sighed with sadness.

He went on, "But the one thing Louise was, was a loving mother." *Now everyone looked at the boys.*

"Louise loved those boys, Joe Jr. and Ricky. She talked about them all the time. She said that was the one thing she did right was having you two boys," he said, looking at the boys.

Now Joe Jr. broke down sobbing with deep hard breaths, which caused a chain reaction with his brother and aunt weeping.

The good Reverend spoke ten minutes more of Louise's accomplishments, and once again asked, "May we pray?"

He quoted a few more scriptures and a verse or two from what he said were Louise's favorites.

We raised our heads, looking up at the good Rev. Shapton who said, "One thing that Louise said jokingly many times, was, when she died she wanted everyone to stand up and sing the old gospel, "Let's Go Out in a Blaze of Glory." She just didn't know it would be so soon or so young. So, if everyone will look up at the words on the monitor, you will notice the Let's is replaced with SHE Went Out in a Blaze of Glory." About that time, the music started and we all looked up in surprise; we stood and sang this tribute to Louise.

Then the good Reverend said one more prayer and told everyone that we were all invited to the church dining room for the meal that several church members had prepared.

"Please join us after the graveside service back here," he added.

The Writer's Club all looked at each other and shrugged. Okay, then, we would all stay.

We were getting our plates full of the wonderful delicious food that the church ladies prepared when Joe Jr. came over to me. He threw his arms around my neck, which took me by surprise in more ways than one, making me about spill my plate, which I had to set down on the table.

"Miss O'Hara, I did hear my mother speak of you. She said that you made it fun to be part of the Writer's Club, you and your friend," he said pointing towards Nora.

"Thank you for remembering, Joe, Jr."

"Please, just Joe. I do know the guy who broke into my house. My mom didn't like him. She thought he was bad for me."

"You mean he's a friend?"

"Well, not really. He's almost twenty and likes to break in and enter homes. I don't do that stuff. Mom said if I kept hanging with him, he would bring me down. I know he has my mother's computer."

"Thanks for telling me," I said.

He slipped me a note with the kid's information, and then he gave me a hug and walked away.

Just as I was reaching for a drink, Harold Stonewall and his son, Oliver, came over to me. I stepped back a little, in fear of another hug. My hands were full again, and well, I didn't want his hug.

I stuck out my elbow for him to shake. He took my elbow gently as not to cause me to spill my food, then Oliver shook my elbow.

Nora, to the rescue, walked over and joined in the conversation.

"So, how does Louise's yard look?" Nora asked. "You keeping it up, are ya?"

"Yep, it's looking pretty good. Oliver and I both are taking turns watering it. It about needs mowed," he said. "Haven't seen hide nor hair of her family, other than Rita, except today."

"I know Louise would so appreciate your help," Nora said.

I excused myself and went to join the rest of the Writer's Club. Nora soon joined us after passing Harold and Oliver off on their neighbor, Carol Hershey.

I was looking for Jeanie Hughes. I saw her at the service, but lost track of her in the dining area. I had not yet interviewed her and, I wondered, was this the time or place? No, probably not.

Nora saw Carol Sue and Bev as they were approaching. Nora shook her head, no, and they made a big u-turn. We didn't want Joe Sr., to know we knew them. Yet!

I glanced around to see if I could see Joe Sr., so I could introduce myself and the rest of the Writer's Club to him, and, of course give our condolences. We were talking among ourselves and getting ready to head out, giving up on Joe Sr., when Nora spotted Jeanie Hughes. She nudged me and pointed toward the coatroom doors that slowly opened. Jeanie came out straightening her hair and smoothing her dress down while Joe was zipping up his pants walking out behind her . . . *What?*

"Oh . . . My . . . God . . . !" I exploded in anger. "Looks like we just might have new suspects for Louise's murder. It just gets better and better," I said to the club, standing beside me in disbelief.

I still wanted to introduce the group to Joe, but no one wanted to shake his hand, and since we didn't know where Jeanie's mouth had been, *no kisses either. Yuck!*

We, as a group, went up to both of them.

I couldn't help myself, I thought about saying, "See you getting some on the side, you sanctimonious asshole." I looked at Jeanie. "And you, Jeanie, had coffee every Wednesday morning with your good friend and neighbor Louise, while bonking her husband. You are disgusting. You both are beyond disgusting. You both make me sick."

But, I didn't say that because I wanted the door of conversation to remain open. I was sick of what I had just witnessed, as was the rest of the Club. But we each smiled and walked over to them.

"Hi, I am Charla O'Hara and this is Nora Weston." Then I introduced all the girls, but no one took the held-out hands of Joe or Jeanie. It didn't seem to bother either of them. I felt so two faced, smiling, but wanting to flatten them both.

Finally, the pompous jackass spoke, "I never liked Louise going to that writer's club expressing her disgust with our marriage and telling family secrets."

Jeanie just hung her head. She knew we knew.

"Oh, really? Louise had nothing but good to say about you Joe," I lied. All of the girls, knowing what I was doing, smiled in agreement.

"Really," Joe softened.

"Yep, good things," Nora confirmed.

Jeanie started slinking away from all of us like the guilty coward she was. *The harlot.*

About that time, Rita and Louise's sons came over to our group.

We shared a few stories and hugged Rita, Ricky, and Joe Jr. before we left. I was glad that that Joe, Sr. had crawled away and went back under his rock.

Nora said, when we reached the parking lot, "You were having a hard time controlling your temper. I could see it in your face, but you controlled it. Yes, you did."

I threw up my hands and screamed, "I am so pissed. The nerve of that low-life S. O. B. to bang or get a blow job in the church coat closet on the day of his wife's funeral. So . . . so disgusting. I would bet this isn't the first time either. That could explain why Louise was in The Key Club . . ."

Then, I yelled, "I just want to hit someone . . ."

The Club, including Nora, backed away. I let out an "OH MY GOD" as loud as I could. Then I let out a horrific scream. With that I bent over and cried. The club surrounded me as onlookers looked.

"You'll get even, Charla. You will make them all pay. I know you will," Nora explained.

All of the Writers' Club were shaking their heads in agreement.

"And we start tomorrow," I said, making plans to meet up in The Cheer Up parking lot.

CHAPTER 17

JACKSON WOULD NOT APPROVE of these shenanigans that I conjured up, not at all. And I didn't want him to find out until it was all said and done.

But first, Nora and I were going to interview Lora Janeson's family, neighbors, and friends.

We wanted to see if we could get a current picture of her to go along with Louise's.

We wanted to show the picture to Louise's Cheer Up buddies, Carol Sue and Bev. Could Lora have been a Cheer Up regular? We lined up the names and addresses so we could go right down the list in Lora's neighborhood.

We knocked on Lora Janeson's front door, noticing crime-scene tape broken and flying in the wind.

"It's a shame that no one thought to pull this stuff down. And it's been weeks since they discovered her body, if not longer," I said, looking over the remnants left from the crime scene.

No one answered the Janeson's door. We walked around the house just in case someone was there. We heard hammering from a shed in the back, so we moseyed toward the sound. A guy was coming out and we startled him.

"Whoa." He jumped back.

"Hi, I'm Charla O'Hara and this is Nora Weston." I handed him our card. "We were hoping you could answer a few questions."

He looked at our card and squinted, "PI's? What's this about?"

"We help the police with different investigations a lot of the times and . . ."

"And what?" he sputtered.

"We were wondering about Lora Janeson. Her death was very much like a friend of ours, and since we're helping the police with our friend's murder, we're wondering if Lora knew the same people."

"I don't know anything about Mrs. Janeson. I only work for her sometimes, a handyman, as it were, for repairs and yard work, and such."

I pulled out my handy dandy notebook ready to write his name down.

"Could we have your name and number Mr. uh . . ."

"No."

"Oh, I uh," I blinked my eyes. I was at a loss for words. I'm hardly ever lost for words.

Nora popped up and said, "We didn't want to upset you, sir, we just want to try to see if there was anything in common with our friend. It would just help us if . . ." Nora noticed him looking at her ginormous boobs.

"Jed Norman. 555 6023"

"Thank you," she said, straightening her shoulders and pulling her girls up and out.

Oh, for god's sake, I thought, writing his name and number down as fast as he was saying it.

"Oh, sorry for staring, but those are magnificent," he said finally raising his eyes to hers.

"Thank you, Mr. Norman. But we could sure use your help if you can give us anything you witnessed, heard, or noticed," Nora said, as gracious as possible.

"Ladies, I didn't work here that day or see anything before or since. Her family wanted me to keep up with the lawn work, and that's why I am here today," he said, trying hard to look in Nora's eyes.

"You have our card if you remember anything at all," I said. "Please give us a call."

"Sure will," he said, looking at Nora's girls.

We turned and walked away.

"You have an admirer," I said. "He's enamored."

"With my . . . girls! He's lucky I'm so nice, as I wanted to reach out and strangle him by pulling his tongue out and wrapping it around his neck until his eyes popped. God, I hate when men stare at my girls."

"His eyes were popped out. People, men, can't help it. I mean they're soooo out there, even when you try to cover them up," I said. "However, I do notice you use them to your advantage by popping them up and out."

"Well, yeah!" she said, adjusting them as we sashayed over to the next place on our list. No one was home. Our luck was the same on the whole block. But at each place we left our business card with a small note simply saying, If you know anything about Mrs. Janeson's murder." Pls call."

Who knows, someone might call.

We decided we would go back to Jackson's house and run through the last of Louise's stories.

As soon as we walked into the house, we went straight to the dining room table to read.

"Nora, do you think Louise kept any records other than these stories? Let's call Rita and ask her to snoop at her sister's a little more."

I dialed her and she picked up on the first ring and a half.

"Rita, it's me and Nora, we have you on the speaker. We got an idea that maybe Louise might have a secret hiding place with information on her Key Club dates. It's a long shot, but we thought it might be worth it if you could find anything at all."

"Okay, I'll go over tomorrow and see if I can find a hiding place. I haven't got time today. I have to go buy something sleazy to wear tonight and I thought I would buy a wig."

"Good idea," we said in unison. "Why don't you ride with us tonight?"

"Actually, I would feel better if I could go with you."

"Be here at half past eight," I said.

We hung up.

"She sounded a little nervous."

"Yeah, but she'll do fine," I said.

"Wait, where's Louise's daily diary we noticed at the beginning? We barely looked at it, before we tossed it over there somewhere," Nora said, pointing in the direction of the dining table.

"The trouble is we've moved this stuff around so much. I've taken it on and off the table for dinner so many times. So, maybe it's buried somewhere in these stories. I'll look for it later."

Nora left to go feed Rick and get ready for our big night of investigation.

I just got through making salmon patties, corn on the cob, and a big salad when Jackson and Bozo came in. One came through the garage door, the other through the doggie door.

"That smells fishy,"

"Meow," Bozo agreed. We sat down to eat, which turned out to be great.

"Jackson, I'm going out with the Writer's Club tonight to celebrate Katy's birthday."

"Oh, is, that right? I was hoping to get a little us time tonight," he said.

"I'm sorry, but we have it all planned out. Nora and Rita will be here, and we have to meet the rest at 8:30."

"Rita?"

"We invited her. She wants to be a part of Louise's friends."

"R i g h t . . . !" he said, stretching it out.

Thank goodness Jackson got a call. He grabbed me, kissed me deeply, smacked my behind, and said, "Stay out of trouble." He left.

I cleaned up the kitchen, petted Bozo, and went to shower.

Before I dressed, I got on the computer to see if I could find a photo of Lora Janeson. I found several pictures of her that had been in the newspaper. I copied the best one to take tonight.

Eight fifteen on the nose, both Rita and Nora arrived.

"Bada bing. Bada boom," Nora said, when I answered the door. "You look A M A Z I N G."

I took her hand and twirled her around and went, "Bada Bing, yourself."

We both looked at Rita. "Wow . . . you pulled off the sleazy Louise look that we saw in the picture with the two hunks without a problem," I said.

"Impressive," Nora said.

"You really pulled it off. I swear with that wig, you will confuse the whole Cheer Up crowd."

"That's the goal. But it costs a lot to be sleazy," Rita said. "Three hundred bucks, and that's not counting these six-inch heels." She pointed to her feet.

I was so glad Jackson wasn't home and I didn't have to explain this to him.

CHAPTER 18

ALL EIGHT OF THE Writer's Club girls, plus Rita, met in the parking lot of The Cheer Up about 8:35.

We were a tad late.

Everyone looked like trouble on the prowl. I believed we could fool a lot of people.

The girls couldn't believe how Rita looked.

Walking across the parking lot, Rita fell off her heels a couple of times. She hung on to Nora who has to have perfect balance all the time due to her permanent front load.

We decided to go through the front door laughing and a few of us a little loud and stumbling around.

We went in as planned, but it kind of backfired as there was only one hunk sitting at the end of the bar, a couple of bartenders and a handful of servers.

We had plenty of room to spread out. We ordered our drinks, still being loud and giggling.

Nora yelled out, "Hey, barkeep . . . got anything special for the birthday girl?" We all pointed to Katy.

"Sure do. Hang around ladies, the action will be here soon. You're the first to arrive," he yelled out over our loudness. "Except him." He glanced over his shoulder to the hunk at the end of the bar.

"You mean we won't have the place to ourselves?" Nora yelled back.

He shook his head no as he mixed and poured Katy a drink. "For the birthday girl," he said, handing it to her. "It's on the house."

Katy smiled and said, "Thanks. What is it?"

"It's a secret, but it's legal." He laughed, almost too loud.

Katy took a sip. "Woolf, this is good," she said, taking another sip.

"Since we don't know what it is, Katy, take it easy," Loraine warned.

"I thought I would nurse it, though it's wonderful; I might pour some of it in the plant over there," Katy whispered. "On the other hand, I might keep sipping," she giggled.

We sat around the bar like we owned it with some of the girls grabbing a few tables. So far, I didn't get the whole hoopla about this place. It was dead and not at all exciting. But we hung out giggling and yelling back and forth to each other just in case business picked up.

CHAPTER 19

"Daniel"

DANIEL NIELSEN SAT AT the end of the bar smiling to himself at the new blood that just stumbled through the door.

"What do we have here?" he actually said out loud.

Buddy, the bartender, answered thinking Daniel was speaking to him, "Looks like a birthday celebration."

"Nice!" Daniel said, looking the new herd over. *Surely one or all would like The Key Club*, he thought, adjusting his boys that were getting excited.

He had already put his key in the hat as he often did when he first walked in. He didn't play The Key Club game every time. Not as often as he used to. But he was anxious to see who would be the lucky lady tonight? Of the regulars left, he had only been with them two or three times. No number fives. Thank goodness, he thought. I really don't like killing them.

Just thinking about it, he had to adjust himself, *again*.

He spotted Rita, "What the hell?" as Daniel took a double take on her. He stared at her.

"I killed you, didn't I?" he mumbled under his breath. "What's going on?"

Buddy, thinking Daniel was talking to him again, though he didn't understand what Daniel just said, looked over where Daniel was looking.

"Well tonight's going to be a BLAST, don't you think Buddy?"

Buddy glanced at Daniel with a half-smile and a nod.

The door opened and several more people walked in.

"Shit, the gang's all here," Daniel said, as he glanced back at Rita. "Hmmm!"

"Who will I get tonight?" he mumbled, still looking at Rita.

He studied her every move. After watching her for a while, he noticed that Louise's moves were different. Not the same.

Then it dawned on him, Louise had mentioned a twin. And when he was with Louise, he thought about how much fun doing twins would be. *No chance with twins, now.* He thought with a cocky snicker.

But why was she here and now? His curiosity was running wild. Keep cool, he warned himself. Keep cool.

CHAPTER 20

FINALLY, THE HUNKS STARTED straggling in, as did the ladies. The guys smiled and nodded their head to us, while the ladies gave us the once-over and over again.

Can you spell *"fear of competition?"*

"Hi, JoJo," the bartender yelled out.

"Hey, Jordan, how's business?" she yelled back to him.

He raised his hand and made a swoop with his hand pointing at all of us. "Better tonight."

"I see that," JoJo said, walking closer to him and looking us over.

A few more presumed regular customers came in. Everyone greeted everyone and they all noticed the new blood. *The Writer's Club.*

Some just stared, and others smiled walking by us.

Bev and Carol Sue came in and saw Nora. They eased back to a table in the opposite corner, not knowing if they should speak or not and if mum was still the word.

After a few drinks, everyone was milling around as was the Writer's Club and Rita.

Carol Sue and Bev had to pass Nora to greet a regular.

Nora stood in their path and said, "Hey, didn't I see you at Louise's funeral yesterday?"

Stumbling with the right words, Carol Sue said, "Why, yes. Wasn't it a nice service?"

"Let me introduce you to Charla," Nora said, reaching for my arm and pulling me into the conversation.

"Hi, nice to meet you both," I said.

"Mum's the word on Louise's investigation here at the bar," Nora whispered.

"No problem," Bev said, and Carol Sue nodded okay, crossing her heart with her finger.

"Look . . . Katy's slurping another drink," one of the Writer's Club girls pointed out.

"Yeah, it's Katy's birthday," we reminded her.

Then turning back to Carol Sue and Bev, Nora said, "We thought since Louise came here, this would be a good place to celebrate."

A five-piece band set up on a little stage back in the far corner started playing a little two-step.

I looked at Nora, grabbed her hand and pulled her to the dance floor. "It's time to party."

"I think we better keep an eye on Katy. She has a head start on us," she said.

"Well, she's getting free drinks."

That's when one of the two hunks in Louise's picture zoomed in on Rita. The double-take was so worth it.

He nudged the guy beside him. Before you knew it, several of the customers were all staring. Finally, the two hunks came over to Rita.

"Wow, Louise, you look amazing. We can't believe it's you," one of the hunks said as we eased over to try to hear.

"Why's that? Because you heard she was dead?" Nora snarled, being protective as we danced and stopped by Rita.

"Well, yeah," he said, as he leaned down to kiss Rita on the cheek. "Nice to see the rumor was wrong."

Rita looked at us, as we gave her the thumbs up and thought, *the guy's really dumb.*

We decided earlier that we would let it ride for a while before telling them the truth. Rita was pulling off the look, but probably not the action. Of course, Rita didn't know anyone's names. Louise always called everyone Sugah, so Rita thought that would work for a while. She'd play that card when it came to it.

The music got louder. Several more of the girls went on the dance floor and started dancing together, laughing loudly, being silly, drawing attention to themselves.

One of the hunks, who had just greeted Louise aka Rita, cut in and started dancing with both Nora and me.

"So, blue eyes, what's your name?" Nora asked.

"Ross. Didn't Louise tell you?"

"Louise just said no one uses their real name."

"Some don't." He swung us out and back around again.

"Actually, Ross is my name. But yeah, a lot of these yahoos don't use their real name."

"Well, to tell you the truth, that's Rita, Louise's twin." Nora told Ross.

"Do tell," he said, as he tried to take a look in her direction as he swung us out, turning us both in a counterclockwise circle and back in toward him.

"Had me fooled," he said, as he looked back over to Rita. He swung us out and back one more time before the song ended, then walked us back to our friends.

Soon the word got out about Rita. Some thought it uncanny, some thought it funny and some, not so much.

The Writer's Club girls were having a such good time that we almost forgot our mission.

All of a sudden, Nora broke out in song . . . "Happy Birthday to you, Happy Birthday to you, Happy Birthday dear Katy, Happy Birthday to you." Everyone joined in.

Then different guys lined up to dance with Katy, who was laughing so hard, having the best non-birthday ever. All of a sudden, a slow dance started, and the guys were asking all of the Writer's Club girls to dance before asking the regular lady customers, who waited with baited breath to dance.

Carol Sue and Bev had met Rita once before. They were amazed at Rita's appearance. They tried to act normal and treat her like she was Louise. *Part of the plan.* But by now everyone knew she was Rita. So they were a day late and a dollar short . . .

Carol Sue got a smile on her face and said to Bev, "It's time to *par tee.*"

"Wait, hold up." Nora said. "Do you know who she is?" She showed them the picture of Lora Janeson.

"Yeah, yeah. She used to come in here, and I think she died a while back.

Didn't know her well."

"Thanks, and mum's still the word."

"We understand," Bev said, grabbing Carol Sue's hand and leading her to the dance floor.

All of a sudden, Jordan the bartender, brought out the notorious hat from behind the bar. Five different guys threw in their keys. The hat went back behind the bar.

After a few more dances, the regular lady customers started talking to us. I squeezed between them at the bar. I said, "Hey Jordan, I noticed you were taking donations in a hat a while ago. How about letting me donate a few bucks?"

The two women I was standing between glanced at each other and started to chuckle.

He laughed, "That's not a donation. Well, I guess some would call it a donation. But it's not what you think."

"Oh, what then? I would like to help."

"Oh, baby, I don't think this is up your alley."

"I don't understand." I acted disappointed.

"Later," he said. "Maybe I'll tell you later, but right now I gotta get back to bartending."

"I came this close." *holding my fingers two inches apart,* "to getting Jordan to tell me about the hat," I said to Nora, walking back in the direction of our table.

"Ah, but the night is young," she teased. "We already know how it works. We just need Jordan, or whoever, to confirm the way it works."

The single hunk, who was sitting alone at the end of the bar when we first arrived, approached me. He held out his hand for me to take for a slow dance. I clumsily took his hand thinking, "*Why did I just put my hand into his?*"

"I haven't seen you here before," he cleverly said, looking me up and down.

"It's my first time," I cleverly retorted.

"Well, I hope it's not your last time," he said, *As Mr. Cool, so confident and smooth* lead me to the dance floor.

"It's looking up," I said, standing there with my hand in his. *Now why did I say that?*

"This could be fun," he smiled placing his hand around my waist, pulling me to him. "What's your name?"

"Charla. Yours?"

"Damon."

He pulled me closer and we danced. I must say he was really smooth and very good. Even the dip at the end of the song was smooth.

A couple of dances later, Damon walked me back to my table.

"Thank you, Charla," then he kissed my hand and walked away.

Nora looked at me and said, "Isn't it funny how some men think a little small talk makes them think they own you?"

"Must be my skin-tight, low-cut red dress," I said.

"You really do look sexy."

"Thanks, but I'm not sure Jackson would approve."

"Hey, you're undercover, and if that hunk you just danced with had his way, you would be under his cover."

"Well, THAT . . . will never happen," I said, pleased with myself, thinking I still had it going on, but then I woke up and realized I could have been dancing with a killer. I took a bar napkin and wiped my hands off, then opened my purse for hand sanitizer.

I looked around the bar for all my friends, making sure they were alright.

One by one I checked off the Writer's Club ladies. "All here," I mumbled.

Katy was leaning over the bar flirting with Jordan the bartender. "Ah, come on Jordie, I'm the birthday girl. Just one more of those secret birthday drinks." Jordan gave in, but made it half the size of the other ones. Katy was enjoying herself and looked like she was getting hooked on that secret drink.

"Nora, we need to keep an eye on Katy."

"Really?" She pointed to Amelia who had her leg up and around some joker who she had backed against the wall.

We walked over to her and gently pulled her off the schmuck.

"Looks like you're feeling frisky, Amelia," I said.

"Well, if it's not Kemo Sabe and her sidekick Tonto. You know I am divorced a year now and it's time to get back in the saddle. Look around, ladies; it's a smorgasbord around here." Amelia slurred.

"Yeah, but you don't want nothing to do with these guys, Mrs. Robinson. You're a little older than some of them. Do I need to remind you why we are here?"

We led her away from some cutie who was young enough to be her son.

"Look, he still has pimples. I bet he just turned 21," Nora said, giggling, "And what, Amelia's 45?"

We led Amelia back to our table and sat her down.

I looked at Nora and said, "I think things are starting to get out of hand."

I glanced over the bar, taking in the whole group.

"Yep, out of hand. Everyone forgot to drink slowly. Looks like we need designated drivers."

Nora watched Damon watch my every move. He couldn't keep his eyes off me.

"Doesn't it creep you out that, that Damon character keeps watching you?" she asked.

"Maybe . . . a little. Actually, I'm worried about all these guys. Hells bells, maybe it's one of these ladies," I said, glancing around the bar. "I just know the key to Louise's death has to be here. I feel it."

Meantime, a short guy came over to Nora and asked her to dance. A slow dance was playing and he laid his head on Nora's bosoms with his eyes shut and a smile on his face. Nora, who had her chest exposed to the elements, rolled her eyes. *Really!* She was thinking. *Really.*

When the song stopped, the short guy put his face into her chest with a noise of gurgling going side to side in Nora's bosom. Nora pushed the little perp away from her, and then she slapped him to kingdom come. He was still smiling.

The perp said, "I just died and went to heaven."

Nora replied, "I can arrange that." The guy slinked away.

I called a limousine service to come and pick up the group to take us home. A limousine was cheaper overall than several cabs.

While waiting for the limos, I moseyed over to Jordan and asked him again about the hat. After badgering him over and over again with a touch of flirting, Jordan gave it up; though he reminded me he doubted I would be interested in partaking.

"Okay, there are about six guys or so who put hotel keys in the hat. The ladies can pull out a key card, read the room number out loud, and the guy it belongs to takes her and the key back to the hotel for a night of pleasure."

"No way," I acted surprised.

"Way. If there are too many ladies who want to dip in for a key, we have to put in blank ones so everyone has a fair shot of getting lucky."

"No-way."

"No really. Way. See that guy that can't keep his eyes off of you at the end of the bar?"

"Yeah," I said, without looking in his direction

"He's always first to drop his key in the hat."

"Hmmm. So how often do you have these drawings?" I asked.

"Usually once a month on the second Friday, occasionally one in between. It depends on the demand. If it falls on a holiday weekend, then the drawing is held the weekend after."

"Huh. You have it down to a science," I responded as I glanced in Damon's direction.

He smiled at me and started walking toward me.

"I see Jordan went over the hat rules with you. You interested? I would love for you to pull out my key."

"I . . . I don't think so," I stuttered.

"Too bad," he turned and walked away. Then half way back to his seat he turned again and said, "Let me know if you change your mind." He smiled the sexiest smile.

I thought this guy could be trouble. He's really movie star good looking.

We witnessed the key drawing and watched some of the pairing of some the couples before the limousine service picked us up.

Everyone would arrive at their home safe and sound.

Nora got out in front of her house but turned, and leaned into the limo and said, "I'll pick you up in the morning. We'll get Rita's car back to her then we'll go to Cheer Up and get mine."

"That'll work," I said. We waved good night to each other.

I had the limo driver wait until Nora got in her door.

CHAPTER 21

I WALKED INTO THE house where Jackson was waiting up. Bozo greeted me, but Jackson just stared.

I threw out my hands and said, "What?"

"Nice dress. Charla, what are you up to? And don't tell me you were celebrating a birthday."

I sat down across from him and told him how we decided to go to the Cheer Up and why. I told him what we learned to this point, leaving out some of the details that I would fill in later.

"Is that all of it?"

"Mostly. I can't help but think that one of those guys killed Louise, and it wouldn't surprise me if the same guy killed your Lora Janeson. Turns out she was a regular at Cheer Up."

"Well now, that theory is interesting," he said.

"Jackson, do you have any cold cases similar to these two? Is there a connection?"

"I'll check it out. This is a very good theory. I am proud of you. Now come here."

Clearly, he was through talking. I got up and walked closer to him.

He stood up. "Though there's not much fabric in this dress, I bet you need help getting out of it." He pulled me close to him, unzipped the zipper and pulled off one shoulder of my dress, then the other. The dress dropped to the floor. I had on matching red lacey panties and bra. I looked as good as Jamie Lee

Curtis in *True Lies* dancing around the bedpost. Almost.

"Whooah." He said, as he picked me up. I laid my head on his strong shoulder, as he carried me to the bedroom.

"I didn't even know you owned such underwear."

"Nora made me buy them," I said softly to him, closing my eyes and snuggling my head into the crook of his neck.

"Remind me to thank her."

CHAPTER 22

NORA PICKED ME UP and we delivered Rita's car then we headed toward The Cheer Up.

"Look, a couple of the girls are here, already." Nora pointed towards them. They were standing by their cars talking when we parked and walked over to them.

"Well, that was fun last night, but I feel a little guilty having such a good time at Louise's expense," Loraine said.

"Not me," Amelia replied. "I like to think it was a farewell party in Louise's honor. I can't remember everything, but I know I was having a good time."

"Yes, yes you were, Mrs. Robinson," Nora giggled. "We had to pull you off a boy toy with pimples."

"Yuuuck," Amelia said. "I don't drink that often. I didn't have much dinner, so it must have hit me hard."

"We all abused our limit," I said. "Katy was sure having a great time."

"Yeah, everyone really did think it was her birthday. Here she comes now," Nora said.

"Top of the morning Writer's Club partiers," Katy greeted as she waved good-bye to her ride. "How's everyone doing? Someone has a hangover," Katy said, pointing at one of the girls who was holding her head, and wearing very large sunglasses.

"Ah, she'll be okay. So, what did any of you find out? Any helpful information?" I asked.

"I think we need to go back," Amelia giggled loudly.

Nora shoved her arm gently. "You don't even remember last night."

"I know I had fun. I think." Amelia said.

"Yeah, but you were no help slobbering over 'Pimple Boy.' Neither were you, Katy," Nora said.

"Actually, girls, I didn't drink that much. I remember everything I did and who with," Katy said. "Maybe, I should rephrase that. Jordon gave me good information. I went home and wrote down everything I could remember." Katy handed me her notes. "I also got some good information from a couple of the guys I was dancing with. It's all right here," she pointed to the piece of paper she handed me.

Nora was leaning over my shoulder trying to read it.

We stood there reliving last night and going over Katy's notes, when, lo and behold, we watched Carol Sue go by in a slow-moving car. It stopped and Carol Sue got out of . . . *WHAT*? Out of Damon's car . . . ?

The car drove slowly back by us, then stopped. Damon rolled his window down and said, "Nice to see you, Charla, and the rest of you ladies."

I threw up my hand in a haphazard wave. The rest of the girls just gawked with smiles. *Damon was really good looking.*

Carol Sue waited for Damon to pull out of sight, before walking over to us.

"What?" she said, spreading her arms out, looking around at all of us.

"Well, what was that?" I said.

She shrugged but smiled.

"You remember the girls?" Nora asked.

"I remember Katy and Amelia," Carol Sue said, "they were having a great time."

"Carol Sue, why?" I asked throwing my hands out as everyone waited for the answer.

"Why, what?" she asked.

"Why this Key Club thing? Damon?"

"I love the excitement of not knowing who I'm going to be with. They are all different. I love the touch, the feel, body to body. It's exciting. No commitment, but all the benefits."

"Hmph," I mumbled looking at the excitement in her eyes, as she explained.

"Aren't you afraid of . . . of disease or anything?" Katy blushed.

"Well, the one thing we have to do is get a routine doctor's checkup and a certified letter saying we are clean, or no keys go in the hat, and no keys are drawn out."

"Hmph!" I mumbled, yet again.

"Yeah, Jordan the bartender is the keeper of the medical records," she said. "But Jordan won't participate. I wish he would. He's so cute, but he's not a player, just the gatekeeper."

"What, a gatekeeper? What does that mean?" I asked as the girls hung onto my every word, not to mention Carol Sue's words.

"The Gate Keeper's in charge of the medical reports, the hat, the keys. He's the GATE-KEEPER."

"Hmph!" I mumbled yet again, as I am lacking an intellectual word.

"The Key Club's the main attraction of The Cheer Up and, has to maintain some kind of dignity, some organization. Jordan keeps records and has to know the players."

"Really?" *Okay, there's that bigger word I was looking for.*

"It's all on the up and up and we are the only known such club in a fifty-mile radius as far we can find out."

"No kidding. So then, Carol Sue, what about marriages? You married? How does that work?" One of the girls asked in great curiosity.

"I am not married anymore. And I am not looking for that kind of a relationship. I just want good sex. And as I said, each of these guys is very different from each other and different in what they want. I enjoy it so much. Though Damon can get a little rough." She said, smiling, rubbing her butt. "But look at him . . . he's so worth it. Some of the guys are married and some of the ladies. Damon's married. I can tell you he doesn't do to his wife what he does to me. Everyone has their reason for getting involved," she continued.

"Sick," I mumbled. Only Loraine heard me.

"Exactly," Loraine mumbled back to me.

"So, what's Damon into?" I asked.

Nora elbowed me in the ribs hard. She gave me the look.

"Domination, control, mostly. But he does have gentleness to him."

"Hmph!" I said. Again with the big words.

"Not to mention he is so good looking and well endowed."

"Hmmmmm." This time it was Nora.

"So, doesn't it scare you on the domination part?" Katy asked.

"Ah, no. I like it sometimes, but I wouldn't want every guy doing the same thing. As I said, they are all different."

"So, Damon's into black leather and whips?" one of the girls asked.

"Yeah, but he's not mean with it. Just likes to take control, but the end result is great."

"Hmph! You're kidding. And you like that kind of stuff?" I asked.

"Oh, hell, I like it all," she stated with a gleam on her face. Clearly a satisfied woman.

"So, you are allowed to talk about sex with these guys? With the other ladies?"

"Of course, we share notes sometimes if someone asks, so do the guys. Who is into what?"

"Really?"

"Ladies, I would love to share more, but I have my son's soccer game to go to. It is Saturday."

Carol Sue got in her car and drove away, leaving us hanging and in disbelief with tons more questions.

We stood looking at each other, dumbfounded. *Soccer?*

"Nora, we need to see if Rita found out any secret activities. Meet me back at Jackson's." Turning to the group I said, "If any of you find out anything, no matter how small you think it is, please call." I said. "We need to figure this out."

Everyone nodded their heads in agreement and headed to their cars as we departed from the group to our own car.

CHAPTER 23

NORA AND I MET up at Jackson's. Neither Jackson nor Bozo was home.

"Rick asked me if you and Jackson would like to go out to dinner tonight?" she said, coming through the front door.

I picked up my cell and dialed Jackson.

He picked up, though I was half expecting Donnie to answer.

"Hey, babe! Glad to hear from you," he said.

"Yeah, why's that?" I asked.

"Oh . . . I don't know. Maybe because you are on my mind, and I was thinking I would like a rewind of last night."

"Really?" I giggled. "Can anyone hear you?"

"No."

"Well, then, maybe we can rewind last night, tonight!"

"Hmmmmm," he groaned. "Something to look forward to," he said. I could tell he was smiling.

"Before we rewind, Rick and Nora want us to go out to dinner with them tonight. Want to?"

"I just have a few things to tie up here and then I am free," he replied.

"Good, we haven't done anything with them in a long while. It'll be fun."

"Okay, later then," he hung up.

We sat down and started going through Louise's stories, moving the piles around, searching for the booklet.

All of a sudden Nora waved the booklet in the air, "Ta dah . . . I found it!"

She read it out loud. I looked over her shoulder to follow along.

"Louise was writing about the dates she had at The Cheer Up, but mostly the women that hang out there and what they have to say about their dates. Sounds like Louise and her friends were comparing notes."

"It sure does. But I'm interested in her actual dates. I know she kept records. She wrote everything down. I'm calling Rita," I said.

I reached for the phone. After a couple of rings, Rita answered.

"Hi Rita, Nora's on the speaker with me, and we were wondering if you had a chance to go over to Louise's yet?"

"I planned on going this morning after you brought my car back, but Joe and the kids are going over to pick up a few things and I didn't want them to see me snooping. I'll go this afternoon. I'll call you when I find something."

"Great. Talk to you later," I said, starting to hang up.

"Oh, wait, you guys; even though I was super nervous, I had fun last night. Thanks for making me a part of your sting," Rita said.

"It was a fun night and you fit right in."

"Thanks," she replied, hanging up.

We were reading through Louise's notes when I glanced at the clock.

"Man, the time's flying. It's time to get ready to go out to dinner."

As Nora was leaving, she turned and said, "Rick and I will be back at seven to pick you up." She closed the door.

Bozo came strutting in expressing his happiness to see me. He jumped up into my arms to get his daily fix on the human touch.

Jackson came home just as I stepped into the shower.

"I'm home," he said, stepping into the shower and snuggling up to me. He was really happy to see me.

Bozo meowed turned and walked out the door.

The phone rang. Jackson said, "Now what?"

I answered. "Okay, un unh, will do."

Meantime Jackson was still soaping my body and I mean *all over* my body.

"That was Nora. Rick made reservations for ShaLadu's."

But Jackson wasn't interested in Shaladu's. He was only interested in the shower.

THOUGH I HAD ON a different outfit, I put on the same jacket I wore to Louise's funeral.

I reached into my pocket and found the note Joe Jr. had given me about the kid who stole his mother's computer.

"Here, Jackson," I said, as I handed him the note. "This could be a lead on Louise's computer."

He looked at it and asked me, "Is this the guy you chased out of Louise's house?"

"Yeah, Joe Jr. gave it to me at his mom's funeral. His memory came back."

"Good lead, I'll get it followed up on," he said, sliding the note into his briefcase.

"Just don't give it to Donnie."

He stared at me a nanosecond then nodded his head in agreement.

He took my hand and turned me around and looked me up and down. "Hmmm, matronly," he said.

"Wh . . . what? You want me to wear the red dress?"

"And have every man look at you and every woman envy you with jealously? So, NO. But you can wear the red underwear."

"I'll be right back," I said going to find something else to wear.

I walked into the living room where Jackson had a game playing on the tube, and I went, "Well?"

"Oh, babe, that's more like it. You can't go wrong in your little black dress," he said, looking me over with approval. "You are wearing the red undies?"

"Maybe and maybe not," I teased as he tried to see.

I was saved by the bell . . . the doorbell. Rick and Nora were here.

CHAPTER 24

WE WALKED INTO SHALADU'S and only had to wait fifteen minutes before being seated.

"I haven't been here before," I said, looking around, "It's beautiful."

"I was here a couple of years ago," Jackson said.

"Really!"

"Charla, yes you have. Remember we had that sting going down with the Bowrey brothers who hung out here all the time. They were meeting several business partners here to launder money."

"I do remember," I said looking around. I spotted Damon with a cute perky lady.

I turned my head away from him, but not before he noticed me. I nodded to Nora and rolled my eyes in Damon's direction.

She nonchalantly looked over, nodding her head in acknowledgment to me.

"This is great guys. We haven't been out together for a long time. I would say we were overdue. Thanks, Rick, for thinking of it," I said, pleased.

"Yeah, Rick, this is great," Jackson said. "I've been working such long hours and I have a lot on my plate. Charla brought up the possibility of a few cold cases with the same MO or similar to these two I am working on. I have Donnie working on it as I speak."

"Hmmm, how does Donnie feel about working a Saturday evening while you're out at a wonderful restaurant with wonderful friends?" My green eyes smiled at him.

Jackson laughed, "I guess seniority ranks after all. Besides I found out she's the one who dropped the ball on Louise's computer."

I gloated at the news.

But instead of gloating out loud, I just said, "Well, enough about work."

We had just finished with our fantastic meal and were waiting for our after-dinner drink and dessert. I ordered, "I Would Kill for Chocolate" dessert. *Seriously, that's what it's called.*

Nora said, "Come on, Charla. Let's go powder our noses."

After dabbing lip gloss on, we stepped out of the Ladies Room into the hallway where Damon was waiting.

He acted like he just happened to run into us.

"Hello, ladies. Nice to see you again," as he put his arms over my shoulders pinning me against the wall. "Enjoying your meal?"

Nora stepped toward him and gently put her hand on his arm to pull it away from me.

She said, "Why, yes, yes, we are enjoying our dinner with my husband, Rick and Charla's boyfriend, the detective."

Damon pulled his other arm away from me and bowed with a sweeping hand court gesture, "My lady, you may pass."

"We better get back to our table," I said. "Nice seeing you again." *Why did I say that?* I felt like belting him.

We walked away and he turned to go the other direction.

"Charla, I am surprised you didn't drop that jerk to the floor. He danced with you a few dances and he thinks he can get by with that kind of thing. What were you thinking allowing him to block you?"

"Oh, Nora, I have my reasons. He's on my radar."

"Creepy," she said.

"Yes, yes, it was." I answered back.

We reached our table and *mum* was the word.

We sat down, and I sipped my Bailey's and coffee. I took a bite of my dessert and it was as good as advertised. I guess I was moaning because everyone looked at me. I looked up and around the table and said, "They should rename this "Better than Sex."

They all reached over with their fork and dug in uninvited.

"Oh baby, this is that good," Nora said.

The guys agreed. They pushed their dessert away and Rick raised his hand to the maître d'.

"Oh, garcon," click click with his fingers.

"Yes sir, how may I serve you," asked the well-dressed maître d'.

"We want three more of that," Rick pointed to my dessert.

He smiled and left to fetch three more "I Would Kill for Chocolate" desserts.

The server returned with the desserts, and I pointed out that they each owed me a bite.

"Oh, my gosh, this is the best chocolate I have ever had," Nora said, salivating. The guys were oohing and aahing out loud themselves.

We were all enjoying eating "I Would Kill for Chocolate" and our time together. I mean all of it. We were laughing at everything by this point.

"I wonder if anyone ever killed for chocolate." Rick asked, laughing so hard that he snorted Baileys out his nose.

"Maybe, drowned," Nora laughed, handing Rick her napkin. Funny thing, we hadn't had much to drink. We were just drunk on a good time and good company.

Damon and his date were leaving; he turned and gave a finger wave. I ignored him.

CHAPTER 25

"Daniel"

DANIEL REACHED FOR THE remote control and clicked on the Sunday football game. He just missed the kickoff and the camera panned the crowd. "Wait, back up," he said, out loud. "Is that . . . Charla?" He wondered.

Dear sweet Vivian came into the room, and Daniel reached for her hand and pulled her down on his lap and kissed her cheek.

"What was that? Wait, back up," Vivian asked him, as Pebble chased her brother Stone through the room.

"I missed the kickoff. They ended up on the 35-yard line. They threw a flag on the Skins and I wanted to see who, I mean why."

"I don't see how you can watch Sunday after Sunday of this stuff," Vivian said, just as the kids ran back through with Pebbles now crying, still chasing Stone.

Vivian hopped off Daniel's lap, "I need to find out what happened," she said, running after her kids.

Daniel got the remote, backed up to the kick-off and watched as the camera scanned the fans again. He put the TV on pause and stared at who he thought was Charla.

"No, that isn't Charla," he said out loud again.

"Who isn't who?" Vivian asked, passing through on her way to the kitchen.

Daniel looked at her, but she walked on through and did not wait for an answer.

Whoooooooosh, he thought. That was close. I've got to stop talking out loud.

Now, he's thinking to himself, thinking about Charla. I can't get her off my mind.

I need to find out more about her. I hope I can find her.

He shook his head no, but was smiling. Stop thinking of her, shut it off, bud. Shut it off and get back to football. He was not concentrating on football.

Chapter 26

"Charla . . ." Jackson called out.

I walked out of the bathroom, towel drying my hair with only a towel wrapped around my body.

"What?"

"I never thought I would ask this, but . . . where's Ryan's poster?" he asked.

I giggled and said, "I thought I would give you a break. He's on my closet door."

"You mean, I don't have to worry about him watching me make mad passionate love to you anymore?"

"That's right, big boy."

"I am at a loss for words. Let's celebrate!"

"Anything for my man," I giggled. "Honestly Jackson, it's no big deal."

"Climb back in bed and let me show you my thanks."

"Can't . . . Rick and Nora are on their way to watch the game with us. Kickoff's in 20 minutes. Better go shower."

I was setting out snacks and drinks when Jackson came in from his shower.

"Oh Jackson, is that something in your pocket or are you glad to see me?"

He put his arms around me and the doorbell rang. The door swung open. Jackson didn't have time to answer.

"Hope we're not late," the crazy redhead yelled out.

"You are just in time for the kickoff. Grab something to eat," Jackson laughed, pushing me away like I was the one with a hard on. He grabbed a paper plate, holding it down over his family jewels and turning until it was safe to turn back around. He was laughing.

"What's the joke?" Nora asked.

"I was thinking of my family," he said, laughing. *My family jewels.*

I changed the subject and led her out of the room.

She looked back at Jackson and said, "Oh . . . Ohhh." And if she could get embarrassed, this might be it.

On the first commercial break, Jackson said, "Hey guys, guess what Charla gave me?"

Nora smirked, "I know what she gave you. It's what she always gives you."

"Nuh-un. You don't know. It is almost as good as sex though . . . Charla put Ryan in the closet, sorta."

"Nuh-un," both Rick and Nora said, looking at me.

"It was an excruciating decision but . . . I thought it was time," I said, smiling.

"Wow, our little girl's all grown up," Nora smirked.

"I just leave the closet door wide open now." I smirked back.

"Game's back on," Rick yelled out as Bozo came in prancing with his tail up and looking at Rick.

"Meow."

"Come on up here, bud," Rick said, as he patted his lap for Bozo to jump up on.

After the game was over and before another game started, Nora and I headed into the dining room to do more research on Louise's diary.

"This isn't quite a diary or a day planner, but it's informative," I pointed out to Nora. "I found it and tossed it over on the side of the table after you left yesterday. I glanced through it, but ran out of time until now to read it. It looks like she kept a record of who she was with, and what they did. It has far more information than what we were reading yesterday."

"Let me see that thing," Nora said practically jerking it out of my hand.

I pulled my chair up next to her so we both could read the ledger at the same time about The Key Club. We started on page one but decided to do a reverse, so the first thing we did was check the end of her diary/ledger for possible clues. Maybe something that sounded like she was upset, or maybe someone she was angry with. We read on, but nothing showed that she was upset. Her last date was a few weeks before her death. She was with Damon. We started reading through it.

Nora read out loud. "Louise said, Damon and I made perfect straight sex. Damon was so gentle and thoughtful. He took his time and made the whole evening and night special. I hardly recognized him."

"Well, that didn't tell us much. No suspicious clues. Sounds normal to me except for the Key Club connection," I said. But we read back several dates just in case there could be a clue. None. No one angry, no one mean, nothing.

We flipped back to the first page which told of the activities of The Cheer Up and The Key Club. It told how to become a participant, which we had already figured out.

"This dates back several years. Look, here's a picture of the first guy she was with. It's that Damon character," Nora pointed out. "He liked dominate sex. Louise said she was submissive. She said, "I did everything Damon wanted."

"Oh my," Nora took a deep breath and continued to read. "Damon tied me up with pantyhose. First he tied each wrist to the bedpost, then each ankle. I lay there naked, restricted in movement. Damon blew a breath up and down over my body. He took a feather and ran it cross my body followed by a whipping with a very fine leather belt. He slapped it down on me lightly and repeated it over and over again, just until I teared up, and then, he stopped. He ran his hand up and down me massaging the places he had just hit with the leather belt. Then said, 'Don't cry. Here I'll make it all better," as he massaged me.

Nora took a breath . . . then continued.

"It actually felt good since none of it was really rough. Damon was gentle. Damon kissed me all over. I mean all over, just before driving me insane, just before he penetrated me. He untied me and rolled over on his back for a break. While he was resting, I showered. Then Damon tied me down again. This time he turned me on my tummy and he raised my fanny up and did to me what he had just done to my front. Only this time he was rougher. I was now really getting into it. When we were done this time, I again showered, put my clothes back on, left Damon on the bed exhausted."

Nora closed Louise's ledger and took a big gulp.

"Wow," I said. "We didn't know Louise at all. That is just WRONG."

"You better look out, Charla, Damon took a shine to you," she teased.

"Fat chance," I said, with a "Yuck," screwing up my face. "Yuck!"

"That was Louise's first date at The Cheer Up / Key Club," she said. "I can't wait to read the rest."

"You pervert," I said, pointing at her. "I only have tomorrow to investigate, then I have two days at the hospital before I can continue on this thing."

"Speaking of the hospital, how's Joan doing?"

"I talked to her a couple of times since she's been home and she said she is doing great. No aftereffects from the accidental insulin shot. She really didn't have more to add to the twins' story."

"Hey, what are you two up to in there?" Jackson yelled after us.

Bozo came wandering in, looking up at me. "What?" I asked.

He went over to his food and water bowls, and I noticed he was out of water. I got him some and he lapped it up fast. "Did Rick feed you too many salted chips, boy?"

"Meow," as water dribbled off his chin.

We walked back into the living room where the guys were still watching football.

"So, who's winning?" I asked

"Skins are up seven, and they're about to go into halftime," Jackson said. "What were you doing in there so long?"

Nora grinned and said, "Hey, Rick, you into dominant, submissive sex?"

"Hell, no," he spattered chips out. "What the hell is wrong with YOU?"

"We were just going over some of Louise's stories," I said. "Some of the stories are pretty interesting."

"Uh-huh," Jackson said, looking at me, and pulling me down on his lap.

"Yeah," I returned his look. I didn't want him to know about the diary. *Yet.*

The game was over and the Skins lost by three. Who knew?

As Rick and Nora were walking out the door, Nora said, "I'll be back in the morning to continue to read Louise's stories."

I threw up a hand in an okay and they went out the door.

Jackson said, "Here, I'll help you clean up."

"Well, thank you, Mr. Detective."

"So, what are you going to do for me?" he asked.

"I put Ryan Reynolds up, what more could you want Action Jackson?"

He chased me down the hall toward the bedroom and shut Bozo out just in time.

CHAPTER 27

THE NEXT MORNING JACKSON left early but with a happy face. *The rewind. Again.*

I took my shower and got ready to face the day. I was ready to meet the world when the doorbell rang.

It was a florist delivery.

"Miss O'Hara?" the delivery guy asked.

"Yes," I answered.

"Sign here," he handed me his IPad.

"I think you have the wrong place."

"Charla O'Hara?"

"Yes."

"Then this is the right place."

He handed me what looked to be an expensive vase with gorgeous roses.

I read the card and it just simply said, "From an admirer."

"Oh, Jackson," I said, out loud.

I set them in the middle of the dining room table, slightly rearranging them with a smile.

The doorbell rang again. Nora threw open the door, "How many times do I have to tell you to keep your door locked?"

"I knew you would be here, asap."

Nora put a bag of Cronuts down on the table with two Starbucks coffees.

"You know this is going to make us fat? And you know I don't like Starbucks as well as Micky D's coffee?"

"Then the next time you can get the coffee," she said, with sarcasm. Then she spotted the roses . . . "What is this?" she leaned down to smell them, she picked up the vase to look at the bottom for the brand name. *Of course, she did.* "Hmmm, Waterford. Very nice . . ."

"They're beautiful, aren't they?" I gleamed. "Wait, Waterford Crystal," I looked closer.

"What's the occasion? It's not your birthday, Christmas, or anniversary," she said.

"Hmph! Maybe Jackson just appreciates me. But I don't think he meant to send them in Waterford Crystal."

She rolled her eyes and set the vase back down.

As we were enjoying the Cronuts and sipping our hot coffee, Nora picked up Louise's diary and was about to start reading.

"We need to check Katy's notes against Louise's info," she said.

"I already did and there wasn't anything in there that we don't already know. At least, it's consistent," I answered.

Nora started to read: "2nd date was with Ross Coveningham. This is one of the two guys in the picture Louise has on her cell phone. He seemed nice. Both of these guys danced with us the other night."

"Yeah, yeah," I said. "Get to reading. I want to hear."

"Oh, don't get your panties in a wad. Louise says Ross is her 2nd date and he's into threesomes."

"Hmph! Ménage a' trois. It just gets better and better." I said.

"Louise said here, Ross brought his friend, Evan Grant."

"So, that's who she had a ménage a' trois with," I said, "Interesting!"

I moved my chair next to her so I could read along.

"She said, 'I liked Ross more than Evan. Evan would massage, caress me, kissing me. He liked rubbing my head which was aggravating to me. Though he was thoughtful of my needs, I didn't need him rubbing my head, twisting my hair. Ross, on the other hand, appeared to be more experienced. Hmmm, perfection. Evan was awkward. But I guess with one you get the other. I guess Evan will learn."

"Oh my," Nora said, as she quit reading aloud.

I leaned in closer to read over Nora's shoulder.

After a few lines, I mumbled, "yeah, ménage a' trois,"

We both blushed.

Nora started reading out loud again. "Evan hung on to my hips and did this flutter thing when he reached his climax. Flutter, can you believe it? I might have to incorporate that style into one of my stories. After we were all done, and everyone seemed to be satisfied, Evan wanted to brush my hair and massage my shoulders. Just when I thought I had seen it all. I did enjoy that part with Evan."

"My third date was with Damon again. This time he brought leather restraints with buckles. He wore a black mask. He also had on a pair of black leather briefs that did not cover his butt or penis. I must say, very impressive. He then put a black leather mask over my head, only mine didn't have a place to see out of. It only had a slit for my mouth, and an opening for my nose, though I was instructed not to talk. This time he wasn't so gentle. He wasn't rough, but more forceful than before. He asked me, "More whore?" I would mutter, more. I guess I am becoming as sick as he is. I now know why there was a slit for my mouth." Nora stopped reading out loud. We both read in silence. Gulping, I continued to read Louise's words, "Damon was yelling, "tell me you love it. I yelled . . . I do, I do."

He took the leather off my face then my restraints. He flipped me over on my back again, and once again he entered me, but this time with the gentleness of a caring groom on his wedding night. "While writing this I have discovered I am as sick as Damon and like it just as much.

I do want more," Louise wrote.

"Woo, I can't get my breath," I said. "Who knew? It takes all kinds. I can't breathe."

"Wow, what an imagination," Nora said. "Who thinks up this stuff?"

"Only it's real. That wore me out."

We had to take a break before we went to the next date.

We did a few jumping jacks along with a couple sit ups and two push-ups. We put on a DVD of Dancing to the Oldies and swung our arms to the rhythm. Five minutes later we went back into the kitchen and had another Cronut.

"Meow." I patted Bozo on the head as he passed through, greeting us. He kept going. *Cats!*

Nora said, "This is Louise's fourth date and it is several months after her last date with that nasty Damon. This date is with a Sonny Thomas. Here's his picture," she said, handing it to me.

"It's that chubby guy that sat at the bar watching everyone. He barely said anything," I acknowledged.

Nora took the picture back and re-attached it. She continued.

"Louise says Sonny was different yet. We arrived at the hotel, he opened the door and there sat a woman in nothing, drinking wine. Sonny said, "Hello honey, meet Louise. Louise this is my wife, Joy.""

"No way!" I said.

"That's what it says." Nora continued . . . again, with a gulp.

"Sonny had me undress slowly. His wife was sitting on the edge of the chair watching.

"Yep, *another un ménage-a-trois*," I said, as I was reading over Nora's shoulder.

We read in silence again and when we were through, we both headed for the Golden Oldies again. "That's it, Ladies, Reach Up as High as You Can, Reach," Richard Simons sang out.

We had to take a long break from Louise's disturbing notes.

CHAPTER 28

WE READ KATY'S NOTES out loud for the heck of it. "Jordan told me about the different ladies that come in. Of course, he thought it was cute that Rita was trying to pull off being Louise, and she almost pulled it off."

"She looked damn good. Very sleazy, but good," Nora interjected.

I continued reading Katy's notes, with *"the look"* at Nora. "Jordan said Rita's actions were not the same as Louise, so everyone figured it out right off the bat, except Mutt and Jeff. *Ross and Evan.*" Katy said she asked Jordan, "Why did it take Ross and Evan a little longer?"

Jordon told me, "Duh! Those two are just in la la land all the time. I think they smoke weed, always moving in slow motion." He also said that most of the women come in two, together. Some of the ladies come in for The Key Club only. They're pretty obvious, he said. Some of the ladies are apparently lonely, some have no excitement left in their marriage, and some bring their husband to drop in his key. He said, "It's a crazy bunch that come in here."

"He also told me, our goal here at Cheer Up was to give the customers what they want, while keeping it aboveboard, and safe as possible. He said I don't think we have had a problem. But he went on to say that not everyone that comes in even knows about the Key Club or even wants any part of it. Just a few drinks, a dance or two and they go home.

I hope my notes help. Love, Katy."

I tossed the notes aside and looked at Nora and said, "I think there is a problem . . . two dead that we know of, and it all stems from The Cheer Up. I just know it."

It was getting late and we neither one of us thought we had another Louise story in us. We were so befuddled, unbelieving. Yet we knew it was real.

I said good-bye to Nora, closed the door, and locked it. I called Jackson. He actually answered himself.

"Hey, babe, thanks for the roses. So, last night was that good?" I teased.

"Yes, last night was that good but, the problem is, I didn't send you roses. I wished I had, though."

"What? Wha . . . then who . . . why . . . ?" I was confused. "Hmph."

"Was there a card?" Jackson asked.

'Well, yeah. It just says "from an admirer" and if they're not from you, then who?"

After further discussion, Jackson and I hung up. I called Nora on her cell. "Jackson didn't send me the roses. Who then?" I screamed into the phone.

"Just cool your jets, sister. We'll figure it out. The good news is, they are beautiful and, a very good caliber of roses, not to mention the vase. Bad news is, we don't know who sent them. But don't toss them. They're beautiful," Nora laughed in a full-out laugh. "I am sure it's no big deal. Someone is just thanking you for something. Just enjoy and don't question a nice gesture. I'm home. Bye."

I held the phone out and looked at it. "*She hung up on me!*"

CHAPTER 29

I WORKED THE NEXT two days at the hospital without incident. While waiting for my cohort, Paul Overland, to give him a ride home, I watched a black BMW pull up.

The dark colored window came down. Damon poked his head out.

"Fancy seeing you here," he said.

"What?" I asked, feeling dumbfounded and surprised to see him.

"I was hoping to see you again," he said. "Did you like the roses I sent you?"

"What, wha . . . you, you sent them to me? But why?"

"I like doing nice things for nice people. You're nice, aren't you, Charla?"

"No!" I sarcastically replied. Thank goodness, Paul walked up just then.

Damon gave me what he thought was a cutesy finger wave and gunned it.

"What was that?" Paul asked.

I'm not sure," I stuttered.

I dropped Paul off at his house and while I was still in park.

I pushed the number three button on my cell phone and called Nora.

"I know who sent me the flowers. I am going to toss them asap," I shouted into the phone.

"Slow down, Charla. Start from the beginning," she said.

I told her what went down in the parking lot.

"You're right. Thank goodness for Paul. In fact, maybe he should ride with you going and coming for a while, just in case Damon is getting, oh, I don't know . . . Possessive!"

"Oh, my God, you don't think . . . ?" I stuttered.

"I'm just saying better safe than sorry. Keep Paul handy when you're working at the hospital and me the rest of the time."

I plugged my cell into the speaker as I pulled away from Paul's house driving towards mine.

"I can't believe this. I shouldn't have worn that red dress the other night."

"Charla, you are probably right, but I have a feeling you could have been in a gunny sack. My money is on the red dress, though."

"Oh, for Pete sake, I'm home now."

"Look over the street and sidewalk, just in case," she said.

"Now you are just trying to scare me." But just as I said that, I spooked and started pulling away and drove around the block just to make sure.

That's when I saw a black BMW parked in a driveway down a couple of houses from me. I thought, *those people don't own a black BMW.*

I pulled down from there and turned off the engine for about ten minutes and waited

Then I started my car and I made my last trip around the block and the BMW was gone.

I sighed out loud. That's when Nora spoke up. I had forgotten she was still on the phone.

"Charla," a couple of beats went by, "make sure your doors and windows are locked."

"I can handle myself. I do carry you know. I can't believe you stayed on the phone this whole time. Say good bye, Nora."

"After you get in the door, and I hear the lock turn. Oh, I heard everything you mumbled. So, keep me on the phone."

"Yes, *Mother.*"

"Hey, you called me," Nora reminded me.

"Oh, my gosh! You're making me paranoid." I took a deep breath. "All clear," I told her as I walked into the house and locked the doors.

Nora kept me on the cell until she heard the dead bolt turn.

Then I went straight to the roses.

"Hasta la vista, baby." I slammed them in the trash. Gone, kaput, out of here. But I carefully set the vase down on the cabinet. It was Waterford after all.

CHAPTER 30

WHILE I WAS WORKING at the hospital, I couldn't turn my mind off the murders and was happy the two days were finally over. Though I love working my shifts, it's so hard when I'm sleuthing. I actually preferred sleuthing and since Louise was such a big deal to me and now Lora Janeson, my mind was reeling.

I stood in the kitchen fixing dinner for Jackson when Bozo came through his doggie door, and as he meowed, I glanced at the doggie door to remind myself it was barely big enough for Bozo, let alone Damon. I felt relief. But the neighbors' pug, Suzy, came in right behind Bozo.

"What's this, Bozo? You're not supposed to have company."

I picked up Suzy and unlocked the front door for Jackson to come in.

"What's going on? You have this place closed up tighter than Ft. Knox," he said.

"Sorry, babe. I just want a little privacy." I handed him Suzy.

"You got it, okay." He sat Suzy down and reached for me and put his arms around my waist. "Nice outfit." He was now making fun of my clown design scrubs. "Sexy."

I threw my arms around his neck and gave him a deep passionate kiss, then leaned back and looked up into his eyes, his brown beautiful eyes. "Thank you for being you," I said, still gazing into his eyes, "But take Suzy home." I picked up and pushed the pug at him, but he sat her down.

Okay, what's wrong?" He asked, moving me out of his way once again, bending over to pick up Suzy.

"Nothing. Can't a girl be happy about having the right guy, at the right place and the right time in her life?"

"Well, ye . . . ah, if that's what it really is." He put Suzy down again, *poor doggie*, and smacked my butt as he turned and pulled two beers out of the fridge, sitting them on the counter, opening them, and handing one to me. "Where's the roses?"

"I tossed them. They were looking bad." *Really bad since I now know who sent them.*

Jackson shrugged his shoulders, glanced at the vase, then picked up a beer and Suzy and went out the door. I locked the door behind him and waited until he was reaching for the door handle to unlock it. He never knew. *Damn Nora. She's making me so paranoid. I'm tougher than this.*

We ate, cleaned up the kitchen and grabbed a couple more Coors Lites. We popped the tops and sat down to watch a little television.

"Did you find any cold cases with the same MO as Louise and Lora Janeson?" I asked him.

"Donnie found a couple of possibilities. We just pulled them out today. We need to study them and see if anything comes up the same. I promise you, though I know I shouldn't, I will fill you in. I know how this is eating at you."

"I might be able to help you out there."

"What do you mean?"

"Carol Sue told me of a couple of girls that died, that hung out at the Cheer Up. It just dawned on me that Carol Sue mentioned it to me Friday night. I guess I forgot. Nora and I'll call her tomorrow."

"You need to let me do my job, Charla. You need to let me do the investigation."

"I can't do that, Jackson. You know I can't." I leaned forward and started to get up.

"Come on, Charla, sit back down," he said, patting the sofa for me to sit. "I don't want to fight. I know you have to be involved. You can't help yourself or your sidekick. Louise was your friend. I know better than try to stop you. I just ask that when you find out for sure, you don't act on your own, but call me. Deal?"

I just looked at him.

He repeated, "Deal?"

I reluctantly said, "Deal." I curled up around him.

CHAPTER 31

NORA RANG THE DOORBELL and waited for me to answer. "I can't make up my mind if I want you safe or just be able to walk in."

"You yell at me every time you walk in and the door isn't locked."

"I'm fickle," she said.

This time Nora brought us Micky D's breakfast burrito and coffee.

"Good girl," I said as I picked up my coffee and handed her a five-dollar bill.

She smirked pushing my five away, then said, "So what's the plan of action today?"

"I don't know if I can take it, but I think we need to muddle through Louise's dates," I said, pushing the five back at her. She finally took it.

We pulled up beside each other and started on date five which was only a month from the last one.

"Here's a picture. I didn't see him there Friday night," I said. "He's African American. It says his name is Roddell Washington. I know that name. He plays professional baseball. This should be good."

Nora started reading out loud . . . "Roddell was probably one of the gentlest lovers yet, or he didn't like me all that much. We had a good time but it wasn't anything different and not that exciting. He has very nice credentials. Nice credentials, short night. This was the first time I was through in a couple of hours. Usually it's an all-nighter. Maybe Roddell has an early baseball game????"

Nora kept reading. "The sixth date was two months later. Who could this be? No picture. Oh, that's because she picked Damon again."

She read on, "Damon tied me up standing in front of a mirror. Here I am a mother of two and the wife of a jerk. I must say, I still looked good. No implants, all natural, butt still plump. I was admiring myself when Damon walked into the room. As he approached me, I could see his manhood getting aroused."

Nora stopped reading out loud and slammed the book shut. "Too much information, too much information. Why can't she have more Roddells?"

"I can tell you this much, if I didn't have Jackson, and my choice was Damon only, knowing what I know, well, I'd probably commit murder by shooting him," I said. "I love the way Jackson loves me. It's more than comfortable. It's way more than special. I can't even think of doing anything like we just read about. Nothing. I guess it takes all kinds. Sicko."

"Oh, I don't know," Nora said. "Some of it sounds pretty good." She snickered.

"You probably would enjoy the whips," I said, but I didn't laugh. *It all made me sick.*

"Only if I control the whips . . ." She joked.

"Always the control freak," I teased.

"Okay, the next story. Oh, Roddell, again. Piece of cake."

Nora once again started reading out loud. "This time Roddell brought some adventure."

"Oh, oh," I said.

Nora continued . . . "He brought a friend. Roddell grabbed my hand and pulled me onto the bed . . ."

"Damn, damn, damn, I don't want to read anymore. Sick, sick, sick. I don't know if this helps in solving Louise's murder. After reading this, do I want to?" I said, shaking my head in disgust.

"I don't want to read the rest. Maybe another time, but I am done, too." Nora said.

"The only thing I would consider is looking at the dates, looking at the pictures and following that line of thinking. I really don't want to think about what sex acts she comes up with," I explained, exhausted and feeling sick at my stomach.

"Well, let's try to work on Lora Janeson's neighborhood this afternoon."

"Deal, you drive," I said.

CHAPTER 32

"WHAT DO YOU SAY we go see Carol Sue first?" I asked as we drove along Route 1.

"Okay, but whassup?"

"Remember at The Cheer Up, Friday night when Carol Sue and Bev said that there were a couple of other Key Club girls that died?"

"Yeah, I'm following you. Good idea."

We headed for Carol Sue's home. She was just walking to her car. She stopped, looked at us, and then walked over as we got out of Nora's car.

"Hey, what a surprise. What's going on?"

"You mentioned a couple other ladies that used to come into The Cheer Up and dabbled in the Key Club," I reminded her.

"Yeah, yeah, but that's been a long time ago, as far back as eight years on one." *She thinks back.* She spoke again. "Probably ten on the other."

"You mean this Key Club has been going on that long?" Nora asked.

"It isn't a new thing. Key clubs have been going on one way or another forever."

"Hmph. I have lived a sheltered life," I mumbled. "I had no idea."

"There are tons of house parties where married couples toss their keys in a large hat or bowl and at the end of the evening the ladies dip their hand in the hat and pull out a key, then go home with the owner of the key."

"No-oh?" Nora and I said in unison, though neither of us was exactly innocent.

"Yes, they do. Sometimes the guy ends up with his own wife. They have to draw again."

"NO!"

"Not only that," she continued, "there are hotel parties all over the city in every city. People show up who want to participate. They meet in a suite, party all evening, waiting with great anticipation to see whose room key they'll pull out. They go to the room with some stranger or maybe someone they have been with before. The next morning, they meet back at the suite and go home. There's a membership fee in that case."

"You certainly know all about perversion style sex. I just thought they were only in the movies," Nora stated.

"Where do you think movies get their ideas? Yes, I do know a lot, because that was what my husband was into, and why I divorced him. Too perverted. I discovered Cheer Up quite by accident. I thought it was a safe place for a single woman to stop in for a drink. I thought it was like "Cheers" in that old TV sitcom. I found out it wasn't, unless, of course, you want it to be. Though it has it's restrictions, I got involved in their Key Club and I must say, they have strong rules, regulations, health guards, safety and security," she said full of information.

"Yet, women seem to be dropping like flies. Maybe months or years between, but something is not secure, safe guarded, or healthy," I didn't hesitate in saying. "So who are the two ladies that you were talking about the other night?"

"I don't remember their names," she answered.

"Can you find out for us? Or take us to talk to Jordan since he knows you and just maybe he'll talk to us?"

"When do you want to go?"

"What time does Jordan work?"

She looked at her watch, "He's probably there right now."

We piled in Nora's car, pulled out and started down the street, but Nora was thinking about what Carol Sue had just said, so she popped out and asked what was on her mind.

"So, Carol Sue . . . you divorced your husband for living a lifestyle you didn't approve of and yet here you are in the thick of things, living the same lifestyle. Why?"

"Strange how the turn of events happens, isn't it?" Carol Sue said, with a straight face. "I found out I liked it, but not my husband."

"Hmph."

CHAPTER 33

WE WALKED THROUGH THE door of The Cheer Up at three o'clock and the place was empty.

Carol Sue yelled out, "How about some service out here?"

Jordan came from the back office. When he saw us, he broke out into a big smile.

"Wow, early birds. I think I can muster up an early bird special."

"Where is everybody?" Carol Sue asked.

"I sent a couple of the guys for supplies, so I'm it. Usually customers start dragging in about five. What can I get ya?"

"I'll have a diet Dr. Pepper," I said, as we all sat down at the bar.

"Me too," Nora chimed in.

"Wow, hitting the hard stuff, huh?" he joked.

"I'll have a Bud Lite," Carol Sue said.

Just as she got her beer, her cell rang. She walked outside to the patio to take the call.

Jordan served us, then turned to answer his cell.

"I can't right now. I'm the only one here and I have customers," he paused then said, "I'll call you back in an hour or so." *A pause.* "Okay . . . later."

He set down a bowl of peanuts in front of us and wiped up some sticky stuff off the bar which was probably left from the night before.

"So, why are you ladies here so early? Let's see . . . Charla and uh, uh Nora. Right?"

"Good memory, Jordan." I said. "Carol Sue was kind enough to bring us in to ask you a few questions."

"Questions? About what?" he asked.

"As you know, Louise Stafford frequented The Cheer Up for a few years and participated in the Key Club. She was killed. And so was Lora Janeson. Then we found out that, over the years at least two or three others died who also were part of the Key Club here," I explained.

"What?" he looked confused. "What's going on?"

"We knew Louise before she was killed. We decided to investigate since she is, uh, was our friend. Now it appears several others who hung out here are dead, too. We just want to know if there is a connection or a strange coincidence. We need to find out," I rattled on.

"The police have been here a couple of times about Louise. I answered all their questions the best I could. It didn't seem to help them much. So, what's your deal?"

"Actually, we help the police out now and again, and with success, I might add," Nora said handing him one of our handy, dandy business cards.

He stared at the small print and grinned. "Personal Investigators."

"Yep, and we do a lot of business, too."

"You don't say?" he smiled.

"I want to talk about Lora Janeson. How well did you know her?"

"Lora was a long time Key Club player. She was a cutesy, bubbly little thing. But I never heard what happened to her," Jordan said.

"She was killed several weeks ago, maybe a month or so ago, the same way as Louise was killed."

"I didn't know. I'll do what I can to help."

"I realize it would be an invasion of privacy for your customers, but Nora and I would like to have a list of your regulars that all of a sudden stopped coming in. I understand there was one about eight years ago, and one a couple years earlier. If you could go back in your books and see if anyone fits the bill, we would appreciate it. Oh, and anything you can give us on Lora since she's pretty recent."

"I'll check into it. I'll do what I can, but I can't make any promises," he said, looking back down at our business card.

"I know you are uncomfortable about helping us, but I can't help but feel there is a connection among these ladies. Everything will stay between us. It will remain confidential. We won't even discuss it with my boyfriend."

"Boyfriend?"

"Yes, Det. Jackson Boxley."

"Oh, yeah, he looks like Ryan Reynolds. He's been here asking questions." Nora rolled her eyes and I smiled.

"I sent Jackson here when I realized Lora Janeson was a regular."

He said, "I probably shouldn't tell you this, but Damon has been asking question about you, Charla."

"Please don't tell him I was here. I have had a couple of run ins with him already and I am not interested." *I think that he's a stalker, comes to my mind.* "So tell me about him . . . if you will. I know Damon is not his real name."

"Well, he's crazy about you. He lights up just saying your name."

"I really don't want him lighting up saying my name or anything else. He's becoming creepy. What's his real name?"

"I shouldn't tell you, but what the hell . . . his real name is Daniel Nielsen. He's been coming here since he turned twenty-one," Jordan told us. "He has never caused me any problems. He's always a gentleman in here. I have no complaints about him. I've overheard different ladies say he likes rough sex. But other than that, I've heard nothing one way or the other except," *he paused,* "he appears to be a lady's favorite."

"Hmph!" I mumbled.

"I need to get back to the books before the crowd starts coming in. I hope I've been helpful. I'll check the records on the ladies you asked about and let you know," he said, as he looked down at our card, waved it in the air, and stuck into his shirt pocket.

Carol Sue came waltzing back into the bar. "Did I miss anything?"

I thought . . . Funny how things work out, especially since we don't want her in the investigation.

"Sorry for pulling you away from your errands earlier, Carol Sue," Nora said, as we drove her home.

"Like I said, I was just going to the store and it could wait. It was fun hanging out with you two."

Carol Sue got out of our car and right into her car and drove off.

CHAPTER 34

WE WALKED INTO THE house and went directly to turn on the computer. We entered Daniel Nielsen's name.

Nora pulled her chair up beside me as I did a search.

Daniel aka Damon came up quickly.

"He lives in Jamerson Estate."

We pulled the house up from the satellite map and went right to the front door.

"Impressive. Look, you can see his BMW parked in the horseshoe driveway. Looks like a couple of bikes lying close to the white columned porch steps. So he has kids."

We went back to his profile.

"He's the CEO of Parker and Parker Architect firm downtown. One of the largest architect firms around. They are famous for their high rises, football and baseball stadiums and five star hotels, among other things. Very impressive, so why in the hell is he hooked on dominant sex?

Why does he sit down at the end of the bar waiting with baited breath for the key drawing?"

"Beats me," Nora said, while she drummed the table with her fingers.

I gently reached over, placed my hand over her fingers, and held them down.

She stopped drumming, but glared at me for a nanosecond.

While skimming through articles, we came across a picture of Daniel and his wife, Vivian, dancing at a Parker Charity Ball. It was a close-up and you could see their sparkly whites smiling from ear to ear as they posed for the picture.

"Wow, they look regal," Nora said. "Mrs. Pervert is very pretty."

"So why?" I mumbled.

We kept reading. There was so much information about Daniel's achievements and lifestyle.

"He has great accomplishments, success in everything he does. He has a great family. I just don't get it. Why is he chasing after me?"

"Makes me wonder," the crazy redhead said, with a gentle shove to my arm.

We read on, Vivian Logan's the daughter of the upper crust Bart Logan. She wed Daniel Nielsen, June 15th, 2001. Daniel came up from the ranks and made it good enough to marry into the Logan fortune.

"He's a go getter, that Daniel is," Nora said.

"Wait. It's too easy to look up information on Daniel. I want to see about me."

I pulled my name up, and it wasn't nearly as impressive as Daniel's. It hardly mentioned my nursing school. There was a little article about me saving a heart attack victim at a movie theater and where I found a bundle of money that I turned in and received a thousand-dollar reward from a very grateful seventy-six-year-old Hilda Simpson who insisted I take the reward. That was about it. But it did mention enough that Daniel could send me roses.

We closed the lid on the computer, and Nora said her good-byes.

"Lock the door behind me and I'll see you in two days. I wish you hadn't said you would work. Remember to keep Paul close. Don't walk out into the parking lot without him."

"Yes, Mother. I will do all the above but the hospital's short staffed this week and I could always use the money."

"Just watch your seven," she reminded me.

I picked up my cell and called Paul. "Hey bud, you working tomorrow and Wednesday?"

"Yeah," he said.

"Seven to seven? I'll pick you up at 6:20."

"Uh, tomorrow will be okay, but I traded hours with Mary Alice on Wednesday so I won't be going in until 7 p.m." Paul said.

"Tomorrow then," I said. "I'll figure out Wednesday on Wednesday."

Jackson came in, hugged me, and then picked me up. "I have to go back to work," he said, as he hauled me to the bedroom for a quickie. Afterwards, he took a shower, grabbed a sandwich and a bottle of water. I walked along with him, throwing on my robe as he walked toward the door. "Sorry for the wham, bam thank you ma'am, but these kitchen murders are giving us trouble. I need to get back to work."

"Funny you always have time and energy for sex."

"Well, yeah, and I make sure you get re-energized, as well," he said.

"Did you check out the cold case files, yet?" I said

"As for your question on the cold cases, we're working on it, but no luck yet. There are so many cold case files . . . so many."

"Check eight and ten years ago."

"Why?"

"A hunch," I said.

"Hmph! A hunch? Okay I'll check out your hunch," he said patting my fanny, stepping out of the door.

Bozo came home, alone. I petted him, fed him and got him fresh water. I locked his doggie door early.

"It's just you and me tonight, bud."

"Meow."

I was having a hard time concentrating. I couldn't get my mind off the "kitchen murders" as Jackson was referring to them. I had to think of working at the hospital for two days. I drifted off to sleep.

After my nap, I called my parents, "Hi, Mom, you and Dad busy?"

Pause

"Uh-huh, he's working. I thought I would come over for an hour or two."

Pause

"On my way."

Okay, bud, you're on your own." I gave Bozo a pat. I grabbed my bag, got my keys and opened, locked and closed the door.

I walked towards my car looking around. My car . . . what . . . on earth. It's not where I parked it earlier. It was sitting there totally detailed, clean and waxed. Sparkling better than a ten-year-old car should.

I pushed my sleeve up and I looked at my watch. How long was I asleep . . . ?

Looking around walking towards my car which was parked on the street, I picked up the card attached to a big red bow and read it.

"Surprise, I hope you like your car. Just a little something for someone special. Damon." I read out loud.

I looked around. When? How? Good grief, don't any neighbors or passers-by ever see anything? He has got to stop this. I called Nora.

"Nor . . . a. He's doing it again."

"What? Who?" she asked.

"Daniel, aka Damon, cleaned up my car, totally, every nook and cranny."

"Stay right there. I'm on my way," Nora demanded.

"No. I am on my way to my parents."

"I'll catch up," she said, hanging up her phone.

I was halfway to my parents' house when I noticed a car speeding toward me. I was just about to slam on my brakes and confront who I assumed was Damon, aka Daniel. Nora came up behind me blowing the horn with everything her Mercedes Benz had in it. She had her arm out of the window waving like a crazy woman drying her just-painted finger nails, which I have actually witnessed her doing.

I pulled over to the side of the road. I gestured . . . "WHAT!"

She got out of her car and came up to me, "Didn't I tell you not to do anything without someone being with you? Didn't I?" she scolded me.

"I have a gun . . ."

"Well, it won't do you any good if it's stuck in your purse and you don't use it."

"On Thursday, I want to go back to the shooting range, and then I think we should try for our PI license. But now, I need to get over to my folks. You coming?"

"Right behind you. And you're right; we need to go after our PI license." She turned and got into her car and followed me.

"Hi, Mom and Dad, I'm here and I brought a guest," I yelled through the door.

Mom yelled back, "Oh, Jackson got to come after all?" She said, coming from the kitchen with my dad in tow.

"No."

"Who then?" my mother stopped and my dad bumped into her just as she saw Nora...

"Oh, Eleanora... How nice it is to see you. Welcome, welcome," my mother said, holding her arms out for a hug for me, then Nora with my dad right behind.

"Hello, Mr. and Mrs. Bordeaux," Nora said, hugging them back.

"Oh, for Pete sake, Eleanora, how many times have we told you to call us Anna and Johnny?"

"And how many times have I asked you to call me Nora?"

"Touché, my dear Nora, touché," my mother said, smiling about being corrected.

My cell rang and I didn't recognize the number so I ignored it, thinking it could be Daniel aka Damon or a salesperson. At any rate, I didn't want to be bothered. I turned the phone off and slipped it back into my pocket.

"Who was the call?" Nora asked.

"Don't know."

"Why didn't you answer?" she asked.

"I just didn't recognize the number . . . Hey, Mother, I just love the way you make your roast beef dinner. It's really good, always a favorite of mine."

"Yes, it's really good, Anna," Nora said, giving me *the look.*

We finished dinner and helped clean up. We were ready to go out the door when my mother said, "Wait," and handed me a to-go bag for Jackson.

"Thank you, Mom, Jackson will love it."

"My pleasure, missy. He works so hard. There's a little something for Bozo, too."

◆》》《《◆

NORA FOLLOWED ME HOME and into the house.

"Nora, you're smothering me. Go home."

"So, where were you taking your nap?"

I pointed to Jackson's favorite Lazy Boy recliner.

She walked over to it, sat down and looked around.

"Look," she pointed to the window. "That's where he watched you snoozing, right through that window."

"Nuh-uh," I said, so eloquently.

"Uh-huh," she retorted. "Though, I don't think he would hurt you. He might be the one who would smother you."

"Why was it, I acted like a wimp when I got the roses? You made me paranoid. Then, he got my car cleaned up and detailed, without my permission. And now I am pissed. He seems to be everywhere I go. I want a face off."

"Hold on sister, don't get too brave," Nora said, gave me a hug and walked out the door. She turned and said, "You may want a face-off, but lock your doors. Better safe than sorry."

I closed the door and locked it. My cell phone rang as soon as I turned it back on.

"Hello."

"How did you like your car? Cleaned up nice, didn't it?" Daniel said.

I hesitated while trying to figure out how to respond. Finally, I said, "Daniel, Damon, whoever you are, though it's really nice of you, you really need to stop. It's just too much. How did you get the car cleaned up so fast?"

"Oh, oh. Someone has been doing her homework," he laughed lightly.

"You found me so I thought it only fair I find you. How's your wife and kids?"

"They are just fine, my fair lady."

"Well, just so you know I'm Jackson's fair lady."

"Just as I am sweet Vivian's gentleman. But yet, interest is there," he said.

"Only your interest, not mine."

"It's early. I feel I will persuade you."

"Aw naw, Daniel. Don't hold your breath. Again, how did you get my car cleaned up so fast?"

"Money has benefits, and I know people."

"Well stop. Good night." I hung up.

Bozo came in; stretched his front paws way out in front of him with his butt up in the air.

"Did I disturb you Bud? Sorry." He rolled over for me to rub his tummy.

"Meow." He was very pleased.

I made sure all blinds were down, all windows and doors were locked. I climbed in bed, beat.

About three o'clock a.m. my cell woke me.

I cleared my throat and answered in a frenzy, "What?"

"Babe . . . I can't get in. You put the night chain on all the doors." Jackson was half laughing.

"Okay, I'll be there in a second," I thought I recognized Jackson's voice but I thought I was dreaming, so I fell back to sleep.

My cell rang again. "Babe, I am waiting to get in. Come on now. I'm really tired."

"Me, too."

"Come on now, wake up and let me in."

I pulled myself out of bed and trudged down the hallway to the front door.

"Meow."

We both looked down at Bozo, "Not time to go out buddy. Back to bed," I yawned.

"Meow."

The next morning, we got up at the same time. Jackson took his shower first then headed to the kitchen. He took care of Bozo, put the coffee on, and the toast in.

Though my knee was on the mend, it was a bit stiff this morning. I dragged my tired body into the kitchen. Jackson handed me my go cup of coffee and two pieces of toast with peanut butter and jam. I picked up my lunch bag, hoping something was in it. Empty.

Hmph. I put my cup down and leaned into Jackson with a goodbye kiss.

"Later, babe."

"Yep, later. Bye, Bozo," I said heading for the door.

Then Jackson said to me, just as I was about to shut the door, "Got your old car cleaned up. It looks great."

"Long story. Tell you later."

I looked around and up and down the street, not because I'm scared, but I just want to be prepared. I got in my clean car and picked up Paul.

CHAPTER 35

TO MY SURPRISE, JOAN Cosby was back and on my floor, again. I walked into her room and she had her leg up in a sling. I looked at her chart.

"What's this?" I asked her.

Joan held her arms out for me to come to her for a hug.

"I slipped on my porch and about went down the front steps. I didn't break anything but I have a bruised something or other, and I guess I sprang it pretty bad," she said, patting her leg. "Because of my age, my kids wanted me to heal with the help of you guys."

"Good idea," I said, looking over her chart. I scanned a note that said her hospital charges were being paid for by an anonymous donor. "Did you know your bill was taken care of?" I asked her.

"That's what I hear. But I can't figure out why anyone would want to pay when I'm on Medicare. I'm just curious. Do you think you can find out?"

"Actually, Medicare Plan B pays eighty percent of your bill and you get the rest, unless you have supplemental insurance. If you do, it will pay the rest."

"No, no, I just have Medicare, but often thought of looking into supplemental insurance."

"I guess we should be happy your bill will be zero when you leave here. I will look into it, if you want."

"Thank you, dearie. I just don't understand."

"Meantime, don't worry about something you can't control. Just be able to walk out of here soon."

I smiled and turned to go check on a patient who had their call light on. "I'll be back," I told her.

I entered room 495 where a fifty-something man was yelling for help.

I walked up to him, looking at the chart that I just took off his door.

"How can I help you Mr. Parker?"

"I feel like I'm going to vomit. Hurry."

I got the bedpan and he up-chucked just as I put it under his mouth.

I poured a glass of water and handed it to him.

"Woof, that was close," Mr. Parker said, rather cantankerously.

"Mm-hmmm, sure was," I said. "Are you feeling better now, Mr. Parker? I'll get you something for your upset stomach."

"First call me Peter," he said.

"Peter Parker," I mused.

"Yes, yes, Peter Parker and, no, I am not Spider Man . . . ," Peter Parker said, with disgust. "That joke is getting old. I'm sure I had my name first."

"Well, Peter Parker, I would never have put two and two, together. Peter Parker or Clark Kent, it makes no difference to me," I zinged back.

"Young lady, we're going to get along just fine," Peter Parker smiled, and a rather nice smile. "I think I need the bedpan again."

I got him all cleaned up, and gave him something for his vomiting. Then after checking on the rest of my patients, I made my way back to Joan.

Nora called my cell, and asked if it was lunchtime yet. She wanted to meet me in the hospital cafeteria. I went ahead and took my lunch hour.

"I just love eating here. The prices are so good, unlike a hospital north of the river, which raised their prices," Nora commented.

"Joan's here, again."

"Really? What for?"

"She slipped and fell. She got a few bruises and banged up her leg. She's here for precautionary reasons."

"You guys do that?"

"Apparently, we do now." I shook my head. "Oh, and we have Spider Man here."

"Spider Man?"

"Yep, Peter Parker himself," I explained. "And he was curmudgeonly."

"What's curmudgeonly?"

"You know. . . bad temper, cantankerous."

"Then why in the hell don't you just say that?"

I just shook my head in amazement. "I have to get back to my shift. Oh, and this is a first."

"What?"

"Oh, you calling me for lunch today. It was nice."

"I felt the need," she said. "I need to watch over you."

"Well stop. I can take care of myself. See you day after tomorrow."

With hugs, we said our good-byes.

The afternoon had gone by fast, and I was back home in no time.

I attempted to read another of Louise's sex stories. I just couldn't get into another sex scene.

I was so tired; I decided to curl up on the sofa, just for a minute. I was all comfortable, when my cell rang.

"How was your day, my lady?" Daniel asked.

"Daniel, you have to stop calling me, and you need to stop sending flowers, and washing my car. This can't go on."

"Oh, my lady, it is my job to do nice things for you."

"No. No it's not, so stop. Please . . . stop"

"You're just tired and testy."

"Good night Daniel," I hung up on him before he could say one more thing.

CHAPTER 36

"Daniel"

DANIEL SAT THERE WONDERING why Charla hung up on him. *Why can't she see I'm only doing nice things for her? I must make her see I mean no harm. How can I get her to accept me?* I realize we only just met, but I haven't felt this way for anyone, ever. Sweet Vivian was just a convenience from a wealthy family. I mean, I met her in the right time in my career. She was an asset. Vivian was beautiful, but sexually she didn't know squat. She was straight laced, and proper. Men just needed more than that. They need, oh, I don't know . . . Whips!

I wondered what Charla needs. I bet she's great in bed. I bet she won't just lay there on her back just going through the motions to get it over with. No I bet she would enjoy it.

I wonder what Charla would think if she knew that I headed up the charity funds for the hospital. See, I'm nice. I chose to help her friend, Joan Cosby. I make a lot of decisions to help others. Why won't Charla let me help her? Why does she always seem upset with me? I must change her mind and make her love me as I love her.

Again, Daniel tried to shake off his thoughts about her.

Just then sweet Vivian walked in ready for bed.

"I put the kids down for the night," Vivian said. "Want to come to bed? You could get lucky." She reached for his hand.

Daniel looked at her, "Wha . . . what?"

"Daniel, you have been so preoccupied lately. I asked you, do you want to come to bed? I also said you might get lucky."

Daniel looked at her and thought, *I guess it's better than nothing. At least I can get my rocks off.*

"Sure, sure," he smiled as he got off the sofa and, set the remote down to take Vivian's hand as she led him to the bedroom.

It took all of ten minutes. Vivian didn't like foreplay. She was doing her wifely duty, and wanted it over with. She didn't disappoint. Same ole, same ole.

While Daniel was in the shower, his mind drifted to Charla again. His eyes were closed and he smiled pretending he was soaping Charla up and down her body and she was loving it. He was kissing her long hard, and deep and she was longing for more.

Of course, Charla isn't there but his imagination allowed himself to grab hold of his swollen erection, and he moaned and groaned with relief, which was more than Vivian had done for him.

Daniel finished his shower and fell into bed. He looked over at sweet Vivian, stared at her a few minutes then rolled over and thought of Charla, pleased with himself and he whispered, "Sweet dreams, my lady," and started to drift off to sleep.

Vivian whispered back, "Sweet dreams, my prince."

Daniel's eyes popped wide open . . . he reached around, patted Vivian's hip. He thought, *not you . . . Charla.*

CHAPTER 37

I WAS WALKING TO my car after my shift ended when I saw Daniel walking towards me. I turned my head and my body stiffened. I looked back at him with a fake smile. I had to order my mental self to do a body shake to loosen up so as not to show my anger. *Appearances, appearances.*

"Hello, Daniel," I said. My stomach tensed when I looked at him.

"Fancy running into you," Daniel smiled.

I bet fancy running into you. You've probably been lurking in the shadows for hours watching my car.

"How long have you been waiting?" I asked him.

"No, no. I just got here. I have a business meeting with the Charity Distributions Committee. I believe you have a friend in here that we just picked up her tab."

"Of course, you did," I said, with curiosity. "Why?"

"What do you mean, why? I love helping people. I'm helping your friend."

"What is it with you? You're always doing things for me and now Joan."

"I told you, my lady. I like doing nice things for nice people."

"Daniel, you seem to be very thoughtful, but I still have a boyfriend that I love very much. You are wasting time chasing after something that will never happen, so STOP!"

"Well, my lady, that too can change."

"What do you mean?" I asked.

He started to answer, but the Calvary drove up.

"Come on, Charla, we're going to be late," Nora yelled out her car window. "Hurry up."

Daniel did the bend at the waist court jester thing, like I was royalty, then he said, "Later my lady, you may pass."

I was shivering as I got into my car, and it wasn't a feel-good shiver. I followed Nora out of the parking lot and home.

We both got out of our cars.

"How did you know?"

"I ran into Paul at the Convenience store pumping gas. He said he was on his way into work.

He said he traded for the later shift. Since it was almost seven, and time for you to be going out to your car, I hustled to get there. I got there just before Paul and looks like just in time for you."

"Take a breath, Nora. Everything's okay."

"What did the pervert want?" she asked.

I filled her in on what words were exchanged between Daniel and me.

"But before Daniel could tell me what he meant by *that, too, can change,* you drove up fast and furious. Though I have my idea of what he meant, I don't like it."

"Hey, I might have saved you from whips or something," she snarled.

"Oh, puhleese . . . Really?" I snarled back. "You think you're so damn cute."

"Maybe not whips, but he's totally infatuated with you. He's stalking you. He's everywhere you are or he watches your every move and not too far away. You need to tell Jackson, now."

"NO," I yelled, "Not yet. I'm not ready. I've got to figure this out."

"Oh, really? You have to figure this out. So, what is this?" she said, throwing up her hands.

"I swear Nora, you couldn't talk without your hands. This!" I expressed with my hands.

About that time my cell rang. "Charla, this is Jordan. I might have those names for you. Can you guys come by Cheer Up about three tomorrow?"

"Yes, and that's great news, Jordan. See you tomorrow."

Nora had her face in front of mine, "What? What?"

CHAPTER 38

JORDON WAS WAITING FOR us when we walked into The Cheer Up. "What do you guys want to drink?" he asked.

I said, "Diet Dr. Pepper, but in a go cup."

"Ditto," Nora agreed.

Jordan set the drinks down in front of us and reached for an envelope that was sitting next to the cash register. He opened it while looking around, checking to see if anyone else had come in.

He pulled out the information and showed us the names of the female customers in question. "Here are the names of the ladies who stopped showing up here." He laid the list down in front of us.

"Jordan, we can't thank you enough." We looked over the list, then I reached to shake his hand in thanks. Nora picked up the envelope and put the sheets of information back in it.

Just before we reached the door, Jordan yelled, "Charla, what have you done with Daniel?"

"Excuse me?" I intelligently asked, as Nora and I both walked back to him.

"Daniel hasn't been back in here since you walked into his life."

"What? What do you mean since I walked into his life?"

Nora edged closer to Jordan, "What do you mean?"

"Just saying Daniel stopped coming in."

"I thought he only came in once a month on the key drawing night."

"Well, yeah. But he also came in several times a week for a drink before heading on home. He stopped."

"Stopped?" Then I thought *that's because he's too busy following me.*

"Yeah, stopped. I told you, Charla, he couldn't stop watching you. In all the years he's been coming in here, I've never known him to dance with anyone let alone watch their every move like he did you that night."

And stalking me.

"Well, I'll have to keep my eyes open." But I thought, *my eyes more open.*

"And I have her six," Nora proudly stated.

We finally stepped out the front door right into Daniel. Nora immediately feathered up. "Just what the hell are you doing here?" she said, with chagrin as she chest-butted him.

"Hold on, almighty protector. I was on my way home when I noticed your car here, Nora. I just thought I would say hello," he said, stepping back from her chest-butting exterior.

"*R i g h t,* so say it and leave," she held up her hand to stop him from moving in closer.

"Seriously, voluptuous Nora, you need to relax. Take a valium. I am not stalking Charla like you think. I just think she's fascinating and I enjoy talking to her. I like doing nice things for her."

"Well stop it. Charla doesn't need your nice things, or anything you have to offer," she was in his face.

"Wait, a damn minute," I yelled. "I'm standing right here and I can take care of myself. You, *I pointed to Daniel,* stop being fascinated with me, and you, *pointing at Nora* stop protecting me. Albeit, you're my best friend Nora, and you're not," *pointing to Daniel,* "both of you are driving me profoundly nuts. Stop, stop, stop. Let me reiterate . . . STOP both of you."

I grabbed Nora and pulled her away with me, but not before I turned back to Daniel, "Go home to your wife. And leave me the hell alone."

We got into the car leaving Daniel dumbfounded. My cell rang.

"Charla, this is Jordan. I told you so. I don't think he'll leave you alone. He has it bad for you."

"Nuh-uh, no, but thanks, Jordan." I hung up.

"What did he want?" Nora asked.

"I told you so," I answered. "Jordan heard us from inside so he called."

CHAPTER 39

To save face, Daniel sat down at the bar in his usual spot. He yelled at Jordan to bring him his regular drink.

"Whew, wonder what's wrong with Charla?" Daniel asked.

Jordan set Daniel's drink down and answered, "I wonder? Excuse me, Daniel, I have paperwork." He went to his office and dialed Charla's cell.

Being alone at the bar, sipping his scotch whisky blend of Chivas Regal, Daniel reflected on what just happened with Charla.

He thought to himself, "*I need to stop her overzealous friend Nora. She needs to butt out. Then I have to get Charla to listen to me. Charla needs to get rid of Det. Boxley. I'm better for her. I can give her more in so many ways. Money, status, love. Everything.*

Daniel started dreaming of him gently laying Charla down on her bed with him caressing every bit of her body, making love to her slowly and deliberately.

Daniel shook his head. Slow down, big boy, as he adjusted his family jewels. Thank goodness no one was there with him. No one could see his manhood growing.

About that time a twenty something couple walked in giggling, hanging all over each other.

Daniel thought, since he watched them pull up in different junk cars, greeting and slobbering all over each other, that it was a rendezvous. I bet he takes her down the street to the no tell motel. It wasn't a nice place but probably all the poor smuck could afford. One thing for sure, he was going to get lucky.

His thoughts turned back to Charla . . . I could do better for Charla. Money's no object. I have plenty and I would wine and dine her in a lavish lifestyle, the way a lady should be treated.

Daniel smiled at the thought. He watched Jordan approached the young cheating couple to get their order. Daniel could feel his arousal settling down. He looked down and thought, as he adjusted himself, *good I can leave now*. He slammed back the remaining scotch, set the glass down, and threw up his hand in a good-bye to Jordan.

Daniel sat in his car and thought he really didn't want to go home to sweet Vivian just yet. "I could be with Charla forever," he sighed out loud. "Charla would be the first I wouldn't want to kill after five times or a million." He sighed again.

He started his car and drove straight to the jewelry store.

He looked at the bracelets and decided he didn't want it to be ostentatious, but not too simple, either. Finally, he spotted the perfect one. He stared at it. The cutesy redhead sales lady had shown Daniel several with great anticipation of a good commission, pulled the bracelet out for him to see up close and personal.

"Special lady?" she asked.

"Oh, yes, special," Daniel smiled.

"This is a 14-carat gold bracelet with three one carats, perfect diamonds in the center of the quarter inch wide bracelet, widening where the three diamonds line up north to south," she said, with an enormous smile.

"I think it would suit her just fine. Ring it up."

The cutesy sale lady smiled about the nice bonus she just rang up, "That will be twenty-one thousand, five hundred thirty-six dollars and 19 cents."

Daniel smiled and said, "For that price, the diamonds should be perfect. They're not."

She looked at the bracelet and said, "They look perfect to me."

Still smiling he said, "Wrap it up and send it to Charla O'Hara at this address, right away."

CHAPTER 40

NORA AND I SAT down and read over the list of names, and information Jordan had just given us.

The first thing I looked for was Lora Janeson. I skimmed down the page.

"Here she is."

"What?" Nora jumped up a bit in her chair with enthusiasm.

"Lora Janeson. It says she had been a Key Club member for six and half years before she was killed. It says her physicals were always good, and she was always healthy. Was. She was married with children. She was a regular Key Club member. The last time she was in The Cheer Up was in June. Jackson said she was killed two weeks later. It also says Louise was killed in late August. Both were shot in the head, while standing in the kitchen. That's why Jackson called them the Kitchen Murders."

"Jordan has three categories, Present, Past or Stop coming in. Oh, and New, so four categories," Nora said.

"I need to give Jackson these 'stop coming' names," I said, making the quote sign with my fingers. "But just the names, maybe some of these names will show up as cold cases. We need to call each of the past members to see if they are indeed, past members, or dead."

"Okay, I'll call the top half, and you call the bottom half," Nora said.

We made a copy of the list and divvied them out. I got my cell and Nora got hers.

A couple of hours went by and I looked over the comments I'd made by the names I had called when Nora came in from the living room.

"How'd you do?" She asked.

"I called all ten names. Six are still kicking. I left two messages on two. The other two phone numbers are disconnected. Two ladies told me to shush as each spoke quietly in the phone. Their then spouse or current spouse didn't know they partook in such diverse sexual activity. And they didn't want them to know." I sighed. "The two disconnects, I am afraid, are not looking good. I'll give those two to Jackson. I asked the ones I talked to if we could meet. They said yes, though a couple hesitated and then said yes when I told them that a couple of their members had been killed. What did you find out?" I said.

"Two are now divorced and made a promise to themselves to behave. Two, like you said, didn't want their spouse to find out anything about their past. They would help if they could keep it on the down low. One married her pervert from the Key Club. Three phone numbers are disconnected. I left one a message and one number has changed. They agreed to meet with us also," Nora said.

"Let's work from here tomorrow and see if we can get any of the exes to come talk to us."

"It's getting late; I need to get home to Rickypoo."

"Jackson's due in a few, too. I need to start dinner before he gets home. So then, we agree to give Jackson a follow up list. I want to interview the other ladies first before turning them over to Jackson. I have to think about how I want to handle this."

"Ten Four, Kemo Sabe," She threw up her hand good bye and reminded me to lock up.

"Ten four," I said back to her as I locked the door.

Just as I turned to walk toward the kitchen, the doorbell rang. I hesitated to answer. I pulled my gun out of my purse and held it behind my back. I peeked out the peep hole. A delivery guy was standing there with a big smile on his face. I pulled the door open.

"Miss O'Hara? Charla O'Hara?"

"Yes," I reluctantly answered.

"Sign here," he pointed.

"No!"

"But, ma'am, I was told not to come back without your acceptance."

"For crying out loud, what is it, and who sent it?" I inquired, hoping it was from Jackson, but knowing that it might be out of his price range coming from this particular jewelry store. I could only hope.

"It doesn't say. But being from this jewelry store, the best around, I bet it's nice," the delivery man said, still smiling.

I slid my gun in the back of my waistband.

I signed and I should've tipped him but hey, I didn't ask for this . . . I closed the door on him and took the beautifully wrapped package and set it down on the table. I stared at it. I walked away, then back several times, looking at the beautiful wrapped box. I picked it up, being very tempted to see what was in it. I sat it back down. Though I was hoping it was from Jackson, my gut told me it wasn't. I started to read the card, but I didn't. I thought, "*that damn Daniel.*"

I walked away from the box and into the kitchen and watched Bozo coming through his doggie door.

He walked back and forth brushing up against my legs and raised his sweet cat face up and meowed.

He kept meowing and walking toward the back door, then walking back to me.

"You have something to show me, Bud?"

He looked at me and led me to the door.

"Okay, Bud, show me," I said as he led me across the neighbor's yard to a tool shed. As I followed him, he would look up at me to be sure I was still following him.

Bozo sat down and meowed and meowed, all the time talking to me.

"What is it, Bud? What's wrong?"

I looked down at a small mound of dirt. I turned around when the neighbor came out with tears in her eyes carrying a little sign. It said, "Suzy was with us 11 years, RIP."

Suzy's owner bent down and placed the marker on Suzy's grave. She gently cried.

The marker said it all. I put my arms around her, and gave her a hug; I asked her, what happened to Suzy?

"The vet said Suzy had a stroke, the best he could tell."

"A stroke?" I looked at her with curiosity. "I'm so sorry."

I sat down beside Bozo to help him mourn his little buddy while my neighbor went back into her house.

"I am sorry, lil Bud," I said brushing over his head and down his back over and over.

He just sat there meowing. It was the saddest thing I have ever witnessed. I cried, too. After a while I stood up to head back home. I picked Bozo up and held him in my arms and the whole time he looked back to his lil' buddy's grave meowing.

I held Bozo for a while to comfort him. I set him down and he went back to his doggie door and meowed. This is the first time I unlocked it for him to go back out. I watched him head for Suzy's grave.

I picked up the beautiful package that had been delivered to me and wondered what was in it. I had no doubt who sent it. I slid it in the drawer just seconds before Jackson walked in the door. I didn't want him to see it. I wasn't in the mood to open the package or deal with Jackson over it. I figured that if Jackson had sent me a present, he would have asked me how I liked it. He didn't ask.

CHAPTER 41

THE NEXT MORNING AFTER Jackson left for work, I called Nora bright and early and told her I was on my way over to her house.

"What a surprise," she sarcastically said. "You hardly ever come over here. I always have to go to your house."

"Well, yeah," I retorted, "I have something to show you."

I grabbed the jewelry package, opened the door, and looked all around for any other surprises. All clear.

I pulled out, drove down the street, looking all around and checking for unwanted company.

I got to Nora's just in time to say hello and goodbye to Rick. *Hug, hug, kiss, kiss.*

Nora came out and yelled, "Get away from my man. You have enough already."

She pulled me into the house and asked, "What's the big secret?"

I stood in the middle of her living room, looking at her beautiful clean house. I noted that everything was in place and there was a place for everything. I sighed and pulled the package out of a grocery bag and raised it up.

"What is it?" she asked.

"Don't know."

"Who's it from?"

"Don't know."

"You didn't open it or read the card?"

"Nope."

"What in the hell is wrong with you?"

"Nothing."

"What are you waiting for? Open up the damn thing," she demanded.

I stared at the beautiful package and glanced back at Nora and said, "I want it to be from Jackson, but he couldn't afford anything from this jewelry store. Soooo."

"Come on," she said.

"I'm afraid."

She reached for the package.

"No." I said, pulling the box back to me.

I slowly pulled the card off the box, opened it and started reading.

"My lady, here is a token of my affection. Wear it thinking of me."

"Oh, my God," Nora said, pulling the card out of my hand. "Open it, open it."

I took a deep breath and exhaled . . . slowly.

I pulled the paper away from the box one corner at a time

"Oh, come on, you're killing me here," she scolded me, reaching for the box.

"No, mine," I pouted.

We both giggled on how childish we were acting.

I took the last of the paper off and opened the robin's egg blue box slowly. By then Nora was right beside me where she could see what was in the box at the same time I did.

We both stared at what was in the box a scooch too long in disbelief.

I held the box out and said, "What on earth? Well, I can't accept this," I said.

"I can," the crazed redhead said, reaching for the box.

I stared at the beautiful bracelet. "He's getting this back and TODAY."

"Hold on Kemo Sabe, at least try it on. That cost him some big bucks. Try it on. Try it on."

I regrettably took it out of the box and slipped it on. "Wow, look how big the diamonds are!

"There are three. If only . . . ? I wish I could keep this gorgeous thing. I wish

Jackson could afford things like this. Just once I wish I could wear stuff like this, like you do," pointing at Nora's gigantic wedding ring that matched her boobs.

"I'll be happy to wear this for you," she said.

"Absolutely not," I said, slipping it off, sticking it back into the box securely and into the grocery bag. "He's getting it back and that's that. Now let's call the ladies in for an interview."

"Ladies?"

"Yeah, ladies from The Cheer Up."

"Got it, we can call from here and meet them here or your place."

"Since everything was scattered on my dining room table, we can meet them at Jackson's."

"When are you going to accept Jackson's place as your place? It has been for years, you know."

"I know, but it's just hard since he bought it way before me. Just call the ladies."

Nora called half of the ladies to meet today and I called the other half to meet tomorrow.

✦»»)«««✦

WE STOPPED FOR LUNCH on our way to *my* place. While we were eating our triple decker chicken salad sandwich on sour dough bread and drinking diet Dr. Pepper, I told her of Bozo losing his buddy and how sad it was.

On the way home, we pulled into the grocery store parking lot, got out of my car when, lo and behold; my stalker, in the flesh, was pulling up in his black shiny BMW, reeking of wealth.

I pulled the robin egg blue box out of the grocery bag and headed toward him with Nora hot on my heels.

Just as I got to his car, he rolled down his window, and I bent down to see him and *his wife*.

"Ooooops, I got the wrong car. I thought you were an undercover cop I know," I stuttered.

No sense in letting the little lady know about the bracelet. After all it wasn't her fault he's a sleaze.

We turned and were several feet away when Daniel turned and spoke to his wife. She smiled with a nod, got out of the car to go into an antique store.

Nora and I approached Daniel again.

"So, Charla, how did you like the bracelet? When I saw it, I thought of you and your sparkly smile."

"Damon aka Daniel," he was smiling at my statement. "I cannot and will not accept this extravagant gift or any gift from you. Please stop the special deliveries. I love Jackson and you don't have a goat's chance with me. Capice?" I said firmly. "Give this to your wife who I am sure is deserving." I pushed the box through the window into his hands.

"Char . . . la?"

"Dan . . . iel, NO!"

Nora pulled me away and flipped Daniel the bird.

"What a lady," Daniel yelled out his window to her. But she just flipped him off again.

Walking away I said, "Thanks for having my six."

We looked back just in time to see Mrs. Damon aka Daniel, give him a kiss on his cheek as he handed her the box. Then, I grimaced when I witnessed a big liplock between them. Daniel was looking right at me. I wanted to pull my gun out and shoot him, but better sense crept in and I took my hand out of my purse.

"Hmmm," I sighed. "I came this close . . . *holding my finger and thumb a fraction apart*, to keeping that gorgeous thing."

"No, you didn't, but you're so badassery, the way you handled him. I saw your hand in your purse."

"Badassery . . . ?"

"Yeah, a new slang word for the year," she said.

"You sure you didn't just make it up?" I asked.

"No, ma'am, I'm pretty sure I could make up better words than badassery. Though, I like saying it."

"Make up one," I teased.

"Okay, aaaah, hmmm, okay . . . panetheus," she popped out.

"Panetheus?"

"Yep, pain in the ass."

"I like it, now if it catches on . . . !"

"We better get home and start interviewing. I already started a list of questions that we need to ask."

"Step on it, Mean Machine," she teased. "Oh, oh, here comes *the look!*"

CHAPTER 42

"THANK YOU, LADIES, FOR coming." I pointed to the dining room. "Have a seat. Does anyone want coffee?" Everyone did.

"Does anyone want sugar or creamer?" hoping they just wanted black . . . !

Everyone wanted one or the other and a couple wanted both. *I don't understand how anyone would ruin their coffee.*

We asked each lady several questions. How long did they belong to the key club, when did they start, are they still active, when did they stop being involved, whose key they drew the most often and how many different guys?

Some of the ladies hesitated to answer and were almost embarrassed. The other ladies acted reenergized just talking about their past activities.

After outlining what each lady said, we could see a pattern forming. Of what, we didn't know.

My focus was on Daniel aka Damon. Damon was how they referred to him and was their favorite. But I didn't care if they knew his real name was Daniel so I told them.

They each had been with him at least once, some as much as four times. They all thought he was gorgeous. They all praised his manhood. Some liked the way he made love.

"Really?" Nora asked, "You into that kind of stuff?"

"It's Damon . . ." One of them said, with a duh!

It takes all kinds.

After they left we looked at our notes. We listed each of the ladies and then listed the guys. We did a tally of how many times each of the ladies had been with each of them and I might say it was very interesting. There were a few guys that were not mentioned in Louise's ledger that we had not heard of until now. It was a slim possibility that Louise hadn't drawn their key or she wasn't impressed enough with their activities or credentials to mention them.

"Don't know why we didn't think of getting a list of the Key Club men. I think it's a good idea we call Jordan and ask him to make a list of the men that have been involved from the start til now," I suggested.

"Good idea," Nora agreed.

I dialed Jordan and told him what I needed.

"I knew that you would want it, so I have it ready if you girls want to drop by," he said.

"We're on our way."

◆❯❯❯◀◀◀◆

WE PULLED UP IN front of Cheer Up by four and, as promised, Jordan had the men's list waiting for us.

"I don't know why I am so willing to help you," he said.

"I do," Nora popped out. "Murder *is* bad for business."

"You have a point," he smiled. "But if there's a way you can keep my name out of this, I sure would and will appreciate it."

I said, "No problem. Your secret is safe with us. That's why we have better luck than the cops sometimes. We don't have to reveal our sources. Jackson said its dumb luck. We do stumble around a lot, and have had a fluke or two, but we do get results. Thanks so much for all your help, Jordan."

"Sorry about Daniel chasing after you. I can't believe after all these years of him coming in here, that he latched on to you. Unbelievable. I know how concerning it is for you, and I feel somewhat responsible. If you want, I will keep you informed if I see or hear anything."

"What do you mean you can't believe Daniel would latch on to Charla? Did you look at her? Especially in that red dress she wore that night. Honestly,

Jordan, you blind?" Nora scolded him thumping her fingers on the bar with anger. "Really Jordan."

"Well, of course, Charla is a knock out, especially that first night you guys came in. No one will forget that red dress. But since then she looks kind of plain."

"Jordan, you should have stopped while you were ahead and before that last statement," Nora said, with fire in her blue eyes as she scolded him.

"Alright, children, enough," I said, to both of them. "Anything you can do, Jordan, will be appreciated."

I grabbed the men's list and pulled Nora out the door. As we were leaving Nora turned and did the finger to eye thing . . . "I'm watching you, Jordan."

He threw back his head and laughed, shaking his head at my over-zealous friend.

Of course, we looked around the parking lot, up and down the street as we walked to my Explorer. I took a deep sigh of relief when I could see it was an all-clear.

We pulled back into the driveway and I unlocked the door. Bozo, who was still mourning the loss of his buddy Suzy, meowed as we came in. He again wanted me to go out with him to Suzy's grave. Nora and I walked behind him and sat down on the ground with him. We sat there for a while and Nora, who never cries, cried just watching Bozo.

"That's the saddest thing I have ever witnessed . . . I didn't realize animals had such feelings," she said.

I picked up Bozo and cuddled him back into the house. He collapsed on the sofa and fell asleep.

Nora kept shaking her head in amazement about Bozo's feelings.

"Come on Nora, let's tally up who did what to who and how many times."

She stumbled into the dining room looking back at Bozo. "He is going to be okay?" she asked.

"He is taking it harder than I thought he would. The poor guy's worn out."

Bozo looked up like he understood, then put his head back down.

We made a list of all the guys and left space to write down the women who said they were with them. It took about an hour to write it all down.

"Tomorrow we have the other group coming in for an interview. It'll be easier with the list of men here already. You should have thought of the men list earlier."

"Me?" she said, with surprise. "You know, a lot of the time Charla, we take two steps forward and one back. We are, after all, unconventional, but we get the job done. Eventually."

"We are amateurs . . . sometimes. But as bad as we are, we are way out in front of Donnie."

"Yep, we are a step above Donnie and sometimes I wonder about that. She's the detective," she said, as she bent over and gave Bozo a loving pat before going out the door. "Lock up."

I started working on a list for Jackson of the women we didn't know about yet. I was anxious to know the outcome when the doorbell rang in a rapid succession.

I peeped out the tiny side window and the crazy redhead was standing with her hands out. "I need a ride."

Laughing, I grabbed my keys and drove her home.

CHAPTER 43

JACKSON CAME HOME AND it was the first time he was able to have an early night in close to a week. His investigation of the Kitchen Murders was going slowly.

He calls them the Kitchen Murders and I call them the Key Club Murders. He doesn't know what I know . . . yet.

I welcomed him with a leap, wrapping my legs around him and hugging him tight.

"This is nice," he said, "But, babe, I am dead tired and can barely hold on to you."

"Rough day?" I said, unwrapping my legs and sliding back down to the floor.

"Rough couple of weeks," he replied.

"I might have something that might ease your roughness," I mused.

"No babe, no sex. You have to rely on Ryan Reynolds tonight."

"No babe . . . it's not about sex."

"What might it be then?" he asked.

I whipped out the list of women's names from the file folder I had the list tucked in . . .

"These names could be on your cold case activity list. I have the dates that they may have stopped in existence. I thought it might help you. Look, Lora Janeson's name as well as my friend, Louise Stafford." I pointed their names out and handed him the list.

Jackson looked over the list. "Where, how did you come up with these names?"

"I have my way."

"Char . . . la!"

"I cannot reveal my source at this time. You know the game."

"Char . . . la!"

"I will tell you when I find out more. You can make the arrest," again I mused.

He wasn't amused.

"I am too tired to argue. I just want to eat something and go to bed."

I made him bacon, eggs, hash browns and toast since I forgot to thaw out anything, *again*.

However, it hit the spot.

We cuddled on the sofa next to Bozo who hadn't moved when we sat down.

"What's wrong with the watch cat?" Jackson pointed to Bozo.

"That's right, you didn't know. Bozo has had a bad day or two. His buddy Suzy died and he's mourning."

"Died? It was just a few days ago that I carried Suzy home. What happened?"

I explained it to Jackson and told him how I had to go to Suzy's grave with Bozo and just today when I got home, he led both Nora and me out there.

"Oh, my God! That is just about the saddest thing I ever heard," Jackson said, quietly.

Bozo stretched and curled back up.

"Poor guy."

Jackson went to bed and Bozo and I cuddled a while longer.

My cell rang. "Good night, my lady."

I shivered and hung up. I looked at Bozo and said, "That was my stalker."

"Meow . . ."

"Exactly."

Bozo followed me down the hall and I slipped into bed beside Jackson and Bozo collapsed on his pillow.

CHAPTER 44

NORA AND I MET with the other group of women and made our notes to follow up.

We listed them beside the men's names. There are a few men who have since retired.

There were several men who had repeat women and some waiting for more action.

We spent the day matching up the information to Louise's diary/log. It was interesting how yesterday's and today's ladies had so much in common with Louise. I don't know why it surprised me, as they were all members of the Key Club. There was a lot of similarity between them and the guys. But grouping them and looking at the list, it was going to be hard to prove any of them were the murderer. My gut of guts still told me there was a connection . . . But how?

While working on the case at home, Nora and I watched Bozo go in and out all day. Each time he went out, he went straight to Suzy's grave. We also noticed that each visit was a little shorter than the last. He was accepting his buddy wasn't coming back.

I HAD A BIG pot roast in the oven with all the trimmings, so I asked Nora to stay and had her call Rick to come for dinner.

The timing was perfect as Rick pulled in right behind Jackson. Rick was carrying a six pack and the guys were laughing when they came through the garage door together.

Rick set the beer down, getting out two bottles, and handing one to Jackson.

Jackson with the cold beer in his hand headed for me. He set his beer down and picked me up and swung me around with gusto. Kissing me, kissing me, kissing me. Swinging me around, he said, "Thank you, thank you, babe. You never disappoint."

"Get a room," Nora said. *Again.*

Jackson looked at me, then Nora, and said, "You two are ah—mazing. You gave us help on a couple of cold cases. They are a little warm now. And just maybe we can connect the dots."

"All in a day's work, after all it's our job to make your job easier. Just wait for the finale." Nora teased.

"The finale . . . ? What finale?"

"Well, there's no finale per se, but there will be," I chimed in. *I hope!*

"Jackson, will you do the honor and pour Nora and me a glass of wine? You boys want wine with dinner or you staying with beer?"

Both said beer as Jackson poured the wine for us girls.

We sat down to a great meal and conversation. My cell rang and I hesitated to answer it. It stopped. Five minutes later it rang again. I answered.

"My lady, you're having a party without me."

I hung up.

"Who was that?" Jackson asked.

"Wrong number," I answered.

My cell rang again, and Nora grabbed it out of my hand and went into the other room to answer it.

"My lady, you hung up on me."

"Daniel, you have got to get a life. My lady is not available," Nora hung up.

Nora walked back into the dining room and handed me my cell under the table.

A bing ring went off. I looked down under the table at the cell in my lap. Hmph, a text message.

I checked it and it said, "My lady, I just wanted to say I miss you."

I nudged Nora under the table and handed her my cell.

Nora glanced down at it and raised her eyes in disgust.

Nora texted him back. "No speaka English."

Daniel texted back "N o r a . . . !"

"What's going on?" Jackson was now curious at my cell going off time after time.

"I keep getting a wrong number. I was nice in letting them know it is a wrong number at first, but when they called back, Mother here took over. I may have my number changed as this guy can't figure out *wrong number*."

"Okay, whatever you need to do, babe," Jackson responded.

All of a sudden there's a roar coming from Nora mouth . . . "*n o o o!*"

Each of us looked at her in shock. "What are you doing?" I asked.

Nora straightened herself up in her chair and said, "Nothing. I just want you to keep your number. That's all. I like it."

"For heaven's sake, Nora," Rick scolded. "What difference does it make?"

She shrugged her shoulders and looking at all of us, said, "What?"

We then had a good laugh at Nora's expense.

Then she said, "Besides, we have our numbers on our business cards and everywhere else. We are going for our Private Investigation license tomorrow and it all needs to match up."

"You're what? Tomorrow?" Jackson was in wonderment.

"Nora's right. With a PI License, we should be able to help you more, Jackson. Having our license will open so many doors for us."

Now Rick was rolling his eyes.

I looked at the guys and took Nora's hand and said, "We didn't want to tell you just yet. We wanted to surprise you after we passed our last exam. We already passed the criminal law course requirements and with the help of a couple of your detective buddies, Jackson, not to mention your help, I believe we are ready to give it a whirl."

Nora nodded her head with great vigor.

"What do you mean with my help?"

"Yep, I asked you tons of questions this past year while taking my classes. I used what you told me and applied it to the requirement test. I gave the info to my partner here." I said pointing to Nora, who also passed.

"We go test out tomorrow."

"Want another beer, Rick? We need to toast our women . . . or get drunk," Jackson giggled.

"Laugh all you want because we are this close to being the newest P I's in this fair city. We will cover your ass with pride," I was now giggling.

CHAPTER 45

"Daniel"

DANIEL WAITED DOWN THE block from Jackson's house for a glance of Charla when she came out.

Jackson pulled out of the driveway heading south.

Daniel had a thought to follow Jackson. So, he did.

"Wonder where he is going? He didn't turn towards the precinct," Daniel said, out loud.

He followed Jackson for quite some distance.

"Where's he going?" he mumbled to himself, but he was anxious. His eyes were darting back and forth.

Jackson turned into the Café on the Corner parking lot.

Daniel said out loud, "What do we have here?" as he pulled over and watched from a distance. Jackson returned to his car with a rather good looking tall brunette.

He watched them get into Jackson's car and pull away.

"Well, well," Daniel still mumbling. "I'm just going to follow them."

He thought how much easier his life would be without Jackson in the picture or that mother hen Nora. Charla would be his.

Daniel made a big decision right then. "I am going to kill Jackson," he said, out loud, almost in anger, pounding the steering wheel with both of his hands. He pounded over and over again until his palms were beet red.

Calming down he muttered, "I'm going to get a car unrelated to me, follow

Jackson to make my move. I'm not unfamiliar with how to steal a car. After all, as a teen, I did more than my share of stealing a car or two, as well as breaking and entering. They were pranks, but nonetheless, I have the experience.

Daniel drove back to his house and got into his gun safe. He chose a different gun than he used in the murder of Louise. He decided on a Glock 9mm. Daniel tossed the gun back and forth in his hands, smiling. He grabbed a box of ammunition and loaded his Glock, then tossed it back and forth again.

He drove his black BMW to the mall parking lot, pulled in and nestled his car between a five-year-old pickup and a slightly older sedan. He assumed he was in the employee parking area. He got out searching around for people. He lurked around looking for just the right vehicle.

Aisle after aisle, he finally found the right car. He saw a piece-of-junk Pontiac that no doubt belonged to a mall employee who had just gotten out of it. Daniel waited until the kid slipped on a store jacket and entered the mall doors. Daniel slipped on a pair of gloves and tried the junker car door, it opened. He climbed in and leaned down to hot wire it and it started. "Good, I haven't lost the touch." Daniel pulled out of the mall parking lot and headed toward where he last saw Jackson. He recognized Jackson's car sitting down the block from the Café on the Corner but nearer an apartment building. He waited.

Daniel, looked around for surveillance cameras. He pulled his hood up over his head and put on a pair of oversize sunglasses for a disguise. He walked down in the alley closest to where Jackson's car was parked and stood at the corner end of it. He waited in the shadows thinking he could shoot, run back to the stolen car, and be back at the mall in no time with none the wiser. He thought he was just out of sight of surveillance cameras. The camera on the corner was dangling down so it was not working, "I couldn't plan this any better," he said, under his breath.

Daniel saw Jackson and the tall brunette come out of the apartment building. The brunette turned and went the opposite direction. Jackson was coming toward Daniel.

"How lucky can you get?" Daniel mumbled in a stage whisper.

He took aim and pulled the trigger, twice. He turned and ran down the alley and jumped into the stolen Pontiac. Just like that Daniel was gone. No one knew.

CHAPTER 46

DETECTIVE DONNIE HARPER TURNED and watched Jackson go down. She rushed back to him. She called for backup and yelled into her cell, "Officer down."

"Jackson, Jackson," she called out his name as she looked up and around for the shooter. She sat down on the ground and put Jackson's head in her lap. "Come on, Jackson . . ."

The backup was there in record time, as were the ME's and paramedics.

Jackson was wincing with pain, trying to sit up, watching the blood pour out of his shoulder and arm. The paramedics helped him sit up, then they got busy cleaning and dressing the gunshot wounds.

"I'm alright," he said, pissed off. "I didn't see it coming. I didn't see anyone," he said, answering the many questions. "Let me up," he demanded.

"No, Detective, you're going to the hospital. Gotta make sure you're okay," the paramedic insisted.

Donnie, who was still hovering over Jackson, agreed with them.

The sirens sounded as the ambulance zoomed towards the hospital.

Donnie called Charla.

"Charla, this is Donnie. Could you come to the hospital right away?"

"Wha, what?" I asked, starting to look pale. Nora grabbed my cell from me, getting the details. Nora handed my cell back to me. "It isn't bad, Charla, Jackson just got shot in the arm and shoulder and he's getting precautionary treatment," my friend told me.

Nora drove me to the hospital. As we headed for the curtain Jackson was behind, we could hear him yell, "I'm alright. Let me out of here."

I felt calm come over me with the sound of his voice.

I pulled the curtain back and was relieved to see he was alright, "Good grief Jackson, I was almost done with my PI test. Couldn't you have waited thirty more minutes before getting yourself shot?"

Then I put my arms around him kissing him, and kissing him.

"Stop! You're suffocating me," Jackson said, pushing me away with his good arm, being badassery in front of his cohorts.

He saw the hurt in my eyes and reached for me with his good arm, and pulled me back to him for a long hug.

Nora said, "Get a room," as she witnessed a very passionate kiss between Jackson and me.

The doctor came in with the Police Commissioner.

The commissioner spoke, "The doc here thinks you need a couple of weeks off to recoup.

"I agreed with him. So, as of now, you are relieved of duty and can report back after your follow-up in two weeks with the doc here, providing he says you're good to go."

We got back home and Nora hung out with us. She called Rick, explained what was going on and asked him to bring us takeout for our dinner.

Jackson sat down to kick back in his recliner. Bozo popped up into his lap. With his good hand, he petted Bozo and asked, "How you doing Bud? You feel'n better about Suzy now?"

It's like Bozo understood Jackson as he looked up at Jackson's face and said, "Meow."

"That's so sweet," Nora said, looking over to Jackson and Bozo.

A while later, my cell phone rang. I answered it.

"So, sorry to hear about Jackson . . . I heard he survived. Good for him and good for you my lady," Daniel said, but was steaming.

"Daniel, how did you find out about Jackson?"

"I was at the hospital at a board meeting when I watched the commotion and inquired what was going on. I happened to see you leaving with Jackson. How fortunate."

"You have got to stop calling me."

"No, no, I don't," he explained. "You are part of my life and I need you in my life, Charla."

"No, no, Daniel, I can't be anything to you. Go home to your wife," I hung up.

"You know he knows where you are at all times. And that's more than spooky," Nora said, clearly concerned.

"I think I will have one of the detectives do a scan on my car. Maybe Daniel has a tracking device attached to it."

"Oh, my God, I hope not," she said.

"Daniel knows everywhere I go. Something isn't right."

The doorbell rang and I jumped.

Nora answered the door with her gun in hand. *That is a sight in itself.*

She threw her arms around Rick's neck and gave him a kiss.

I said, "Get a room."

Jackson, who was on pain pills, woke up, lifted Bozo off his lap, and tried to get out of his chair.

"Oooh, that smarts," as he fell back.

"I thought maybe you were comatose the way you were out," I said, relieved.

"Yeah, I guess the pain pills have more than just pain relief in them. I feel woozy."

Nora brought Jackson a plate of KFC and sweet iced tea.

"Thanks, but I need Rick to help me down to the little men's room first," he said.

Rick got him down and back with only a few stumbles into the hall wall.

Before Jackson had one piece of chicken eaten, he fell asleep, again.

"Looks like we are going to be working from here for a while," I said.

Jackson's cell rang. It was Donnie. "How's our boy doing?" she asked.

My green eyes were getting red. *Our boy.*

As nicely as I could muster, I said, "Woozy, he's having a hard time staying awake."

"Well, that's to be expected. He's in a lot of pain?"

"He feels no pain," I giggled.

CHAPTER 47

JACKSON FELT BETTER AS each day went by. I took time off from my nursing job to nurse him.

I even gave up trying to write. My focus was on him.

Jackson made a few calls and found out that Nora and I had done well on our test. The only thing we had left to do was to test out on the gun range. Jackson made an appointment for both of us to finish our testing in the next couple of days. If we passed, we would get our PI license then. It was so close we could taste it.

Meantime, detectives and boys in blue were popping in and out as the brotherhood of police do, bringing well wishes from the guys that couldn't show up and bringing casseroles with every kind of cooked dish you could think of.

Nora and I worked endlessly on contacts from the list we had built over the weeks of investigating. Leaving Jackson in good hands, Nora and I reviewed Louise's neighbors, Lora Janeson's neighbors, as well as the Key Club group again and again. We knew if we kept at it, we would find out who the killer was.

Donnie kept us informed on how the attempt on Jackson's life was going. It was going as well as the Key Club murders. Zilch. Zero.

Donnie, with the help of Scott Edward, junior detective, was still working the Kitchen Murders aka Key Club murders.

I reminded Donnie that the names of the ladies I turned over to them were all part of the Cheer Up crowd. I told her I felt there had to be a strong connection and to check them out against any cold cases.

Jackson overheard my phone conversation with Donnie.

"You know Charla, you and Nora just might be on to something," Jackson said, trying to get out of his recliner. As he stood there, I showed him the chart and the connection from who was with whom at the Cheer Up. I told him how I felt about the Key Club being the main connection to the murders.

"So, all the time I called these cases the Kitchen Murders, you and Nora were calling them the Key Club Murders."

"Yes, but we haven't been able to connect the dots, yet. We feel it all stems back to The Cheer Up and the blasted Key Club. I keep looking at all our notes but come up with zilch."

I looked at Nora, who was bringing in sandwiches and diet Dr. Pepper and nodded towards the diary/log that Louise kept. She understood that I wanted to show it to Jackson. He had read bits of it before, but now it was time to fill him in all the way.

"Char . . . la, Nor . . . a, you have been holding out on me," he glared.

"Not holding out, just holding up telling you. Now's the time," I said, as I fluttered my eyes at him.

He hugged me with his good arm and patted Nora on the head. "Good job."

"Tomorrow, Nora and I will finish testing for our PI license while you go to the doctor." I reminded him. "Who is taking you?"

"Donnie."

I rolled my eyes in dismay. "Really? Not one of these guys?" I said looking at the guys in blue still strategically standing or pacing back and forth.

"These guys need a break and Donnie volunteered."

"I bet she did."

Changing the subject, he said, "This will put a whole new light on the case." He swept his good arm across the table. "I am thrilled you have all these notes and I can't wait to read Louise's diary, completely."

"I think you will find her diary, well . . . very interesting," I said, gulping.

"Oh, I don't know. Jackson will probably like it," Nora snickered.

The phone rang. I put Rita on the speaker so we all could hear her.

"Sorry, I still haven't been able to find anything else at my sister's house. Funny thing is, Louise's computer's back."

"Really?"

"Yep, Joe Jr. does know who took it from the description you gave him. He convinced the guy to return it. Joe Jr. said to tell you he was sorry he lied to you and it took so long," she said.

"While we were at Louise's funeral, Joe handed me a note with the guy's name on it with how to find him. I haven't been able to locate him yet. Bad thing is," I said, "I had my gun out and could've shot him."

"I'm pretty sure the kid knows it. He told Joe Jr. you about caught up with him and he did see your gun. He also said he felt sure if you hadn't tripped, you would have taken aim."

"Thanks, Rita. Keep in touch."

Jackson just stood and stared at me, then Nora. "You have been busy," but he was clearly pleased. "Now that you are a PI, our working together will be easier."

"You know something I don't?" I asked.

"Just a feeling," he teased.

"Read," I ordered, "you have a lot to catch up on."

We watched Jackson's reaction as he read the first couple of dates Louise had described.

He read a little more and then set the book down and said, "Woof."

"I have to confess, after several dates, Nora and I stopped reading it. We just read the first line or two to see how many times she was with each guy and basically skimmed over the rest."

"Fascinating read," he muttered.

The phone rang again. It was Amelia from the Writer's Club. We hadn't talked since Jackson was shot and home. I filled her in which was practically no different from the two weeks before. I told her that we were concentrating on Louise's murder and wouldn't be back to the Writer's Club for a while. I asked her to keep us informed if they heard anything.

She said she would.

CHAPTER 48

"Daniel"

SITTING IN HIS HOME office, Daniel was wringing his hands. "Shit! How could I have botched the shooting so badly? With a Glock 9 mm I should have killed Jackson without a problem, but instead, I botched . . . the kill. I rushed the shot. Now, Charla hasn't left Jackson's side. So many cops around their house, I can't even call her. Good thing I planted a GPS in her car. I'll know if she does leave. I can't wait to see her. I can't wait to talk to her. Why does this girl affect me like this?

Daniel was in turmoil thinking about her. His mind was reeling.

He checked his computer again to see if Charla was on the move before he went down to his wife and family.

"Just as I suspected, she won't leave Jackson's side, the lucky stiff," he said, out loud.

He turned off his computer and meandered down the stairs feeling down in the dumps.

Rock and Pebbles ran to him hoping to get some attention, but instead he looked at them and said, "Not tonight. Dad doesn't feel good."

Dear sweet Vivian said to him, "You haven't felt good in a while. If you keep this up, you will need to see the doctor."

"Shut up, Vivian, shut up. You have no idea. I have problems and they don't concern you."

"They do concern me when you ignore the kids and, in fact, me. I mean we haven't had sex in a while now."

"If that's what you call sex . . . ! You just lie there and I can't tell if you are enjoying it or not. Your expression is the same."

"Well, I never."

"That's right, you never."

He grabbed Vivian's hand, yanked her up off the sofa, and yelled, "Rock, watch your sister. Mommy and Daddy have some business to take care of."

"Okay, Daddy."

Daniel pushed Vivian through the bedroom door; then shut and locked it.

"Daniel, what are you doing?"

"I'm making sure you just don't lie there."

He ripped her clothes off and threw her on the bed. He put his hand over her mouth . . . "Not a word, Vivian. Not a word. This is way overdue."

He tied her hands to the bedpost with the panty hose he'd just torn off her. He took a pair out of the chest of drawers and tied her feet to the other post. He stuck a sock in her mouth.

He got undressed, his manhood enlarging at the thought of what he planned for his wife.

He pulled out one of Vivian's narrow belts and rubbed his manhood over her face, her breast, and tummy. He moved down between her legs and as he slid in her, he started slapping the belt across her tummy, first soft then harder. She was twisting and twisting from the pain. She whimpered.

"I said not a word Vivian. Not a word."

Tears started rolling out of her eyes and down towards her ears as she turned her head side to side trying not to say a word, as warned. But she couldn't stop the whimpering from the sting he was applying as it got harder.

"This is what it's supposed to be Vivian. Emotions! It has to have emotions. Not just lie there."

He pulled out of her, and reminded her not to say a word when he untied her. He flipped her over and retied her. He did a slow soft spanking then increased the pain. She whimpered and he shoved the sock back in her mouth. "Shut up, Vivian. We are doing it my way."

He pulled a scarf off the end of the bed that minutes earlier he had taken off her. He pulled it softly across her body. She got chills. Then he slapped her butt with his hand hard several times.

She was crying.

"Shut up, Vivian. Shut up."

He pulled her head back by her hair. He raised her butt up and he jammed his manhood into her hard and rough.

"This is what men want, DEAR SWEET VIVIAN. No man wants his wife just lying there like it's great. Well, it's not great. This is GREAT, Vivian. This is great." He was pumping her long and hard. He was getting into it. She cried.

Finally, the finale. He rolled off her and slapped her butt as she dropped flat on her stomach.

"Now that's how it is done, Vivian."

She sighed, sobbing. She couldn't talk. She just lay there.

"Well, that looks familiar," he smirked. "Just lying there, but this time I got my rocks off, and good."

There was a soft knock on their bedroom door. "Yes," he answered.

"I'm hungry, Daddy," little Pebbles said.

"Sorry, Daddy, she got away from me," Rock blurted out.

"No problem, kids, we'll be right there."

Daniel jumped in for a quick shower then pulled on his sweatpants and a tee. While Vivian just lay there.

"Come on, Vivian you have kids to take care."

"Go to hell," she cried.

"Yeah well, sometimes I feel like I'm already there."

Vivian got out of bed and looked into the mirror. She had stripes of blood all over her body. There were none oozing, but blood had come to the surface.

She cried, "You son of a bitch."

"Leave my mother out of this," he replied, as he went out the door.

CHAPTER 49

NORA AND I GOT to the gun range bright and early to test. We passed with flying colors.

The car was still moving when I got out, running toward the door. I slammed through the front door, jumping up and down, then side to side waving the papers at Jackson. "I'm a PI now. I'm a PI now. La de da . . ."

Nora was a few minutes behind me, jumped right in. "La de da."

"In case you wondered, the doctor said I'm healing pretty well, but wants me to stay home one more week," said Jackson.

"I'm sorry, detective. How insensitive am I?" I put my arms around him and said, "I'll make it up to you tonight. I'm on top."

"Forgiven," he grinned. "The closet door will be shut."

Nora rolled her eyes.

"That's right, big boy, no Ryan Reynolds allowed."

Nora rolled her eyes, again.

Out of the corner of my eye, I saw movement. I pulled my gun out, turned and took my stance as taught in PI school.

"Whoa, horsey," Donnie said, throwing her hands up in fear of getting shot.

I put my gun down and back into my purse, shaking my head.

I threw my hands out like *what the hell.*

"Oh, yeah, Donnie's here," Jackson mused.

"I now know. Anyone else here to surprise me?"

"No, just Donnie. I'm having her help make heads or tails of your notes."

"So, I checked out two of the ladies that once upon a time were members of the Cheer Up. Both were part of the Key Club like you said. They both said they didn't want to let anyone, especially their husband or kids, know," Donnie said.

"Why did you interview them? You need to concentrate on the ladies that have since come up missing. I don't have the resources to check them out, but you do," I said. "That's why I gave you the names."

"Sorry, I clearly upset you. I didn't mean to step on your toes. If it weren't for you and Nora, we wouldn't have this much to go on," she said.

"Then check out the names that I gave you that are missing. We need addresses, phone numbers, etc. We need to know if they are dead or alive."

"Aye, aye, sir, ma'am, will do." She glanced at Jackson and shrugged her shoulders.

"Let me introduce you to two of the most recent Private Investigators to get their license, Charla and Nora," Jackson said, with pride to Donnie.

"Well, well, congrats you two," she said, reaching to give both of us a group hug and a fist bump.

"Thanks," we both said, in unison, trying to back away from her.

Donnie gave her salutes and walked out the door, followed by Nora who went home.

"You mean to tell me Donnie's going to be here from now on while you recoup?"

"Oh, babe, it's her job. She's my partner. We have to work together."

"Well, so do we. I just . . . just don't care for her. She gets on my last nerve."

"I couldn't tell," he goaded me. "Seriously, she's not you, babe, but I do need her on the job."

"I know, but she rubs me the wrong way. Why can't she just look into the ladies that are missing to see where they are and if they are alive. And stay out of the obvious."

"Charla, she is the police and she has to investigate where she can, to help solve this case."

"Then tell her to stick to the plan."

"Babe, we all have a plan."

I threw up my hands. "I know I should be working with the police, not the police working with me. I'm going to fix dinner." I started to stomp off.

"I'll help," he said, getting out of his chair.

"Okay, one arm man. Set the table."

Zing, zing. Kerplunk, kerplunk. Something flew, crashing glass through our front window close to where Jackson was just sitting. We ducked and hit the floor.

"What the hell was that?" I asked.

"Sounded like gunfire . . ." he said, looking around.

"Oh, my God, Jackson, someone wants you dead. Or me?"

We crawled across the floor and called 911 from the kitchen phone that Jackson pulled down from the counter. He told them who he was and what was going down.

Since the boys in blue had been dismissed from hanging out here, but staying close by, they were here in a matter of minutes. They came running through the door. "Anyone hurt?" one of them asked.

"No, not this time," Jackson said, now standing up trying to help me up with his good arm.

"Someone's relentless. It looks like a 9mm again," Jackson said, pointing to the slugs in the hall wall.

"You're right, Detective," one of the officers said, digging out both bullets.

I meandered over to the window where the shots came through. I looked it over, not because I knew what I was looking for, but because someone deliberately shot into our house so I looked outside through the hole. I could see a couple of officers talking to the neighbors. One of them bent over and picked up what looked like shell casings and slid them into a latex glove. Apparently, he didn't have any evidence bags with him. So, good call on the gloves.

"Good, maybe they'll find out something," I thought out loud.

The officer brought in the casings, dropped them in a plastic evidence bag, and handed them to Jackson.

"I would bet these are from the same gun that was used in shooting me." Jackson said, sounding very concerned.

After a couple of hours, the investigator and crime unit were done.

"Detective, the Commissioner wants to put a man on both your front and back doors, again. Or you can go to a safe house."

"I think we'll be fine right here. We can't uproot now. Too much going on,"

Jackson said, reluctantly. "Beside we have Bozo."

Bozo heard his name, meowed, prancing in to us through his doggie door.

"Thank goodness, you are safe, Bud," I said, picking him up in relief. I snuggled him as he purred from all the attention.

❖》》《《❖

AFTER ALL THAT JUST happened, I didn't feel like cooking so, we ordered pizza. We shared it with the three officers that were hanging out here now.

Nora, Rita, Amelia, my parents and Jackson's parents, all called and wanted to come over when they heard the address on the news. The news didn't mention our names, just the address. They were warned by the commissioner no names or hell would have to be paid. Plus, they didn't want to jeopardize Detective Jackson Boxley.

Donnie came riding up on her white horse, a day late and a dollar short, but here she was.

She looked like hell . . . wearing sweats, her hair a mess and no makeup on. I was in hog heaven. She was ugly. I mean ug-ly. Hallelujah. The heavens opened and the angels sang. "She is ugly."

Jealously was gone, the red in my green eyes, gone. I loved her. Hallelujah. She's ugly.

Jackson watched the smile come across my face and I know he had to wonder, what on earth?

I stuck out my hand to thank her for coming and she took it. I put my arms around her. Hallelujah, she was ugly, I kept hearing in my mind. She was ugly.

Jackson looked confused.

When Donnie left with relief that her partner was all right, I danced with joy.

CHAPTER 50

I FIXED BREAKFAST FOR the boys in blue, and we sat down to a great meal while one officer walked the perimeter of the house. I took him a hot coffee and a breakfast sandwich. He was glad to have the coffee as this was the first frosty morning of the season. However, because there was a rotation, none of the guys had to stay out more than thirty minutes at a time.

And for the most part as they were guarding us, Bozo was guarding them.

Nora pulled up and came through the door with a big bang. I started happy dancing. I grabbed her arms and I swung her around making her happy dance with me.

"What's with you? Get some last night?" she asked.

"No. This is way better than sex."

"Chocolate?"

"No better."

"What could be better than sex or chocolate?"

"Donnie . . . without makeup. She's UGGG—LY. I swore when I saw her, the clouds opened and I could hear the angels sing Hallelujah. She has no eyebrows. Without her false eyelashes, she was ugly. "

"Watch it, missy," Nora said, glaring at me.

"Oh, but you look good without your false eyelashes," I stuttered. "A natural beauty."

"It's getting deep in here. Though, I doubt you have ever seen me without them."

I thought for a minute, "Once when you were in the hospital and had your appendix out. And you were yelling for someone to bring your makeup bag, but no one did."

"Yeah, yeah, I remember. So, Donnie's all false?"

"Appears so. Hallelujah," I sang out.

I no more got that out of my mouth when Donnie walked in. Nora looked her over.

Donnie stopped and asked Nora, "Do I have something on my face?"

Nora gulped. "I just like the color of your lipstick," she said, lying.

Nora was saved by the bell. Both Donnie's and Jackson's cells went off at the same time.

Donnie looked at Jackson, and they whispered a second, and then she left.

"What's going on?" I asked, closing in on Jackson with Nora on my heels.

"Another kitchen murder," he answered. "They are going to call me back with more details in a minute."

"Kitchen murder?" I repeated.

"Char . . . la . . ." he said looking at Nora now, "no."

"Jackson? It sounds like it's part of the Key Club murders."

His phone rang. "Yeah, mmm hmmm. Right. Keep me informed."

Nora and I were right in his face.

"Spill, buddy, spill," I said, staring him down, as did Nora.

"Back off, you lunatics," he threatened. "Give me room . . . Get me space. You both are hovering. I can't breathe," as he pretended to grab his neck. "Capisce?"

"The audacity of it all," Nora said.

"What?" he looked at her like she was crazy.

His phone rang again. It was Donnie, who I am no longer jealous of.

He hung up and looked at both Nora and me.

"You're going to find out anyhow, so here goes," he said, with a frown as he knew he couldn't leave the house yet.

He gave us all the information he had gathered to date.

The first thing Nora and I did was walk over to the dining room table and look at the list of women from Cheer Up / Key Club.

"Hmph! Her name isn't on the list anywhere," I said, looking at Jackson, then Nora.

"What do you think's going on? Is she new to the Key Club or is this a copycat?"

"Okay, you two are biting at the bit, so here's the address. I'll call the detective in charge, which appears to be Donnie at this point, and tell her you are coming to help."

We both threw our arms around him in a group hug and thanked him.

"Watch the arm . . ." He pointed out. "The arm, the arm," he said, screwing up his face.

I reached over on the table to get a handful of business cards out of the box to take with us.

Nora stopped me and said, "I got new cards printed and just picked them up. I haven't even opened the box yet to look at them." She pulled the box out of her designer bag.

She opened the box and they were two tone pink. "No, no, no. This isn't what I ordered."

I looked at one and its light pink with Charla O'Hara, with my phone number in the upper left corner, and in soft medium pink, Nora Weston with her phone number in the bottom right. And to finish it off, hot pink in the middle with Private Investigators printed in black.

"No, this isn't going to fly. These are ugly," I said, shaking my head no.

"Okay, I'll take these back tomorrow and get new ones. Grab a few of the old ones."

One of the boys in blue stepped up to get our attention. "Do you have any card stock paper?" he asked. "I can whip you out new business cards in a jiffy."

"Yes," I said, reaching over to the hutch where I kept office supplies and reams of paper. I pulled out plain white card stock paper.

"Okay then, how do you want them to look, and what do you want them to say?" he asked, excited to do something other than just pace.

We showed him what we needed and sure enough, abracadabra, we had new business cards.

All we had to do was cut them to size. I pulled out the paper cutter.

"We can't thank you enough," Nora said giving him a hug, "that was fast."

"Ah, that's alright. Glad I could help," he blushed.

Chapter 51

We pulled up to a gated neighborhood where an officer on duty was manning the gate. He called Donnie for permission to allow us in.

We pulled into the driveway of the mansion which looked like it spread out for miles.

"So, this is how those who have the big bucks live?" Nora said, pulling into a parking space on the curved driveway. Her eyes were wide, darting left and right, trying to take it all in.

We walked through the front door like we belonged. As we looked around, an officer directed us back to the kitchen where the poor victim lay on the floor.

Nora grabbed my arm, stumbling back a couple of steps when she looked down at the victim. She looked pale all at once. For a minute I thought she was going to be sick and pass out. I held onto her and helped her regain her balance.

"Don't let her barf on the victim. Take her out of here." The senior Medical Examiner said, looking up at us.

I assured him she would be okay and she wouldn't mess up the crime scene.

"Take a deep breath and exhale slowly," I suggested, holding her steady, nodding to the ME working right below us.

I had been on a site like this a few other times while on a date with Jackson, when he was suddenly called out on a homicide. *Though I wasn't supposed to be at any of them.* But this is Nora's first in the flesh dead body up close and personal. However, no one can ever get used to seeing this kind of thing. After all, she's dead and someone killed her. She was someone's daughter, wife, mother, sister and she didn't deserve this kind of death.

The medical examiners were working furiously and were just about done when the CSI team walked in to take over the crime scene, nodding to us in recognition.

Nora started coming out of her slight comatose condition, and was able to stand on her own again, but wouldn't look back at the victim. She moved toward the breakfast nook and started checking things out.

As I stood there and looked around, it was clear this was like the Key Club murders. As far as I knew nothing describing the Key Club murders was out there for public knowledge. So, was it the same killer? This was a mystery for sure. And it looked like the same .22 caliber pistol was used. Whoever shot her was a little sloppier. It's strange they didn't pick up the casings. *Hmmm,* I thought out loud. They must have been in a hurry and fearful of getting caught . . . I would assume.

I saw Donnie out of the corner of my eye, walking toward me.

"So, PI's, what do you think . . . ?" she said, looking down at the body, then over to Nora. "Her husband said she was fine when he left to take their kids to school. When he came back, he found her like this. We've been questioning him. Care to take a shot at it?" she tossed her head and pointed toward the living room where another detective was still questioning him.

I decided not to interrupt. "I don't think this is connected to the Key Club murders. It appears to be the same M O, but something's not quite right."

"Key Club murders?" she questioned.

"Oh, that's right; Jackson refers to them as the Kitchen Murders," I said.

"Hmph! Key Club murders?" she repeated.

"Donnie, that's why I wanted you to concentrate on the list of missing ladies from The Cheer Up, to see if the names matched the names in your cold case file."

"Sorry, I didn't connect it. I guess I dropped the ball," she said.

"Yes, you did. Yours is not to reason why, yours is to do or die," I spluttered out without thinking. I took a deep breath, and continued. "I can't tell you enough how important it is to our case. You can start now."

"Our case?" she said.

"Yes, our case," I glared at her.

She nodded her head in agreement, and left to make a call. *No doubt to Jackson.*

Nora and I put on our latex gloves and started wandering throughout the house, being careful not to touch anything, but taking a lot of pictures.

Nora was clicking away when Donnie came back to us. "Whatcha doing?"

"It's one of the procedures we had to learn since we can't touch with or without latex gloves, we have to snap tons of pictures. We can't knowingly interfere with a police investigation."

"That's considerate. Most private eyes I know interfere and touch everything."

I thought to myself, *just how many Private Investigators do you know?*

"I'm not saying we won't, but we sure will try to go by the rules."

Jackson said you would. He just told me you two have done more for the Kitchen Murders, ooops! I mean The Key Club murders, than the whole task force has."

"Only because our friend Louise was killed," I said.

I looked up just in time to see Nora start up the huge curved staircase. I said, "Excuse me," to Donnie and followed Nora who was snapping away.

We went into the master bedroom. It took my breath away trying to take in the over-all view.

"We could put Jackson's whole house with the backyard in this bedroom," I said, with envy.

We both walked into the gigantic walk-in closet.

"Look, does this look right to you? Snap a picture," I said; pushing the clothes apart.

"The safe was standing wide open." Nora snapped a picture of it.

"I'm going down to get Donnie."

Nora stood watch outside the closet until I got back with Donnie and an officer.

We walked into the closet to show Donnie what we had found.

"What on earth? The safe door is closed," I said.

"I didn't move from here," Nora said, swearing. "No one came through here. No one."

The officer, Donnie, Nora and I, started searching every inch of the closet when, quite by accident, Nora stumbled into the wall and it gave away. She yelled out, "Here, come here."

We followed her voice and found her half in and half out of the closet.

We helped her up, and the officer stepped into an alcove leading away from the closet.

He came back and said, "It leads to another closet, which leads to another bedroom, but ends in the main hallway." He led us back through the maze, and sure enough, it came into the main hallway, to a small staircase that came out in a hidden door to the kitchen pantry.

We checked with the officer who came around the corner to see if he had seen anyone coming down the steps. He hadn't.

We went back upstairs the way we came, and started searching the other bedrooms and a huge library. We opened the French doors off the library which was off the master suite and we stepped out onto an elegant veranda.

"Anyone could have come and gone through here," I said, "Then climbed down this trellis."

"But who?" Donnie asked, who was now clearly impressed with Nora and my investigative skills.

"Someone who knows this house," I replied, as I watched Nora taking pictures everywhere. *No stone unturned.*

We returned to the downstairs and walked into the living room to talk to the husband who was sitting with his head in his hands, shaking his head in disbelief. Since the husband was still talking to the other detective, we once again passed on questioning him and headed outside.

CHAPTER 52

"Daniel"

DANIEL WALKED OUT INTO his yard, curious about what was going on next door to him.

He was stepping from one foot to the other, watching the police circus.

"What's going on?" he said, out loud. "Is that, that, wait . . . that is Charla? And Nor . . . a . . . ?"

To see better, he walked closer to the wall that divided his property from where all the action was.

He couldn't stand his neighbor's whiny bitching mouth, always yelling at her kids, and her husband.

I just did them a favor by offing her. I just got my 22, aimed, fired and dead.

Daniel thought he was lucky no one saw him sneaking across the yards earlier that morning. He thought killing his neighbor would throw off any of the Key Club investigation. If someone other than a Key Club lady got killed, then the police would hopefully go another direction. He was hoping it would throw them off the trail. Though he didn't think the police had a clue.

He watched Charla walk around the yard, looking up at the French doors. She walked over to the trellis, took ahold of it, stepped upon it and shook it several times. She went up a couple of steps and stood there for a minute bouncing. She stepped down and walked along looking at the ground. She bent over, appeared to be studying something, then picked it up and slid it into an evidence bag.

Daniel watched her, trying to figure out what she had just picked up. Could it be something he lost, messed up on? Without taking his eyes off Charla, he watched her every move. He rubbed his temple, but his mind was going crazy trying to figure out what he possibly forgot.

Nora walked over to Charla, and took the bag out of her hands, looking it over. They stood and talked for a few minutes, then called Jackson's partner over to them. Daniel's chest grew heavy with worry.

Charla handed the evidence bag to the detective who headed toward her car with an officer on her heels. Charla and Nora started walking in Daniel's direction.

"Be still my heart, my lady is heading my way," He actually said, out loud. But instead his heart was speeding with excitement.

All of a sudden Charla and Nora turned, and headed back toward the back of the house.

"Damn," he said, out loud.

Just thinking of Charla, he had to adjust his family jewels. It seemed he had his hand there adjusting or relieving himself on a regular basis, since the second he met Charla.

Out of the corner of his eye, he watched Vivian, who was still angry with him for the spanking he had given her, walking toward him.

"How long are you going to be out here?" she asked sarcastically. "The kids want to come out and play."

"Fine, send them out," he growled.

"Well, that is a piss poor attitude," she said, then turned, and walked away.

The kids came running out just as Charla and Nora walked back towards him.

"The timing couldn't be worse," he said in a low voice.

"What, Daddy?" Rock questioned.

"I said it's about time you got out here on this beautiful day."

They giggled as he chased them to the back yard, pretending to be a monster.

"Get me Daddy, get me," Pebbles begged.

Daniel thought how could anyone suspect me of murder? Just look at me being a normal dad. I can fool anyone, any time. They will never connect any of these murders to me. Never.

Daniel, who was now more narcissistic than ever, pushed Pebbles on her swing. She did a deep belly laugh with excitement. He listened to his little girl laugh, but he couldn't shut his mind off. He pushed his daughter harder and harder until she yelled, "Stop Daddy, stop. I'm going to fall out. Stop, Daddy, please," she cried, begging.

He didn't hear her because he couldn't turn his thoughts off. His thought were louder than his daughter's cry. *I haven't talked to Charla since I shot Jackson. I can't believe I missed him sitting in his chair. Two shots and I missed. I am losing my touch. Or maybe its Charla . . . She makes me so horny I can't concentrate.*

She's been his nursemaid from the beginning. She finally left his side and here she is.

I love her so much it hurts. Why can't she see that? I think I'll call her . . . now!

"Daddy's going to be over there," he said, now hearing Pebble's scream to stop. He slowed her down and stepped away from the swing and pointed to the other side of the yard.

He dialed Charla, "Hi, my lady, miss me? I've missed you," he said staring, at her.

"Daniel, I'm busy."

"I know, my lady. I've been watching you."

"Watching me?"

"Yes, my lady, I live next door to the murder scene. I watched you and Nora walking around the yard. You find anything of interest?"

"Daniel, I'm on my way over,"

His heart sped up. My true love is coming to see me. He patted his chest. "Pitter pat," he mumbled.

He waited and he waited. Finally, Vivian opened the back door and said, "Daniel, the police are here."

"The police are here," he said out loud. "Come on, kids," he called to them, thinking, *I want you to meet the woman of my dreams.*

They walked into the back door where Vivian, Jackson's partner, Donnie, Nora and Charla, stood waiting with a couple of officers standing by the front door.

Donnie took the lead. She held out her hand to shake Daniel's, looking him up and down. "Hi, Mr. Nielsen, I'm Det. Donnie Harper."

He smiled, but looked at Charla.

"And this is Charla O'Hara and Nora Weston, Private Investigators helping the Police Crime Unit," Donnie continued.

"Really," he said, still looking at Charla. "How may I be of assistance to you?"

"Did you see anything unusual at your neighbors' this morning?" Donnie asked him, pointing in that direction.

"No. I heard the neighbor screaming at her family at the top of her lungs, yet again."

"Did that happen often?" Donnie said, hunting for a pen to write in her notebook.

"Yes, every day you could hear her screaming at someone in that house. They argued all the time. They rarely got along," he told them, expressing disgust. He reached for a pen from the cabinet and handed it to her.

"Did they get along with their neighbors?" she asked, finally taking the pen.

"So-so, for the most part. About like all of us, I suppose," he replied, looking at Charla.

"Did you know them well?"

"As well as the rest of the neighbors," he replied.

"So, not well then, huh?" Donnie said.

"Nope."

"So, you don't socialize with your neighbors?"

"Once, a long time ago when we moved in, there was a neighborhood BBQ," he offered.

"Only once?"

"That's it."

"Why is that?"

"Just for this reason," he said, still looking at Charla.

"What?" she asked.

"I don't want to know any of their business, and I don't want them to know mine."

"I see. You're a private kind of guy?"

"I try."

Daniel looked at Vivian, and asked, "Have you been questioned?"

"Yes, just before I called you in."

Daniel scowled.

"Mr. and Mrs. Nielsen, thank you for your cooperation. If you hear anything that would help us with this case, please call," Donnie said, as she handed him her card.

"I have a question, Mr. Nielsen," Charla said.

"Fire away Miss O'Hara. Fire away," he said, smiling on the inside, making sure no one picked up on his excitement that Charla had spoken directly to him.

"There are foot prints in your neighbor's yard that lead to your fence and it looks like the footprints stopped and someone hopped over to your yard. Can you fill in the blanks?" she said, staring at him.

Daniel's heart fluttered, but he tried to cover it up by coughing into his hand.

"Why, yes, Miss O'Hara, I can answer that. I hopped over the fence to retrieve my son's ball. I got it and hopped back over to my yard."

"Dad."

"Don't interrupt Rock," Daniel stopped his son.

"But, Dad," Rock tried to speak.

"Shhhh, Rock," Daniel warned, squeezing his son's shoulder.

"Thank you. Call if any of you remember anything," Donnie said, extending her hand.

Daniel walked them to the door making sure he was by Charla, so he could put his hand in the small of her back while leading her to the door. He got excited just touching her.

Daniel excused himself from his family, and headed to the shower where he thought of Charla and relieved himself. "Char . . . la," he moaned.

CHAPTER 53

As we walked toward Nora's car, she stopped, and then turned to me, putting a hand on each of my shoulders, looking me straight in the eyes.

"Charla, you're going to have to watch your back. That guy's obsessed with you. You are going to have to keep your eyes wide open from now on. You can't be alone, and you need to tell Jackson."

"You're right."

"Well, wow . . . , how does that taste coming out of your mouth?" she asked.

"What?"

"That I am right," she bantered.

"I already decided to tell Jackson everything as soon as I get home. Daniel just now convinced me. I sensed his obsession was stronger than ever, especially after placing his hand on my back just now. I felt a difference in his touch. It was strange."

"Good for you and I will help you . . ." she said. "Wait, he touched you?"

"Yes, he touched me, but gently like he was guiding me. Good lord, I didn't want to make a scene, so I just acted like it didn't happen." I paused and took a deep breath, "When I tell Jackson, you can listen, but since you have a tendency to exaggerate, you absolutely cannot say anything. I mean nothing. You understand? Nothing."

I grabbed her arm and pulled her back from going toward Daniel's. So, she flipped him the bird as I got her turned back to her car.

"You know that was a wasted bird as I am sure he didn't see it." I scolded her.

She frowned and said, "Just in case."

We pulled up, and Jackson was sitting on the front steps talking to one of the guys in blue, while another one walked the perimeter. They stood up when Nora and I approached.

"Should you be on display for the next pot shot? They might get lucky with you out in the open," I barked at him.

"Officer Finley, meet testy Charla, the newest member of the PI's," Jackson said, pulling me into him with his good arm. "And this is her partner, Nora Weston. You will be seeing them around more now that they are legit."

"Nice to meet you both," the officer said.

We both nodded with a smile.

"Jackson, right after lunch, I need to talk to you. It's important," I said.

"Not too important if it can wait until after lunch." He teased.

"Depends," I said, guiding him inside before I started to explain things to him. "I'm hungry. I want to eat first." I started putting out lunch meat for sandwiches and diet Dr. Pepper for drinks. Jackson got himself a cold Heineken. We sat down at the dining room table.

"How's your shoulder and arm?" I asked.

"Much better. Looks like I can go back on active duty next week. I can't wait. I hate sitting around here all day and night. I don't know how anyone does it and likes it. Oh, the bullets they pulled out of the wall here matched the one they pulled out of me. And the blues found the casing in the alley near where I got shot."

"I thought they couldn't find the casing," I said, reaching for the bread.

"The blues went back to check one more time. Just as they were about to give up, the sun hit just right, barely catching the casings. Perseverance and a job well done," he said.

"That's great news, but whoever was shooting at you was sloppy. Doesn't seem to be a pro," I deduced.

"I probably pissed off some perp and he's trying to get even. We'll figure it out. Now, what did you want to talk to me about?"

Nora who was biting her lower lip, spoke up. "Charla has a stalker."

Jackson did a double take on me, "Talk."

I glared at Nora. I started by telling him that he was right, that we had not gone to a birthday party for Katy. "We went there to spy. We wanted to know why Louise would hang out at a place like Cheer Up. We wanted to find out about the Key Club. As I told you before, we were having fun while trying to find out why, what and who. The guys were helpful and friendly."

"I bet," Jackson said, staring me down.

"It was her red dress," Nora interrupted.

"I could see how the red dress would attract some yahoo. I didn't even know she had that dress or the underwear. Oh, and thank you for that, Nora." He gave her a quick smile.

"Okay everyone, let's stay on track. Anyway, we danced a lot with each other and some of the guys. One guy sat at the end of the bar and just watched. After a while, he came over to me and asked me to dance. I did, and several dances later he walked me back to my table."

"Several dances . . . go on." Jackson motioned with his hand, now sitting straighter in his chair.

"While asking the bartender information about the Key Club, this guy Damon walked over to me and asked if I was interested in joining the Key Club. I found out most of the guys didn't use their real name."

"Well . . . what was your answer? Did you want to join the Key Club?" he asked. "Well?"

"God, no, Jackson! And I told him that. This guy, Damon, turned and walked away. The next morning, we were picking up our cars when he pulled in and let Carol Sue out. Several of the Writer's Club girls were picking up their cars and we couldn't help but gawk."

"Who is Carol Sue?" he asked.

"Carol Sue and Bev were friends with Louise. They hung out together and were all into the same thing, variety sex. We met them at Louise's funeral. Well, Nora did."

"Variety sex?" Jackson said, with curiosity.

Nora sat there and listened to me explain everything about the Key Club and about Louise's diary/ledger which I tossed towards Jackson again, since he had read some of it earlier.

"It is all in there. Who she was with and what they did. I must warn you it is very descriptive and no stone left unturned, as I am sure you may have discovered."

"Yeah, I got the descriptive part already. Hmph! Where does the stalker fit in?"

Nora spoke up, "Damon, aka Daniel Neilson, the guy at the end of the bar has been stalking her. He's everywhere Charla goes. He sent her the roses, cleaned up her car, and bought her a diamond bracelet. It's spooky."

Jackson who was proud of me for being able to take care of myself and who has a certain je ne sais quoi, was now showing signs of getting . . . uh, I don't know . . . pissed. He sighed with repulsion.

"Yes but, I saw him in the mall parking lot with his wife. The wife got out of the car, and went inside. I pushed the bracelet through his window and told him to give it to his wife. I didn't want it. We watched him give it to her when she got back into the car."

"She did, Jackson, Charla pushed it through his window, and told him to stop giving her things, and stop following her." She was throwing her hands in all directions with clear excitement.

Jackson was not amused.

I went on and told him of the phone calls. Even about the night at Shaladu's.

Jackson was looking more and more upset twisting ever so slightly in his chair. And I could see his knuckles turn white from making a fist in each hand.

"And, to top it all off, Jackson, he lives next door to the lady who was killed this morning. So, we were in his house questioning his wife and him," Nora told him.

"Okay, Charla. I'll get someone to pay him a visit and warn him to stop following you," Jackson said, now rising to his feet to get his phone. "He'll get the hint when we put pressure on him for every wrong turn or anything we can harass him over."

"NOOOOOOooooooo," I growled, grabbing his phone out of his hand.

He did a double take on me and then glanced over at Nora.

"What the effing is going on . . . ?"

"Look, Jackson, I've been working on a plan. I . . . I . . ."

"What? You, you what?" He said, clearly agitated.

"I can't go into it right now, but Nora and I have a plan."

Nora's mouth gaped open as she looked at me with a "*WHAT?*"

"Ye. . .ah, we have a plan," she stuttered.

"Okay, give," he said.

"We are fine tuning it, and I'll let you know if it works," I said, with confidence. "I will take care of Damon, aka Daniel."

"Yes, we will," Nora said with a confused look on her face that Jackson didn't see, as he was busy staring me down.

"I hope you use good judgment and, if you need help, no shame in yelling uncle," he said.

"Roger that," Nora said, smiling at him, trying to conceal her confusion over what I said.

"Oh, brother . . ." he snorted. "You . . . two . . . driva me nuts. Just be careful, and be smart and above all do not get into something you can't get out of. Keep me posted."

"Roger that," I said.

He grimaced and threw up his hands. "Ten-four, good buddy and all that bullshit." He gave up.

We walked out of the dining room. "What plan?" Nora asked.

"A plan as we go plan," I giggled.

"Oh, for a minute I didn't think you had a plan."

"Tomorrow, I want to go back to the mansion where Daniel's neighbor was killed and check it out one more time. Something isn't gelling," I told her.

"Okay, I'll pick you up at eight," she said.

Jackson and I were watching TV, and I could see the wheels turning in his head. I had a feeling he would not back off. I looked at him and asked, "What are you thinking about?"

"Oh nothing. Just watching TV"

"Why do I NOT believe you? You promised me you wouldn't interfere with my plan to find out about Damon aka Daniel in my own way."

"I didn't promise anything. I just reminded you, there is no shame in yelling uncle," Jackson said.

But he can say what he wants; I know he won't let me out there without a watchful eye.

CHAPTER 54

THOUGH IT WAS AN unusually warm day, I grabbed my jacket and went out to Nora's car when she honked.

"Got a plan yet?" she asked, when I only had one leg in the car.

"Nope," I answered, pulling the other leg in and closing the door.

"Greaaat. Buckle up."

"I plan uh . . . uh, to keep an eye on Daniel, and not let my guard down."

"Great plan, yeah a great plan," she reiterated.

"I just don't want Jackson to jump the gun. He's got enough on his plate. I feel we can handle Daniel."

"We?" Nora questioned, putting the car in gear, looking both ways before pulling out onto the street.

"You betcha, plan as we go plan," I reminded her, still trying to connect my seat belt.

WE PULLED UP INTO the mansion driveway close to where Donnie was standing with her left hand on her hip, and her right hand on her gun that rested at her waist, staring in Daniel's direction.

"Whatcha lookin at?" Nora asked, walking toward her.

Donnie took her hand off her gun and pointed.

"Oh, for God's sake," Nora said disgusted. "What's wrong with you? He's a pervert."

I could barely hear the two of them talking as I walked toward them. I looked into the direction they were staring and saw Daniel bend over, then stand straight up and stretched upward to clip a broken branch.

"Oh, baby," Donnie said, fanning herself with a flyer she had just picked up off the driveway.

"Look at his biceps, his pecs, his six packs, and his buns. Everything's perfect, even his perfect flawless tan," she said, still gawking.

He reached over and picked up his shirt and started to put it on. I heard a low growl. "No, don't," Donnie said, begging under her breath.

I grabbed Donnie and turned her around while Nora shoved her toward the house. "What is wrong with you Donnie? Get a grip," I scolded her. "He cheats on his wife and is into dominating sex, among other things. He's a . . ." I was interrupted with, "Charla, wait up," Daniel yelled over to me, walking in our direction still putting his shirt on.

Donnie stopped, turned and looked at me. I could tell her wheels were spinning.

"Yeah Daniel, what's up?" I inquired, trying to maintain dignity since I couldn't stand the guy. Nora stood there ready to step in, if needed.

Daniel leaned in to kiss my cheek.

Just as I started to push him away Nora moved in "Back up, slick," she said, stepping in between us.

"Just saying hello to my lady," and he swooped his arm down and around. *The court jester crap.*

"Again, Daniel, my lady is off limits," Nora snarled. "How many times do I have to tell ya?"

He smirked at her, ignoring her comments, then said, "So, what are you ladies doing here?"

Donnie who was as clearly impressed with Daniel's looks, spoke up, "Checking out the place one more time in case we missed something before."

Sweet Vivian came out and yelled for Daniel. She threw up her hand with a wave hello when she saw him with us. Then she said, "Hurry up, we have to get

Rock to his doctor appointment." She waved to us again, turning to step upon her porch to go back in.

Daniel turned and just before he walked away, again leaned in to kiss my cheek. I stuck my hand in his face to stop. Nora stepped in between us and pointed for him to walk away.

"Relax, Nora," he said, clearly agitated with her interference. But he walked away.

I pulled out an antiseptic wipe and swiped at my cheek and hand.

Donnie turned and faced me. "What the hell was that?"

"What was what?" I said, innocently.

Nora spoke up and asked Donnie, "And what was that? Why are you drooling over Daniel today and not yesterday?"

"No shirt today," she said, in a matter of fact tone. "Again, what was that?" She turned and looked at me.

Nora spoke up again, "He's Charla's stalker. He thinks he's in love with her."

"Spill," Donnie said.

So, Nora spilled it, and told Donnie too much. I cringed because I felt Donnie was the enemy. Nora talked too much. I kept trying to interrupt and I tried changing the subject. But Nora was hell bent on spilling it all.

"So, does Jackson know any of this?" Donnie asked.

"Yes, but not the in-love part. I would appreciate it very much if we could keep that part quiet for now. Nora shouldn't have told you," I said, glaring at Nora. "And if Jackson says anything to me about it, I will know where it came from. I will be forever pissed at you."

"I wouldn't mind having your problem," Donnie said, still watching Daniel walk way. "I promise Jackson will not hear it from me."

I said, "Stop it. Didn't you hear me say that Daniel belongs to the Key Club and is in to dominant sex? Didn't you hear me say that, that was Daniel's wife over there? Stop reliving him with his shirt off. For Pete's sake, Donnie, get a grip," I said, slightly shaking her at the shoulders, but I really wanted to slap her across her face and hard. *If only.*

Now Nora took Donnie by the shoulders and said, "Snap out of it. You're a cop."

"Okay, I'm back, but I am just finding out this stuff so show me some slack," she said, as she adjusted her gun and walked toward the front door, motioning for a couple of officers to come with her.

Nora and I walked toward the back of the house. Something was eating at me about the safe being open, then closed and no one there. There had to be an answer.

As we walked, I said, "Nora, you have a big mouth. You have to be careful about what you say and who you say it to. I didn't want Jackson's partner to have ammunition on me if ever needed. She could use that against me and I would be in big trouble with Jackson. Daniel isn't the only one Donnie has a crush on, and she could really play this up."

"I wasn't thinking. I just thought . . . cop. Sometimes my mouth overrides my ass," Nora said, hanging her head.

"Trust me, I know, so watch it. But for now, let's get to work on the problem at hand. How did that safe get closed? And how did they get out of the closet and away without anyone seeing them?"

We pranced around to the back of the house and as we reached the backyard, I noticed someone standing at the opened backdoor, and it wasn't the murdered woman's family. Whoever it was, they were being cautious and sneaky, moving very slowly. The person looked around and was startled when she saw us and tried to dash away in the opposite direction. But Donnie and a boy in blue came out of the door and were right there to grab the sneaky perpetrator.

"Where do you think you're going?" Donnie demanded, pushing the female intruder back in the door. We followed them into the kitchen, where we saw traces of the CSI dusting powder all over everything and the remnants of tape where the victim lay on the floor.

"Please let me go. I'm not supposed to be here, and I'm going to be in so much trouble," the young Hispanic woman pleaded.

"You think?" Nora said, stepping toward her.

"What are you doing here?' Donnie asked.

"I . . . I was looking for something."

"What?"

"When I worked here before, I lost something important to me."

"Can you elaborate? What was it you lost? What's your name? And what was your job?" Again, Donnie was leading the questioning, not letting her answer one, let alone multiple questions.

I stepped closer, not wanting to miss a word.

"My name is Maria Garcia. I was one of the maids. My job was the north wing of the upstairs. I recently lost the cross necklace my grandmother gave me when I was child. I thought it possible I dropped it somewhere here," she rattled off as fast as Donnie had asked.

"Uh-huh. You think you lost it *IN* the safe? When?" Nora asked, taking over.

"About a month ago, when the Missus caught me with the uh . . . the Mister. I thought I might have lost my necklace in the closet. Perhaps the Missus put it in the safe, is all I am saying."

"You were fired? For screwing the Mister?" Nora said, with outrage.

"Uh-huh, I was fired."

"So, Maria, how long did you work here?" I asked, finally getting a word in.

"Just under three years."

"How long were you doing the Mr.?" Nora continued.

"About two years. It was right after my twentieth birthday."

"Did the Mrs. know the whole time?" I asked.

"No, no. She just caught us. Told me to get my things and get out. That was when I think I lost my cross."

"Miss Garcia, did you come back yesterday and kill Myra Cunningham?" I asked.

"No, oh no, I didn't. She was already dead when I came back here. I snuck up upstairs to check for my cross. I heard a noise and I ran to the Mrs. closet and hid. After a few minutes, I thought it safe to come out. I saw you and you." *Pointing at Nora and me.*

"When we searched, you weren't in there," Nora said. "The safe was open and then it was closed."

Maria Garcia looked around the room and said, "Oh, I was there. I watched you and was afraid you would catch me. Here, I'll show you," and she led us to a panel in the pantry that moved when she pushed it. "I don't think the Mrs. would mind me showing you this now."

We all followed her through the door where a spiral staircase went upstairs. It was another secret passage.

We followed her up where there was a landing big enough to handle all of us.

Maria turned a brass handle and the door opened right into the closet. A chest of drawers moved to the right and we walked in. The chest had been moved when Nora fell through the wall the day before, apparently from Maria Garcia's hurry to get out of there.

We went through the secret passage yesterday, but this was an additional route.

"Well, I'll be damned," I said. "Who knew?"

"I'm sure all the housemaids, the Mr. and maybe the kids," Maria Garcia said.

Of course, that wasn't what I meant when I said, who knew? But it was nice that she filled us in.

"So, Miss Garcia, if you were here yesterday looking for your cross, why did you come back today?"

"You scared me yesterday and I didn't get to finish searching. I panicked and accidently closed the safe. I came back today hoping to get lucky."

"Miss Garcia, this is your lucky day. I am taking you in for further questioning," Donnie said, as she slapped the handcuffs on her.

"Detective, I didn't do anything . . . nothing," she said, as she squirmed trying to get her hands loose from Donnie's clutch.

"Watch it or I will arrest you for resistance," Donnie said, yanking Maria's hands back.

"After you were fired, you were here yesterday and today without anyone home. I believe they call that breaking and entering. That alone gets you cuffs," Donnie said as she read the Miranda to Miss Garcia. Donnie handed her over to an officer.

As we followed the officer walking her down the front staircase toward the front door, the door opened and *the Mr* . . . Bill Cunningham walked in, taking a double surprised look at Maria, and I could see panic creep into his face.

"What's going on here?" he asked.

We gave him the quick version.

"Does she need an attorney?"

"Depends," Donnie said. "I'll let you know."

We closed the front door behind us, and followed Donnie to the 405 Precinct.

"Do you think she shot Myra Cunningham?" I wondered out loud.

Nora answered, "Don't know. Could be, but that would be too easy."

CHAPTER 55

DONNIE CONTINUED TO QUESTION Maria Garcia at the precinct. We listened from the other side of the one-way mirror, where Nora and I kept looking at each other with disgust from the way Donnie was interrogating her. She asked numerous questions at once without giving the suspect a chance to answer.

Garcia never wavered from her story, even though Donnie tried to intimidate her by slamming her fist down on the table and yelling "Tell the truth." After several hours of brow beating Garcia, Donnie finally let her go.

As Nora and I were walking through the 405, different detectives and officers gave us the thumbs up sign or just smiled with a head nod.

"Funny how much respect we're getting now that we are certified P.I.'s," Nora said, holding her chin up and shoulders back.

"Sure is," I said, filling up with pride.

"Where we headed now?" she asked. "We have a couple more hours left this afternoon."

"I thought we could head back over to Louise's neighborhood to check a few possible witnesses. I sure would like to interview a couple of potential witnesses. Someone somewhere has to have noticed something."

Just as we pulled up in front of Louise's house, her neighbor Harold, came out to greet us.

"You're doing a bang-up job keeping Louise's yard looking nice. How's it's going Harold?" I yelled, walking toward him.

"Well, if it's not the sleuthing twins," he said, shaking his head. "Going okay, I guess."

"I see you are still keeping your word about taking care of Louise's yard. The fall roses look great. They are such a bright, beautiful orange," Nora said, pointing to them. "Just beautiful."

"Well, I can't take the credit since Louise did all the hard work getting them in a couple of years back. A few of the neighbors are pitching in to help; even my son's helping out. Not hard to do if you can keep the cops from stomping around on it."

"So, Oscar's still staying with you?"

"Yup, yup, but not for long. Seems the lil Mrs. and him are working things out."

"That's great," Nora mumbled.

"Harold, do you know any neighbors with the names that are in Louise's stories? A Jesse Bains, Marilyn Crain or a Joan Hannity? Is there anyone other than Oscar that has moved back here?"

Harold scratched his head, nodding it up and down then said, "Not as I recall. Why?"

"They're just a few names that came up and we were hoping to check them out."

"Sorry, I just can't recall," he said, shaking his head no. "I know most everyone around here and those names don't stick out or ring a bell. Sorry, I'm no help."

"If you do happen to remember anyone, call us," Nora said, handing him a brand-new business card.

"Well, well. You're legal now," he said, as he read the bigger print. "Congrats." We both said, "Thanks."

We left Louise Stafford's home and pulled into Lora Janeson's neighborhood and again knocked on a lot of doors. One little old lady answered, but said she was in Florida at the time, so she wasn't any help.

We knocked on a few more doors. Finally, we heard a bang, clatter and someone rolling to the door. A seventy-year old man answered, tugging and fighting to pull open the door. He said, "What the hell do you want? Can't you see I'm sitting in a wheelchair and how hard it is for me to answer my door?"

"Sorry, sir, but we are trying to find out if any of Lora Janeson's neighbors saw anything or notice anything unusual the morning she was killed?" Nora said.

"I seen you two snooping around here, from that window," He said irritably, pointing toward his front window. "I didn't see anything, don't know nothing. Too early for me anyway. Now get the hell out of here and don't come back," he snarled and he started pushing himself back from the door.

Before he got too far back through the door, Nora tossed our business card where it landed in his lap. "Call if you remember anything . . ." she yelled after him.

"Go away," he said, trying hard to shut his door on us.

We turned and walked down the handicap ramp toward the street.

"Today was the first time anyone answered their door. I swear if I was a thief, this would be the first place I'd hit. No one's ever home," Nora said, looking around.

"Or no one wants to get involved and just won't answer their doors. Janeson's caretaker hasn't even been around the last couple of times we've been here."

Nora looked around and looked toward Janeson's house and covered her girls.

I had to laugh at her.

We finally gave up and left Lora Janeson's neighborhood.

Nora needed gas so we pulled into Serve Yourself Convenience Store. She put her debit card into the slot and started to pump the gas, then went inside to get us a diet Dr. Pepper. I stood there keeping an eye on the gas pump and checking my cell for a text or recent calls that I might have missed, while we were trying to catch people home. I glanced up just in time to see Daniel by his car. I immediately started to get pissed. I turned away like I didn't see him.

I watched Nora walking back across the parking lot carrying our drinks, when I felt Daniel's presence. I elbowed him, flipped him over my shoulder, kneed him in the groin, then an upper cut to his jaw, tossing him to the ground, twisting his arm behind him, and then I sat on him.

"Hold on, my lady, it's me, Daniel," he whimpered, trying to catch his breath.

I stood up, leaving him rolling around on the ground in pain, grabbing his crotch and then his ribs.

Nora started cracking up and said, "That's what you get when my lady doesn't like being snuck up on."

"Shut up . . . Nora," he said, rolling around trying to get up with a bloody nose where I buried his face in the concrete. "I'm sorry. I didn't mean to scare you, my lady." He stumbled trying to get up holding his ribs, then his crotch, then his head. He stood half bent over having a hard time standing parallel while brushing gravel and dirt off his suit, while blood dripped from his nose. He hurt all over and didn't know what to sooth first.

"Oh, you didn't scare me," I said, pleased with myself, but I still wanted to kick him again.

"Clearly you can take care of yourself," he said, wiping the blood off his face with a coarse paper towel he grabbed from above the window washer solution.

"What are you doing here?" I asked him flippantly.

He pointed to his car. "Getting gas, then I spotted you. I wanted to surprise you, but I got the surprise instead." He said, holding the paper towel to his bleeding nose and trying hard to stand erect.

"I didn't know if you were friend or foe," I said, with disgust.

Nora snorted and said, "Foe" . . . *jerk*. "Hey slick, you need an ambulance. I'll call one for ya," she said, still laughing.

He did a double take on her. "I think you know better, Nora. I have the upmost respect and care for Charla and no to the ambulance," he said, clearly agitated with her comment. "I'm Charla's biggest fan."

She glared at him and said, "You need more fans and you need to get a life."

He looked back at me with pleading eyes.

"Okay, this is how this is going down, Daniel. If you happen to be in the same place as I am, then you need to announce yourself while maintaining and keeping a distance between us. Or this will happen again," I said.

"Just stay away, Daniel. Charla's not interested in you. Stop showing up," Nora said, no longer laughing.

Daniel continued to do a stare down with her.

"My gas just cut off. I bid you a fond fair well, my lady," he said to me. "Nora," he said, not so fondly as he started gimping away holding a paper towel to his nose with one hand, and holding his ribs with the other. He started to turn back toward me, but had second thoughts.

"Nice job, Charla."

"I actually saw him put the nozzle in his gas tank before he saw me. I pretended not to notice him. I turned my back on him, so I knew it was Daniel when I felt his presence. I wanted to flip him and do him some damage. It was such a great opportunity. Ohhhhh, that felt goo . . . d!"

We got back into her car and pulled out, still smiling about what I just done to Daniel.

"And he doesn't even get mad at you. You could haul off and hit him or kick him in his balls, oh wait, you just did that and he just says, that's okay, my lady. And by the way, what the hell is this 'MY LADY' crap?"

"Don't know. He started saying it the night we went to The Cheer UP. He took me back to our table and did the bend and court-jester thing. He just does it and I have no clue. He must think it's cute and he's prince charming."

"Well, it's no prince charming and sure in the hell's not cute. Maybe sexy but not cute," she said, changing the radio station. "And he needs a haircut."

"Really? That's the best you can come up with? Is he needs a haircut!"

"He's so perfect to look at, that's all I could find wrong with his appearance," she said. "His physical is appealing, but his mental is screwed up. He's the true meaning of you can't judge a book by its cover."

"Meantime, he's stalking me, cheats on his wife, and is into dominant sex among other nauseating things. He's creepy," I said. *I wonder about Nora sometimes.*

A little while later my cell rang and I recognized the name . . . Jordan, from The Cheer Up.

"Hey, Jordan. What's up?" I answered.

"I have a customer here that has a bloody nose, bent over and said his ribs are killing him. He said you nailed him, my words, not his. Anyway, I had to get him ice for his nose and for his lower anatomy. And he asked for two extra bags of ice. What gives?"

"You his baby sitter now?" I asked.

"Funny you should say that. He stopped coming in. Hasn't been in here since that time you came in. What . . . Week or so ago. He just stopped. The ladies here keep asking about him. They miss him. He's a lady's favorite, you know."

"Really? So I heard." I said, not really caring.

"Just now he said he only stopped in for ice for his nose and," Jordan laughed, "his balls. Didn't even order a drink. What have you done to him?

Ever since he met you, he's all messed up."

"Not my problem," I said. Then I gave him a brief version of what happened at the service station.

"Ohhh, nice job. And for the record Charla, I don't blame you. He has it bad for you," Jordan said. "Beware."

"I am not interested. I'm already taken by the detective hunk."

"He's walking back this way, so I'll let you go. I wouldn't want Daniel to know I called you."

"He won't," I told him as we hung up.

Nora, who couldn't wait for me to fill her in said, "Well? What did he say?"

"Jordan said Daniel's there icing his wounds."

We both started laughing at the thought of Daniel sitting there icing his nose, his ribs, and his balls as we pulled up to the house.

Nora let me out and watched as I entered through the front door. I turned and waved.

"Hey, babe," I greeted Jackson with a big kiss when he walked up to me. "How was your day?"

"Interesting," he said as he hugged me tight.

"What's wrong?" I asked.

"Oh, I just heard how effective you are with your, our investigation. Donnie filled me in. Even about your stalker."

"I told you not to worry about me. I could handle Daniel."

"Oh, I know that now."

"What do you mean, oh, you know that now?"

"God, I hate to admit this but I had a BOLO for you and did have you followed. Well, not followed per se, but the blues are keeping an eye on you. So, they're not following you, but if they see you 'Be On the Look Out' they are to observe for a while."

"I can't believe you, Jackson. You promised."

"I know, I know. And after the report about your takedown at Serve Yourself Convenience Store, I know you can handle yourself. If I was that Daniel Nielsen character, I think I would think twice about following you." He wrapped his arms around me again.

Bozo, my big ole Tom Cat, came in and wanted me to follow him.

"Ooh oh, boy. What's wrong?" I asked, as both Jackson and I followed him to the back door.

We went out the door where our neighbor stood with a brand-new Suzy, a baby pug.

We followed Bozo over to her as she sat the pug down, who then started bouncing toward Bozo.

Our neighbor said it has been like that every time she brought her out to potty train. Bozo has been sitting at her door just waiting each time for little Suzy to come out.

"Oh, my God," I said, patting my heart. "Bozo's so human." Then I reached down and patted him, then Suzy, who was still bouncing around him. "You have a new buddy. I think I'm going to cry."

We visited with our neighbor while watching the old cat and the baby pug play.

"It's time for dinner," I said as we headed back into the house. That perked up Bozo who was ready to come in, too.

We sat down to eat and I asked Jackson, "What has your crew found out about the Key Club ladies that we couldn't find? Did you find any cold cases on any of our missing ladies?"

"Funny you should ask. I have a whole stack of cold cases on my desk with descriptions along the lines we are looking for. One was shot in the head, but is hanging on after all these years. She's in a wheelchair and has no memory of how she got there. However, she does have sketchy memories before she was shot or at least parts of it. She's in hiding. Her parents after all these years still won't say where she is. We could be interested in that one. Anyway, that is what I was told when I called in this morning."

"Do you think I could go to the station and see what they have and compare notes?"

"Yep, tomorrow. I'm planning on going in for a while. Test the waters. Starting Monday, I'll be on desk duty until I get my gun hand strength back."

"You were shot in the left arm and shoulder, you're right handed. So, how's that fit?" I asked.

"It's the protocol, I'm limited. But tonight, we celebrate."

And we did.

CHAPTER 56

I WENT WITH JACKSON to the precinct and as we walked into the dark, stinky squad room with its dingy, filthy windows, a loud hurrah went up with a lot of fist bumps and hand and finger explosions with a few "Love you, man," from his cohorts.

Donnie crossed the room and went right into Jackson's arms. I rolled my eyes though I know she's ugly. *Really ugly.* Donnie backed away and gave me a glance and then said, "Hi Charla. Jackson looks great."

"No different than when you saw him yesterday."

Donnie shrugged her shoulders, and made a turnabout face and walked back to the coffee machine. She yelled across the squad room, "Charla, do you and Jackson want coffee?"

Hmph, trying to make up to me?

"Why, yes, we do, two sugars in one and the other black. Thank you so much Donnie." *But I thought, Bitch; you'll probably screw that up too.*

Everyone settled down after greeting Jackson one way or the other. He sat down at his desk and started going over the tons of paperwork that was waiting for him. By the looks of his desk, I don't think that a dust cloth had once touched it while he was away, if ever. I blew a place off and moved a pile of files closer to us. Lo and behold, there was a stack of cold cases staring back at me.

"Jackson, can I go through these?" I asked, picking up the stack.

"What is it?"

"Cold cases."

"Let's look at them together," he said, pulling me and the stack closer to him.

We went over them one by one without anyone of them standing out. I couldn't believe how many cases went unsolved. It was a very sad state of affairs. We both pushed through the stack and finally *boom,* one name popped out. I pulled the folder out from the stack and read her name . . . "Rosalind Hayward," I said out loud, as I pulled the Key Club list out of my bag to compare names. I spotted Rosalind Hayward's quickly.

Jackson looked over my shoulder and read exactly what I was reading. My cell rang.

"Hi Nora . . . ," I answered, and waited for her to finish yelling at me.

"Yes, Mother, I'm okay. I came in to the office with Jackson. Why don't you come down and pick me up and we can go over the cold case I found that looks promising."

We hung up. "Nora's on her way here," I told him.

"Sounds like she's really upset with you?"

"Yes, mainly because I forgot to tell her I was coming down here with you. She feels left out."

"With all these yahoos hanging out here, they won't get much work done if she comes in here with all her, ah her, glory hanging out," He laughed.

"Welllll, she's on her way."

"I just hope these guys can handle it," he said looking all around the squad room.

We continued going through the stack of cold cases and just at the end of the last stack I ran across another name on the Key Club list. "Gloria Arrassmann."

"What?" Jackson asked me.

"Looks like we found two of the three victims, and if the lady in hiding is the third victim, we have a connection. We will be ahead of the game. These two were shot in the head early in the morning and found dead in . . . *he kitchen,*" we both chimed in.

"The kitchen murders," he said.

"No . . . The Key Club murders." I said, making it clear to him with a little punch in his good arm.

Jackson's desk phone rang. "Yo?"

"Jackson, I have a voluptuous redhead down here giving me what for. Says you're expecting her," the sergeant said looking her over with a big smile.

"Send her up Sergeant," Jackson smiled from ear to ear.

We both set our eyes on the squad room doorway, waiting to see Nora's entrance. We couldn't peel our eyes away. It seemed forever, but here she came waltzing in. . . . Thank goodness she had a black all weather coat covering all her glory, so all anyone noticed was her false eyelashes, all her jewelry dripping off her and her big red hair.

She came in swinging her designer bag while she looked over the room, and said with a nod, "This place is disgusting."

She now had everyone looking her way and then she peeled off her black all weather-coat.

"NOOOOOoooo!" "Keep your coat on. We're going," I said rushing over to her trying to pull her coat back up on her shoulders.

"Get a grip," she said, pulling her coat off her shoulders.

I held my breath and relief fell over me when she dropped her coat on the chair, and was wearing a black turtleneck, long sleeve *designer* sweater with skin-tight black jeans. *Woof, that was close. It's not like these guys haven't seen hookers on display or anything.* Thank goodness it was getting cold out.

With a great deal of relief from both Jackson and me of Nora's attire, I showed her the cold case files on the two Key Club members.

"I think we need to go over this again and again. There has to be answers hiding in here," She commented.

"Jackson, can we make copies of these two files?" I asked.

He did a double take and started to say no, but in midstream of shaking his head no, switched and said, "yes," with a bunch of rules and regulations added.

Nora and I went into the breakroom while the squad secretary, *as they still called her,* copied the parts we could have and would need from the files of Rosalind Hayward and Gloria Arrassmann.

We waited in the breakroom, eating a stale donut, and drinking godawful coffee, until Donnie came in to join Nora and me.

"So, Charla, I've always wanted to know how you got the name O'Hara. Is it your maiden name?" Donnie asked.

Filling the time waiting for the files to be copied, I felt charitable. "My maiden name is Bordeaux. My grandfather was a stowaway on a ship from Belgium. I am a second-generation Belgium. He married a Dutch girl half his age and my dad was one of six kids, one girl and the rest boys. My dad met and married my mother who is Irish."

"Oh, that is how you got the name O'Hara, your mother's maiden name."

"No," I said, but I continued. "I was married to Patrick O'Hara for just under two years when he was shot and killed."

"Shot and killed?" Donnie asked with great curiosity.

"Yes. We were driving down old 71 when random shots came into the car. Patrick was hit in the leg. He was able to pull over; I treated his leg and called 911. The problem was, he was also hit in the neck and fell forward on the steering wheel and bled out before the ambulance got there. I didn't even know he had been hit in the neck."

"Random shots?" She asked, shocked.

"Yeah, some asshole had been taking target practice on moving vehicles for several weeks. The police hadn't been able to catch him, until Patrick was killed. There were near misses and cars shot up. They finally caught a seventeen-year-old with the help of the tips line. Someone turned him in. He stood trial and is now serving time for murder in the second degree."

"Oh, Charla, I'm so sorry."

"Me, too, I was so young when I married Patrick, and though I miss him still today, it's going on seven years since he died and now I have Jackson," I said with a mental eye roll. *Ha, ha, I have Jackson.*

The squad secretary came in, and said the copies were made as she handed me the package. We stood to leave the break room when Donnie threw her arms around me with a hug. I gave Nora an actual eye roll when she looked confused. I pulled Donnie's arms away, and turned to walk away but did say, "Thanks, Donnie." *Cause I'm nice.*

I looked around and, when no one was really paying any attention to us, I leaned down and gave Jackson a kiss on his cheek.

"Babe, be careful out there. Eyes all around," he said pointing his finger in a complete circle of the squad room.

"No problem, hondo. I got Charla's six," Nora said, with pride.

Jackson gave her the thumbs up, and we took our leave saying good bye to numerous detectives and guys in blue.

We stepped out onto the street and started walking toward Nora's car.

Looking down at the sidewalk, I said to Nora, "Did you see that?"

"Yep, I did. Mr. Good Looking Pervert is on the other side of the street, acting like he's checking his cell phone. Not obvious or anything," Nora responded, looking down the street toward her car.

"He's everywhere. Doesn't he have to work?" I snarled. "I am so tired of watching out for this guy."

"Ten-four good buddy. I so agree."

We got into Nora's car and watched Daniel bend down, acting like he was picking up something then get into his car.

We pulled away from the curb. Daniel pulled away going the opposite direction.

I half expected Daniel to do a U-turn back in our direction. He didn't. But why?

Later, as we approached our home-made office at Jackson's, we could see Daniel's black BMW a block away.

But he just stayed back and then left.

We went in and put the pictures of Rosalind and Gloria up on our new Murder Board we had assembled a couple of days before.

We stood back looking at the board, trying to make a connection between all of these murders.

"The connection between the four Key Club murders has a common denominator, 'The Key Club.' The Cunningham murder victim didn't belong to any club that we knew of. Sooo, why was she killed the same way and what's her connection to these other four? And where's the fifth missing Key Club woman?"

"Jackson told me of a woman who was in hiding. Apparently shot in the head. But he didn't have any information on her. Her parents are on the hush-hush. They are keeping the secret to themselves. It could very well be connected to this case

Bozo came in, followed by the new Suzy.

"Whatcha got there, Bozo?" I looked down at Suzy and asked, "Where's your mom?"

My neighbor, Mary, was already knocking. I walked back to the backdoor and let her in.

Suzy wiggled over to Mary with a little bark.

Bozo followed meowing, like, "I told you so." It was so cute.

Mary picked up baby Suzy, "Shame on you, you can't follow Bozo home. Bad girl," Mary said, rubbing the little pug's head. "I have some training to do and soon won't be soon enough. Problem is Suzy doesn't understand what I am saying yet," she smiled.

Mary left and the house phone rang at the very same time.

"Oh, hi, Rita, how have you been?"

I put her on the phone speaker for Nora to be involved in the conversation.

"Hi Rita," Nora blurted out.

"I was wondering if we could do lunch tomorrow. I was going back through Louise's closet, and I found a couple more notebooks stuck inside a pair of knee high boots. I don't know if they will help you, but who knows, maybe."

"Sure, we can do lunch tomorrow. Do you have a place in mind?"

"There is a new little place called, "Rabbit Mesa.""

"Never heard of it. Do they serve rabbit?" Nora snorted sarcastically. "Rabbit Mesa? Hmm yum."

"I think that will be fine, Rita," I said smacking at Nora.

Rita said Rabbit Mesa is the owners' name, and then rattled off the address. We agreed to see her at 11:30 tomorrow.

"That's interesting. I wish it was dinner tonight. I want to see those notebooks," Nora said, wringing her hands like the devious witch that she can sometimes be.

Nora left to meet Rick and his parents for dinner. A rarity if there ever was one. Rick's parents have been in Australia for a month on vacation. They just got back two days ago and after resting those two days, thought it time to share their Australian adventure with Rick and Nora. Nora wasn't a fan. But she trudged off towards the Australian adventure of Mod and Rod Weston. *Rod and Mod* was what Nora called them behind their back. It was actually Rod and MaDonna.

✦》》《《✦

I STARTED AN EARLY dinner and waited for Jackson to walk through the door.

"Hi there big boy," I greeted Jackson as he came through the door. Bozo came waltzing in thinking I was referring to him as big boy, which I often do. Poor kitty was confused when I ignored him, hugging Jackson.

We unhugged and Jackson noticed the murder board that Nora and I had moved closer to the dining room table for the first time. We had Louise's stories and ledger sitting open and out with the cold case files.

He looked at it with approval.

"Uh-huh, you got a little Rizzoli and Isles going on here. Looks right on," he said, rather pleased with the setup.

"Yeah, we took a page out of your book. Looks a lot like the 405 murder board, doesn't it?"

I left Jackson standing there studying the board, while I finished dinner.

In thirty minutes, I yelled out, "Dinner's ready."

Jackson came to the kitchen table carrying the cold case files to study them while we ate our dinner.

"You know Charla, you are on to something here," he said, flipping through the pages.

"Thanks. I think so," I replied, sipping a little Chianti. "I wish I could put two and two together."

"We will, babe. We will."

CHAPTER 57

RITA WAS SEATED AT a table when we walked into Rabbit Mesa and immediately Nora said, "Grab your purse, Rita, we're not staying."

Rita stood up and started walking toward us and asked, "Why?"

Nora pointed at a brown roach crawling up the wall, just above a table that we walked passed.

"Whew, that's sickening. In broad daylight to boot," I said.

We all three walked out of Rabbit Mesa shaking out our clothes and bags. An employee ran after us yelling, "Why youse leaving . . . ?"

"Roaches." Nora yelled back at him and we kept walking.

"I thought you said this was a new place," Nora commented to Rita.

"I heard it was. The guy's nickname is Rabbit, and he just opened it a month ago. Boy, I'm disappointed," Rita explained. "I was anxious to try the new place out."

"Follow us Rita. I know just the place."

We pulled up in front of Taco Bell.

"Really?" Rita said, spreading her arms out after she stepped out of her car.

"Really," Nora snarled with a laugh. "It's our fallback place."

"Fallback place?" Rita looked confused.

"We like to fall back on it when we run out of time or ideas of where to go to eat," I said. "We like Taco Bell."

"Well, okay then, Taco Bell's as good as the next place. It's cheaper too, and, since I'm picking up the tab, well, thanks girls," she said.

"At least, we haven't seen roaches here," Nora said, grabbing Rita and me through the arms and hustling us toward the Taco Bell door.

We got our order and sat down in a semi-circle booth making small talk when Rita pulled two small notebooks out of her purse, and handed them to me. *I was sitting closest to her.*

I took a bite of my taco, sipped my diet soda, and opened one of the notebooks.

"Well, this doesn't make sense," I said, flipping through the pages. "It's in code or something. I think its English but other than that, I can't make it out. It's jibber jabber."

Nora reached over and grabbed the other notebook and said, "What the fudge? What kind of code is it?"

"Apparently, Louise didn't want anyone to know her secret," Rita suggested.

"Well, good lord, her secret's out and spread out in her ledger/diary. We know her secret. There's no secret left. What was she thinking?" Nora stated. "KGB? It just doesn't make sense."

"I think that's the whole idea," I said, taking the last bite of my taco. "Wonder what Louise was hiding?" *We found out later it was a fake secret code between her and her high school friends that she kept all these years. It was supposed to confuse whoever read it, even them.*

I took both notebooks and stuck them into my gun bag. I had moved to a slightly bigger gun bag, since we became certified Private Investigators. You know, I had to have room for the cuffs, pepper spray, Taser and a back-up gun, pen and tablet, lipstick, mascara, tweezers, finger nail file which I rarely use, flashlight, wallet and calendar, the works. Not to mention my regular gun I had strapped just inside my jacket at my waist. Nora's bag is even bigger. Of course.

I looked up and saw Daniel walking through the door with his two kids. *Coincidence or planned?* With Daniel one never knew. I just knew that every time I turned around, he appeared. I gave a head nod in Daniel's direction. "Look."

Nora and Rita both turned to face the entrance.

Daniel tilted his head with a smile when he noticed us. Nora and Rita quickly turned around, but since I was facing him I just averted my eyes.

I could see him in my peripheral vison lean down to talk to his daughter and put their order in.

Thank goodness, we were pretty close to being done eating. We stood up to leave when, lo and behold; Daniel and his kids came waltzing over to sit in the booth next to us.

"Where are you going so soon?" he asked, as he pushed his daughter into the booth. "I was hoping to talk to you, Charla."

"Daniel, do you have a GPS on Nora's car? Or is this just a coincidence that you show up everywhere I am?" We started picking up our tray of trash to empty, and then leave.

"Oh, my lady, I assure you, this was a coincidence. This is one of Rock's and Pebble's favorite places to eat."

The three of us looked down at the children, smiled, then turned and started walking away. The children waved to us. *After all the children are innocent.* We gave a little wave back to them.

Daniel said, "Have a nice day. I'll be seeing you soon." He gave the finger wave that we ignored.

We got out in the parking lot; I turned and yelled, "Shit, shit, shit . . . this happens too much." Then with calming inhale/ exhale, I continued, "He's everywhere I go. We go. Either he follows us or he has bugged our cars. Nora, I want to check your car out, but not here."

Rita was looking around. "What's going on?"

"Oh, Daniel, aka, Damon, thinks he has a huge crush on Charla. He seems to be everywhere she is."

"Well, you could do worse," Rita snickered. "Do you see how gorgeous he is? Did you see how every woman, young and old, looked at him just now?"

I looked at Nora and then Rita and said, "Did you see how gorgeous Ryan Reynolds aka Jackson is?"

Nora rolled her eyes as Rita answered. "Yes, yes I have, and you are right. Jackson's gorgeous and he does look a lot like Ryan Reynolds. Very nice indeed. Though I think Jackson's a tad bit cuter."

"He is, isn't he?" I said, proudly.

"What's with you guys?" Nora said, still rolling her eyes.

"Nora, you're going to have to stop rolling your eyes before they get stuck," I giggled.

I turned, and looked at Rita . . . "Then you know what I am talking about.

I don't need a dominate overbearing guy hanging all over me. He's sick and into whips. No, no way, nada, zero, zip, would I ever want to be with him. Unh-uh," I said, with an actual shiver at the thought.

Rita followed us to the mall parking lot, a few blocks down from Taco Bell, and out of sight of Daniel.

Nora got out, opened her trunk and pulled out a large plastic sheet. She spread it on the ground, half under the car and half on the outside of the car. She slipped on a pair of latex gloves.

Rita watched in awe and spoke up, "What on earth?"

Nora got down on the ground and didn't hear Rita, so I answered.

"Nora hit a dog a few years back. She stopped and picked it up, hurried it to the vet. She saved the dog's life, but messed up the inside of her Mercedes interior with doggie blood. Though she hasn't hit another animal, she's always prepared now."

"Uh-huh," Rita said, shaking her head in amazement.

We both looked down at Nora who was clearly having trouble getting under the car. It was comical.

"My damn girls won't flatten enough for me to slide under," she said, trying to adjust them to the side. She pulled her head out and looked up at me. "Your girls won't have any problem."

She scooted out and I lay down in her place.

"Wait," she said, handing me a pair of latex gloves. "This is not for your fingernails to keep from getting dirty, but if you find anything under there, you won't get your prints on it."

"Always prepared," I grinned.

"You betcha, ever since I hit the dog."

I searched under that side of the car and I couldn't find anything.

Nora, being Nora, said, "Look again."

"Still nothing. I thought bugs or whatever were always planted near the rear wheel well on the driver's side," I said, sliding out from under the car.

"Check the other side."

She picked up the plastic sheet and dragged it to the other side of the car.

All the time Rita watched us work and listened to our constant bantering with one another.

I slipped under the car on the passenger side rear wheel. I couldn't see as well on that side of the car, "Nora hand me a flashlight."

"I don't have a flashlight."

"You don't have a flashlight . . . ? You have everything in that luggage you call a bag."

"Oops, I took it out for Rick to work under the sink. I guess I forgot to put it back."

"Okay, okay, I am here to save the day," Rita blurted out. She pulled out a two-foot-long flashlight from her car.

She leaned down and handed it to me.

I turned it on and it lit everything under the car from front to back and side to side. I looked from left to right. Nothing.

"Nora, there's nothing under here. I think I'll look up under the front bumper." I once again crawled out from under the car.

Nora and Rita quickly picked up the plastic sheet and spread it under the front bumper.

Sliding back under the Mercedes, I again turned on the two-foot-long flashlight. I looked and felt my way through the under carriage. My left hand hit something slightly protruding. I turned the flashlight that direction and yelled, "Found it."

I pulled the device gently off and stuck the gismo into the plastic bag Nora handed me. She took it from me as I pulled myself out and up off the parking lot blacktop.

"Yep, a tracking device."

I had mixed emotions looking at it in the plastic bag. I wanted to jerk it out of her hand and stomp it flat, but I knew better.

"We need to turn it in to check whose fingerprints are on it, if any, or stick it on the soccer mom's van sitting over there," Nora said, pointing at the van.

"There probably aren't any prints, because usually people who stick tracking devices on cars do so with gloves on. So, my money's on planting the device on the soccer mom's van. That will confuse the hell out of Daniel or whoever's tracking us," I smirked.

We looked at Rita and she giggled, "Let me plant it."

Nora gave her a pair of latex and Rita looked around to see if anyone was watching. She stuck the device under Soccer Mom's van then ran back to us as fast as she could, giggling.

"We're good to go," she said, still giggling like it was the first time she ever did a mischievous thing in her life.

"All clear," Nora said, with amusement.

"Now let's go see if there's one on my car." I said.

Rita followed us to the house where my new engine in my ten-year-old Explorer set waiting for some action.

Since my car set up higher, Nora spread the plastic sheet out on the ground and lay down on it and tried to slide under.

"Damn these things," She yelled out.

"Almost, this time. Just a few more inches higher and you would have had it made," I teased. "Get out."

"You two are so funny," Rita spoke with enthusiasm. "Funny, funny, funny."

I couldn't see Nora's face, but I heard her say, "Sometimes."

I was using Rita's big flashlight again.

"I need to get one of these for my car," I mumbled.

"What?" Nora asked.

"A flashlight like this," I said, raising it up and out from the car. "And I could use it as a club."

"Good idea," Nora said.

Rita listened and chuckled. We clearly were entertaining her.

"Seriously, it would be a great addition to my guns, pepper spray, Taser, and cuffs. My little flashlight I carry in my gun bag, serves its purpose, but this thing could do some major damage," I took a breath. "There it is . . . found it," I said, detaching it from the car's frame.

I handed the tracking device to Nora who put it in the plastic bag with her gloved hands and sealed it. I stood up and stretched.

"This one we'll have checked out," she said."

"Damn straight! Anyone up for wine?"

They both thought it sounded great. We walked single file to the front door where I noticed something on the porch.

I picked up the package and it said, "For My Lady."

"Okay, this is just too weird. I am not going to get upset. No, I am not going to get upset. No, I am not. The hell I'm not. I'm not going to acknowledge I even got this present from Daniel."

"Oh, give it to me," Nora said, ripping the package out of my hand.

As soon as we got into the house, she tore the paper off . "Oh, baby, this is beautiful," she said, with gusto.

I wasn't going to look, but Nora with her oohing and ahhing got Rita and me curious.

"It's a book of poetry with a note saying, Love verses for MY LADY. What the hell is so beautiful about this?" I asked.

"Nothing, but I made you look," Nora said, with a deep bellowing laugh.

"You two made my day," Rita said, as her belly bounced up and down with laughter.

"No matter what . . . I am not acknowledging I ever got this. If Daniel asks me, I going to say what gift? Can you imagine a book of sonnets? Really . . . !" I said, pacing back and forth.

The two girls were bent over laughing.

"I personally don't think it's a laughing matter."

Nora straightened up and hit her head on the corner of the table. "Ooh, fffffu," she just stopped short of dropping the F bomb. "That hurt."

"Now that's funny," I said, with zest. "Oh, sorry girlfriend. Are you all right?"

"No . . . Oh . . . a." She said, with a tear in her eye. She took a sip of wine that I had just poured for her. She was massaging her head. I patted her shoulder, still laughing.

"You are so insensitive, you ratfink," But now she was laughing still holding her head. "Get me some ice, will ya?"

I pulled a bag of frozen peas out of the freezer and handed them to her.

"I decided that from here on out, anything Daniel gives me or sends me, I'll ignore it. I'll save it all in a box where I will have proof of his stalking me or I may decide just to send them all to his wife with his notes. I'm still keeping track of his phone calls on that gismo you gave me."

With a hand towel wrapped around the peas Nora held it on her head while a tear or two ran down her cheeks. "That's actually a good idea," she said.

We sipped our wine and just before we had a second glass, Rita said she had to go. "Thanks, girls, for making my day. It's been a while since I just laughed." She stretched her arms out for a hug and after giving each of us a hug, she left, still laughing.

Nora stayed and I replaced the bag of peas with a bag of frozen corn on her bump. I opened the peas and put them on to cook. Why not?

CHAPTER 58

"Daniel"

DANIEL WAS BEAMING IN on the tracking device.

"What the hell?" he said out loud, as he drove back and forth in the mall parking lot looking for Nora's car. He couldn't find it. Finally, he orbited in on a van.

"What the hell . . . ?" He was again speaking out loud.

About that time, he watched a woman with three kids come walking up to the van.

Daniel sunk back into his seat with disgust. He felt betrayed and whispered, "Nor . . . a."

He acted like he was going to park across from the lady's van.

She looked up and smiled at the good-looking hunk watching her.

"Sorry, lady. You're not my type," he muttered to himself.

He stopped and turned off his ignition. He stared into space pounding his hands on the steering wheel, getting angrier by the second.

"Charla and that pesky Nora figured out I've been tracking them," he was muttering out loud.

"Charla," he said out loud again. "Oh, Charla, I love you so much. Why can't I win you over?" Daniel put his face in his hands and thought, *I'm charming, I'm better-looking than most guys or so all the ladies say. I have money, status in the community, why can't you love me back?*

These are the things he kept thinking over and over again, just about every time he saw or thought of Charla. *Why not me?* He started pounding the steering wheel again.

Getting frustrated and pissed off more than ever; he started his BMW and drove toward his house. He entered the house and checked on the kids. Seeing Rock, he told him to keep an eye on his sister for a while.

Daniel walked into the kitchen and grabbed sweet Vivian's hand and pulled her up the backstairs towards their bedroom.

"No, Daniel, no. Stop it. You're scaring me," she pleaded.

"Shut up, Vivian, you're my wife and I want you here and now." He threw her on the bed, pulled off her jeans and tore her buttons off her shirt. He pulled her shirt open and saw she wasn't wearing a bra.

"What's this, dear sweet Vivian? No bra. Were you expecting me?"

Knowing she could do nothing or there was nothing she could say that would change what was about to happen to her, she replied, "Why, yes, Daniel. I knew you would be home soon. And here you are." She spread her legs wide open, acting out the role that Daniel apparently wanted her to play.

Daniel was going through the motions but for some reason, he suddenly stopped. He looked at her and pulled away.

"What's wrong, darling, isn't this what you want?" she asked, thinking she just dodged the bullet of his abusive love-making he's all of a sudden into.

He stood up, pulled on his jeans and a shirt. "You disgust me," he said.

He left the bedroom and she smiled.

He went down to watch TV and to relieve Stone from sister duty. Only he was not paying attention to Pebbles. His thoughts are of Charla. "Charla," he mumbled.

He yelled up to Vivian, "Watch the kids, I have an errand to run. Be back soon."

Vivian yelled down, "Bring home milk."

He ignored her.

CHAPTER 59

BOZO CAME IN THE kitchen with Suzy following close on his heels.

There was a knock on the backdoor. I looked out and opened it. "Hi neighbor. I think I got what you want," I bent over and picked up the baby pug and handed her to her owner.

"This is becoming a problem," my neighbor said.

"It's okay. Suzy can only come in with Bozo. Bozo needs a new friend and I don't mind, but I know you want to know where she is."

She took the pug and said, "I'll probably be back again," waving her hand good-bye.

"So, big boy, you need to have a talk with your new little buddy that she can't follow you home every time. One of these days I'm going to walk in, and you both will be in here and her mom won't be able to come in and get her."

"Meow."

"You know what I'm saying, don't you?"

"Meow."

"Of course, you do."

I walked over to the murder board with all the players on it and gave it a thorough going over. I looked down at the ledger.

"There has to be an answer here," I said out loud. "Daniel dated these women . . . but then he has dated most of them. He's a lady's favorite, you know. He's also clueless. I really think he thinks he's going to win me over. But he won't." I sighed in revulsion.

I got cross eyed looking at it. My head started to hurt.

"Why can't I make the connection?" I said, still talking out loud and massaging my head.

Bozo came up and rubbed against my legs. I bent over and picked him up, then glanced out the front window.

"What the hell?" I saw Daniel drive by the house very slowly. I checked the door and double locked it. I pulled the blinds, still holding Bozo. I went to the backdoor and made sure it was locked, then made sure the garage door was down and locked as well as the door coming into the house. I leaned over and locked Bozo's doggie door. I walked back to the front and looked out at my car, and no one was putting a tracking device back on it. I felt relieved. I took my car keys and pointed out the window to make sure the doors on it were locked.

I jumped when I heard my cell ring. I looked at it and it was Daniel. I ignored it.

A little while later my cell rang again and again. It was Daniel.

I finally listened to the messages, and it was the same old thing.

"Where are you? Why won't you talk to me? Why don't you meet me? I miss you, Charla. Please call me," he was pleading. No, he was whining.

"Good grief! He's making me sick."

I added the message to the device that Nora had gotten me a few weeks ago. I had so many such messages from Daniel. I am glad Nora loved gadgets. I was building a harassment and stalking case. Stalking was so hard to prove and I wanted to be ready.

I decided to call her. I put Bozo down and he looked at me like "why?" but he wandered off instead.

"Hi. Jackson's back in the swing of things and is working late again. I thought I would go visit my mom and dad this evening. Want to go with me?"

As I talked to Nora, I looked out and around outside, watching for Daniel, who had, hopefully, given up.

"Let me see. Go help Rick or go with you to see your parents. What to do? Rick could use me since he's working on a brand-new account, but can probably handle it without me. He does have employees with him. He just wants to make sure the first time on this new account is done right. Soooo."

"Oh, for God sake, Nora. Yes or no? Make a decision."

"Oh, don't get your panties in a wad. Of course, I'll go with you."

"Good, because Mother invited us to have dinner with them."

"What's she having?"

"What difference does it make? It's free and my mom's stuff is always good. She made chocolate meringue pie."

"Yum, my favorite. So yes . . . what time are you picking me up?"

"Good grief, I thought lemon meringue was your favorite. Six."

"Yes, they both are. I'll be ready."

I picked her up at exactly six and pulled into my parent's driveway at six twenty.

And for the first time in a long time, I honestly felt I didn't have anyone following me. Not a nonchalant boy in blue or Daniel.

We passed out hugs and kisses between my folks and us.

"How's Jackson feeling?" my father asked me. "Back to work full time, eh?"

"Yeah, he's doing better and in the full swing of things. I think he's glad to be back to work and away from me."

"Oh dear," my mother said.

"No, no. I mean, I fussed over him so much when he was down, I'm sure he's glad to be back to a routine with his job. That's all. We're good."

"Thank goodness." My mother sighed with relief. "I really like Jackson. "How about you, Nora? How are you and Rick?"

"Why? Did you hear something?" Nora took an inquisitive look at my mom. "We're good."

Then Nora elaborated about Rick's big new account and how important it was to him.

"We'll make more money from this one job than any three others."

"I know you and Rick work hard to grow your business," my mother said.

"Cha-ching. As business grows so does the money and we're doing great."

"That's nice dear."

My mother served stuffed cabbage, mashed potatoes and gravy, and a huge salad with the works. And as promised, my mother brought in her chocolate meringue pie.

I sat back, rubbing my tummy from overstuffing myself on my mother's food which was always good."

"Dinner was really good, Mrs. Bordeaux. Thank you for including me," Nora said.

"Anna, dearie," she replied.

"Dinner was good, Anna, exceptional, especially the pie."

"Yeah, Mom and Dad, thanks for having us." We stood to clear off the table and carried dishes and leftovers to the kitchen.

"Here, dear," my mother said, handing me a care package for Jackson and a little something for Bozo just as we were leaving.

"Oh, Mom, thanks. Jackson will love it, and you, for thinking of him."

"Always my pleasure, dear."

Hugs and kisses around and we were on our way once again. I started checking my rearview mirror and looked all around me.

"So, Charla, why the nerves?" The crazy redhead asked.

"I got a couple of phone calls from Daniel this evening which I ignored, and he drove by my house, slowing down, and looking up at the house. I'm just sick of it. I might decide to run him down with my car."

"Did you copy the messages off onto the new whatchamacallit I got you?"

"Yes, yes, I did. I am building a case one way or the other," I replied.

"Good, but if you decide to run him down, be sure I'm with you."

I laughed. "You know, Nora, I am not afraid of Daniel. I'm just not quite sure what to do or how to handle it. I am afraid, however, that if I get a restraining order etc., he'll come back at me tenfold. So, because of that fear, I am holding off."

"Oh, I don't think he would ever hurt you. But I do think he would like to hold you, caress you, kiss you and maybe even whip you," Nora was now being preposterous trying to get me in a lighter mood.

"Who need friends when I have such great enemies?"

"Do you think Daniel is schizoid? I do think he's narcissistic." She asked for my opinion.

"Oh, Lord, I have no clue. But schizophrenics don't have relationships, can't get close to anyone. They are generally not into social activities. Daniel loves attention and to be noticed. He's into Satanism. Anyway, that is what I call his style of sex. Who knows what he's capable of doing. He's enigmatic, narcissistic and any other adjective you can think of. Yeah, I can see Daniel never taking blame. He loves power and prestige. Yeah, he's narcissistic. I just don't understand his infatuation with me and I think he thinks he's winning me over."

"I guess if we could figure it out, we'd have a lot more answers," Nora said, with all her wisdom.

"Any answer on Daniel would be nice or even Louise's murder. I studied the murder board earlier today, and all I got was a headache. I felt my eyes actually cross. That's about the time I looked out the living room window and saw Daniel driving by. Anyway, I know the murder board has the answer, but I just don't know what it is. I wonder if Jackson's team found any info on the cold case of the last missing person. I think I'll try to pull up information on the computer tomorrow morning. I am beat tonight. I think I will just fall in bed."

"We're here," Nora said.

"Where?"

"Good grief, Charla. Where are YOU?" Nora sounded concerned. "You're tired. Why don't you let me drive you on home, and I'll bring your car back to you in the morning, though driving your car is beneath me." She giggled. "So I will sacrifice driving your car since I don't think you should and you're so preoccupied."

"Oh, I can make it. I'm just tired. I thought my mother's strong coffee would keep me awake, but I think I could fall into bed and go right to sleep."

"Alright, but call me after you get home, inside and locked up."

"Yes, Mother."

I made it home and inside with the doors locked. I quickly called Nora. "All is good."

I greeted Bozo and started down the hallway where I heard soft music playing, and the lights dim. Jackson was laying across the bed in all his glory, *naked*, with a handful of flowers right in front of his manhood. He was sound asleep. *Romantic.*

I tiptoed around to put his care package into the fridge, and then changed into my oversized T-shirt. I slid into bed and pulled the cover up over both of us. I left the music and dim lights on, and I fell asleep.

About five a.m. I felt Jackson's arm go around my waist and he tugged me to him. We spooned and then all his glory woke up. I rolled over and said, "Looks like you're glad to see me."

He kissed me. And then . . .

He took his shower first and though we just got through making love, I was feeling pretty frisky. I climbed into the shower with him.

"My turn, big boy."

Meow.

"Not you, Bozo. This Bozo," I giggled, shutting the shower door and putting my arms around Jackson's neck. "Want me to soap your back aaannnnnn-nddddd this?"

Jackson groaned, "ohhhh, yes."

CHAPTER 60

WHILE I FINISHED GETTING ready for the day of who knows- what, the phone rang.

It was the hospital.

Jackson handed me a cup of coffee and then he handed me a bacon, egg and toast sandwich.

"Who was the call from?" he asked.

"It was the hospital. They are short personnel today and wanted to know if I would help out in the ER for four hours."

"Are you?"

"I said yes, but not before I reminded them that I'm on leave. I would do the four hours only."

Jackson smiled at how I caved. "So, when do you go in?"

"I'm on my way as soon as I change into my scrubs," I said, taking my coffee and sandwich to the bedroom with me.

I ARRIVED AT THE hospital about eight thirty. Good timing. I would leave at twelve thirty. *Only* . . . all hell broke loose.

"Fire victims coming in," someone yelled.

"Gun shots coming in," someone else yelled out.

I had forgotten how chaotic it got in the ER, and I now remembered why I didn't work it. I looked over to the E R entrance and watched Daniel come through the doors half carrying and half dragging his neighbor, whose wife was found shot in the head just a few days ago. Though I couldn't believe what I was seeing, I did rush to him and yelled for a gurney.

"Daniel, what happened?" I asked, "Isn't this Mr. Cunningham?"

"Yes, I found him collapsed in his driveway. I did CPR and decided, since he was breathing a little better, I'd just drive him in. An ambulance would have taken too long. I did what I could."

I was looking at Daniel a whole new way. I felt softer towards him. I smiled and told him,

"You did good, we'll take it from here."

"Charla, will you keep me informed?" Daniel asked.

I glanced up at him and answered, "I will."

As I pushed my patient back to the ER room, I heard Daniel say, "I miss you, Charla."

That's when my mental alarm went off as to why I shouldn't feel soft toward the nice gesture, he showed by bringing in his neighbor. Pervert.

The ER was buzzing and more disasters kept coming in. I was not going to be out of here in four hours or even eight.

After the ER doctors and technicians left Mr. Cunningham, I went to check on him.

"How are you feeling Mr. Cunningham? Do you remember what happened to you?" I asked.

"No. I think I passed out."

"Your neighbor Daniel Nielsen found you in your driveway and brought you in to the ER."

"Daniel . . . ?"

"Yes, Daniel Nielsen found you. He said he gave you CPR."

"No, I don't think Daniel did that. But I really don't remember. That doesn't sound like Daniel."

I thought, *You got that right.* "That's okay Mr. Cunningham. If you remember why you passed out, or how you were feeling just before you passed out, let me know. Meantime, a hospital team will be down to take you to get a series of tests done. We'll get to the bottom of what happened to you."

Mr. Cunningham, who was now appearing to be a little more alert, looked at me and asked, "Aren't you one of the detectives that's investigating my Myra's death?"

"Still investigating."

"Still?" he asked.

"Mr. Cunningham, your wife was killed and the forensics should be coming back soon. We'll know more then.

"Only Mr. Cunningham, I'm not a detective. My partner, Nora, and I are Private Investigators."

He looked strangely at me and then looked me up and down.

Knowing he was curious as to why I was there and in scrubs, I filled him in.

"Mr. Cunningham, I am also an RN, as well. I work for the hospital and I investigate. My boyfriend's the lead detective on your wife's case."

He looked confused then he crashed just as I was going to ask him why he was acting like he just found out about his wife's death.

"I need help in here," I yelled as I started pounding, and pumping Mr. Cunningham's chest. Staying alive, woe, woe, woe , woe, staying alive . . . The crash cart got there and everyone went into action saving Mr. Cunningham's life.

With everything looking good now, I decided to relax a bit. I sat down and put my face in my hands and mumbled, "I hate working the ER."

"What?" I heard someone ask. I looked up and my sweet man was standing in front of me.

"What a surprise. What are you doing here?" I asked him, giving him a big hug.

"I wish I could say I came by to check up on you, but I'm doing a follow up on the shooting that came in earlier. I came in to check on the condition of the victims to see if I could interview them. Unfortunately, one died and the other one is hanging by a thread," Jackson said, down in the dumps and clearly tired.

"Oh, babe, I'm sorry they couldn't pull your victim out of it. Maybe the other one will pull through."

Donnie came in swinging the door wide open and walked up to Jackson.

"Hey, Jack," she said. "The update's a tad bit better on the survivor. Thought you would like the latest info."

What was she doing and why did she sound like she was a B character out of a B movie? I looked at her with curiosity and did a shoulder shrug. "Yeah, Jack," I smirked. *I just can't help myself sometimes.*

He patted the top of my head and turned to leave. He turned back and asked me, "Your four hours up yet?"

"Yeah, about three hours or so ago. Busy day. I'm heading out in a few minutes. See you at home?"

He told me he didn't know what time he'd be home with all the open cases he was working on. He took a deep breath, "Now, this shooting." Just before he turned around to leave he said, "Thank your mother for the stuffed cabbage and pie. Even cold it was good. I gave the watch cat his too."

My poor guy was so beat. I watched him slump off.

Before leaving, I checked on a few of my patients and then Mr. Cunningham, who had just come back from a series of tests on his cardio and a blood workup. He lay nearly unconscious and didn't hear me walk into his cubicle and look at his chart.

"Miss O'Hara?" he said softly, trying to catch his breath.

"Yes, Mr. Cunningham."

"Please call me Bill."

"Okay, if you call me Charla."

"Deal. Would you do me a favor?" he asked.

"Sure, what do you need?" but I could barely hear him.

"This happened to me this morning; I don't think my kids know where I am or why. Could you call my son for me?

Both he and his sister, Caroline, are old enough they don't need a sitter but . . ." he trailed off.

"Sure, I'll be happy to. Name and number?"

"Scott Cunningham, 555-5251."

"I'll call him right away."

"Thank you."

I put his chart down then I asked him, "Would it be okay if we went back to your house to investigate?"

"Sorry about earlier when I acted like I was surprised to hear my wife was killed but my head was foggy for a bit. When do you want to go?" he asked.

"As soon as possible. My partner Nora, and I are trying really hard to help solve your wife's murder."

"Hmph! What about your job here?" he asked.

"Ah, I'm just helping out today. I'm actually on leave for a while."

"Here's Maria Garcia's phone number. She can help you get in."

"What? I thought your wife fired her for ah, ah . . ."

"She did, but I hired her back," he whispered.

"Really," I said clearly surprised. Now I remembered . . . He's another sleaze.

"How was your wife's funeral?"

"We haven't been able to have it yet. It's supposed be this Friday."

"Why so late?"

"First, the autopsy wasn't done on time. Then the out of town guests needed more time to get here. I just hope I'm out of here in time."

I bet. You just want to get back to banging Mariaaaaaa.

"Okay, I'll call your son and then I'll call Maria."

"Thanks Charla," he said. But I thought, call me Miss O'Hara.

✦》》《《✦

I CALLED NORA WHEN I got home.

"Thank goodness Jackson filled me in this morning or I would have thought you were tied up in a bed somewhere getting spanked."

"Oh Nora, oh Nora, oh Nora. I don't need this today. I'm beat."

"I'm sorry, Charla. I'm too feisty for my own good sometimes. How was your day?"

I filled her in and told her that we were going over to the Cunningham's tomorrow.

"Oh gripes, I forgot to call the Cunningham kid. Pick me up at nine tomorrow." I hung up.

The phone rang. I was afraid it was Daniel. I looked at it and relief came over me. Nora.

"Hello."

"Do not ever hang up on me again," she scolded.

"Ah, Nora, I didn't. I was done. Pick me up tomorrow. I am hanging up, now."

I called Scott Cunningham. "Zup?" he answered.

"Scott, this is Charla O'Hara. I am an RN and I'm calling you to tell you your father is in the hospital."

"You're kidding, the poison finally kicked in?" he said laughing. "That's the least the old cheat deserves."

"Excuse me?"

"Yeah, yeah, my sister and I wanted to scare the old bastard, so we got some drugs from my mom's bathroom cabinet and ground them up in his oatmeal. Don't know what they were, but we knew it would cause some damage to the old cheat."

"Okay, Scott, listen to me. I am on my way over and I want you to get me those meds. The side effects could cause your dad to die, and then you and sister both will go to prison."

On the way out the door, I called Nora. "Grab your coat. I'm on my way and will explain when I get there."

We got to the Cunningham's house where Scott and Caroline were waiting, scared. Scott handed me the bag of meds.

I scolded him again and said I would see both of them later.

As we pulled out of the Cunningham driveway, Nora called Jackson. He said he would have the kids picked up right away.

Nora and I rushed the drugs to the hospital. We explained to the doctor on call what had happened. He looked at the prescriptions and said he would be back in a bit.

We waited and waited. Finally, the doctor came out and told us it was under control and he would take care of Bill Cunningham immediately. He thanked me for being so swift in getting the prescriptions to him.

"Woosh, that was close. I don't like the guy but, I don't want his kids to be hurt because of what they tried to do to their dad. Though, I don't blame them. We saved the jerk by the hair of his chiny chin chin, and I really don't think he'll press charges on his kids. At least, I hope not. The kids will get more than a slap on the hand. I don't want them to do jail time. I would like to see them do community service until they are twenty-one and, of course, probation that long. It'll be up to the courts to decide," I was so tired that I rattled on and on.

"Didn't you say the kids didn't intend to kill their dad, they just wanted him really sick, to pay for the way he treated their mother?" Nora asked.

"Scott and Caroline didn't know how much it would take to make their dad sick. They got carried away."

"No kidding," Nora replied.

"I'm beat. I'll drop you off and then I am going to bed. If it wasn't for the Cunningham's, I would have been asleep a couple of hours already."

"Have you eaten?"

"I forgot."

"We can do a drive through, I could use some fries."

After we ate our hamburgers, I dropped her off and drove home.

I fed Bozo and fell into bed. I was asleep for thirty minutes when my cell rang. I opened one eye and turned the ringer off. "Can't take you tonight, Daniel," I mumbled falling back to sleep.

I heard Jackson come in about three o'clock. He gave me a kiss on my forehead and went to take a shower. Fifteen minutes later he too fell into bed exhausted.

The next morning, I put a note on the counter, "coffee is in the thermos, bacon's in the microwave. Love you." Nora picked me up and I left the house, letting Jackson sleep in as long as he could.

My cell rang. It was a hospital number. I hesitated to answer after the day I had yesterday.

"Hello," I answered less than enthusiastically.

"Charla, this is Bill Cunningham. I heard what you did for me. I can't thank you enough. I will be able to go to Myra's funeral after all. I was worried I wouldn't be able too. Thanks again."

"Mr. Cunningham."

"Bill," he said.

"Mr. Cunningham, I did it for your kids. It's that simple. I want you to be understanding and handle this with kid gloves. The court will apply the punishment. You will not. I don't want them to get into any trouble or I will be at the funeral on Friday and I will tell everyone there about Maria Garcia. That's the first thing and the second . . . You have to fire and get rid of Maria immediately. Hire her ugly cousin, but you have to get Maria out of your house. She is a constant reminder to your kids what you two did."

"Message received, Miss O'Hara."

"Oh, and Mr. Cunningham, Nora and I will still be popping in at your house today."

"Fine," he said. He was not so friendly now.

I took in a deep breath and exhaled slowly, hanging up the phone. "I just don't understand some people's way of thinking."

"He's a prick," she said, and I agreed.

CHAPTER 61

NORA AND I PULLED up in the Cunningham's driveway where Maria met us with her bags packed.

I smiled in satisfaction.

"Mr. Cunningham is having his sister stay here until he hires my ugly cousin," she smirked while some spit blew out of her mouth.

Nora giggled. I stared holes through her for laughing.

"Miss PI's, I cleaned the mess up that your people left behind."

"Great. Now get out . . ." Nora said, displeased with Maria still hanging around.

Maria started toward her car, and I yelled after her, "Stay in town. We're not finished with questioning you."

Maria turned around and sat her bags down. "I'm here now. Ask away," she said, with a smart mouth and a very strong Spanish accent we hadn't heard her use before.

"Oh, brother," Nora said, in a stage whisper. "Now she's the victim."

"Look, Miss Garcia, Myra Cunningham was killed a few days ago in her home, then her kids tried to do away with their father. You were first fired by Mrs. Cunningham for banging her husband and now fired for just bad taste. So lose the attitude, because you are smack dab in the middle of Myra Cunningham's murder. Stay close. We will be in touch." I said angrily. "Oh, and Miss Garcia, did you find your cross necklace?" I yelled after her.

Maria shook her head no, and traipsed toward her car. She turned and said,

"Emma, Bill's sister is waiting for you. I mean Mr. Cunningham. I'm still going to see the Mr."

"Not on my watch," I curtly said to her.

"Slut!" Nora yelled after her, but not too loudly. "I bet she never had a necklace."

We watched Maria pull away.

My cell rang. "It's Jackson," I said, as I pressed the on key.

"Hi babe, did you get enough rest last night?" He asked me.

"Yes, how about you?"

"Thanks for letting me sleep in a little. Where are you?"

"Nora and I are at the Cunningham's."

"Donnie and I are on our way there now," he said, then hung up.

"Jackson and Donnie are on their way here."

"We better get busy. We need to beat them to . . . whatever," she said, pointing as she turned in a semi-circle toward the front door.

My cell rang again.

"What, Daniel?" was how I answered.

"Oh, my lady, sounds like you are having a bad day. I am watching you and you don't look happy."

I turned to see if I could see him. He was pulling out of his driveway. He did the finger wave.

"I've got to go, Daniel."

"Have a nice day, my lady." He pulled onto the street and drove away.

"Daniel, huh?" Nora asked.

"Yeah. Come on. Let's meet Emma."

We knocked and Emma answered. We did the usual introductions, and she held the door open for us to enter.

"This is such a mess," Emma stated. "I know Bill's my brother, but he can be such a, a jerk. He didn't treat Myra right. And that piece of trash that just left here, well I could go on forever about her."

"Don't hold back, Emma," Nora said, half laughing.

"Oh, I am sorry to hit you with this right off the bat. I just don't understand Myra getting killed, the kids trying to kill their dad and their dad committing carnal sin. Now I have to go get the kids out of juvy."

"Emma, slow down. To be clear, the kids wanted to make your brother sick, not dead. They wanted him to pay for having Maria back in the house."

"Can't say as I blame them."

"Clearly, you don't think much of your brother."

"Actually, you're right. I love him because he's my brother, but I dislike all that he does. He has no morals. He treated Myra awful."

"Do you think he was capable of killing Myra?" I asked.

"Yes, I sometimes think so, but did he? Absolutely not. He's a lot of things, but not a killer. Do what you have to do around here," she said, swooping her hand in a semi-circle over the house. "I have to bail the kids out."

Emma put on her coat and walked out the door just as Jackson and Donnie pulled up. They said something to her and she just pointed toward the house as she got into her car.

They joined us and the first thing Jackson said to me was, "Congrats on saving Bill Cunningham's life." We did a little fist bump. "Nice save."

"Thanks, but the kids were the ones who came through with the meds." Another fist bump and explosion.

The four of us separated to different directions of the house for better coverage.

I was coming down the stairs from what I hoped was a final investigation of the upstairs bedrooms when Nora came running into the foyer from the kitchen holding a baggie.

"Look what I found stuck in the corner of the kitchen cabinet door hinge where Louise had to be standing," she said, holding up the bag containing what looked like a piece of blue fabric, although, it was very small in size.

"Good job in seeing it, Nora. It's so small; I can understand why it was missed before. Or else one of the kids or their jerk father might have torn it off since Myra Cunningham's death. We'll have them run the DNA on it."

Donnie and my man walked in from the living room area.

"What do you have there?" Jackson asked, as he took the baggie from Nora.

Jackson examined the teeny tiny fabric through the baggie, then stuck it in his pocket to be turned in for analyzing, as Nora explained for the second time in so many seconds where she found it.

"Good eye, Nora."

"That reminds me," I said. "Have you heard anything about the piece of glass I found out in the yard?"

Jackson looked at me and said, "Refresh my memory."

"I gave it to Donnie . . ."

"Wha, what?" Donnie looked taken aback. "I . . ." she was clearly thinking . . .

"*Donnie* . . ." I am visibly annoyed. "The last time you, Nora and I were here investigating, I found a piece of jagged glass that looked like it had a shoe imprint on it. I put it in an evidence bag and handed it to you."

"I, I, oh, yeah, now I remember . . . I stuck it in my glove compartment so nothing would happen to it . . ."

We followed her out of the house and watched her approach her car.

"Oh, my God, I forgot about it," Donnie was stammering as she reached into her glove compartment to pull it out. She raised her head out of her car and held up the bag of glass . . ."Here it is," she said, proudly.

"Jackson, she's incompetent. First, she forgot Louise's computer which was back at Louise's house, *but not because of Donnie*, and I bet there was no follow up done on the kid that took it or the return of it, and now this. What else has she forgotten or else didn't follow through with? Has she even followed up on the important cold cases?"

I didn't wait for Jackson's response as I ran to the side of the house where earlier in the week, I discovered footprints. Relief hit me when I looked down and around. The tech had been there to get the imprints. He left the telltale signs of the goop he used to raise the prints. *No thanks to Donnie.* I was the one who called the guy over to get the imprints and, since I thought he would do his job, I had turned to join Donnie and Nora to go to Daniel's house, to ask him and his wife questions. So yeah, I was relieved when I saw it had been done.

Jackson walked up to me with Nora.

"Whatcha looking at?" he asked.

I pointed and explained. "I'm almost sure that if I hadn't called the tech over myself, this imprint wouldn't have happened," I said, still irritated with Donnie who was now running up with the glass.

I took the glass from her and handed the bag to Jackson.

"This should have been processed, and if it had been, we would be closer to finding out who it belonged to, but thanks to *her*," now pointing to Donnie, "it's going to take even longer, and it could be good evidence. The Key. Oh, I don't know . . . something . . ."

"I just forgot," Donnie said, throwing up her hand exposing her midriff.

I rolled my eyes. I had no more words for her. I looked at Jackson as he slid the glass in a larger bag along with the bag with the tiny fabric. "I promise this will not be out of my sight and I will get it turned in today."

We all pulled off our latex gloves and slid them into our pockets.

Jackson put his arms around me to partly show me support and partly to calm me down.

Nora and I started toward the front yard as Jackson hung back talking to Donnie.

"Boy, I would love to be a ladybug flying over those two right now to hear what Jackson's laying into Donnie about," Nora said.

I stopped, cocked my head and looked at her, "A lady—bug?"

"Well, yeah, flies are nasty and everyone slaps at them. But ladybugs are cute and everyone says, oh, look at the cute ladybug. No one smacks at them, and if they did, they would get dyed red."

"What?" I am truly confused at this point, shaking my head in disbelief at the crazy redhead.

"Focus Nora."

"I just mean I would love to hear what Jackson was saying to her."

"Me, too. I have a few choice words I would like to say," I answered.

We glanced back at Jackson who was still talking at and not to Donnie as she hung her head. We continued to walk to the front of the house where we saw Emma pull up with the juvenile delinquents.

"Court's in six weeks. That's as soon as it could be heard," Emma said, as she shook her head in shame of her niece and nephew. "Meantime, these two aren't leaving this house except to go to school and back. It will be easier to keep track of them and I will be here to see that it happens, or until their dad is on his feet and strong enough to take them and pick them up."

Now the kids hung their heads. Emma nudged Scott. He nudged her back. Then she flipped him on the back of his head. He looked at her and said, "Miss O'Hara, my sister and I are very sorry. We only wanted to make him sick, then maybe he would have time to think about what he's doing to this family."

"Thank you, Miss O'Hara, for acting so fast with our mother's uh, prescriptions and saving our dad. We do love him. And you saved us too," the sister said, crying huge crocodile tears.

I stood there staring at the two juveniles, trying to figure what to say next and how to say it, whatever it was. Both had tears in their eyes.

Now, Nora nudged me toward them. "Well, I hope you neither one will do any juvy jail time. I heard it's really bad," she told them.

I looked at Nora, giving her the eye. *Really!*

I patted each kid on the shoulder, then told them, "I'm just glad you stepped up with your mother's prescriptions in time. That's a good sign for you and I am sure the judge will recognize it."

"Thank you, Miss O'Hara," Scott said, and his sister chimed in with her thanks.

Emma said, "That's more like it, now move it."

They headed for the front door and we headed for our car. Meantime, Jackson was still talking to Donnie.

Nora and I stopped at Taco Bell and there he was again. Daniel.

We didn't think he saw us so we slipped into the ladies' room, used the facilities, and then Nora peeked out.

"Yep, he's still out there."

While hiding out in the ladies' room with nothing else to do, we both pulled out our guns and checked them. We each took out the bullets and looked down the barrel then put the bullets back in and closed the chamber. Some lady with her two little kids came in and stared at us a fraction of a second then said to her kids, "We're going on down to Burger King."

We put our guns back in their respective places, dabbed a little mascara on and fresh lip gloss.

Nora peeked out again.

"Looks like he's cleaning up his table and getting ready to leave."

"Good," I said, "I'm getting tired of hanging out in the jonnett."

We waited another couple of minutes then stepped out and no Daniel.

"We got lucky this time."

"What did you get lucky about?" Daniel asked, as he walked up behind us.

"Where did you come from?" Nora asked him as I tried not to look at him.

"Men's room," he said, halfway pointing toward the men's room.

"Oh," she responded. "Well, we're about ready to go. Hurry up and order," she said, nudging me in my back. "Remember to get it to go."

We got our food and headed for the door.

"What's your hurry, my lady and her sidekick?" he asked.

"Gotta eat on the go. Got a . . . a dentist appointment," Nora stammered.

"Well, I can take Charla home," he offered.

The dentist appointment's for Charla. That's why she can't talk."

"But she can eat!" he exclaimed.

"Well, yeah. On the left side of her mouth. It's a soft taco." Nora said, leading me out the door.

I threw up my hand and beat him to the finger wave, and I smiled a lopsided grin.

He finger waved back a little, but seemed a little curious about what just happened.

Out of earshot, I said, "That whole thing was weird, but fast thinking about the dentist."

"Good job on twisting your mouth," she pointed to my mouth.

We pulled into the north side of the mall under the shade of an old maple tree and started eating our Taco Bell before our tacos got soggy.

"I wonder if Jackson is still bending Donnie's ear. I believe he was really upset with her."

"She deserves all the chewing out he can muster up," Nora said, shrugging her shoulders.

"Besides, she's looks really ugly without her makeup," I came back childishly.

"So, you keep telling me," she replied.

"I told you Donnie was ugly before?"

"Only about every day. Let's pull up to the mall doors. I want to check out some new sunglasses," Nora said.

"I'm kind of broke. I got a few dollars for vacation time when I took my leave from the hospital, but that was just a couple of weeks of pay, and I haven't been paid for my last shift in the ER yet. Investigating and not getting paid is a bitch."

"I forgot you have to earn a living. Sorta."

"Not all of us have a husband who is the King of Clean successful cleaning business," I countered.

"Hey . . . I helped him start that business. I worked my fake fingernails to the bone helping him get it going."

"Whoa, horsey. Don't get your panties in a wad," I lightly punched her shoulder. "Now let's go look at those sunglasses."

We hung out in the mall and Nora, in fact, bought a pair of Vera Wang designer sunglasses. She wanted two different pairs but settled for one pair, feeling sorry for me not being able to buy even a cheap pair. *What a friend.*

Truth is, I love her to pieces. She's of the haves and I am of the have nots. But it has always worked for us.

I accept her being near rich and she accepts me as being near poor. *But the secret is, I'm not.*

The truth was, Nora came from a poor upbringing. She has done quite well. I am very proud of her.

We walked out of the mall toward the car and I grabbed my mouth like it was really sore and stuffed tissue in it as I watched Daniel walking toward us.

"Doesn't that man ever work? Did he lose his job? What on earth? He's looking right at you."

"My Lady," he said, swooping his arm down and around. "Is there a dentist in the mall nowdays?"

Nora spoke up. "No, the dentist appointment went well. Show him Charla." *I shook my head no.* "We just had to stop in for a minute to pick these up," she said, showing her sunglass purchase.

"Can I drive you anywhere, Charla?"

I shook my head, no.

"I take it your tooth is better now."

I held up two fingers.

"Oh my, two teeth."

I nodded my head, yes.

"Yes, two teeth. The one was hurting her really bad. The tooth next to it had a cavity as well, though not so bad. Dr. Hill took care of both of them. Charla's doing great now and will be back good as new when the novocain wears off."

He started to approach me, I assumed with a hug, and I shook my head "no" pointing to my mouth.

"Okay, then," he said. "I'll catch up with you later."

Nora did the finger wave to him. He smirked and walked towards the mall doors.

I took a deep breath and pulled out the soggy tissue out of my mouth. "He is getting on my last nerve. I feel something's off with him beside his sex hobby, his stalking me, and showing up everywhere we are even after we found the bugs."

"I think we need to check more into his background," Nora said. "Cause something about him is off."

"He checked out as a good family man, does well in his job, socially acceptable, and absolutely successful. We can't find one thing wrong with him other than his dominance sex hobby, cheating on his wife and his obsession of me. Everything else turned up all good. That in itself is spooky."

"I need to get home to Rick, so let's move it."

"Now you want to move it," I shrugged.

"Unfortunately, his folks are coming over."

"I like them."

"I don't."

"Shame on you," I said.

"Hey, they are the ones who tried to sabotage our wedding. They didn't think I was good enough for their baby Ricky-poo."

"That was years ago, and now they think you are better than rice pudding."

"Really? Rice pudding?"

"Yes, and you know they love you."

"Okay, okay, point taken. They love me. Now get a move on," she said, trying to hustle me to the car.

CHAPTER 62

"Daniel"

DANIEL CAME OUT OF the mall, opened his car door and tossed his packages into the passenger side seat. He got in and buckled up.

He put his head in his hands and got tears in his eyes.

"I have to win Charla's love. She's clearly not there yet. So, think, Daniel, think," he said out loud then started to bang his head against the steering wheel until his forehead turned red.

He pulled himself together and started the engine. He looked around before backing out and saw dear sweet Vivian walking across the mall parking lot with a rather nice-looking guy, though a little nerdy.

Daniel stopped and assessed his wife, and the guy.

So, he backed out, pulled up, slammed on his brakes and jumped out of the car in front of her.

"What are you doing here?" Vivian asked Daniel, a little shocked at seeing him there.

"Shopping," Daniel said, "More importantly . . . what are you doing here with that . . . that man?"

"Take it easy Daniel. I've been seeing a," *she swallowed hard,* "a sex analyst. Dr. Fitzpatrick, meet my husband, Daniel," she said, looking at Daniel's forehead where blood was surfacing. Daniel looked at Vivian then stuck his hand out to shake Dr. Fitzpatrick's out-reached hand.

"Doctor," Daniel said, pleasantly. "So, where's your office?" as Daniel looked around the parking lot.

"Yes, yes. I can see where this could be unusual. Your wife was my last appointment of the day. Since I needed to pick my car up from the shop, she offered to take me."

Daniel stared at one then the other. "I don't see a car shop here."

They both looked at each other, then at Daniel in a very awkward moment.

"Dr. Fitzpatrick's car wasn't quite ready for pick up and since the mall was on the way to the shop, I asked him if we could stop at the mall for a minute."

"Well, let's see what you have in the bag," Daniel said, grabbing the bag from Vivian's hand.

"It's embarrassing," she said. "I actually had to have Dr. Fitzpatrick help me pick out the right one."

Daniel pulled out a book and smirked. "How to get into Dominance Sex with Your Spouse." Then, in smaller lettering, "How to accept being submissive."

"Interesting," Daniel said. "Why do you need a book like this?"

"You like that kind of sex. I just want to try and understand."

"I don't like that kind of sex. You sick or something?" Daniel was now pointing at Vivian angrily.

"But Daniel," she said, embarrassed.

"But nothing," Daniel said. He looked at the doctor who was clearly confused. "Dr. Fitzpatrick, Vivian will no longer be in need of your service. Take the book back, Vivian, and I'll take the good doctor to get his car."

"But, Daniel," she pleaded.

"Take the book back before someone sees you with that trash, Vivian." Daniel pointed and motioned for her to go on.

"I think I'll walk from here. It's not that far. Thanks for the offer," The good doctor smiled and started to walk away.

"No. No, I will drop you off."

The good doctor reluctantly got into Daniel's car, and told him where to pick up his car.

They pulled up in front of the dealership and as the good doctor got out of Daniel's car, Daniel reminded him that Vivian would no longer need his services. The doctor nodded that he understood.

Later, when Vivian walked through the front door with the book hidden, Daniel was waiting for her. He had arranged for the kids to go to their grandparents." Daniel took Vivian's hand and pulled her up the stairs to the bedroom where he had it all set up for Dominance sex.

"Okay, Vivian. You want to know about Dominant, submissive sex. Well, let the master show you."

She screamed. She cried. She hurt. She passed out. She came to. Daniel didn't leave one technique out or a page unturned.

"Need I show you more?" he asked her.

"No, Daniel."

"This is how it's going to be from now on. I am Dominant. You are submissive. Got it?"

"Yes," she whimpered.

"What? I don't hear you."

"I said YES, Daniel. YES."

"Now that's better. Remember you started this," he said.

"No, you did."

"You only had a taste a couple of times. You went and talked to the good doctor, then you bought a book. Why, Vivian? Why?"

Vivian yelled, "Because it's sick, Daniel. Sick!"

"Well, that's where we differ. I love it, and you'll learn to love it."

Vivian ran to the bathroom and stepped into the shower.

Daniel slipped in behind her, turned her around, then started making gentle sweet love to her.

She melted, then cried even harder. "Why, Daniel? Why?"

"Why not?"

CHAPTER 63

I UNLOCKED THE DOOR and to my surprise, both Bozos were home and waiting for me. Man Bozo wrapped his arms around me and kissed me hard, then gently. Cat Bozo rubbed my legs for attention.

I looked at both of them and said, "Which bozo do I pet first?"

"Me, me, me," Jackson said, jumping up and down like a little kid.

"Meow, meow, meow," Bozo said, pressing against my legs.

"Oh boy, choices," I said, giggling.

"Choices nothing. That bozo can't give you what I can give you, babe," said the gleaming Jackson.

"Meow."

"It's like he understands . . . uncanny," Jackson said and stared down at Bozo the cat.

Then he grabbed me and pulled me to him.

"Can Bozo the cat do this?"

"Hmm," I moaned.

"Can Bozo the cat do this?" he unbuttoned my shirt.

"Hmm."

"Can Bozo the cat do this?" he unzipped my jeans.

"Hmmmm."

"And can Bozo the cat do this?" He picked me up and headed to the bedroom.

"Sorry, Bozo the cat," I hmmed again, just as Jackson shut Bozo the cat out of the bedroom.

A while later Bozo the cat was lying patiently outside the bedroom door when we both stepped out.

Bozo the cat started up where he left off . . ."Meow."

"Okay, big boy."

"You 'talkin' to me?" Jackson asked.

I lovingly hit his arm. "Wrong big boy."

I leaned over and picked Bozo up and carried him to the kitchen where I locked his doggie door for the night. I fed him his kibble and bits and gave him fresh water.

The pizza delivery came and we popped the top off a couple of Buds. *Now this is life.*

We sat down to watch a little reality TV and got sick of it pretty quickly. Since there wasn't any football on TV, we tuned in on Quigley Down Under. Always a good watch.

When it was over, I did the thing I didn't want to do, but did it anyway . . .

"So, about Donnie?"

He pulled me closer to him and looked into my eyes, "We had a very long talk, and we came to a mutual agreement that she has made a lot of mistakes and missteps. She needs a bit more training. So, as of now, though I think she has great potential, she knows she needs to have a bit more understanding on how to conduct a murder investigation. She is going to be with another partner who has to go through training and she will go through extensive training with him. The department was in too big a hurry and rushed her to be my partner since mine died suddenly. She just wasn't ready. So, she stepped down. Tomorrow I will know who my new partner will be. I hope it's someone who won't hold me back and slow me down."

"Wow, I hope I didn't cause any of this," I looked into his eyes.

"No, you didn't, so don't worry your pretty head over it. Okay maybe a smidgeon," holding his thumb and finger barely apart then turned to kiss the top of my head.

I knew I contributed to Donnie being demoted, and I was glad. And I didn't care.

"I hope your new partner's ugly."

"Really, Charla?"

"Well yeah . . ."

"Okay, I will tell them to send me someone ugly. Wait. Let me call my department now to let them know I want ugly," Jackson teased.

"Okay, call."

Jackson pulled me to him and my robe came open. "Oh, oh, big boy, you up for another round?"

"Sure am," he said, as we raced down the hallway, dropping my bathrobe on the floor outside the bedroom door. He didn't wait to get me on the bed. He turned me around, held my hands against the wall. I jumped and spread my legs up and around his waist, we slid down the wall and never did make it to the bed.

The next morning, we both woke up naked. We heard something and Jackson popped up, slipped on sweatpants and grabbed his gun.

He came back laughing.

"What?" I asked, still trying to find something to pull on.

"In our haste to get it on again . . . and falling asleep after, we forgot to turn the TV off."

We both laughed, but I thought something seemed off, so I glanced around the room and noticed a picture of Jackson and me turned face down.

"Jackson, did you leave the picture of us this way?"

"No, babe, I haven't looked at it in awhile."

"Hmph, this isn't the first time I found it face down," I said, wondering.

"What?" he said.

"Oh, nothing," I said, dismissing the thought.

Jackson left to meet his new partner, and I told him as soon as he knew who it was, he had to text me the partner's picture. Not that I could do anything about it, but still . . . I wanted to know.

Jackson also wanted to go by the CSI lab to be sure they were running tests on the glass footprint and the piece of blue fabric.

Jackson texted me, and said that the lab was behind and shorthanded. Unfortunately, they wouldn't be able to run any tests today, but promised to get to it as soon as possible.

I texted him back. *Damn that Donnie.*

He sent back a =).

I love that man.

Nora drove up in her Benz, and it sounded like someone had set a bunch of screws lose in her motor. I ran out and threw my hands up in "what the hell?"

She parked it in the driveway, got out and said, "Someone stole my cross-over pipe."

"Crossover pipe? Really?"

"Oh, I don't know what it is. Sounded good though, didn't it? As much as I hate riding in your ten-year-old Explorer, I'm going to need a ride back from the dealership."

I did the Bozo thing, got my jacket, put my gun in my bag and grabbed a handful of PI business cards. A girl can never have enough business cards. I double checked the locks and pulled the door closed and tested it. I can't shake the bad feeling someone was coming in the house unbeknownst to us.

I pulled in behind Nora and listened to the racket all the way to the dealership. They told her they would check it out and hoped to have it ready for her by five.

She got into my ten-year-old Explorer that purred like a kitten getting its tummy rubbed.

"So, what's on the agenda?" she asked.

"I so want to interview all of the Key Club participants again. I want to start with a one-on-one. I have a list of questions and, by cracky, I want answers. I have a list of their names, addresses and phone numbers in this folder." I handed her the folder. "But first I want to run by the 405 and see if Jackson's in his office."

That's when I told Nora about Donnie getting demoted.

"Happy dance," Nora made around about with her hands. "The airhead!"

"So, I want to check out Jackson's new partner. See if they clean up as nice as Donnie did."

"You jealous already?"

"Aah, no. Aah, yes. Aah, I hope not."

CHAPTER 64

WE PULLED UP IN front of the 405 and, as luck would have it, Jackson was walking down the steps with a younger looking Jackson. *A mini me.*

"Well, that's double trouble. Two Ryan Reynolds, if that's his new partner. I can handle that."

"I can, too," Nora was truly drooling.

"Wait a damn minute . . . You too?"

"Well, yeah. I may not agree about the Ryan Reynolds' look, but there isn't anything wrong with Jackson and now a little Jackson."

"Oh, oh, Jackson spotted us. And he's headed this way along with his new partner."

Nora straightened up and fluffed her girls.

"Really?" I said, "You can't tell me that you don't use those things to your advantage."

"Well, duh!" the crazy redhead responded. "If you got them, is all I'm saying."

I bantered, "Not fair."

I was able to pull into a spot that really wasn't a parking spot. But, hey, I wasn't parking, and I wasn't leaving the car unattended.

I threw my arms around Jackson's neck and we did a quick tiny kiss and then broke away from each other.

"Sorry, I forgot we were in front of the 405," I said.

"Nora," Jackson nodded his head to her. "Ladies, I would like for you to meet my new partner, Zack Alexanderson." He was younger by a few years than Jackson and Jackson had about twenty pounds on Zack. *Twenty pounds of muscle.*

I smiled, "Enchante, Zack," holding out my hand.

"Yeah, what she said," Nora said, "Enchante," fanning herself.

"I have to apologize for the girls. They are easily distracted when they see a good-looking guy."

Zack smiled back, "Nice to meet you both."

I leaned in to Jackson, "I am a happy camper. Zack doesn't wear makeup."

"Okay, you checked out my partner, now get out of here before I have to ticket you for parking illegally."

We left and headed for The Cheer Up. We needed to talk to Jordan again.

◆))) (((◆

WE PULLED ON THE door handle of The Cheer Up to go in, but it didn't open. Locked!

We knocked on the door, knowing that Jordan was doing inventory or the books. We knocked again, then watched a shadow walk across the front window.

Jordan answered the door and looked bewilderedly at us. He seemed reluctant, but let us in. We soon found out why. A little perky redhead came bouncing out of the backroom, straightening her top and pulling her ponytail tighter. She smiled, patted Jordan on his butt, and said, "See you at home, baby."

He tossed his head with a, yes.

"Uh?" We both looked at Jordan.

"You probably won't believe this, but that little lady is my bride of five years. She's a doll, isn't she?"

We looked at him, then each other and back at Jordan.

"We didn't know you were married," Nora said, staring at Jordan.

"No one does. We keep it that way when it comes to the bar business. She helps out here with the accounting and helps me keep track of the Key Club."

"I see you got a bonus just now," I giggled.

"Yeah, it happens, now and again. I guess I should also tell you, as with all your snooping, you'll find out anyway, I am part owner of The Cheer Up."

"I figured that out, already," I said.

"You didn't tell me," Nora whispered, leaning toward my ear.

"Sorry, the thought came and went."

"So, Jordan, who's the other part owner?"

"That would be Kandi's dad, Mike."

"Kandi?"

"My wife."

"OOOHHHH," Nora said, a little loud.

"I've known Mike for years. He's been my dad's buddy for most of my life. One day he said he didn't want to work the bar as much and asked my dad if he would want to partner up. Dad said no, but I said yes. The last time I'd seen Kandi was before she went away to college. She came back, we got reacquainted, and the rest is history."

"So, your father-in-law started the Key Club?"

"Yes, but I didn't know until after I signed on. It's really good for business."

"It's not good for all your business," I said.

He interrupted and said, "You know, I've been thinking about that. I did a few inquiries and found out that the one lady, who was shot, apparently didn't die. She was shot in the head, but survived and is in a nursing home in a small town just outside Pittsburg, Kansas. Her family hid her for fear someone would try to kill her again, to do away with her. They legally changed her name to Zoey Collins. She isn't very old, maybe forty or so. But she isn't always in this world. My source tells me that some days are good, and some days are really bad. She stares into space, and doesn't say much. When she does talk, it's mostly mumble jumble.

"I figured this would come up in your investigation, so I asked my mother, who happened to be friends of Zoey's mother, if you two could try to talk to her, and she said you could try. To get access to Zoey, the family said you have to use the password before the administrator will let you see her. The administrator is the only one with the password. And remember you can't tell anyone."

Nora did the turn the lock on her mouth and threw away the key. "Okay, the password, please," Nora asked nicely. She crossed her heart and said, "Cross my heart, hope to die."

Sometimes I just have to ignore her.

"So, come on, Jordan, the password please."

"Ivanhoe." Then he gave us the directions how to get to Amber Haven Nursing Home.

I looked at Nora . . . and we both said, "Road trip."

"Thanks, Jordan," I said and turned to walk away but turned back to him and asked, "Jordan, when were you going to give us this information?"

"I only found out late yesterday, and believe it or not, I was going to call you today," He turned, picked up our card off the cash register to show us how close he was to calling to us. "After Kandi left."

Jordon slipped our card into his pocket patting it, as we said our good-byes.

Before leaving The Cheer Up parking lot, I called one of the Key Club used-to-be's from my cell and made an appointment to go see her in about an hour. Nora contacted our second appointment from her cell phone.

We did a McDonald drive through to get a bite for breakfast just before the time roll over for lunch.

We sat in Micky D's parking lot enjoying Micky's coffee, *or at least I was,* when my man and his new partner pulled in and spotted us.

We followed the two hunks into McD's and waited while the guys got their lunch, then joined them with our breakfast burritos and coffee.

Nora and I explained to the two detectives our new-found information and told them we would be going to see Zoey tomorrow.

"I swear you two should go to the police academy and become detectives yourself," Jackson said, leaning over and kissing my cheek, pleased about what he had just heard.

"No!" Which sounded like a lion's roar from both of us girls in unison.

"Cops have too many rules and regulations. They have to go by the book. I just couldn't do that. Why heck, I don't even like following the cookbook directions. I bend the recipes to fit my needs. The same with private investigation, I don't have to follow an exact recipe."

"Nicely put. Great metaphor," Nora said, giving me a high five.

"You're right, it would be hard for you to go by rules and regulations. I've watched you stress over recipes," Jackson said, winking at me. "Besides, you are great at outside police help, you and your partner over there," now pointing at Nora. "I know Nora has even more difficulty pulling back the reins."

Nora took that as a truly good compliment. I did not.

Then Jackson turned to Zack and said, "These two, though a bit unorthodox, seem to get the job done, or else come up with something that guides me in the right direction, especially since they became certified Private Investigators."

"Ah shucks Jackson, you make me so proud . . ." Nora giggled, blushing a bit and giving him a shoulder punch. He winced a bit, as it was his injured shoulder that was still tender.

I nodded my head slowly up and down wondering what Jackson was up to. Then here it came.

"Okay, I'm going with you tomorrow," he said.

"Jackson, it's supposed to be a secret, so let us feel this lead out and see if we get anywhere before you waste your time. Our source says Zoey isn't altogether together. So we can check it out and I promise you'll be the first to know if any useful info comes out of it. Besides, she's still afraid of men."

Jackson said after a few moments' thought, "Okay, I understand. See you at home tonight. It's taco Tuesday." He and Zack stood to leave.

"Righhhhhtttt! Rick and Nora are joining us."

With a thumb's up in approval, he patted me on my head and kissed my cheek, waved to Nora, and the two hunks left the building, followed by us.

We interviewed the two appointments we had, and found nothing different. We were hoping the more we pumped the Cheer Up crowd, that something different would pop out. It didn't. Yet!

We went by to check out Nora's Benz. The mechanic said that someone poured sugar into the gas tank. They flushed it out and there was no damage. He said it was running smoothly.

Nora threw up her hands in disgust and said, "Well clearly someone was sabotaging my car. The bug didn't work, so now this." Nora was thoroughly ticked, stomping off to settle up the bill.

And I don't blame her. I just wish we could catch Daniel or whoever . . . But someone was trying to do harm . . . !

CHAPTER 65

THOUGH NORA'S BENZ SOUNDED normal again and was running great, we decided to take my ten-year-old car to Pittsburg. After all, since it does have a new engine, the gas mileage wasn't bad. A good thing, since the price of gas was so high.

We headed towards a small town just outside of Pittsburg, Kansas, where Amber Haven Nursing Home was located. We put on some seventies hits, and sang along.

All of a sudden Nora turned down the music. She turned to me and said, "So, I've been watching the way you and Jackson interact with each other. You are so darn cute together. He truly loves you." She paused, "Do you truly love him?"

"Oh, Nora, I am gaga over him. I love him so much. I always want to be with him. It is just meant to be."

"Then why haven't I heard wedding bells?" she inquired. "It's been five years."

"Seven, and five with Jackson."

"Tomoto, *tomato*,"

"Sure, some day. We don't talk much about it. He asked me to marry him awhile back, and even pulled out a big beautiful shiny diamond ring. But after I hesitated on the answer, he closed the box and put the ring up. He said he's patient. When I'm ready, just pull the ring out and put it on. He said then he'll know that will be my answer. I have pulled it out and looked at it a few times, and even tried it on but, it just doesn't feel right, yet."

"You know your hubby's been gone a long time now. Don't you think it's time to move on?"

"Yes, and I am, but I don't want, oh I don't know what I want. I guess a little more time."

"You act like a poor little church mouse. When are you going to break into that life insurance money Patrick left you?"

"I guess I think if I don't use it, he's not really gone."

"But he is gone and for a long time now. So if you love Jackson so much, why can't you be fair to him?"

"You do have a point. Maybe soon."

"Does Jackson know about all your money? That you're really rich?"

"Nah, not yet. Heck my parents don't even know."

"I am honored to be the only one to know your dark secret. All that money."

"Well, you have been with me through thick and thin."

I turned the music back up and we started singing again.

I looked into the rearview and had a strong feeling someone was following us.

"Nora, I think we have a tail."

She got into her big bag of tricks and after searching and throwing things out onto the floorboard, pulled out a pair of binoculars. She undid her seat belt and turned to see if she could make the car out.

"Oh . . . my God, Charla. It's Daniel."

I slammed on my brakes, and pulled off the road and waited.

"He can't know where we are going. Call Jackson for me and explain that it just got complicated. See if he can get Daniel picked up for suspicious behavior, or some damn something."

"Ten-Four, My Lady," she said.

"Smartass, just call Jackson. Tell him we are just outside of town and try to give him the exact location. We haven't been on the road all that long."

"Jackson," I heard her say as I stepped out of the car.

I slammed the door and leaned on it just waiting for Daniel to pull up.

Daniel was smiling from ear to ear when he stepped out of his BMW and walked toward me. I watched him, but then gave myself a head slap and stopped looking at him.

"My lady, do you have car trouble? May I help?" he asked.

"No, Nora's a bit sick. I had to stop and let her hang her head out of the car window. She just barfed and barfed."

Daniel stepped back a little and said, "Tell Nora I am sorry she is ill. I best be on my way. Until morrow comes, my lady." With that he turned on his heels, headed to his BMW, and drove away.

I opened the car door and leaned in to tell Nora, what was said.

"Call Jackson back and tell him to nix the reinforcements. All we have to do is threaten to barf and Daniel's gone."

She dialed Jackson . . . again.

"He wants to talk to you," she said, handing me her cell.

"Hi Babe."

I filled Jackson in and he laughed, "You girls do have a way of handling any situation that pops up. Are you sure you're free of your stalker?"

"Yep," I said, as I watched Nora pick up all her things off the floorboard, and rearrange her bag.

I hung up from Jackson and told her to buckle up, then pulled back out on the road.

I cranked up the tunes, and we started singing, again. Loudly.

In spite of Daniel or anyone else, we made good time pulling into Amber Haven.

We asked for the administrator. A tall matronly woman in a navy-blue pantsuit and sensible shoes, came around the corner holding out her hand to each of us. Looking around to see if anyone was close enough to hear, she asked for the password.

"Ivanhoe," I said, just as cautious.

She led us down a long hallway with colorful wreathes hanging on different doors for the personal touch. We made a turn left down another long hallway that was painted a happy green, and again adorned with colorful door ornaments. The smell was a bit antiseptic.

"Here we are," she said, and introduced us to the nurse on duty.

"I'll be right with you as soon as I give Zoey her insulin shot. She's a diabetic," the nurse explained.

I watched Nora slide a box of chocolates back into her bag. "Don't want to make her sick. I'll just give it to the nurse's station."

As we walked over to Zoey, I noticed a sixty something regal woman stand, and walk out of the shadows of the room toward us.

With an outreached hand, I said, "Oh hi, I'm Charla O'Hara and this is Nora Weston."

Nora handed her our card.

"I'm Zoey's mother, Virginia, she said. "Zoey this is Nora and Charla. They have come for a visit with you."

"Nice to meet you both. I hope we didn't come at a bad time," I said.

"No, no. There are rare good times. Zoey's so-so today. I don't know how much good she will be to your case, but all you can do is try."

"Thank you, Virginia."

We both sat down by Zoey and gently talked to her. She made eye contact a couple of times and blinked a time or two for an answer.

I showed her pictures of the different ladies from the Key Club. Zoey's eyes softened and she got a pleasant-half smile, like she recognized one or two of the past members. Thinking there was a light bulb going off, I decided to take a bigger step and show her two of the cold case ladies' pictures.

She clearly studied them. While she stared at the pictures, I took another step and mentioned The Cheer Up and the Key Club.

Zoey became extremely upset. She just kept shaking her head and saying "No. No. No. No," for several minutes.

Virginia went over to Zoey to try to settle her daughter down.

We slipped out the door and waited in the hallway until Virginia could come out and talk with us.

After five minutes, we could hear Zoey's sobs subside, and Virginia came through the door.

"We are so sorry that we upset Zoey."

"Don't worry about it. We're always protecting her, although we hope something will jar her memory. You know what happened, don't you?"

"Yes, we know she was shot in the head."

Virginia filled us in on the details on what happened.

"Apparently the intruder thought he shot Zoey in the back of the head, but just as he pulled the trigger, something startled her and she turned ever so slightly and went down. The intruder left her for dead. But as you can see," *pointing towards Zoey's room,* "she was shot in the temple above her ear. Her father and I found her, apparently right after it happened, and we went into action. He's a doctor and I'm a nurse. We worked fast and the paramedics got to her in record time, or we could have lost her." She wiped a tear away. "That was ten or eleven years ago. I lost all sense of time. Her father and I have since retired. We spend our time with Zoey now. He will be back in the next hour."

"She really looks good." *Other than a bit of a droopy eye, she looked normal.* "We just want to know if we can keep coming back. Maybe she will recognize someone in a picture that will trigger her memory," Nora said.

"Oh, she remembers. While she was still out she talked in her sleep. I try not to judge her, but she said unbelievable things. *Unbelievable things.*"

"So, then you know she belonged to the Key Club?" I asked.

"Yes, I know just enough to know what went on. I don't even want to talk about it."

So, with that we stepped back into Zoey's room to say good-bye. After all, she has feelings, and she can hear, and she can see. And someday soon, she will talk.

Virginia walked us out more for exercise than politeness.

"You know, Virginia, Zoey was one of five that were shot in the same way, possibly six. A couple of the dead ladies were found recently in cold case files with the police department. After investigating we found they have a connection to the Key Club. The others died on the spot. Zoey is the only one who survived."

"I didn't know if they were all connected. We DON'T want anyone to know she's here," she said.

"Nora and I have spent a good deal of time on this since one of our friends was found shot to death just weeks ago. Yesterday, we started questioning all over again. We just talked with a couple of Key Club ladies that stopped participating. They still couldn't shed any new light on the case. We feel strongly there is a connection that stems from the Key Club, we just haven't been able to put our finger on it."

"Was your friend a member of the Key Club?"

"Unfortunately, yes. We didn't have any idea she was involved until her sister gave us a journal to read. It's full of information about the dates, the sex, and so much more. It made us so sick reading it that we had to put it down and work from a murder board."

"A murder board?" she asked.

"It helps us stand back and look at the victims and all the players. We are hoping that something will pop out at us. Nothing has, yet."

"I need to get back to Zoey. I hope she will be able to help one day."

We turned to walk away, when something dawned on me that Virginia had said. I called out to her.

"Virginia, when you found your daughter that morning, did you see anything unusual or someone who didn't belong outside your home?"

"I don't recall. I'll put my thinking hat back on. I'll let you know if something comes up. See you tomorrow?"

"Tomorrow's good." I said. We left.

"You drive tomorrow," I shoved Nora gently, as we walked towards the car.

We headed for the city and pulled up in front of Nora's just as it was getting dark. The days were shorter and colder now that we are going into winter.

I shuddered when Nora opened the door and stepped out of the car to go to her prince charming, King of Clean, waiting at the front door. He threw up his hand in a wave to me, and then they embraced. I smiled and drove away.

CHAPTER 66

SINCE IT WAS LATE and I was too tired to cook anything, I opted to pick up sub sandwiches on the way home.

I pulled into the driveway behind Jackson's unmarked car. I smiled at the thought that Jackson beat me home. My cell rang a text alert. I looked down and saw that it was Daniel. *"My Lady, contrary to your belief, I was not following you. I had a client meeting about ten minutes down the road from where I saw you. Please rethink me. OXOX, Daniel*

"Yeah, I'll rethink you." I said out loud, and then I turned my cell off.

I walked through the back door proudly holding up my bag of subs.

"Oops!" I started laughing out loud.

Jackson had just spread out the subs, chips and cookies he had picked up. "Brewsky or soda?" He asked reaching in the fridge.

"Diet Dr. Pepper."

He looked up out of the fridge and laughed when he saw the duplication of subs.

"Great minds think alike," he said, setting our drinks down then grabbing me for a passionate kiss.

"Meow," Bozo announced himself, walking through the doggie door with baby Suzy's head trying to poke in behind Bozo.

"Oh, no, you don't," my neighbor said, grabbing the pug's hind end, and pulling her out just in time.

I watched her through our backdoor window walk back to her yard with the pug in tow.

"I bought Bozo a cup of spaghetti with just a bit of sauce," Jackson said.

"Aah, that's so sweet, Jackson."

He set the spaghetti down on the floor and sure enough, Bozo approached it with great care and nibbled slowly away as he purred.

"The lab's trying to get the footprint off the piece of glass you turned in, but it's not clear enough and they're having a problem identifying the actual make of the shoe," he said, taking a bite of his sub.

"I don't understand it. I could see the imprint with my naked eye."

"I know, but the imprint didn't come through good enough."

"Maybe they should use that new superglue vapor chamber I watched on the TV show, 'Forensic Files.' It does wonders."

"I will pass that along, Miss Detective. So how did your meeting go down in Pittsburg?"

"Oh, Jackson, it was so sad. I just don't understand how one person can do that to another."

"How bad is it?"

"Well, Zoey's hanging in there. Her mother said she has a good day ever, now and again, but I don't know what Zoey's good day consists of or what the heck is ever now and again."

"So, Zoey wasn't having a good day?"

"No, though we brought out a few pictures of some the Key Club ladies that were involved back then. Zoey gave a smile on two of them. Then, when I mentioned the "Key Club," *I put up the quote sign,* Zoey starting saying no, no, no over and over again until her mother calmed her down. She felt that Zoey remembered back then. She said when Zoey was in the hospital, she talked in her sleep and it was disturbing."

"But now Zoey doesn't talk much?" he asked.

"No. Her mother said she shut down right after she started coming around, probably because she remembered something too horrible. We're going to keep going back as much as we can, and hope beyond hope something will shake her up, that she'll be able to talk about what happened to her. We're going back tomorrow."

"I know I've told you and your sidekick before how much I, myself, and the police department appreciate your help . . ." he said.

"But?"

"But, now that you're certified Private Investigators" *he did the finger quote,* "I can't tell you enough to watch your step and watch the boundaries of the law," he half warned and half said with pride.

"Boundaries? You mean there are boundaries? What's this boundaries crap?" I teased.

He threw up his hands and said, "That's right, you know no boundaries,"

"I wouldn't feel right if I didn't mention again, how important it is that Zoey's name doesn't get out," I reminded him. "That's my only boundary. Her safety."

"Oh, Charla, unlike you, I know boundaries," but he smiled.

"Duh! You're the police, you have to, butttt, I don't," I snickered.

CHAPTER 67

NORA PICKED ME UP bright and early, and since neither of us had breakfast or coffee yet, we pulled into The Hot Cakes Café, which was located halfway from home and Amber Haven.

We ordered and acted like we never had biscuits and gravy before. *Delicious!* Melt in your mouth homemade biscuits and the tastiest sausage gravy. Closest to my grammy's that I ever had in a restaurant.

The server said, "This," she moved her hand over the menu, "is ninety-five percent homemade." Then she showed us the pie menu which was all homemade.

"Chocolate meringue pie is today's feature, followed by lemon meringue," the server said.

"I have died and gone to heaven," Nora spouted. "Chocolate meringue, not chocolate cream. Lemon or chocolate meringue . . . what to do?"

We asked the server to save us a whole chocolate meringue pie to go and we would pick it up on our way back through in a couple of hours.

"So far, this has been a productive day," I said, rubbing my belly.

"We haven't done anything, so how can it be a productive day?"

"We ate biscuits and gravy with a huge homemade cinnamon roll. Then we're stopping back by here to pick up homemade pie. All of this will have produced fat on my hips, productive!"

"God, I hate it when you talk logic," she laughed.

We were stuffed. We paid the server for our wonderful breakfast as well as for the pie. We tipped her and waddled out of the Hot Cake Café.

We pulled up at Amber Haven, where Virginia was waiting for us.

"I'm so excited. Zoey has been smiling a lot today and she put several sentences together. It's progress. Come on and see for yourself," she beamed.

We followed her to see Zoey, who was sort of talking to the nurse who was testing her blood sugar.

The nurse drew out insulin in a syringe, checked the amount, flipped it with her fingers to get any air bubbles out. She used an alcohol pad to swab Zoey's arm.

"Stick," the nurse said.

"Oh, ou . . . ch," Zoey said, with a halfcocked smile.

Virginia and the nurse looked at each other and started laughing.

"Well, my my," Virginia said, clearly happy, as she high fived the nurse.

"You have witnessed another first," she said to us.

We didn't want to jump right into questioning, so on a casual note we shared our experience at The Hot Cake Café and how great it was to visit with Zoey and her mother. Zoey raised her eyes, showing interest. We heard her do a little hmm.

Gently we started talking to her about the pictures of her friend's that we showed her yesterday. We did most of the talking, but by showing her the pictures again, it softened Zoey more today.

Then we pulled out Jordan's picture.

Zoey looked at it and appeared to study it, but nothing registered.

"Wait, I have a younger Jordan in here, somewhere," Nora said, going through her bag, pulling out another handful of pictures and bingo. "Do you recognize him?" Nora pointed at the picture.

Zoey took the picture out of Nora's hand and dropped it. Nora picked it up and handed it back to her. She studied it. After a couple of minutes, she smiled.

"You recognize Jordan?"

"Yeesh," Zoey slurred. "Ni. . .ce," she said hugging Jordan's photo.

"Yes, he's nice," Nora smiled.

Zoey had a spark now, but didn't resist Nora taking the photo away from her.

We decided to take a walk. *We needed to walk off the biscuits and gravy,* Zoey acted like she would like to go. With her mother's permission, Nora took one arm and I held her up with her other arm, and we walked up and down the hallway. Zoey was acting like she was enjoying herself. She got tired before we made it back to her room. The nurse, who had been watching us, hurried with a wheel chair, slid it under her and rolled her back to her room.

Virginia told us that this was another first for Zoey.

"Another first?" I asked.

"Yes, another first. She hasn't been out of her room without me or a nurse. I guess she just needed you two to open her eyes, sort of speak. I don't know what's going on, but I like it."

Virginia was just beaming.

"I'm glad we could help, but honestly we don't know what we did."

"I think it's because you are talking about things she knows and recognizes, but I ask you to please proceed with caution. I see improvement both yesterday and today, but use caution on trying to get her to talk too much, too soon."

"Virginia, we are under a deadline. I really would like to get relevant answers in the next few visits."

"I understand, but again, proceed with caution. I already see a big difference, but, be careful. Who knows, it may not take as long as first thought," Virginia said, "and thanks for that."

"We'll come back tomorrow, if it's okay with you?" I asked.

"It most certainly is and I might have you bring me a biscuit and gravy," Virginia giggled. "I bet Zoey would love some too. In fact, here's some money to pick up the B & G's."

"Oh heck, that's okay, we'll pay. That's the least we can do." Nora said, but still took the money when Virginia pushed it toward her a second time.

We drove back to the Hot Cake Café and picked up our chocolate meringue pie. The owner was nice enough to cut it perfectly down the middle. Nora ordered two B &G's to go for tomorrow.

"So, we're eating here tomorrow?" I asked her.

"Yes, we're coming back."

"Okay, but I'm getting oatmeal."

"Righttttt."

CHAPTER 68

ON OUR WAY BACK to see Zoey, we once again stopped at the Hot Cake Café; Nora got another B&G. I did not. I got two poached eggs, two slices crisp bacon, and whole grain toast, light on the butter.

"I can't believe you are being so good," she said.

"I know we're going to be back here a time or two more so, I don't want this investigation making me into a two ton Lizzy."

"How'd ya like that chocolate meringue pie, ladies?" The server from the day before asked, as she walked up to our table.

"We don't have any left. It was excellent," Nora said. "We had a slice and then kept whittling away until . . . well, I'm ashamed to say this, but Rick and I ate it all and wanted more."

"Jackson and I ate half of it and saved half for tonight. I know I compare your cooking to my mom's and my grams but it's true . . . can hardly tell the difference between yours and my mom's. That's the best compliment I could give you. Mom's is awesome."

"You saved some pie for tonight?" Nora asked unbelievingly. "If I'd known that, Rick and I would have been over to finish it off for you."

"Yeah, well, Jackson said he has plans for the pie and it doesn't include a fork."

"That's disgusting," Nora said. "You are going to waste that awesome pie."

"Get a grip, Nora. I waddled out of here yesterday, and I just couldn't handle anymore starch or carbs. The pie is safe."

"I knew that," she said, hitting at, but missing my arm.

We paid for our breakfast and paid for the B&G for Virginia and Zoey, then drove to Amber Haven.

I noticed how the scenery was changing so I said, "The fall colors are going to be beautiful in the next week or two. They'll be in full color by next weekend and then the leaves will fall off. It's going to be grey and dingy and that's depressing,"

Nora was half enjoying the drive until I mentioned the upcoming winter, then she started to get sad.

"Till it snows," I added. "Here we are. You almost passed it up."

"Snow, now that's depressing," she said, as she parked the Benz.

By now the staff at Amber Haven just looked at us, smiled and waved as we headed on down two long hallways to Zoey's room.

"Oh, Zoey, looks who's here. And look what they brought us," Virginia said, with a big hello smile.

"Actually, Zoey, your moth . . . er," I had to stop in mid-sentence.

Virginia shook her head no. Later she told me she wanted Zoey to think the food gift was from us and not ordered by her. I didn't understand why she just didn't say it was from her.

"Look, Zoey, the girls brought you biscuits and gravy. Your favorite"

The nurse heard and immediately tested Zoey's blood sugar.

"Ouch."

"Good to go, Zoey. Enjoy."

"Oh my," Virginia said. "I keep forgetting about Zoey being a diabetic."

"So how long has she been diabetic?" Nora asked.

"All her life."

"And you forgot? . . . Ohhhh, I didn't mean to sound sarcastic," Nora apologized.

"No, no you didn't. We watch her sugar intake, like candy, cake, cookies, soda and things like that, but I always forget the carbs aren't good for her either. Zoey loves carbs. Biscuits and gravy are her favorite."

"I didn't realize carbs would raise blood sugar," Nora said.

"Once and awhile won't hurt her. Carbs turn into sugar," I stated. "So, you do need to watch your intake of starch and carbs as well."

Virginia looked at me for a nanosecond and started to say something, but I interrupted her.

"I'm a nurse too," I said, as I slid the sera-foam plate across to Zoey who was sitting at the little kitchen table. Virginia joined her.

We chitchatted while they ate.

I explained, "Lately I've been doing more investigating than nursing, but I like both and both are rewarding."

Virginia said, "Sounds like you have a full schedule."

Nora chimed in, "Yes, we do."

"Are you a nurse also, Nora?" Virginia asked.

"No, my husband and I have a cleaning business."

"Do you clean homes?"

"No, mostly industrial businesses," Nora said.

Our attention turned to Zoey, who interrupted the conversation by trying to push away from the table and trying to say "good" while rubbing her tummy.

Virginia got her settled and we gently went into The Key Club homicides again.

You could tell Zoey was starting to relax with us as each visit went along. She smiled more and was putting more words together for sentences, although it was a slow process. She pointed to a picture and said a name, then looked at the next one.

We showed her more pictures and she seemed to be holding her own, but her mother had warned not to push, and we didn't want to overstay our welcome, so we told Zoey we had to go. She seemed upset, but we reassured her that we would back.

Zoey reached for us. We each leaned down and hugged her.

"You have just witnessed another first. She has never reached for anyone before this minute," Virginia said, with excitement of her daughter's progress.

Then Zoey stood up on her own, got her balance, and started walking with us. Her mother beamed. "Another first," she whispered.

Zoey was tired from our visit so she didn't walk far. The nurse slid a wheelchair under her and we said good bye.

✦⟫⟫⟪⟪✦

We went back to Amber Haven a couple more times and each time was better than the last.

With Virginia's permission, we wanted to press a little harder.

This time we brought different pictures with us and had a few more questions to ask Zoey.

She beamed when she noticed us come through the door. We did our usual greeting before gently going into the things we had talked about on our last few visits.

We showed Zoey a couple of new photos of some of the guys that were around back when she was involved in the Key Club, that we found in Louise's ledger.

"Zoey, here's a couple of different pictures of a guy that seems to be a fan favorite, who still goes to The Cheer Up. Here's a younger one of him and one of how he looks now. Not much difference. He's still very much into the Key Club activities. Take your time and look at him, see if he looks familiar," Nora said, as she handed her the pictures.

Zoey slowly looked at each picture and after a few seconds of staring at them, horror came into her eyes and you could see her make a connection. She started shaking and stuttering. "Himmm, himmm shooo, sho, shot meee. Dammmmmon."

"Oh, my God," her mother said, pulling the photos of Daniel out of Zoey's hands to look at them.

Virginia shoved the pictures to me. "Take them away."

I took the pictures, stuffing them into my coat pocket. I leaned over and put my arms around Zoey, holding and rocking her, but I was torn between holding her and wanting to go call Jackson.

"I am so sorry, Zoey. I am so sorry," I cried with her.

We hung onto each other rocking and crying, I looked over at Nora and Virginia who were now holding onto each other and crying as well.

"Zoey, I am so, so sorry to put you through this, but now with your help we can put this douche bag away where he belongs. We can't thank you enough," I said, still holding and rocking her.

I finally stood. I looked down at Zoey who looked like she had relief coming across her face.

"Are you alright?" I asked her.

"Ye . . . s, ye . . . s. Think . . . Th . . . ank you."

Because we didn't want to be rude by just leaving after finding out the horrible truth, we hung out for a while longer, trying to comfort both Zoey and her mother. I was feeling the pressure and needed to call Jackson.

Though it appeared they had both found peace, Virginia and Zoey were holding onto each other.

Controlling our anxiousness, we said our good-byes and walked out of the nursing home door, then busted into a run to the car.

"I knew it. Daniel. Oh, my God, it's Daniel." I bent over, holding my stomach, and started to sob.

Nora put her arm around me and said, "We'll get him. And it should be easy the way he's always around you. Piece of cake! He's a cooked goose."

CHAPTER 69

TAKING A DEEP SIGH, I again said, "Oh, my God. I knew there was a connection," I was still holding my stomach and now pacing, pacing, pacing. "I need to call Jackson to get the ball rolling. Daniel needs to be arrested, ASAP. The second thing I want to know, how many times Zoey was with Daniel, then Louise, or Lori Janesen and the other two. How does it tally up? Why them and not the rest of the ladies he's whipped? What about Myra Cunningham? How does she fit in?"

"Charla . . . slow down. Your head's going to fly off with all the thinking you're doing. The spinning is making my head hurt just listening to you and watching your brain work. Call Jackson."

"Okay, I'll call Jackson and you call Jordan for the tally."

She walked a little ways from me and called Jordan, while I called Jackson. Jackson answered on the first ring.

"What's up, babe?"

"I know the killer. You have to go after him. He's dangerous and he's my stalker."

"What? You're saying it's Daniel."

"That's exactly what I am saying. Daniel Nielsen's the killer."

"Okay, Charla, this is what I want you to do. Don't come back the same way you went. Actually, wait right where you are. I'm coming to get you. Step back into Amber Haven and hang out until I get there. I'm sending a patrol car there as we speak. They'll watch after you until I get there."

"Okay, but you're scaring me."

"You should be scared. It's Daniel and he's obsessed with you. I'm on my way."

"Jackson, I think it's wise to get away from Amber Haven. I don't want any harm to come to our witness, Zoey. We'll head for the Hot Cake Café and wait."

"Smart. I'll see you there."

"Jordan's calling me back after he checks the information," Nora said.

We drove to the Hot Cake Café and parked in the lot. We got out to stretch our legs.

Nora got a call. "It's Rick," she said, putting her earpiece into her ear while she took the call. She was busy talking and throwing her hands around, no doubt telling Rick everything we'd just found out to this point.

I called my mother for a minute and explained a fraction of what was going on. I told her I would fill her in later. As I hung up, I turned to see if Nora was through talking. I didn't see her. I walked toward the Hot Cake Café, and as I came around to her side of the car, she was lying on the ground.

"Nora, Nora . . ." And the lights went out.

CHAPTER 70

I SLOWLY OPENED MY eyes and whispered, "Nora, are you . . . o . . . k . . . ?"

"Oh, my lady, you're awake. Welcome to our new home."

"Wha . . . ?" I was lying on a sofa. I tried to sit up while holding my aching head that was spinning around. My eyes were fuzzy and my ears muffled. I could hear talking but it sounded distant. I couldn't figure out what the voice was saying.

Finally, I heard faintly. "I built this house as a spec. for an older gentleman as a futuristic style home."

What home? What gentleman? I didn't understand. No, that's the problem, I didn't understand, but the voice kept talking.

"He had a grandmother who had Alzheimer's and a bad case of Sundowners. The sun went down and the grandmother's agitation went up," the voice said, offering me his hand to get up.

What's he saying. Alzheimer's?

Pushing his hand away, but hitting air, I said, "Wha, what?" Again, I held my head, trying to sit up and understand what on earth he was saying. He's just rattling on and on. I fell back down on the sofa.

The voice went in and out of my poor head, but he kept talking, talking . . . "His father was in the beginning stages of Alzheimer's. He had fear his father would lash out and start hitting someone or burst out in a non- stop verbal cursing fit, so he decided to build this house where the sun shined all the time.

Okay he needs to shut up. But he kept going on and on.

"The poor gent's airplane went down before he could take possession. His parents were with him. So, I kept it for myself. Little did I know that you and I would be living in it."

He was still reaching for me to help me up.

"Wha . . . what?" I said, still pushing his hands away. "What are you saying? I don't understand what you're saying."

"You'll understand when your head clears."

"I'm going to be sick," finally sitting up. My head was dizzy but my vision was slowly coming into focus. My brain started to connect, then it dawned on me that the voice that rattled on and on was, oh, my God, Daniel!

"Here use this," he said, handing me a wastebasket.

He left and came back once again, reaching to help me up. I refused his help.

"Here drink this. It will help you wake up and then you'll understand," he said.

I took the glass and started to throw it at him, when I realized whatever it was would be better than this cotton in my mouth. I sipped it. It did help me come around pretty quickly and things started clearing up. Even my tummy settled down.

"What's this stuff? What are we doing here?" I asked.

"First, this *stuff* is a concoction that I made to counter the chloroform I unfortunately had to use on you. Don't worry, I didn't use much. You'll be fine. I didn't use much on your buddy either, and she's going to be all right, as well."

"Nora?"

"Yes, Nora's going to be just fine. Honestly, I don't understand how you put up with her. She's such a pain in the ass. I wanted to get rid of her so many times. Butttt, she's your best friend, so I stopped short . . . every time. Let me tell you, it would have been easier pursuing you without her always being there interfering. I really don't like her. I came this close," he said, holding his thumb and finger two inches apart, "to finishing her off. This close," he repeated.

"Where is she? How?" I asked, looking around.

"I happened on you by chance. I, however, was prepared as it was my plan to take you at some point. Sooner than later."

"Where are we?" I half yelled.

"My lady, you are not listening . . . but . . . no problem. As I was saying, Nora is, I am sure, doing just fine. By now your detective has reached her." *He took a deep breath.* "This is our new home. Let me show it to you."

Our new home. I don't think so.

As he tried to pull me up on my feet, I started wheeling my arms and managed to connect a couple of left hooks on his face, only I was still in a weakened stage and I barely touched him. *Too bad.* I feared for my life when the voice of reason connected with me. Nora's voice said, *"Charla, you can do anything to this guy and he will just say that's ok my lady. He won't hurt you."*

Feeling brave, I shoved him away from me and managed to get up right. I felt it best to play along, for now. *I cannot, and will not show fear, only anger.*

Then I remembered how many times I cried myself to asleep with my gun under my pillow wanting him to stop this crazy obsession he has for me.

"You're in deep thought, my lady. I pray it's about me," he said, reaching for my hand.

"Oh, it's about you," I said sarcastically, slapping his hand away and managing to take a step.

"In time my lady, you will come around," he said, sure of himself. *Delusional!*

He motioned for me to follow him. Reluctantly, I did.

Proudly he said, "Here is the state-of-the-art kitchen. As you can see it has all stainless-steel appliances, a restaurant size refrigerator, and a top of the line electric range. I know a lot of people prefer a gas range, but this is an all-electric house." He paused, looking around the kitchen, "Look at the beautiful granite countertops. I got the top of the line cooking utensils, fine china, crystal, and all the things I knew you would like. Look, I have a fully stocked refrigerator and pantry," he said, opening the refrigerator and pantry doors.

For Pete sake, what's he doing? I don't give a rat's ass about this kitchen, this house, or him. Leaning against the counter, still trying to find my sea legs, I said, "Aren't you afraid this stuff will spoil?"

"No. The non-perishables will keep, and, of course the frozen food will remain frozen. While you were out on the sofa, I stopped by the store and bought eggs, milk and such. "I hope you're happy about the selection I have chosen for you."

"Whatever! If you're into that kind of thing." I said, sarcastically, with a lot of anger.

"This will go better if you lighten up on your attitude. I know this will work, but only if you co-operate."

"REALLY? You knocked me out. You took me against my will. You imprisoned me AND it will only work if I CO-OPERATE. How dare you!"

Ignoring me, he said, "You're getting tired, testy. Let me show you to the bedroom." he pointed in the direction he wanted me to go. "You need to rest."

I gulped, and said, "Really. You think I need rest. I just came to. Thanks to you, I had rest."

He took my arm and led me along for the tour, but I clenched my fist so hard I thought I felt blood.

"I realize this was sudden, and you're probably not ready to share our bed . . . yet. So, here's your room. I hope you find it to your liking."

There will never be any bed sharing with you. Never.

He opened the door to *my* bedroom. I must say it was beautiful. All my favorite colors. But I would never tell him that. I looked around and shrugged. "It's alright."

"Look," he said, opening the closest doors.

"Step back, Jack . . . Are these my clothes?" I asked, clenching my fist, again.

"Yes, some are and some are brand new. I took the liberty of stepping into your home while you slept, and I watched you and Jackson while you were sleeping. I pulled out my favorite outfits of yours. Look, here's the red dress you wore the night I first laid eyes on you."

Note to self . . . Remind me never to put that dress on again. Burn it! Wait! In my house watching us sleep. I will get him back for the intrusion. How dare that slim ball.

I fought back tears and turned my head so he couldn't see my weakness in crying. I just couldn't show fear. But the anger was building and I had to be tough.

He opened up the chest of drawers.

"I bought you brand new underwear and night clothes. As you can see. I have the red lace underwear that you had in your drawer and a nightie with robe that you had on the back of the bathroom door. I took the liberty to wash them."

"You shouldn't have, Daniel" I said, rolling my eyes and thinking, *no you really shouldn't have, you delusional piece of perverted trash.* I did a smug smile.

"I hope you like everything. I really tried hard to get what you like. Here, come and see the rest of our home."

Looking around, I could tell I couldn't escape. Since I didn't have anything else to do, I followed him as he showed me every nook and cranny. One problem I noticed right off the bat, and it didn't take a brain surgeon to figure it out . . . there were no doors going out. No front door where a front door should be.

"I noticed there aren't any doors to go outside. How do we leave?"

"Oh, my lady, that's the best part. We don't."

"What on earth? What do you mean we don't leave?"

"I should rephrase what I just said. You don't leave. I have to go to work."

"I'm a prisoner?"

"No, my lady, I wouldn't say you're a prisoner."

"If I can't leave, and you have me locked up here all day and all night, then I am a prisoner."

"I will give you a phone to make a call to your parents and one call to that pest, Nora."

"So, you're throwing me a bone."

'No, no bone, just a nice gesture."

"Okay, let me call them now, so they'll know I'm fine."

"In due time, my lady, in due time. I have a special phone that will only call the two outgoing numbers I have programmed, no incoming calls. And no tracing of calls is possible. You can call Nora and your parents every other day for five minutes each."

"Well, I guess, thanks for that," but I was thinking, *delusional jerk, you just screwed up.*

"Now, now my lady, no need in getting upset, yet again."

"I'm just trying to understand the ground rules of your house."

"Our house, need I remind you."

"What's out here?" I asked, walking to a window.

"Your view."

"I have a view?" I pulled the curtains back and clearly it was a remote control outside scenery. Lights would come up in the morning and go down in the evening. Clever. It's early evening now. I think.

"So, you've thought of everything."

"I've had time planning our life together. And thanks to the creativity of the gentleman who wanted sunlight for his father, voila, here we are."

"Just so you know, I know you're into dominant sex. Whips and things. I'm not."

"My lady, I didn't think you were. When you are ready, I will make sweet unbridled love to you. You are worthy of the best love making ever. You will be very satisfied. Only skanks need dominance. And you my dear are no skank."

Gulp! I just stared at him, then looked around when I saw a slight deviation of the wall. "What's over here?" I said, rushing toward the wall where I gave a slight push and discovered it opened into the garage where Daniel's car was parked. But I could see no garage doors going out.

"So, if there is no way out, or apparently in, how did your car get in here?"

"Oh, there is an in and out. It's a secret and you may never know. It depends on if I can win your love whether or not you will win the secret."

Knowing I will never learn to love Daniel, I said softly, "I will never learn to love you."

He just leaned against the wall and stared at me. "I'm patient, I pray you will."

Knowing this argument could go on and on, I decided I was hungry.

"I feel like a hamburger. How about we go get one?"

"Nice try, my lady. The refrigerator is full."

"I don't feel like cooking," I said.

"That's fine. I will fix us something. I love to cook."

"Of course, you do." I sat and watched Daniel play chef. I must say it smelled unbelievable. At least, I wouldn't starve while I'm a prisoner. Of course, I wouldn't let on how great it smelled.

"How about a cold beer?" I asked.

"How about a nice Pinot Noir?" he countered.

"Chilled?"

"I am sure you know most wines are served room temperature," he scolded.

"Yes, I know, but I like most wines chilled."

Daniel pulled out a cold Heineken and a glass. He set them down in front of me.

"Lime?" he asked, smiling.

"Why, yes, lime would be nice."

He sliced a lime and rubbed it around the rim of the glass.

I took the lime and dropped into the bottle and took a long draw.

"Boy, that hits the spot."

He just looked at me and probably wondered what I was going to do to the hamburger.

"Here you go, my lady. A cheese hamburger made to order."

He passed the burger to me on a China plate, followed by the condiments to dress my burger on another china plate.

Hmmm, I thought as I looked at the knife he had just passed me, *No, not sharp enough*. I spread mayo on both sides of the bun, but used my fingers to place a piece of lettuce and a slice of tomato on one side of the bun and the cheeseburger on the other. I slammed the two sides together and had a big bite.

"Hmm, good." I said, still chewing.

"Chips?" he asked.

"I don't suppose you have fries with ketchup?"

"Next time," he said.

"Okay, I guess chips will do."

Daniel joined me. He dressed his burger, cut it in two and sipped his wine.

I took a long pull of my cold beer, then burped.

"Well, Charla, you are trying hard to be inadequate, but we both know it's an act."

"You're half right. Hamburgers aren't like eating a seven-course meal. It's a hamburger. You take it in both hands and dig in, therefore a beer goes well and I'm about ready for a second." I held my almost-empty bottle toward him.

Daniel got up and got me another bottle and a slice of lime that he stuck into the bottle.

"Thanks," I said handing him my now-empty bottle.

Daniel started cleaning up the kitchen while I wandered around, looking for an escape route.

It didn't matter where I wandered, as I couldn't go anywhere. I was stuck in a luxurious four-bedroom prison. I pulled back the curtains and saw the auto daylight turning into dusk. I couldn't wait for the moon to come out or the sun to come up. This was going to be a very, very long night.

CHAPTER 71

THE OFFICERS FOUND NORA on the ground beside her car. The Hot Cake Café patrons couldn't see her lying on that side of the car. One of the officers found her as he was checking the perimeter, walking from one side of the car to the other. He yelled out to his partner, "Over here. She's over here."

He stooped down, shook her and she moaned. "Are you alright?" he asked.

Moaning, she still had a smart mouth. "Yeah, right, I decided to take a nap . . . ! Do I look all right? Get me up, get me the hell up," Nora demanded.

"Well, no, ma'am, you don't look all right," he heaved her up off the ground

"What happened?' she asked, leaning on the officer. She touched her head that had a tiny stream of blood trickling down from her hairline.

"Looks like someone drugged you and knocked you out." He looked at her head and said, "Whoever did this hit your head or you hit it on the ground when you fell."

"You think?" she said, sarcastically, taking a long pause. "Wait, where's Charla?"

"I was just about to ask you about Miss O'Hara. She isn't here," he stated.

"What? She's not here?"

"No."

"Let go of me." she said, pushing the young officer away from her. "I have to call Jackson."

He opened the car door for her to sit down.

"Where's my cell?"

The officer looked around the car and found it just under the car by the front tire, mashed!

"It's broken," she said, thoroughly upset. "The buffoon made sure it wasn't going to work!" She said, frustrated.

Here, use mine," The officer handed her his phone.

"It's dead." She said, in a panic.

The officer pulled out his nifty charger and attached it to the phone. Voila, it powered up.

He stood by her while she dialed Jackson. The other officer ran into the café looking for Charla and for help.

Shortly, the other officer came running out with a server and the cook following close behind. The officer yelled, "Charla O'Hara isn't in there."

"Well, duh," Nora mumbled. "Charla wouldn't just leave me here." Then Jackson answered.

"Jackson," . . . *Nora's voice dropped,* "Something has happened to Charla."

Jackson pulled over to the side of the road and sat there, stunned.

"Jackson, Jackson. Are you there? Charla's missing."

Jackson snapped to. "What did you say? Charla's missing?" Jackson was reassessing what he had just heard. "So, Charla's missing."

"Yes."

"Missing?"

"For Pete's sake, Jackson, get a grip. Missing."

"Then she's not dead. She's missing."

"No, I don't think so. I think Daniel found her. Looks like he surprised us. He knocked me out and now Charla's gone."

"I'll be there in a minute." He took a deep breath, pulled himself together, looked both ways and pulled back out in traffic.

One of The Hot Cake Café servers came out with a glass of ice water and a cup of coffee. Hanging her head, Nora took the coffee and passed on the water. She looked at the server and said graciously, "Thanks."

More officers drove up and conducted a search in and around the area to see if there was any evidence left behind.

Jackson pulled up after breaking the speed limit with his lights and siren blaring. He made it in record time with Zack hot on his tail.

He put his arms around Nora, who was now sobbing heavily.

"Oh, Jackson I know he's got her. I told her over and over again I had her six. But I didn't."

Then he pushed Nora away at arm's length and looked her in the eyes.

"Nora, it's Charla. She's a survivor. She will survive. She will find a way. We have to hold it together and help find her. And we will," then he pulled Nora back to him and hugged her again.

◆❯❯❮❮◆

ON THE WAY BACK to the city, Nora rode with Jackson, crying all the way. Jackson's partner, Zack drove Nora's car and one of the officers drove Zack's car back.

Nora went home to the comfort of Rick's arms. Jackson and Zack stayed back at the 405 where they met with other detectives and off duty police officers who wanted to help in any way they could. It was very comforting to Jackson and gave him hope. *After all, it's Charla.*

The first thing the detectives were going to do was find out all they could about Daniel Nielsen.

Everyone got their assignments. While some detectives and officers surrounded Daniel's home, others went to his place of business. Jackson and Zack started their interrogation at The Cheer Up.

Though it wasn't a Key Club night, The Cheer Up was very busy and loud. Jackson had to yell over the crowd to get Jordan's attention.

When Jordan approached Jackson and Zack, he could tell something terrible had happened. He took the two detectives back to his office.

"What happened?" Jordan asked.

Jackson, with the help of Zack, explained.

Jordan said, "You know, I was just talking to Nora a couple of hours ago. She asked me to check out how many times each of the victims had been with Daniel. I was about to call her and tell her what I found out, but since you're here, I'll tell you what I figured out."

"Go ahead and fill us in," Zack said.

Impatient, Jackson started drumming his fingers on Jordan's desk. Jordan looked down at Jackson's hands, realizing Jackson was anxious and probably didn't even know he was drumming. When Jackson noticed what he was doing, he dropped his hands in his lap.

"Go ahead," Jackson said, encouraging Jordan.

Jordan laid out the notes in front of the detectives and proceeded to tell them, "Each of the five women had five dates with Daniel. I don't know why he allegedly killed them after five dates, but five seemed to be the common denominator. Going through the files, they died within a few weeks after their fifth date with him, but no one had any idea he was involved. Allegedly." He said, being careful of his assumption.

"Oh, we are 100% sure he's the one. I'll update Nora on your finding," Jackson said, getting up and extending his hand to Jordan.

"Nora's all right, isn't she?"

"Yes, she is. She's tough. Thanks for all your help," Jackson said, pulling his hand out of Jordan's.

"I'm glad to help in any way you need me." Jordan took in a long breath, and then said, "I know Charla will be alright. I probably shouldn't say this to you, since you're Charla's boyfriend . . . but I don't think Daniel will hurt her. He seems to think he's really in love with her. He met her and he stopped everything else to concentrate on her. She'll be fine."

Jackson gave a long cold stare at Jordan, then said, "Thanks again," as he and Zack turned to walk out of Jordan's office.

When they approached the car, Jackson gave Zack a quizzical look. Zack got into the driver's side, forcing Jackson to get in the passenger seat. He looked over to Jackson and said, "You're so stressed that I thought I should drive." Then he said, "Interesting and weird. Sorry, man."

Jackson shook his head. "Yeah, weird. Punch it, Zack."

Zack hit the gas.

CHAPTER 72

NORA, WHO COULDN'T JUST sit there, needed to be proactive. She decided to call Rita to see if she was willing to help her find Charla, be her backup and help with the investigation. Nora couldn't stand the thought of being alone, because all she did was cry. She knew she would show a strong front if she had a temporary sidekick. She needed to be "Tough as nails."

Rita agreed and said, "I'm happy to help even though I've never investigated a thing, not even what dog left poop on my lawn. But I'm willing to do all I can to find Charla."

Nora picked her up and they headed for the Writer's Club, which just happened to have a meeting that day.

Nora spoke to the group . . .

"Ladies, it hasn't been mentioned in the news yet, but what I am about to tell you is on the low down, so I ask you to keep it classified for now."

They anxiously waited her to say more, but it was like Nora had a hard time talking about Charla. The club first looked at Nora, then Rita, then back to Nora, who finally pulled the lump out of her throat and continued.

"It's not a 100% fact, but what we know in our gut, and what the police feel," *she sighed* . . . "we feel that Daniel Nielsen has Charla. He's obsessed with her. He knocked me out and took Charla yesterday. That's our gut feeling, but, for sure, Charla's missing."

You could hear a pin drop while everyone looked around at each other.

"I am asking you to keep your eye out for Daniel. We think he has Charla hidden. If someone sees him, call the police and stay put. Do nothing but watch, and watch from a distance. He's dangerous"

Nora handed out her and Jackson's cell numbers.

The Writer's Club ladies were clearly upset and some were even at a loss for words. After thinking about what they just heard for a nanosecond, they said they were willing to help any way they could, then after looking at a street map, they decided to pair up and hit the streets with eyes wide open, searching for their friend and Writer's Club groupie.

✦❯❯ ❮❮✦

"THE NEXT STOP IS Daniel's home. Are you up for it, Rita?" Nora said.

"I'll do whatever it takes to find Charla. So yeah, I'm up for it."

Pulling up in Daniel's driveway, they noticed all of the police action going on in and around his house.

"Donnie!"

"What?" Rita said.

"You remember Donnie. She's an incompetent investigator. She botched the evidence from every crime scene she ever worked, she's an airhead and Charla doesn't like her, so I don't either. One more thing . . . she's Jackson's ex-partner and his ex-partner because she's incompetent." Nora pointed toward Donnie. "Remember she messed up with Louise's computer?"

"Are you sure that's why Charla doesn't like her? Because she's a good-looking gal!"

Nora looked at Rita like Rita had a screw loose. "Yes, if not for her makeup, she's ugly."

The two of them traipsed up to Daniel's door. Ringing the bell, Donnie saw Nora and started running up the steps.

"I thought I would hang out with you, Nora."

"NO!"

"But . . ."

"But nothing," Nora reiterated. "What are you doing here?"

"I volunteered to help."

"Well, don't help. Go back home."

By then, Vivian Nielsen answered the door with tears in her eyes and recognized Nora. She held the door open for her and Rita to come in. Donnie followed. *Damn!*

"The police have been here since last night. They are waiting for Daniel to show up. But he won't. I am so embarrassed. "

Nora pulled a Charla, and touched Vivian's arm, showing trust and caring. After all, it wasn't Vivian's fault what Daniel was or what he'd done.

Vivian sat down and invited Nora and Rita to sit, too. Nora introduced Rita and explained who she was. Donnie stood there, hovering over them, and trying to hear every word.

Looking at Rita, Vivian said, "I am so sorry that Daniel killed your sister." She hung her head and whispered in a distraught way, "if he did." Raising her head, she looked at Rita who had tears in her eyes., "I'm sorry for your loss." Rita couldn't respond.

"Vivian, did you have any idea what Daniel was capable of?" Nora asked.

"No, not until lately. He has been so preoccupied for weeks now. He . . . he's been mean to me."

"Mean? Did he hit you?"

"No, no . . . well . . ." Vivian hung her head yet again. *I can't even hold my head up from all the shame my husband has caused. The sick bastard.* She thought to herself.

"Well, what?"

"Well, he's agitated all the time. Lately, when he comes home, he pulled me to the bedroom and pushed me onto the bed and . . . and he does terrible things to me. He told me I had to like it. He whipped me." She said, looking around to see who might have heard her.

"Whipped you?"

"I'm so embarrassed . . . he's into dominant sex and, yes, he whipped me," She said.

"Oooh-o . . . So, he's just been into dominant sex with you lately?" Donnie said, interrupting.

"Yes, and I hate it. He left marks on my back. It's so degrading."

"What else have you noticed different about him?" Nora asked, glaring at Donnie.

"He seemed to talk out loud or mumble all the time. He's gone so much, and just left at the drop of a thought."

"Did you know he's been following Charla around and showing up wherever she was?"

"No, not at all. I just found out. I knew something was bothering him, but, of course, he wouldn't talk to me about it. That poor woman. I hope he doesn't hurt her."

"No, I don't think he'll hurt her. I don't mean to sound insensitive, but did you know he texted her all the time that he loved her, he couldn't wait to see her. He has sent her extravagant gifts. He's obsessed with her. He showed up just about everywhere she was." Nora said, looking at the diamond bracelet on Vivian's wrist.

"Oh, Vivian, I don't mean, I mean." Nora stumbled with words, touching Vivian's hand.

Vivian pulled her hand away and hung her head. She started sobbing. "He only married me for my family's money, to further his career. He loved just enough, but not good enough. It's always been that way. I tried and tried to get him to love me completely. He has always been emotionally distant. I just don't do it for him. But, but your friend Charla . . . I've seen her and she's gorgeous. I watched the way he looked at her, the way he always tried to touch her. I heard how she talked to him, when she was here. I don't think she would take his crap. She looked like she would stand up to him. I suppose that's what he needs."

"Mommy, Mommy," Stone tried to get his mother's attention.

Vivian pulled her son close and asked, "What is it, Stone?"

"Daddy didn't go get my ball . . . He was coming back from Scott's backdoor . . ."

Nora called Jackson immediately and filled him in. Hanging up, she said, "Vivian, can I see Daniel's gun collection?"

Wiping her eyes, she said, "Why, yes, but he has sold several, or so he said. Maybe he just took them with him."

"Does he have a list of his gun collection?" Nora asked.

Vivian stood and started walking to Daniel's office. Nora, Rita, and Donnie followed her to the gun cabinet.

"It's locked. He keeps his gun serial numbers, makes and models list in there. See, you can barely see the edge of the paper sticking out," she pointed.

Donnie, forever playing the big shot, called an officer over and asked Vivian's permission to get into the cabinet.

"Donnie, wait for Jackson," Nora warned.

Donnie said, "No, no I got this." She wrote into her notebook, then asked Vivian to sign for the permission. *In writing.*

Nora wasn't sure that was legal, but it was done now, and Rita and Nora witnessed the whole thing.

Jackson arrived. Holding out his hand to Vivian Nielsen said, "Nice to see you again, Mrs. Neilsen. I'm sorry it's under such circumstances."

She smiled weakly, "I'm sorry Detective, about Charla. I liked her."

"You mean like . . ." Nora corrected. "Vivian, would you mind if Stone tells Jackson what he said about Daniel coming from the Cunningham's?" Nora asked.

"Stone . . ." She called out to her son.

Stone came running in, "Yeah, Mommy?"

Kids are so clueless sometimes, Nora thought.

"Stone, will you tell Detective Jackson what you said a minute ago, about Daddy coming across from Scott's?"

Jackson smiled. "It's Det. Jackson Boxley," and handed her his card.

"Sorry, Detective," she said, fumbling with his card. "So, tell him, Stone."

Stone told all he could remember about that day. Jackson took a lot of interest in Stone's words.

Jackson and Nora stepped aside and Jackson said, in a loud voice, "Now we know Daniel killed Myra Cunningham, we just need a motive."

Nora agreed, "And evidence would be good."

Jackson called in for a search warrant. "The warrant will be here directly," he said.

He told the officer who was still trying to get into the gun cabinet to stop and wait for the warrant.

Jackson studied Donnie and with nod of his head, motioned her away from the gun cabinet. Her shoulders slumped and with a sigh, rolled her eyes and stepped back.

Vivian's parents entered the house and looked around at all the chaos. Pebbles let go of her gram's hand and ran to her mother with eyes wide open, looking at all the commotion going on.

Stone came around the corner from the kitchen and jumped into his papa's arms. For a minute Vivian felt a touch of normalcy.

The warrant arrived and the officer continued to try to get into the gun cabinet, while Jackson and Zack went into Daniel's closet. They pulled out all of Daniel's shoes. Jackson spotted a blue sweat shirt with a slight hole in it. He pulled it off the hanger, shoving it into an evidence bag. Zack helped him put all the shoes into several evidence bags. Jackson looked at Donnie, and then looked away, deciding he would just hold on to the evidence bags and give them to the crime lab himself when they got there. He carried all the bags into Daniel's office, set them down, and. started going through Daniel's desk. He bagged Daniel's computer. He stuck a stack of files in a bag and gathered all blueprints that were rolled up on the desk into evidence bags. He pulled open a desk drawer and bagged everything he found that could possibly be a clue, including flashdrives.

Finally, the officer got the gun cabinet opened. He yelled, "Detectives."

Jackson pulled an officer into the office to stand guard over all the evidence bags while he, Zack, and Nora with Rita, went running into where the officer stood, pleased with himself for finally breaking the code on the gun cabinet.

Jackson first went through the guns, matching them against the list and checking if they were loaded, before he bagged and handed them to Zack. Jackson took the list of serial numbers and descriptions and slid it into his pocket.

The police and forensic techs were dusting and going through things with a fine-tooth comb.

Finally, after they collected all they could, they packed up and hauled it all back to forensics.

Jackson put a rush on all of it. Speed was of the essence. Charla was still alive and everyone had to act with haste to get her free from a madman.

CHAPTER 73

I CLIMBED OUT OF bed and stepped into the shower, using the lavender bath soap Daniel had provided. I washed my hair in the shampoo he brought from my own bathroom.

I pulled open the chest of drawers and elected to wear my own underwear. I threw open the closet doors and again elected to wear my own clothes, jeans and a tee. I put on my tennis shoes, unlocked the door and ventured through it, walking softly. I wandered into the kitchen, starving, though Daniel had a small stocked refrigerator in my room. *Why not?*

I entered the kitchen where scrambled eggs, sausage links, and toast awaited on a lidded warming platter. A couple of different pastries were sitting on a fine china platter with a lid over it.

I frowned when I read his note.

"My Lady, sorry I couldn't join you for your first breakfast in our new home. Next time. Meantime, enjoy the breakfast I prepared for you. I shall return a little later. Unfortunately, I have to go into work today. Learn to love me, my lady. Soon, D"

"Okay D, I won't." I said out loud, tossing the prepared food in the garbage disposal.

I pulled out the eggs and a brand-new roll of sausage to prepare my own breakfast.

After I finished, I cleaned up the dishes by placing the dirty china in the new stainless-steel dishwasher. I wiped down the electric range and counter-top.

"Geez, I hope fine china can go into the dishwasher. Hmph. We'll see," again talking out loud.

I went into the TV room to watch the news. *Hmmm, no news on me.*

I pulled the curtains back and saw that it was raining, only to remember that it was a video. Lightening was a nice touch.

I turned on music with surround sound and noticed all the video cameras watching me.

Even when Daniel wasn't with me, he was with me. I ignored them.

I tried all the windows and walked along the walls pushing and pulling, checking out any give. Nothing, but I wouldn't stop trying.

I went back to *my* bedroom and stood in front of the window. I felt safe there, as safe as anyone could under the circumstances. There were no video cameras in this room. I picked up the small wooden chair and hit the window as hard as I could. The chair broke, but the window didn't.

I wandered into the dining room. Whoa, a cell-phone. I picked it up and headed back to my room.

I turned it on and checked it out. Two numbers were programmed into the phone as promised.

I called my parents first.

I rattled off as fast as I could, "Hi, there. I have exactly five minutes and then the phone cuts off. I just want you to know I love you and I am all right. Daniel's treating me good, but won't let me out of his sight. Call Jackson and tell him I can only make a call to you or Nora every other day for five minutes. If he needs me to know anything, he can let you or Nora know to pass it along to me day after tomorrow or have him stand by. Tell Jackson I love him. I know Jackson and Nora are working hard to find me. I can tell you I am in a four-bedroom new house inside, what I think is a warehouse. I can't figure out how to get out of here."

"Charla baby, we love you too. I will pass this along. I will be better prepared for questions day after tomorrow. I will have Jackson standing by. Charla . . . BEEEEP! The call was cut off. Five minutes as promised. I wonder how Daniel pulled off having a controlled phone. *I guess money can buy anything.*

I called Nora. She sounded shocked. I explained the cell phone deal to her.

"Tell Jackson the situation. I know you are doing all you can. I think the next call I will call you, then my parents. I will fill you in and then finish with my parents. You can compare notes. You can call my mother when we're done. There's a remote video on the outside of this house showing sunrises and sunsets with all the weather in between. Funny thing, the trees don't bend and the leaves don't fall. Is it raining? Oh, never mind."

I explained to her the living arrangements and what I thought about the whole thing.

Nora said, "Hold on. Daniel killed Myra Cunningham. Jordan found out about the four ladies killed plus Zoey, all had five dates and several weeks later they were killed." Beeep!

The five minutes were up. It wasn't a very long time when you have so much to say.

I would have to plan better and have questions ready for my parents, as well as Nora, day after tomorrow.

I walked out of my room and starting searching every nook and cranny. I was shocked when I saw Daniel standing in the kitchen.

"My lady, I hope you are finding everything accommodating. I hope you enjoyed your breakfast."

"Actually, I tossed it down the disposal."

"Well, that is too bad," he said, reaching for a pastry. He took a bite. "Good." He took another bite of the jelly filled donut.

"Okay, you made your point." I said.

"My lady, you don't have to worry about poison or sedation as you can't leave here anyway."

"What are you doing here?" I asked.

Clearly, I hit a sore spot as Daniel's face was growing red.

"Your detective sabotaged my office, my home and all my favorite places. I can't go home or to work or anywhere. If I need to buy groceries, I will have to put on a disguise. Not how I had all of this planned."

"Since you're such a smart guy, you should have planned better . . ." I said, rather hatefully.

"My lady . . . what an attitude," he said, trying hard to not to sound angry, but he was.

"Just saying . . . By the way, thanks for the cell. It was nice to talk to my parents and Nora." Though the words sounded nice, the way I said them wasn't.

"Oh yes, Nora. I may have to rethink Nora."

"What do you mean?"

"She's such a pain in the ass. She drives me nuts with her oversize mouth and oversize everything else. I know she knows it was me that brought you here."

"Well, if she didn't know before, she does now," I snorted.

"My wife called me, crying about Nora and your detective showing up at our house, going through my things, hauling everything out. Ah, but alas, I don't care about those things. I have you, my lady."

"What about your kids?" I said, with less enthusiasm.

"I will bring them here in due time."

"Ah, but alas, they have school."

"Ah, but alas, you can home-school them."

"Ahh, but no."

"My lady, I pray you will go along."

"Don't hold your breath. You may have me locked up here, but nothing can change how I am or how I believe."

"I have hope of all hope."

"Hope all you want, but it's not going to happen," I said, with a great deal of anger. "So, let's talk about the murders."

"What murders?" He inquired.

I stared him down for a minute, then I rattled all the victims' names to him.

Calmly, without feeling bad about any of it, he said, "As you know I don't like clingy. I can't stand women who whine."

"That's not a reason to kill them."

"I suppose not, but at the time, I couldn't let Vivian know."

"Know what?"

He hung his head . . . "I'm ashamed of my past behavior."

"So, clear your conscience. Tell me everything," I said, sitting at the kitchen bar with my head resting in my hands.

Once again he hung his head. "Why? I don't know. It is just what it is," he paused.

"Daniel, I can't leave. Waiting is what I have. Tell me."

He got control of his voice and said, "Five. Five was the magic number," he started.

"Five, why five? What's the significance?"

"I had to start somewhere, so my rule became five times and then it ended. Which does not apply since I found you. WAS is the key word. When a lady of the Key Club pulled out my key on the fifth time, I had to do away with her."

"For Pete's sake. Why?"

"I found that when it's number five, they get possessive and cling to me. They thought more was going to happen. They wanted a relationship with a bond. I just couldn't allow that to happen. So when they drew my key on the fifth time, I wasn't dominant with them. Instead I made love to them, sweet love. Then when I thought it was a good time, I slipped in behind them and ended their miserable little life."

"So, let me get this clear. You hate women."

"No, no, contrary to your belief, I liked them all for the most part. It's just . . . Oh never mind, that was the old me."

"You're into dominance and you want them submissive. Then they get clingy. Then you treat them to great straight sex, and then kill them?"

"When you sum it up that way . . ."

"Alright, what about Myra?"

"Ah, you learned a lot from your phone calls this morning. I may have to rethink the phone call deal. Hmm." He said, looking at me.

Acting like it didn't matter about the phone, *which it did*, I probed him further. "So why Myra?"

"I did her family a favor. She screamed at those kids constantly. She called Bill every nasty thing she could come up with . . . all the time. She was one nasty woman. She went around with her clothes too tight her shorts too short, crop tops showing everything possible. She bleached her hair and lay in the sun all the time, and got toooo tan. She was nasty. I did her family a favor and put her out of her misery, out of their misery."

I ran my fingers through my blond highlights. *Whew!* I thought, fighting to stay composed.

"You can't be judge and jury. Besides, Bill was the sleaze. He was bonking the maid." I told him.

"Really?" he said surprised.

"Yep. So, you killed Myra the same as the Key Club ladies. Why?"

"To throw off anyone who might have figured it out."

"You got careless, Daniel."

"Yes, yes, I did. But now, my lady, no more mistakes. I will spend the rest of my life loving you and trying to get you to love me back. I am a changed man, thanks to meeting you."

"Speaking of meeting me, Daniel, why me? I have never shown you any interest. I don't understand your infatuation with me. I tried to discourage you in every way. So why?"

"Oh, my lady, the night I met you, you were a knock out in that tight red dress. Every hair in place and, by the way, I love your hair down." *He sighed.* "Your makeup was beautifully done and not overdone. I was immediately drawn to you. You felt right in my arms when we danced. You acted like I was no big deal. Most women I show that much attention to think it's a lasting relationship. They want more and fall all over themselves getting my attention. But you showed indifference. That intrigued me even more about you. I had to find out about you and the more interest I showed you, the less interest you had in me. I had to win you over."

"Yet you haven't mentioned my intellect, Daniel. Why is that?"

"Au'contraire, my lady, that's what got my attention in the first place. You're the whole package."

"It didn't work, Daniel. I'm still not interested. What makes you tick, Daniel? You're a good-looking guy, you have a wonderful family, a great job, everything going for you, so why dominant sex."

"The dominant sex started when I was fourteen. I was more mature for my age than most boys. My mother's best friend noticed. She took me under her wing and taught me all about dominant sex."

"Oh my God, that's sick," I said, annoyed and somewhat shocked.

"Maybe," he said, pushing his hair out of his eyes before he continued.

"She showed me how to be rough with belts and restraints. I didn't like the pain at first. The spankings got a little too hard sometimes, even brought blood to the surface."

"Didn't your mother notice?" I asked.

"I was fourteen so only my arms were showing. She just thought it was normal boys' play."

"But it wasn't, was it Daniel?"

My mother's friend also covered for me."

"I bet, the sick bitch."

"Of course, I didn't realize it was sick until later. She just said it was our secret. By then I learned to love it. She even taught me how to pull a feather and scarves across my body, gently sending chills. I especially enjoyed the gentle straight sex," he sighed, "and the oral sex. It's a variety and I never tire of it," he said.

I could tell by the bulge growing in his pants that he was reliving it. *Yeah, I looked.*

"Disgusting!" I said. "Did your mother ever find out about her friend?"

"Maybe, now."

I shivered at the thought of how a woman could take advantage of a kid like that and teach him such sadistic sexual acts. I wanted to vomit. Now though, I needed him back on track and not going down memory lane.

"Since the police have closed in on you, how are you going to pay for all of this?" I asked.

"I am a fortunate man to have so much knowledge and wealth."

"Really," I said, turning my head looking around the room.

"Oh, my lady, I have it all in order. I have bank accounts in the Cayman Islands. I have fake identification, passports, everything imaginable for us when the coast is clear, and when you have accepted me and our life together. We will never want for anything. I have it all covered."

"Daniel, it will never happen." I glared at him with hate.

"I can wait," he said, "but since I am in a confessing mood, I suppose I should tell you I killed that yipping pug next door to you."

"You killed Suzy. My God, Daniel, why? What's wrong with you?"

He stared at me for a few seconds, and then said, "Nothing is wrong with me, it's that she simply barked too much. Many times she was outside when I came to check on you. The pesky, yipping dog got on my last nerve, and she became a nuisance, so I ended her life," he said.

Trying to grasp what he just said, I remembered my patient Joan Cosby.

"Daniel, since you're in a tell-all mood, what about Joan Cosby? Did you do her any harm?" I asked.

"Contrary to your suspicion, I did not do harm to Mrs. Cosby. She is a sweet old lady. I do not know what happened to her. The staff is still investigating, so rest assure my fair lady, I did not do anything to her," he reiterated.

"No, just to poor innocent dogs. Oh, let us not forget the Key Club clingy ladies," I reminded him.

"I assure you there's NOT one lady among them. It was the Key Club after all. Char . . . la, you worry for naught. Eat now, before it gets cold."

I pushed my plate away.

CHAPTER 74

NORA TOLD JACKSON WHAT Charla said about the possibility of the house being surrounded by a warehouse. Jackson spread the blueprints that he had gotten from Daniel's home and office over the conference table. Nora leaned over, trying to understand the blueprints, and asked, "Whatcha looking at?"

He answered as he studied every fraction of them, "I figure Daniel's the designer of the place he's keeping Charla, so I am going over every single design he ever put on a drafting table, or computer screen, down to the smallest of scales."

Nora looked over to Zack. "What's Zack working on?" "Zack is working with Tom, who is an expert hacker, are going over Daniel's computer. I have Ron over there working on Daniel's texting and his cell phone calls. Trying to see where the cell towers are located I asked Rick to come in and work on the thumb-prints since he's familiar with the latest new age gadgets."

"My Rick?" Nora said, as she looked around the room and saw her sweet King of Clean way over to the left, helping out. She smiled, giving the Queen's wave to him as he looked up. He smiled and waved back with a salute.

"Here's a warehouse that could be the one," Jackson said. He picked up the phone to get a warrant ready for the address.

"Since the judge was anxious to stop Daniel Nielsen from more killings, he's basically sitting by the phone ready to sign off on a warrant." Jackson said. "I'm glad he's on our side. Plus, it doesn't hurt that he knows Charla and her parents."

Zack looked up and motioned for Jackson, "Come over here, Jackson. You have to see this."

"Whatcha got there?"

"Looks like Nielsen had a tracking device on Charla's and Nora's cars."

Jackson turned to Nora who was standing behind him listening, and Nora started to shrink.

"Noraaaaa."

"What?"

"You knew about being tracked," he asked. "For God sake, Nora, you two are so, so frustrating."

"The bug we found under Charla's car we bagged and turned it into Donnie."

Without another breath, he yelled, "D o n n i e eee, GET IN HERE. NOW!"

"Yeah?" Donnie asked, walking up to Jackson.

"Go home, NOW!"

"But?"

"Go NOW and don't come in until you get a call from this office. You're suspended for failure to follow through and for dropping the ball yet again. We don't have time to babysit you. GO!" he pointed toward the squad room door. "Now."

Donnie obeyed. She left with tears in her eyes and her head down. She knew better than try to talk Jackson out of it. She messed up one too many times.

Finally, the warrant came through and everyone saddled up.

They pulled up and surrounded the warehouse with a bullet proof armored vehicle. They rammed and opened the doors without a problem. Jackson and two dozen cops charged through while Nora did as she was told and stayed in the patrol car, waiting.

After they totally searched the inside of the warehouse, they all came out, defeated and deflated.

Nora popped her head up when she heard them coming out of the warehouse. She got out of the patrol car and ran to Jackson.

"Sorry, kid, wrong warehouse. There will be another. Go home and get some rest. We've been at it all day."

Nora looked at her watch and realized she hadn't been home since she had taken Rita home.

It was eleven and it dawned on her how tired she was. She looked at Rick, who had come along to show support to her and Jackson. She leaned down and gave her man a good-night kiss.

"Hey, want me to check on Bozo?" she asked Jackson.

"Please. I'm going to be at it for another couple of hours. I'll send Rick home in a bit."

CHAPTER 75

IT WAS ABOUT ELEVEN thirty when Nora pulled up to Jackson's house. She used the extra key he had given her and opened the door. She flipped the light on. Bozo stretched and meowed, but stayed on the sofa.

"Hi bud. Your mom will be home soon. I promise."

Nora saw movement out of the corner of her eye and her heart skipped a beat. She turned to see Suzy, the baby pug just in time. She released her gun and pulled her hand out of her bag with a sigh of relief.

"Woof, woof," Suzy barked.

Nora grabbed her chest, "Suzy you have got to stop coming in with Bozo. Did you tee tee anywhere?"

Nora looked around on the floor, the sofa, then went from room to room, but didn't see any accidents.

"You know, Bozo, if you went back out, she would follow you. Do you think you can do that the next time?"

Bozo stretched and barely opened his eyes before he curled back up and went back to sleep.

The neighbor saw the lights and called.

"Hi, Charla. This is Mary. No one was home, so I couldn't get the pesky pug," she giggled.

"Oh, hi Mary, this is Nora. Come on over, Suzy's here."

In exactly three minutes the doorbell rang and Nora let Mary in.

"Where's Charla? Is she working at the hospital?"

Nora explained to Mary what had happened.

Mary fell back on the sofa in disbelief.

Then she said, "You know, I've seen someone prowling around several times. A couple of times it was real late at night when I had to let Suzy out."

"Did you say anything to Jackson or Charla?"

"No. Since Jackson's a cop, I didn't think about an actual prowler or break-in."

"Don't worry about it. Nothing you can do about it now."

"I feel so bad. I could've warned them," Mary had tears in her eyes. She bent over, picked up Suzy, and said goodnight.

Nora picked up Bozo to hug him, and then put him down, fed him, and gave him fresh water. She made sure she locked the doggie door.

Nora walked up to the murder board, looked it over, and shook her head, realizing how the pieces fit together now. She sat down at the dining room table putting her head down on her arms, and sobbed.

Bozo came in and jumped on the table.

"Meow," Bozo tried pushing Nora's head up, then again.

After Nora realized what Bozo was trying to do, she raised her head, pulled him to her, hugging him to her chest, for what seemed to be hours while she sobbed.

Nora's cell rang with Rick's special ringtone. She set Bozo down and emptied her bag over the dining room table, going through it to locate her phone.

She answered, sobbing, "Hey."

"Honey, where are you? I just got home and you aren't here." Rick sounded so worried.

"Oh, I lost track of time. I'm spending time with Bozo."

"Time to come home, honey. There's a lot to do . . . tomorrow."

"On my way."

She picked up Bozo one more time and with a hug said, "Good night, Bud."

CHAPTER 76

I WENT TO BED fully clothed but I didn't cry myself asleep this time. I had a feeling Jackson would be busting in any time and I wanted to be ready.

I finally got out of bed about six a.m. I took a shower and put on clean clothes. *My clothes.* After brushing my hair back into a ponytail, I decided to pull the curtains back and see what the video had in store for the day.

"Hmm, the sun's coming up over mountains. There are no mountains in mid-Missouri. Not like these. These look like the Rockies." I started laughing and wondered when I would see Hawaii, the ocean, Victoria Islands, or even the Golden Gate Bridge. I unlocked the door and stepped out into the hallway.

I heard Daniel putzing around in the other room. I hurried down the hallway toward the noise. He was coming out of the pantry.

He saw me and smiled as he put the fresh donuts down on the counter with Starbucks' coffee.

"What's this? Starbucks' coffee? Lamar donuts?"

"Nothing's too good for my lady. Have some fresh coffee and just out of the oven donuts."

"Wait, where did you come from?" I ran to the pantry and started pushing and pulling anything and everything I could grab hold of. Nothing. I came out of the pantry where Daniel was leaning against the counter with his arms across his chest in a tight pair of jeans and a black tee. He looked . . . good. OMG! I have been here too long. *Hey, I'm only human . . . I'm mad, not blind,* I thought, then gave myself a head slap and reminded myself *he's a killer..* I regrouped and my thought changed to thoughts of Jackson. I turned my back to smile, wishing Jackson would hurry up and find me, and he would.

I noticed sunglasses, a baseball hat, a wig and beard sitting on the table. I picked them up and looked at Daniel.

"Today's disguise . . . I know how you love your donuts."

"I prefer McDonalds' coffee and apple fritters are my favorite. So maybe you don't know me as well as you think."

"If you look into the bag you will find apple fritters. My mistake on the coffee. I'm still learning about you. I did see Nora carried Starbucks into your house."

"Starbucks is Nora's favorite." I said, taking a bite of a fresh, still warm apple fritter.

He smiled and said, "I won't make that mistake again."

Daniel started toward me and I stepped back.

"I can wait," he said, backing away from me. "I'll keep trying."

"You'll wait a long time, like forever," I said, spitting out a little fritter. He handed me a napkin that I swiped out of his hand.

I heard Daniel's cell ring. He answered "Yes, she's fine. No. I said NO." He hung up quickly.

"Honestly . . . you hung up?" I pointed to his phone. "Who was it?"

"Oh, my lady, it is of no concern of yours. I shouldn't have answered it. I fear it was a big mistake. The cell tower could bring your detective close . . . but, he will never figure out how to get in here."

Daniel, who . . . was . . . it?"

"Vivian."

Before I could ask another question, Daniel pulled out a hammer out of the bottom cabinet drawer. He put the cell phone down on a wood block cutting board and POW. He flattened the phone in one hit. No longer of use.

He looked at me. "There, that's done."

He went to the pantry, got a box off the shelf with a new cellphone. "For an emergency."

I approached him with my hand out for the phone. He had several such phones, but all were parent locked, so I couldn't use them anyway.

He shook his head, no. "I'll control this."

"Hey, I don't suppose you will let me have tomorrow's calls today, will ya?" I asked as I turned to walk to the living room and turn on TV local news.

"Look Daniel. We're famous," I said, pointing at the TV.

"Umm," he groaned low. "This isn't going as planned."

"Daniel, cheer up. It'll be over soon."

"They will never find us. I can live here with you, forever."

My God, as hard as I try, I couldn't get this guy mad at me. This guy was completely delusional. I am out of here PDQ or faster. *Come on, Jackson, hurry.* Then my mind drifted to the cell-phone Daniel had in his pants pocket. I pictured the drawer with the hammer and other tools in it. I pictured the knives and other cooking utensils, the pots and pans.

I started day-dreaming, but first things first. I needed to find the exit. Once I found the exit, I could take a knife and ram it into Daniel, bash his head in with the skillet or maybe the hammer. Man, he trusts me by having everything in the world available to defend myself, all but my gun. *Man, I could use my gun.*

I can dream about everything, but the fact is, I can't do anything until I find that exit and Daniel knows it.

I decided that I would get up earlier in the morning and sneak out to catch Daniel leaving or coming back. I needed to see where he comes and goes and more importantly how he does it. Right then I started asking for Mc Donald's coffee.

"So, think I can have McDonald's coffee tomorrow?"

"We'll see."

There's a split picture of me and Daniel on the TV Screen.

Under my picture, which wasn't a bad picture, it said, "Victim, Charla O'Hara." No doubt Nora chose the photo.

Under Daniel's, it said, "Suspect." His picture showed his good looks. Of course it did.

A stand of microphones came into view. At the bottom of the screen it said . . .

"Stay tuned for Chief Anton and Lead Det. Jackson Boxley."

I glanced at Daniel who was watching and taking a deep breath.

"Turn it off."

"I can't. I have to hear."

He started to get up and move to the TV to manually turn it off.

"Daniel, no."

He looked at me, but recoiled and allowed me to watch and listen. *Why I don't know.*

Chief Aton did his usual spiel, then turned the news conference over to Jackson, who looked so tired and started with his pleasantries of welcoming the news media.

"Charla O'Hara is a pillar of the community. She is strong and fearless. She's a survivor. We will find her and we will prosecute Daniel Nielsen to the fullest. Questions?"

"Detective, does Nielsen have Miss O"Hara? And do you know where he's holding her?"

Duh, what ridiculous questions, he thought, then answered, "Yes, we are closing in on Daniel as I speak. I feel sure it will all be over soon," he said, playing to the camera.

"Where are they, can you tell us?"

"No, I cannot divulge that information. Thank you for your questions and your concerns."

Then Jackson looked into the camera and said, "Charla I am coming for you."

Out from behind Jackson's back Nora popped out, leaned into the microphones, looked into the camera, and pointing her finger said, "Daniel, we are going to get you . . . Your goose is cooked," she smiled.

"Oh no, you won't," he pointed back at her. "I'll get you first," he said perturbed.

Daniel looked at the TV like he was there in front of her and said, "Look at you with your cleavage hanging out. Shhh it. It's disgusting. I just don't get how you two are friends," he said turning to me.

Laughing, I said, "Okay Daniel, pack your bags. We're leaving here soon."

"Seriously, my lady, let me remind you, they will never find us. Your detective was blowing smoke."

As I was doing a happy dance in my mind, I said, "Tell me, Daniel, what are we supposed to do day after day, let alone hour after hour?"

"Honestly, Charla, I'm content just being here with you."

"Honestly, Daniel, that just isn't good enough for me. I need entertainment. Things to do, places to go. I need a life. How can you be content just being here with me? It will get old quickly. You are worldly, active in the community; you can't just shut everything down and everyone out."

He studied me and thought about what I had just said. Without saying anything, he got up and turned off the TV and put in a movie for us to watch.

"Here, I have a favorite of yours, Blind Side starring Sandra Bullock."

"Okay, what are we going to do after the movie's over? Watch another movie?"

"Yes."

"You don't plan on hurting Nora?"

"Shhh, watch the movie. This is my first time to see it."

He sat down beside me and I moved across the room to a single overstuffed chair.

"In time my lady, in time."

He keeps saying "in time, my lady." I know there's not ever going to be enough time.

⟫⟪

THE MOVIE WAS OVER and again I loved it.

Daniel, who was slumped into the recliner end of the sofa, nodded his head up and down slowly and said, "Good movie. I can understand how you like it so much."

Like a child I hopped up and asked, "Okay, okay, now what are we going to do?"

"I have an idea but unfortunately you're not ready . . . yet."

I ignored him.

I walked over to the window; pulled the curtains back and the blind up.

"So, can you make it look like fall? I need to see fall colors. I don't want to miss the leaves falling."

Daniel got up off the sofa and walked over, picked up a control, and pointed it in the direction of a shelf by the fireplace.

"Let me show you how you can change seasons, locations, and sky lines, even movement. Whatever you want, any time you want."

Cautiously, I came closer to see the remote as he handed it to me.

He stood behind me putting his arms around me holding the control in front of me.

"Too close, too close." I pulled away.

He pulled his arms from around me and stood next to me while he showed me how to operate the remote.

I discovered this could be fun.

"How does this work? Is it around the house? Like surround sound? Did you have to put a satellite on the roof or antenna? How do you get reception?"

Apparently, I caught him off guard.

"I designed a solar panel to rotate on the roof. This control will move the panels when needed to catch the sun. It holds on to enough energy to last several days, even if it storms or it's cloudy longer than usual. It's one of my favorite designs."

"Can I try? How about a sunset in the fall, from a New York City high rise?"

"Yes, but it takes a little more programming. Here, let me show you."

I watched him put in a series of numbers into the control. Immediately the design of what I wanted started forming. First, he plugged in the background with fall colors, then a sunset and finally the New York City skyline with a high rise.

"This is beautiful. But, of course, the real thing would be better."

"Oh, my lady, for a moment you were paying a compliment."

"You have to admit, Daniel, the real thing would be better."

"I suppose."

I thought he was moving out of the way, only he just changed position, so when I turned and caught him off balance, he fell, bringing me to the floor. We were face to face and body to body. I felt his manhood growing. *Really?*

"Oh God, get off me, get off me," I yelled, "You're trying to cop a feel," I pushed him with all my might. He was bigger and stronger than me, lying on top of me.

He didn't move. He was caressing my face, pushing the strands of my hair out of my eyes. I squirmed and shoved him the best I could. "Don't, Daniel, don't." But the more I squirmed the more his penis grew.

He was reacting on impulse, but then he realized I wasn't enjoying his impulse. He lifted himself off me, but sighed and said, "Sorry, my lady. I was caught up in the moment. You clearly weren't." He extended his hand to me and I actually took it, letting him lift me up with ease.

He stretched and adjusted himself, then asked, "How about some lunch?" Like nothing had just happened.

◈◈◈◈◈◈◈

WE HAD LUNCH, THEN watched The Proposal, starring, again, Sandra Bullock and of course, Ryan Reynolds. *This was the movie I fell head over heels for Ryan Reynolds.*

This movie was another first for Daniel and he approved. *He apparently raided the movies from my collection.*

Finally, dinner was over and I was bored and tired of this charade. He didn't want TV on. I did. He won.

"It's too early to go to bed. Do you have anything to read?" I asked him.

"I anticipated you like to read, so with a little snooping in your house, I found a few books that I feel sure you would like. Sorry if I picked any that you recently read."

I tried to act like I didn't notice what he just said. I was getting angrier by the second. Trying to compose myself, I looked over what he had just brought me, and, yes, I liked these books and, yes, I had recently read a couple of them. Always a good read. Then I exploded.

"What is wrong with you? You know Daniel, I sensed someone around numerous times, when I was asleep. You are intrusive. You had no right . . . !"

"I like to watch you sleep. A couple of times your detective was in bed with you. I've watched you make love and I pictured myself with you and not him. Mostly, I waited for him to leave and just watched you. Bozo got used to me coming in. He's an interesting pet."

"Daniel, how dare you? How did you get in?"

"I came through the backdoor, straight through the kitchen into the living room, then your bedroom. You really need better locks on the window by the backdoor. I just jimmied the lock on the window and reached in and unlocked the door."

"Oh, My GOD. What is wrong with you? You even made Bozo a traitor, and when I see him again . . . I'll love him." I got tears in my eyes. Daniel didn't see the tears as I turned them off as fast as they started. I couldn't be weak. I wanted to hit him with everything in me, but if I did, I couldn't run from him as there was no way out . . . ! I was stuck.

"How dare you watch Jackson and me? I feel so violated."

I pulled my cardigan sweater tight across my chest, guarding myself. I felt nauseous.

I sat in silence and watched the remote-control sky line with the sunset and fall leaves. I didn't want to let Daniel get under my skin. I wouldn't let Daniel get under my skin. I kept repeating it. I felt like I needed to stay in control of my thoughts and actions. I couldn't dwell on his intrusion of Jackson and my bedroom. Above all, I needed to maintain distance from this guy.

"You're quiet my lady. What can I do to make it up to you? I would say I am sorry for what you think was intrusion, but I cannot say that I am sorry, because I am not."

"You should be. You crossed the boundaries. That's unforgivable."

"I will win you over, this I promise you."

"No, you won't. This I promise."

"My lady is testy. You're tired. Shall we call it a night?"

"That's a great idea." I reached for a book and headed to my bedroom. I locked the door, and pushed the chest of drawers in front of the door for extra security.

I showered, and dressed back into my street clothes. I fluffed and leaned the pillows against the head of the bed. I started reading, trying to fight back the animosity I held for Daniel.

After reading a couple of chapters, I started thinking of my two allowed five-minute phone calls the next day. I hoped I didn't mess up that privilege. Hurry up, Jackson, come get me. I cried, thinking of Daniel's intrusion in Jackson's and my bedroom. I drifted off to sleep with tear stained cheeks.

I woke up a little before six. I pushed the chest of drawers back and unlocked the door as quietly as I could. I crept down the hallway with hope of catching Daniel going or coming back. He came through the pantry door. He didn't see me. I backed away a couple of steps, then let out a cough and yawn to let him hear me coming. It was too late to see how he came or went.

"Good morning, my lady. I hope you slept well."

No thanks to you. "I have a big favor to ask of you Daniel."

He shrugged, "Ask away, and then drink your McDonald's coffee before it gets cold."

"I would appreciate it, if you would stop saying, my lady."

"Why, I don't know if I can. I think of you as my lady and, and well . . . I'll try."

"That would be great. What did you bring from Mickey D's?"

"Just coffee. I am going to cook our breakfast today. No donuts. What would you like?"

"Donuts!"

"My a . . . Charla . . . seriously?"

"Okay, two poached eggs, two crisp bacon strips, one slice of whole grain toast, hold the butter and OJ."

"Someone's watching her calories."

"If no donuts, then this is what I want."

Daniel's an excellent cook. He appeared to be good at almost everything. He's so self-assured of everything he does. I just don't understand why the killings, or his dominance, or his obsession with me. Why me? Then I heard Nora's voice in my head, "why not?" I absolutely laughed out loud at that thought.

Daniel glanced at me. "What thought made you laugh? My uh Charla?"

"Nora."

"That thought had to be a nightmare, not worthy of a laugh," he said with disgust.

AFTER BREAKFAST, IT WAS finally eight o'clock, time to call Nora and my folks.

"Daniel, I would like to call my parents now."

He went to his coat pocket and brought out the throwaway phone I had used the last time.

"Thank you. But I would like privacy. I'll just go into my room."

Daniel didn't say a word. Just stood and watched me with a smile on his lips.

I closed and locked my door, and then I went into the bathroom where I locked that door as well.

"Hi, it's me. Listen. I think there is a solar panel on the roof that operates a remote scenery thing. I'll explain when I see you . . ."

"That's my girl."

"Jackson, thank god. Anyway, it's a house inside a warehouse with solar panels on the roof. I believe the solar panels are quite large. Hopefully, you will see it from the air, we might get lucky. Also, Daniel comes in and out through the pantry somehow, but I have pushed and pulled everything and I haven't figured it out yet. I miss you. I love you. Tell Nora to watch her back. Daniel's pissed at her comment on TV. He may come after her."

"Good work. Nora is never alone. We got her covered. Rick's also helping out at the 405. Keep up the good work. I love you and we will find you soon."

"How's Bozo?"

He's fine. He misses you. I do . . ." Beep. The time is up.

I called my parents and told them as much as I could before the beep ended the call.

I unlocked all the doors and walked out to Daniel and handed him the phone.

He reached out to me, grabbed my hand and pulled me to him. He placed his lips on mine and gave me a gentle kiss and then he let me go. I didn't have a chance to react other than shock.

"Sorry, my — a, Charla. I have wanted to do that since I first laid eyes on you that night at The Cheer Up." He reached for me again, but I declined and held him at a distance.

"You feel so natural in my arms just now. You belong in my arms."

I interrupted him . . . "Daniel, I love Jackson. I will always love Jackson. This thing you want between you and me, will never work. You can hold me here against my will for twenty years and I will still love only Jackson."

"I can convince you to love me. I know I can."

"No, no you can't. You're wasting your time, so you might as well let me go."

He reached for me again and said softly, "Charla."

I shook my head no. Again, I was able to hold him back from me. *He's so delusional.*

CHAPTER 77

IN THE SQUAD ROOM at the 405, Jackson had pinpointed three warehouses that Daniel designed.

He was up in the helicopter at the break of dawn looking down at one location after another.

He decided to check each roof of each warehouse first, just in case more than one had the solar panels.

"Shit, they all have solar panels," he muttered. "Let's take it down and go regroup."

The helicopter pilot set it down. Zack and Nora rushed over to Jackson.

"Well?" Nora asked anxiously, holding onto her hair from the wind of heli-blades that were just starting to slow down.

"All three warehouses have solar panels. I have no choice than to get warrants for all three."

They headed back to the 405 to start the procedures and organize the search to find Charla.

Jackson divvied up the orders among the officers and detectives. Everyone accepted their assignment with exuberance and was anxious to get going.

"I have a swat team sitting about two blocks away from each warehouse waiting for the word to strike. As soon as the warrants come through, we move," Jackson said, pacing. He was anxious.

"Come on, come on," he said, looking down at the phone. "Ring, damn it, ring."

Meanwhile, Rick, along with a couple precinct scientific minds were going through every single piece of information they could, trying to find some slipup on Daniel's secret passage to get to Charla.

Another hour went by.

"The judge has been in court all day and is just now signing off on a warrant for one warehouse," the detectives yelled out the address across the squad room. Everyone rushed to grab their equipment and raced out of the 405, leaving it just about empty. Rick was still there working away.

Jackson called the swat team to give them the address, but asked them wait for him before going in.

"On my count," Jackson said. "Three . . . Two . . . One . . ." he pointed toward the warehouse and the swat team, every officer, and detective rushed the building, with someone going into every window, door or opening possible. They even rammed the concrete walls to make way for other personnel to go through and with any luck, find a house.

Nothing. Empty. About that time, Jackson's cell played, "When the Saints come marching in."

He answered it.

"Jackson. I think I found it"

"Found what, Rick?"

"The warehouse with a house built in it. It appears to be very, very elaborate. The design is unlike anything I have ever seen. It has "Joseph Willis futuristic home" written on the band around the rolled up blueprint. It has a note saying Willis wanted it built for his parents."

"That's great, Rick," Jackson's mind was reeling and he thought for a moment while still holding the cell to his ear. He pointed and motioned to Zack and a couple of other detectives to come to him. In the phone he said . . .

"I want you to call all the media, and have them go to the other location for a false alarm, but they don't need to know that. I want to send them to one warehouse while we go to the other one."

Jackson got the information from Rick on both warehouses and shared the information with each department head.

"Sorry, I know you all want to be in on Charla's rescue, but some of you need to do a false run and go through the actions and motions of breaking into the warehouse with the news station reporting with vigor, while the rest of us go to the correct location and do a surprise entrance."

Nora, who stayed back unusually quiet, had chewed her fake fingernails off. She approached Jackson and said, "As much as I want to be there when Charla comes out, I think it would look more realistic if I am there when the TV station shows up. You know they will have it televised, and with all hope of hopes Charla and Daniel will be watching, thinking we are hitting the wrong warehouse. Daniel will be smug. He'll just think you're behind a ram or something. So hopefully he will be concentrating on me."

Jackson reached for Nora, put his arms around her and gave her a big brotherly hug.

"Smart thinking on your part, sister. Charla knows how you love a good sting."

"While we're going through the actions here, as soon as you get Charla, promise to let me know ASAP. Promise?" she said.

Jackson made the promise to Nora, then brought everyone together and gave them their final instructions.

"I'm calling the warehouse Charla's in, warehouse one. You, Zack, will go to warehouse number two and wait for my instructions. When I get to my location, I will call you to get your team in place."

Jackson still had Rick on the phone getting information about the warehouse.

Jackson and his team pulled up a couple of blocks away from warehouse one as Zack arrived at warehouse two.

Jackson borrowed a cell from one of his detectives, and called Zack while still hanging on every word Rick was telling him on his cell.

"Jackson," one of the detectives called out to him, "the Judge has both warrants coming and I just got word the blueprint of this address is going to be here in a jiff."

Jackson tossed his head that he heard the Junior Detective.

Now, it was a waiting game. He told Rick he'd call him back when he received the blueprint.

In thirty minutes both warrants were delivered at both locations as well as the blueprint to Jackson.

Jackson called Rick and Rick told him where he thought the weak spots were.

Jackson called Zack and told him to move in close to warehouse two and wait for his orders.

Finally, when everything was in order and everyone was in position, Jackson called Zack.

"Hold on, Rick," he said. "Zack, when I am ready, I will count from three down to one, then we simultaneously hit both warehouses. The news cameras will be on you while we hopefully surprise Daniel here."

Both Zack and Jackson had the warrant in hand. With everyone in place and both warehouses surrounded, Jackson called Zack.

"Three . . . two . . . one . . ." Both Jackson and Zack pointed . . . and charged both warehouses.

CHAPTER 78

WATCHING TV I NOTICED Daniel start to sweat and fear come across his face as we watched the Swat team surround the warehouse and ram-charged it time after time breaking into the warehouse side. The news camera was busy filming a live feed. Nora was hanging back, but Daniel saw her. He started to pace from one side of the room to the other.

"Your friend looks like she's going to pass out," Daniel said, smugly, pointing to the TV. "She's all nervous and the funny thing is it's the wrong warehouse."

Daniel jerked his head around at the noise he heard just outside. He paced and kept saying, "It's the wrong warehouse. They'll never find us."

I rose and smiled, "Yet here they are. I told you we should have packed."

"They can't get in," he said. He pulled me to him and held my hands behind my back where I couldn't move. I tried as hard as I could to get away. His eyes widened and he showed anger. With his free hand he pushed my face to his, and then kissed me with every bit of passion a sick serial killer could muster up. With my eyes wide opened, I kneed him in the groin as hard as I could, but he acted like it didn't even phase him as he tightened his grip on me and pulled me closer.

About that time the warehouse wall came down and the side of the house came open.

I kicked him in his right knee just hard enough, that his leg started to buckle. I felt my chance to break away from the kiss and struggled to pull away from him. I said, "So, Daniel, guess you were wrong."

Daniel started to panic, dragging me around with him as he looked around for something to fight with. *He had a knife. A skillet. A hammer and other kitchen gadgets.* Daniel was still holding onto my wrist when Jackson with a few of his closest friends burst through the exterior and interior walls.

"What took you so long?" I yelled out to Jackson as Daniel let go of my wrist.

Jackson didn't answer me. He charged Daniel in his gut and took him down in a tackle any pro football player would be proud of. Daniel got to his feet and retaliated by charging Jackson and driving him back into the kitchen counter. Jackson was able to throw a right hook across Daniel's left cheek which knocked him back a couple of feet. That didn't stop Daniel as he charged and Jackson went down. A few choice curse words were exchanged as they rolled around on the floor. They both were able to get on their feet, only to go down again. Finally, Jackson was able to get up. He yanked Daniel to his feet where Jackson delivered the mother-load of all hits across Daniel's nose and we could hear it breaking as he hit the floor. Blood went everywhere as Daniel shook his head from the blow he'd just received. Two officers stood over Daniel as Jackson turned toward me.

"He broke my nose,' Daniel screamed to the officers. "You saw him. That son-of-a-bitch broke my nose."

Only one officer answered as the other stood silent. "Sorry man, I only saw you slip and fall into the counter."

Daniel has always taken pride in being able to keep his composure. Today, he did not. All of a sudden Daniel hung his head in defeat.

I ran and jumped into Jackson's arms and wrapped my legs around him, never wanting to let go of him.

He swung me around, hugged me tight, and said, "I have someone who wants to talk to you," and he handed me his cell. My feet hit the floor. *So much for never letting go.*

I heard Nora screaming to Zack and everyone, "Jackson has her."

I yelled, "Hello. Where are you?"

Nora was now blubbering and sobbing something awful and I could hardly understand her. I laughed.

"Stop it. You had me scared to death," she screamed into the phone.

With her cell phone up to her ear, talking while she cried, an officer took her by the elbow and led her to a patrol car to bring her to me.

By now the TV stations had figured out what was going on and they headed to warehouse one, where the real story was.

Jackson pushed me away from him gently and said, "I've been looking forward to this."

Jackson walked up to Daniel who was now on his feet.

"Daniel Nielsen, you have the right to remain silent . . ."

I leaned in and looked at Daniel, then Jackson, and said, "Book him Dano."

Daniel hung his head and Jackson smiled as he slapped the cuffs on him.

"You know Jackson, Daniel has been in our house and watched us sleep and watched us have sex."

Without a word, Jackson drew back his fist and *bammmm* right into Daniel's nose again. More blood sprayed as Daniel's knees buckled. The two officers pulled him to his feet and led him out. Daniel had nothing to say, just hung his head.

Tears started to form in my eyes as I thought of all those poor women who now had justification. The Key Club Murders were solved. The sick, sadistic, pervert, insane man was out of business.

As they walked Daniel out through the hole in the wall, he turned to me and cried out, "My lady, I love you, and I never would have hurt you. You are my life . . . Next time I will plan better. Wait for me." Due to his broken nose, his words were muffled but I understood what he said.

"Looks like you're going to get life," I snarled, "Life! You hear me, Daniel? Life! There will be no next time."

Nora came running up to me and about knocked me over. She hugged and hugged me. We jumped up and down, going around and around like two school girls that just got appointed to the cheerleading squad.

CHAPTER 79

MY PARENTS, THE WRITER'S Club, Rita, Jordan, even Harold were waiting outside when I walked out of the warehouse. A loud cheer rang out. Paramedics rushed me. I assured them I was just fine.

The TV stations and reporters crowded around me as I tried to walk toward my parents. I gave the media reporters a brief summary of what happened and then waved them off. It surprised me that they turned to interview the unsuspecting detectives.

"Now that's what I'm talking about." Nora put her arm through mine as we headed to my parents. Then I watched Jackson's parents approach with their arms outstretched to me.

Jackson put his hand on Daniel's head, pushing it down and shoving him into the squad car, then returned to me.

"As much as I would love to celebrate with you, I have tons of paper work. The DA wants to make sure every t is crossed and every i is dotted. So, I may not see you until morning."

"I understand and I am so grateful you have t's to cross and i's to dot, because I am no longer with that sick bastard."

Jackson kissed me long and hard with a lot of passion. I had a feeling Daniel was watching and I admit it, I peeked to see and he was watching our every move. I closed my eyes again.

I heard Daniel screaming for something for his nose that kept running blood.

After we both looked over at Daniel, Jackson turned back to me and said, "You'll need to go to the 405 to make a statement."

"Can it wait until tomorrow afternoon?"

He squeezed me and said, "Okay, I know where you live."

"I have a couple of people to see in the morning and then I can come in."

Who are you going to see?" he asked

"Zoey and her mother."

Nora sung out, "Road trip . . . Biscuits and gravy here I come."

I smiled with a big thank you as I made a full circle and pointed at all my friends and even Harold along with Donnie standing next to him. I hugged my parents, then Jackson's parents again. Rick pulled up, got out, and ran straight for me. He hugged me and Nora yelled, "Get away from my man. You have enough. Ooops! You're down to one." She was just hee-hawing.

"She thinks she's so damn cute."

"Yeah, she does," Rick turned to Nora and wrapped his arms around her, and then he shook Jackson's hand. "Man, that was a tough one."

"Glad to have had your help."

"Rick, do you know how Daniel came in and out of there?" I said, pointing toward the house.

"Sure, I finally discovered it written ever so tiny by the pantry on the blueprint; here let me show you . . ."

Nora, Jackson and I followed Rick into the kitchen and then into the pantry.

"See," he said, directing us to a can of Campbell's Mushroom soup in the very back of the shelf. It was among several cans and was basically undetectable.

"See the can's hollow and sits on top of a lever type handle, and when you turn the can left, then right and then left again, this part of the pantry opens right into the garage where Daniel's BMW was still parked."

"There's a door on the other side of the kitchen that he left open for a second, and I could see his car. Later I tried the door, but it was locked up solid as a rock. It wouldn't budge," I said, showing him what I was talking about.

Rick said, "The soup can that opens the pantry has a two-minute delay. After two minutes the garage door opened and he could drive in and out all he wanted to. There's a sensor that automatically closed the door. There's a control over by the door that you said was open when you saw his car. It's in the garage, hidden, and only opened from the garage and not from within the house. That's why you couldn't get it open."

Rick took us all out into the garage and, sure enough the garage door slid open to one side. From the outside in the street or parking lot there was no physical sign of a garage door. Looked just like a brick wall.

"Look . . . Daniel also has an elaborate setup in his car."

We bent down to see. "So, he could come in and out of the pantry, or he could enter the house from that door. The area around the warehouse is deserted. So, no one knew he had this set up. Apparently, he didn't have any drug dealers or homeless hanging out around here," Rick explained. "Daniel built this for some billionaire whose dad had Alzheimer's and he didn't want his dad to get out."

"Or anyone. As much as this is fascinating, I am tired of this place and just want to go home," I mumbled.

"The officer will take you and Nora to her car. We'll finish checking this out. Go home babe," Jackson said. "We'll catch up later," he winked.

"Love you Jackson," I hugged and kissed him good-bye.

We walked toward the patrol car just as the car Daniel was in was pulling away.

Daniel gave me the finger wave and threw a kiss to me. *Oh, brother!*

CHAPTER 80

I HAD ONLY BEEN gone three nights, but it felt like a lifetime. I was anxious to see Bozo. Nora drove me home and my parents followed.

I unlocked the door and a thought came to me as I stepped in . . . How great it was going to be that I could sleep in my own bed with Jackson, without someone sneaking around, spying on us, invading our privacy, our intimate times *and* on top of it all, making friends with my cat!

Bozo came slowly working his way to me. He sniffed. He walked around me.

"Look at that, Charla, he's not sure it's you. He's being cautious."

"Hey, big boy . . ." As soon as he heard my voice he meowed and meowed, rubbing against me. He placed his paws up on my legs. I bent down, picked him up and, he nuzzled into my neck.

"Yes, I missed you, too. But I understand you betrayed me."

"Meow, meow."

"What do you mean he betrayed you?" Nora asked. My parents stepped closer to hear.

I told them what Daniel said about sneaking in and watching us, me. How Bozo paid him no attention. "He probably let him pet him."

My parents gasped. Nora wanted to go bloody Daniel's nose, again.

Nora looked at Bozo and said, "What kind of watch cat are you?"

"Meow," he said, as he narrowed his brow in disgust.

"Really, that's all you have to say for yourself," Nora sweetly scolded Bozo.

"Daniel killed four women. Zoey was supposed to be number five. Then, he killed his neighbor because she was annoying and he thought he was doing her family a favor. In addition, he was trying to throw off the other killings by killing Myra. Who was, in fact, number five? He killed Suzy because she dared to bark. He met me, sneaked around my house, touched my things, moved them around, and then he became obsessed with me. He shot Jackson and then tried again, all the while stalking me. He kidnaped me, hid me out in a secret home which was inside a warehouse, and with a remote, controlled the weather all around the house, and all in a matter of weeks." *I took a breath.* "Of course, that's what we know. Hard telling how many others he possibly killed. He's so narcissistic that he thought he would never get caught. For someone so intelligent, he was clueless on the obvious. He didn't think I was intelligent enough or couldn't give me credit, that when he gave me the phone to call you, I wouldn't give clues. Well, duh on him."

"He probably thought you were coming around to his way of thinking and that you wouldn't give him up," my crazy redhead friend said. "Wait . . . killed Suzy?"

"He said he felt charitable and told me about Suzy. Of course, he didn't know I would be free to tell anyone else."

"Good grief, why? She was cute, and well, that's just wrong. She didn't bother anybody."

"Apparently, she bothered Daniel. He said she barked too much when he came around to check on me."

"Are you going to let Mary know?" she asked.

"No sense in getting her upset over something she really can't do anything about," I answered.

"You're probably right," she said.

"You know, Charla, you probably saved other women's lives. If he hadn't met you, he might have killed more unsuspecting Key Club women," my mother said. Then she pulled me to her and hugged me tight and long.

"Okay, break . . ." I told her, as I patted her shoulders and gently pushed her to arm's length. "I'm here and I am just fine."

Though I was glad my parents and Nora were here, I couldn't wait for them to leave. I needed some alone time. I had been smothered enough.

I started toward the door and tried to nudge them out, throwing hints like,

I need a shower and rest. Reluctantly, my parents took the hint. They kissed and hugged me good bye, but Nora hung out.

"Nora, I love you, but I meant for you to go, too."

She acted deflated. "I'm just so glad everything turned out okay, that you're home safe."

"I know, but we can talk on our way to see Zoey tomorrow. I am beat. I need to shut my mind off."

Nora finally and with great hesitation, opened the door and stepped out, then said, "I'll pick you up at eight."

She turned to walk away, but turned around and said, "Lock up."

"A lot of good that did," I growled as I closed the door and locked it.

I took a shower and put on my sweatpants and tee. I looked at the bed which hadn't been made since I left.

I straightened it out and climbed in. I pulled the covers up to my neck and snuggled in for the night. All of a sudden, I jumped out of bed and pulled back my curtains to see the actual sky with stars and the moon at half-crest. I smiled, closed the curtains, and climbed back into bed.

I woke up with a gentle kiss and whisper, "Honey, I'm home." But it sounded like Daniel. Startled, I opened my eyes wide, sat up on my elbows and looked around the room, my bedroom.

I realized it was a nightmare and after a few minutes of searching my brain on why I had fear just now, I took a deep breath and slowly exhaled, then repeated it several more times. Being calmer now, I laid back down. "Silly dream," I said out loud.

I was just about to drift off to sleep again, when I heard a slight noise. I opened my eyes in time to see Jackson walk softly toward the bed. He dropped his clothes on the floor where he stood. I pulled back the cover and patted the bed to welcome him in.

CHAPTER 81

I GOT UP EARLY and was anxiously waiting for Nora to pick me up. Letting my man sleep, I kissed him goodbye, and whispered to him that I would see him in the afternoon. As I walked out of the bedroom I heard him, "hmm" and he went back to sleep. I spent some time with Bozo before unlocking his doggie door. I heard a woof, woof. I opened the door and saw little Suzy waiting for Bozo. Mary was on Suzy's tail, so to speak.

"I apologize again for Suzy always being here, but she just loves Bozo," Mary said.

"No problem. Bozo kind of likes her, too."

"Charla, I'm glad everything turned out good for you. It scared me the other night when Nora was here and filled me in on your capture. I'm, oh, you know, I'm happy for you."

"Captured! I hadn't thought of it like that. Now that's scary. I'm glad it's over, too."

I looked at the clock and found I had a little time before Nora picked me up. "Mary, would you like to come in for coffee?"

"Yes, I would love it."

The baby pug came waltzing in and Bozo wanted to go out. But they stayed in.

Mary and I visited over coffee for the first time in I don't know . . . ever.

A half-hour later I said to Mary, "Nora's on her way and I have to leave. It's been a pleasure to visit with you and it was long overdue."

She agreed and picked up her pug and left. Bozo followed.

Nora picked me up at eight sharp. She knocked on the door, then yelled as she opened it . . . "How many times do I have to tell you to lock up?"

I gave her a hug and a smile. "Last I checked it didn't stop Daniel from getting in."

She gave me an upper arm punch. "Let's go."

I put on my coat and we started our drive to Amber Haven.

"Wow, the fall colors are at their peak. I wasn't sure I would be able to enjoy this again."

Nora reached over and patted my leg. "Real fall colors is better, huh?"

We stopped at Hot Cake Café, and got our B & G's, and answered what seemed to be a million questions about my kidnapping. We ordered pie to pick up on our way back.

Nora ordered a whole pie for her and Rick. I stayed with the half pie. We also got a couple of B & G's to take to Zoey and her mother.

We walked into Amber Haven and all the staff, including Zoey and her mother were standing by the front door to greet us. A roar and applause rang out with, "that a girl!"

We gave the B & G's to Zoey and Virginia. While they were eating, we filled them in on Daniel's takedown.

We told them that we could not have pulled it off without Zoey pointing the finger at Daniel.

Virginia said, "We were watching TV and watched them bring Daniel out. Oh, my gosh, I have a hard time with someone that good looking with everything going for him, to turn out to have tried to kill my daughter and killing those other women. It makes me sick. We're so happy you caught him, but sorry you had to go through such an ordeal, Charla. But thanks. Thanks to you both."

Zoey was squirming in her wheelchair but finally got the words out, "Tha . . . than . . . thank yoouu, gi . . . girls" and she reached her arms out to us for a hug then started to stand.

"I'm sorry you had to go through this ordeal, Zoey, living in fear, all these years," as I held my hand out to steady her standing.

"The doctor said, if Zoey keeps this up, she will get to go home soon," her mother said.

"Zoey, that's wonderful news."

Zoey, with Virginia's help, walked with us down the hallway toward the front door.

The Amber Haven staff was waiting for us. They were smiling and taking turns giving Zoey a high five on a job well done, walking with only her mother's help.

The administrator said, pointing to Nora and me, "Thanks to you two we don't have to worry about Ivanhoe again."

While the staff looked weirdly at the administrator for that comment, Virginia, Nora and I laughed.

"We'll keep in touch, Zoey," I promised.

We left feeling pretty darn good about Zoey's recovery.

We headed out to pick up our pie, which Nora had thoughtfully brought a cooler to put our pie in. We then headed to the 405.

CHAPTER 82

As we drove I felt a calm come over me. "Do you feel that?" I asked my redheaded friend.

"What?"

"No looking over our shoulder or under our cars."

"Peaceful, isn't it?" she said.

Nora and I walked into the 405 and cheers went up. Jackson was standing with a cake in his hands to celebrate. It said, "Thanks P.I.'s"

We cut it and passed it out to anyone who wanted a piece of celebratory cake.

Nora gave her chain of events of what had happened, then she went home. I stayed to give my statement.

There was one thing left to do. I would have to face Daniel one more time . . . *at his trial!*

Jackson took me home. The first thing he wanted was a little bed time with me.

He unlocked the door and picked me up to carry me over the threshold. Just then we heard "Surprise!"

The house was full of friends and family; even Donnie stood there with her arms wide open.

The beer flowed, the wine was poured. Everyone brought potluck and there was so much food.

We relived the last several days over and over, but at last, the subject was changed.

"Charla and Nora," my mother said, "My Red Hat ladies are planning a trip and we want our daughters to join us."

"Daughters?" Nora questioned.

"Why yes. Charla, her sister and you. We would love to have you."

Nora blushed and clearly had a tear nearly ready to drop from her eye.

I excused myself, went to the bedroom, then returned carrying the box with the engagement ring in it and handed it to Jackson.

I got down on one knee and announced, "Yes, Jackson, it will be my honor to accept your proposal of marriage."

Smiling from ear to ear, he slid the ring onto my finger, lifted me up and then kissed me like never before.

"Oh . . . get a room," my best friend said, as a roar went up in congratulations. "Meow."

ACKNOWLEDGMENTS

Thanks to the Woodneath Writer's club for reading and critiquing as I worked on this my first novel.

Author's Note

My writing may reflect some old-fashioned comments or ideas that I blame on my mother. I do have a very young, modern soul and write with a younger perspective. I enjoyed writing this book so much that I wished I had started writing years ago.

I have two more books in the works and can't wait for you to read them as well.